Satan's Treasure

Satan's Treasure

Lou Volpentesta

Front cover image: Courtesy of Shutterstock and Fotosearch
Front cover design: Shankari Mano
Back cover photo: Gary Tannyan

Issued in print and electronic formats.

ISBN 978-1-988387-00-0 (paperback).—ISBN 978-1-988387-01-7 (hardcover).
—ISBN 978-1-988387-02-4 (epub).
—ISBN 978-1-988387-03-1 (kindle).

This is the original print edition of *Satan's Treasure*. An unpublished draft of the novel won an Honorable Mention in the 2000 Magnum Opus Discovery Awards, in affiliation with the Hollywood Film festival.

To my parents, Arcangela and Alessandro Volpentesta, who sacrificed everything to provide their children with a better life.

And to my dear friend Michael Murphy and my brother-in-law Vince Bruno, who both left us much too soon.

Chapter 1 — Friday, June 13, 1997

The Guardian heard a twig snap near the gate of the citadel. Holding his breath, he leaned out of his sentry box and peered intently into the murky darkness. He had little difficulty in pinpointing the location of the disturbance, for his formidable powers not only included the strength of a grizzly and the cunning of a fox, but also the visual and auditory acuity of a panther.

The intruder was a succubus, a creature of the night whose demonic evil was hidden beneath a veneer of physical beauty. She slipped past the gate and paused, sensing His presence. She was tentative, frightened, but her predatory instincts compelled her forward, toward the inner sanctum, seeking out the souls of the men and children sleeping there. She proceeded slowly, her breathing ragged, her right hand groping blindly in the darkness.

Stepping out of the sentry box, the Guardian crept to the center of the passageway, planted his feet firmly on the cobblestones, and uncoiled his sleek, sculptured body to its full, magnificent height. His muscles rippled. His nostrils flared. Narrowing his eyes, he extended his arms and waited for the intruder to fall into his deadly embrace.

The succubus stopped abruptly, sensing His proximity. She gasped. Her heart began to pound, partly from fear, partly from sexual agitation. Trembling, she pressed her body to His and unbuttoned the top of her bodice. She bent her head to one side and offered up her slender neck.

Enveloping the creature in his powerful arms, the Guardian lowered his mouth to the soft, smooth flesh. He snorted sharply as her scent — a commingling of sweat and perfume, desire and dread — assailed his nostrils. Baring his razor-sharp teeth, he snarled and sank—

"Frank. Hey, Frank! Are you getting in, or what?"

Frank Ryman clenched his fists as he stepped into the elevator and turned to face the door. Behind him, a trio of smirking co-workers began to exchange hushed whispers. Ryman pictured their mangled bodies under the wheels of a speeding subway train.

The door closed and the elevator began its 22-storey descent. Ryman overheard his co-workers discussing their plans for the weekend — a family barbecue, a baseball game at Yankee Stadium, an afternoon at Jones Beach. Mundane pleasures for insignificant men, he mused, sneering.

After what seemed an eternity, the elevator finally jerked to a stop in the crowded lobby of the Bell Liberty Bank Building, home to the accounting firm of Roswell, Adams & Dickerson, Ryman's employer. His colleagues rushed past, tossing off a series of mumbled goodbyes. Ryman knew they were going for drinks, a Friday night ritual; he also knew they didn't want him along. The sentiment was mutual. Shoptalk was irritating enough, but attempts at being "one of the boys" — especially the endless blathering about sports and sex — made his head throb.

The door closed and the elevator continued its descent to the underground garage. Ryman stepped out into the cool, dank air and hurried to his blue Volvo. Tossing his briefcase onto the passenger seat, he climbed behind the wheel, started the engine, and steered the car up the ramp to join the traffic jam wending its way along Pearl Street, in Manhattan's financial district. The drive home always took an eternity, but it was better than being squeezed into a subway car with a horde of surly, sweat-stained commuters.

Ryman lived alone in a two-bedroom apartment on the Upper East Side. Housed in a recently sand-blasted brick building near the intersection of Lexington Avenue and East 90th Street, the unit faced west, offering up spectacular sunsets and a panoramic view of the area's diverse mix of Beaux Arts, Art Deco, Modernist, and Post-Modernist architecture. Normally, such an apartment would've been beyond the reach of someone earning a CPA's salary, but a string of astute stock acquisitions in the early nineties had provided him with a considerable nest egg.

Ryman parked the car, stopped to pick up his mail in the lobby, and rode the elevator up to the 10th floor. The day's tensions began to melt away as soon as he stepped through his front door. This was his refuge, an oasis in an increasingly frenetic and incomprehensible world. Setting down his briefcase, he strode into the kitchen and poured a glass of grapefruit juice, which he sipped while flipping through the mail. He then entered the bedroom and changed into his swimming trunks. Tossing a wool robe over his shoulders, he grabbed his goggles and a bath towel, and went down to the pool for his evening swim.

Since it was the supper hour on a Friday evening, and unseasonably cool for mid-June, he had the pool to himself. He felt relieved; swimming with others made him feel inhibited. Disrobing, he put on his goggles, plunged into the cool, clear water and with a couple of powerful strokes churned his way to the bottom. Twisting around, he gently settled onto his back and stared up at the surface. Beyond the point where air met water, reality seemed distant and tenuous.

These quiet moments, insulated from the harsh and ugly sights and sounds of scrabbling humanity, filled him with rare contentment.

*****

Ryman stood naked before the full-length mirror in his bedroom, admiring his 26-year-old physique. It was a good body. Tall, lean, broad-shouldered. A swimmer's body. But it was his face that pleased him most. Smooth, supple skin, piercing blue eyes, short, sandy hair combed straight back, and a strong chin. He didn't like his mouth, however. The lips were too full, verging on effeminate.

After dusting his body with talcum and spraying on some deodorant, he put on a clean white shirt, a thin blue tie, a double-breasted black suit of raw silk, and a pair of black patent leather loafers. He hated slovenliness, even when there was no one around to notice. And he always dressed for dinner, which he usually ate at home.

Tonight he would be dining on Tandoori chicken and curried rice, ordered from an Indian restaurant that had just opened down the street. In the meantime, he would tinker with the 5,000-piece jigsaw puzzle that lay spread out atop half of the dining room table. It was a reproduction of a remarkable painting he'd found in an art book purchased during his last visit to the Guggenheim, Jean Delville's *Les Tresors de Satan*. When he first saw the painting, with its golden nudes splayed at the feet of the dark lord, he felt like the artist had peered into his very soul.

Puzzles — of every kind — were Ryman's favorite pastime, and had been since childhood. Originally, he had turned to them as a way of occupying his mind so *she* couldn't creep into his thoughts. Now he not only found them calming and intellectually stimulating, but also an excellent tool for honing his powers of deduction and concentration. And he was an excellent solver. It had taken him less than twelve seconds to figure out Rubik's Cube.

After supper, he went into the living room to watch a video. His collection was extensive — over 200 titles — stacked alphabetically in an ebony cabinet. Movies were Ryman's second passion. He preferred films that portrayed family life, ideally with a strong mother figure, like *Mrs. Miniver*, *A Tree Grows in Brooklyn*, and his all-time favorite, *The Grapes of Wrath*. Regrettably, no one seemed to be making such pictures anymore. Now it was all gunplay, special effects, and projectile vomiting.

He, of all people, knew that ugliness existed in the world. He didn't need to see it plastered on a two-story-tall movie screen, in glorious Technicolor and ear-splitting Surroundsound.

As he scanned the rows of titles, his thoughts began to drift, causing him to close his eyes and lean against the wall. An image coalesced in his mind. A citadel, bathed in darkness. Footsteps approached the main gate, and then stopped. The intruder was a beautiful woman...a woman intent on doing evil....

Ryman shuddered and opened his eyes. His heart was pounding. He needed to get out...to find a release for the pressure that was building up inside him. Picking up a copy of *The New Yorker*, he turned to the 'Goings on About Town' section and found the name of a jazz club on West 44th Street. He jotted down the address and called for a taxi.

*****

Ryman felt relaxed as the cab motored south along Fifth Avenue, between the verdant foliage of Central Park on the right and the brightly lit shops, hotels, and apartment buildings on the left. He was always calm when he set out in search of a sexual partner. The problems — which recently had been getting worse — occurred later. He took a deep breath and silently intoned the mantra he'd been repeating since leaving his apartment: *this time will be different; this time will be different; this time....*

Suddenly, the cab screeched to a halt. Ryman glared at the back of the driver's turbaned head, then turned to look at a knot of nervous pedestrians standing in front of the Metropolitan Museum of Art, waiting for the traffic light to change. They could've been a delegation from the United Nations. Black, Caucasian, Oriental, Latino — even a Hassidic Jew complete with black felt homburg and temple curls. A snapshot of New York City. More Italians than in Venice, more Puerto Ricans than in Ponce, more Irish than in Dublin, and more Jews than in any other city in the world.

The light turned green and the cab continued on its journey, leaving Central Park behind and entering the most exclusive shopping strip in the United States — possibly the world. Tiffany & Company, Van Cleef & Arpels, Cartier, Saks Fifth Avenue — the list seemed endless.

Ryman glanced at his watch and shifted position. As he did so, he noticed a billboard. It depicted a scantily dressed brunette with bee-stung lips, a mammoth bosom, and a leering smile, draped over a red Ferrari.

"Look at that," he said, grimacing. "What a disgusting display."

The Sikh driver, surprised by the unexpected outburst, glanced in the rearview mirror.

"Women who flaunt their bodies that way are no better than whores," continued Ryman.

"Sir?" said the driver, uncomprehending.

"Why is society so obsessed with a woman's physical appearance? You can't open a magazine, go to a movie, or watch television without some brain-dead Amazon shoving her breasts into the camera. You'd think that being beautiful was an accomplishment rather than just an accident of birth. Such women should be condemned and ostracized for their despicable behavior but instead, society treats them like goddesses and showers them with money and prestige."

Ryman clenched his jaw and balled his hands into fists. "And don't think these creatures aren't aware of their power. Oh, no. They exploit it for all it's worth! When are people finally going to wake up and see these evil, manipulative, money-grubbing she-devils for what they are! If I had my way, I'd—"

He caught a glimpse of the driver's startled expression and realized he'd gone too far. Taking a deep, restorative breath, he settled back and reminded himself that he had to maintain his self-control in public or risk being sent back to the hospital.

Taking out his pen and the black notebook he always carried, he jotted down the word 'Ferrari' and the location of the offending billboard. Tomorrow, he would send the company a scathing letter.

*****

The woman Ryman had chosen from among the half dozen unaccompanied females who were in the jazz club turned out to be a dental hygienist. He almost gagged when she told him. How could anyone stand poking around inside wet and rancid mouths all day, week after week, year after year? Some people would do anything for a paycheck.

Her name was Tanya Holt, a redhead, born in Queens, now living and working in Chelsea. As usual, it hadn't taken him long to strike up a conversation. Women always responded favorably to his pick-up techniques, which he'd learned from studying the romantic leading men from Hollywood's Golden Age. His conquests credited his 'bedroom' eyes and his willingness to listen. It was amazing how much women were willing to reveal about themselves to a sympathetic listener — even the most intimate details of their sex lives.

Not that he cared. In fact, their inane babbling bored him to tears. But he had to feign interest because nightclubs were his only option when it came to picking up women. Prostitutes, a vile, disease-ridden species that should be placed in permanent quarantine, were out of the question, while women who used personal ads and dating services were usually looking for a relationship. Ryman's needs were strictly short-term.

Up on the stage, the fat black tenor sax man finished his solo and the rest of the combo kicked in for the finale. Tanya Holt crushed out her cigarette and leaned across the table.

"You're not a native Noo Yawker, are you Frank?" The mumbled rush of her pronunciation left no doubt about *her* origins.

"No. I was born in New Orleans."

"Really? You don't have an accent."

"I guess it wore off."

"How long you been in town?"

"Almost five years."

She nodded and took a sip of her pink lady, the third she'd had in the last half hour. "So, the Big Easy, eh? That must've been a fun place to grow up."

"Not especially."

"No? How come?"

Ryman's jaw muscles tightened.

"Sorry," she replied, making no attempt to hide her annoyance. "I didn't *mean* to pry."

Ryman forced himself to smile while he struggled to block out the memories that were massing on the borders of his consciousness, threatening to pour out of his ears like malignant pus. He needed to bear down. Concentrate.

"Are you okay, Frank? You look a little seasick."

"I'm fine. Just a touch of indigestion, I guess."

"Have some more brandy."

"Good idea." He caught their waiter's eye, motioned for another round, then turned back to Tanya. Her legs were crossed and she was listing to one side, peevishly sucking on her cigarette. Ryman frowned. He needed to regain the ground he'd lost.

"Tanya?"

She cocked her head and studied him through narrowed eyelids.

"Did anyone ever tell you that you've got magnificent hair? Not just the color, which is gorgeous in its own right, but the texture. It looks as soft and light as butterfly wings. May I touch it?"

She finished her drink and placed the glass on the table. "Sure, why not."

Frank slid his chair closer and gently placed his hand on the back of her neck. He lingered a moment, then fanned his fingers and pushed them slowly up toward the top of her head. As he massaged her scalp, he leaned forward and gently brushed his lips against her ear lobe. She didn't pull away. Emboldened, he stuck out the tip of his tongue and began to lightly lick her ear.

Tanya closed her eyes and moaned softly.

"Why don't we get out of here," he whispered, squeezing her arm.

"Okay. We can go to my place. It's just a few blocks away."

*****

Tanya Holt's living room smelled of incense and lemon deodorizer. It was furnished with a black leather sofa, a pair of rattan fan chairs, and a rattan coffee table with a glass top. It also had a fake fireplace with a dozen ceramic gnomes arrayed atop the mantelpiece and enough plants to make Tarzan feel at home.

Ryman leaned back on the sofa and watched uneasily as Tanya used a credit card to shape a small mound of cocaine into two long, narrow rows.

"Sure you don't want some?" she asked, placing a rolled-up dollar bill to her nostril.

"No, thanks." He had declined once already, citing sinus problems. In truth, he wanted nothing to do with drugs. Unlike alcohol, which he drank in moderation, they loosened his grip on reality — and opened doors that needed to remain closed. He also feared drugs because they'd killed his mother. Regrettably, not before the wretched woman had already infected him with her peculiar form of madness.

Tanya leaned forward and snorted up both lines of cocaine in one quick, fluid motion. Shuddering, she sat back and made a series of rapid sucking noises with her nostrils. She then wiped away the residue with her fingers and finished her drink.

"Honey," she said, snuggling closer, "you don't know what you're missing."

Ryman placed an arm around her shoulder. Murmuring, she ran her hand along the inside of his thigh and turned toward him. Their faces drew nearer. She parted her lips and closed her eyes. Ryman's heart began to pound as his lips touched hers. Her tongue immediately slid into his mouth, lunging, probing. It tasted of tobacco.

For one brief moment, he thought it was going to turn out all right. Then, with unrelenting familiarity, the emotional maelstrom he had dreaded began to take shape, fueled by a combination of disgust and claustrophobia.

No! Not again! Not this time!

He tried to resist by concentrating on the way he felt in his fantasies. Strong. Virile. Commanding. The master of all he surveyed.

It was no use. Nothing could stop the tidal wave cresting inside his skull. His ears rang. His body tensed. His eyes rolled up into their sockets. There was a moment of calm, and then the wave broke, channeling his emotions into an almost overpowering rage.

"Noooo!" he cried, clapping his hands to his ears. He turned to glare at the woman, who sat cowering at the far end of the sofa, gaping at him in fear and confusion. She reeked, like some loathsome creature dredged up from the primordial ooze. A voice inside his head, strange yet familiar, urged him to smash her, pound her, turn her face into a bloody pulp.

Beads of sweat broke out on Ryman's brow as he strained to regain his self-control. He clamped his eyes shut and gulped for air. Not daring to look at the woman again, he jumped to his feet and rushed toward the door.

*****

Back in the privacy of his bedroom, Ryman threw himself onto the mattress and buried his face in his hands. The psychic battle that had started at Tanya Holt's apartment continued to rage, making his brain feel like a sponge being wrung out.

Moaning, he rolled onto his side and tried to concentrate on the titles of the novels stacked along the bottom row of his bookcase, hoping the effort would take his mind off the pain. But he couldn't get his eyes to focus. He sat up, intending to get a couple of Tylenols from the bathroom. But as he rose to his feet, a series of powerful spasms ripped through his body, knocking him back onto the bed and causing him to bounce and flail like a rag doll. Then, as quickly as it had started, the paroxysm subsided.

Ryman, his face now serene and his eyes wide and alert, blinked and slowly got to his feet. Stripping off his clothes, he entered the walk-in closet, grabbed the handle of a cedar trunk — the only item left behind by his mother — dragged it out into the open, and unhooked the latch. His body tingled with anticipation as he slowly raised the cover.

Humming a song from his childhood, he reached into the trunk and pulled out a garter belt, lace panties, a pair of silk stockings, and a padded brassiere, and laid them neatly on the bed. He admired the items for a moment before putting them on, then reached into the trunk again and took out a white, strapless, ruffled tulle ball gown, a gossamer vision bedecked with crinolines and ribbons. He wriggled into the dress, then stepped into a pair of black, open-shank pumps. A long, layered blonde wig, parted on the left, with bangs that swept down then back over the right ear, and a necklace of black pearls with matching earrings, completed the transformation. Ryman picked up the makeup bag and glided into the bathroom.

A few minutes later, he returned to the bedroom and stood in front of the mirror. The reflected vision caused him to gasp with delight. "Francine, honey, if only mamma could see you now. She'd be so proud of her baby girl. A shimmering southern belle of the first magnitude."

Ryman carefully lay down on the bed, sighed like someone who'd just shaken off the weight of the world, and fell into a deep, restful sleep.

Chapter 2 — Saturday, June 14

Frank Ryman woke up with a start. He'd had another nightmare, the same one that had been haunting his sleep for the past six months. It began with him sitting on the floor in the middle of a white room, surrounded by dozens of grinning, naked women slumped against the walls, dark-eyed and lifeless, like a collection of demonic porcelain dolls. It always ended with the women crawling toward him, their jaws snapping and their hands extended like claws.

Shuddering, he threw off the covers and staggered to his feet. Something soft brushed against his face. He reached up and was surprised to find himself grasping a handful of long, blonde hair. "What the—" he mumbled, as the wig slid off in his hand. His surprise gave way to dread as he glanced down at the expanse of white tulle covering his body. "Oh, God. Not again."

Repeatedly hissing the words "I am a man!" through clenched teeth, he quickly stripped down and jumped into the shower. Why couldn't he keep that... that...thing from creeping into his brain? The doctors had promised that she'd never bother him again. But now she was back, and she seemed to be getting stronger with each appearance.

Trembling with rage, he grabbed a washcloth and violently scrubbed his face until it ached, hoping to wash away his tormentor's presence along with her make-up.

His thoughts turned to the incident at Tanya Holt's apartment. It was the fifth consecutive time the prospect of sexual intercourse had filled him with revulsion, then rage. He could no longer ignore the truth. He'd allowed the needs of his body to override the strictures of his intellect. He'd been fooling himself into thinking he could get away with it by holding back his orgasm, thereby preventing the women he slept with from robbing him of his life force. Instead, he'd fallen right into the enemy's trap.

Gritting his teeth, he angrily twisted the faucet to its hottest setting and aimed the spray at his genitals. He needed to be reminded that the world was full of female predators who hid their rapacious natures behind beautiful smiles and used the promise of sex to cajole men into doing their bidding. Like succubae, they haunted the night in search of prey. Once they had what they wanted, they discarded their victims like so many empty shells.

Ryman stepped out of the shower and began to towel off. He felt certain life would be safer and less complicated without sex. He'd have his work, his hobbies, peace of mind. It was simply a question of willpower.

*****

After a lengthy swim and a light breakfast of orange juice and buttered toast, Ryman felt like himself again. It was time to take care of his correspondence, a duty he performed every Saturday. He retrieved his notebook from his suit jacket and strolled into the office he'd set up in the second bedroom. Half a dozen floor-to-ceiling-high bookcases, containing hundreds of neatly stacked directories and reference books, lined the walls and a computer workstation stood next to the window.

Ryman sat down and turned on the computer. Clicking the mouse, he called up his personal file and selected the folder containing the template he had created for his 'special' correspondence. The letterhead featured an illustration of a knight in golden armor protecting a young boy against an enraged hydra. Each of the creature's nine heads had the face of a leering, straggly haired woman. Arrayed in an arc above the illustration were the words 'THE GUARDIAN' in 36 point London type.

Using various directories to find the snail mail or E-mail addresses of the companies whose advertisements had offended him that week, he spent the next few hours composing a number of letters expressing his displeasure. He never ranted, however. He wanted the recipients to take his opinions seriously so he always worded each letter carefully to make sure his tone was polite and his arguments cogent.

When he finished with the advertisers, he dashed off a number of letters to the editors of New York's daily newspapers, reiterating his arguments against the cult of female beauty in general and the use of vacuous, half naked women in advertisements in particular. None of these letters were ever published because he never signed them. He preferred to remain anonymous in order to protect his much-cherished privacy.

Ryman finished his correspondence by 3:00 p.m., leaving him with an hour to spare before the start of his favorite radio program, *Molinaro on N.Y. Ninety-Nine*. The three-hour-long show — which also aired weeknights at 8:00 — provided a forum for discussions about contemporary culture. During the first two hours, callers were allowed to express their opinions on any relevant topic while the last hour featured a guest interview.

Ryman, a regular participant, had so impressed the show's host that he'd been given a special phone number that allowed him to bypass the station's main switchboard. Apparently, only a select few had received this honor.

Turning his mind to what topic he would discuss, Frank Ryman walked into the kitchen for a snack.

Chapter 3 — Monday, June 16

Detective Sergeant Lionel Jackson placed the cardboard box containing his belongings on the desk that had been assigned to him and sat down. Most of the other desks were vacant, which didn't surprise him. New York City homicide detectives carried heavy caseloads that continually kept them on the move.

Jackson lit a Camel and checked out his new surroundings. Like most squad rooms, the one used by the South-Central Detective Area Task Force, headquartered in the 15th Precinct, had all the atmosphere of a linen closet. The walls, painted an ugly green that looked even ghastlier under the buzzing fluorescent lights, were covered with maps, calendars, wanted posters, duty rosters, Legal Bureau bulletins, and departmental memos, some taped directly onto the cinder blocks, others pinned to various corkboards. There was also a large, elaborate chart showing the weekly results of the station's fantasy baseball league standings.

The room was furnished with a dozen gray metal desks, each equipped with a coffee-stained IBM Selectric III typewriter. The squad's lone computer was nestled in an alcove created by two rows of seven-foot-tall file cabinets, sharing the space with a water cooler and a coffee machine. Two additional rows of file cabinets stood against the opposite wall, flanking the holding cell. The C.O.'s private office occupied the far end of the room. Next to its door was a metal stand holding a large clothbound ledger, the Green Book, which contained a record of every homicide case — time, date, location, circumstances — handled by the task force so far that year.

Jackson watched a pair of flies, tired from playing a noisy game of follow the leader, land on the corner of his desk, preen themselves, then zip off again. Yawning, he leaned forward and peered into his box of belongings. Sitting on top was a brass frame holding a photograph he'd taken the previous summer, of his wife and two daughters posing with Mickey Mouse at Disney World. He placed the photograph on the desk and took a deep drag on his cigarette.

The squad room door opened. Tensing, Jackson looked up. It was his new C.O., one Lieutenant Jim Hawthorne, a six-foot-five, bull-necked behemoth with penetrating green eyes, an unruly tangle of curly brown hair, more decorations than a Russian general — at last count, 42 departmental citations and awards, and membership in the Honor Legion — and a reputation for having the tenacity of a wild boar. And, with a B.A. from Columbia and a law degree from New York University, he also happened to be the best-educated man on the Task Force. Rumor had it he spent as much time lecturing at John Jay College of Criminal Justice as he did on duty.

"How's it going, Lionel?"

"Just settling in, Lieutenant."

Hawthorne grabbed a nearby tube chair and dragged it across the cracked linoleum. Sitting down, he pulled a package of Juicy Fruit gum out of his shirt pocket and dangled it in the air. Jackson shook his head. Unwrapping a piece, Hawthorne shoveled it into his mouth, then leaned back and fixed Jackson with a steady gaze.

"I'm not going to bullshit you, Lionel. Things are going to be tough for a while. Some of my people still have an attitude about your role in that hostage incident, even though everybody knows you were officially cleared of any negligence. So you can expect a few cold shoulders at first. I know it's not fair, but then again, if people always did the right thing, you and I would be out of a job, right?"

"I guess."

"I should also warn you that like a lot of other cop shops in this city, we've had our problems with race. Officially, the department takes a dim view of such crap, but as we both know, only individual officers are privy to what goes down on the street and in the squad room. And since cops are notoriously tight-lipped...."

"How 'bout you, Lieutenant? You got a problem with my record, or my color?"

Hawthorne's gaze didn't waver. "That's a fair question. As for your record, I know what it's like to be in a tough spot. I have no doubt you did what you had to do. Your color is irrelevant. The only thing I care about is how good you are at helping me improve this squad's homicide clearance rate."

Jackson lit another cigarette with the butt of the one he was smoking.

"Like I was saying," continued Hawthorne, "things are going to be tough for a while. But you just do your job and try to stay cool until the others get to know you. In a few months, you'll be in like Flint."

"I'll do my best, Lieutenant."

"I expect no less," replied Hawthorne, sliding out of his chair.

Jackson watched him go, then began to put away the rest of his things. He knew the C.O. was right about staying cool, even if it strained his patience beyond endurance. A homicide detective relied on his colleagues, so he needed to win their respect. Without it, you became invisible, a non-entity.

In police circles, newcomers were judged according to a series of simple criteria. Did you have a backbone? Would you take the lead in a dangerous bust? Would you do so every time, or would you temper your courage with common sense? Would you be loyal and, if so, to whom? If you were loyal to the brass, you became a pariah. If you could balance your loyalty between the rulebook and the street, you made the grade.

Every cop had to face this judgment if he wanted to be accepted by his peers. There was no other way. In Jackson's case, the task would be even more daunting, not only because his status — at least in the eyes of some — had sunk lower than that of a rookie, but also because he was black. For despite all the recent noise about the NYPD's reforms, it was still one of the least racially integrated urban police forces in the country.

*****

Jackson didn't leave the station house until 9:30 p.m. Although his first day had been uneventful, he'd seen no point in rushing home to an empty apartment. He hated the solitude; as one of seven children raised in a cramped and noisy Brooklyn flat, it was alien to his nature. In fact, he'd never lived alone in his life. After being accepted into the police academy in 1980, he'd shared an apartment with a couple of fellow cadets. Two years later, he met a beautiful coed named Alyssa Ellison, a Chicago native who was spending her summer vacation with her brother in Harlem. They were married in 1983 and immediately started a family.

Now both Alyssa and the children were gone and Jackson was discovering what it was like to be alone. It was a problem he'd have to fix. A dog, maybe — assuming his new building allowed pets.

Thanks to some string pulling by a retired desk sergeant he'd done a few favors for back in the South Bronx, he'd wrangled a relatively cheap one-bedroom unit in a co-op on the Upper West Side. It was a lively, multicultural neighborhood of huge Victorian apartment buildings where intellectuals and artists lived side by side with shopkeepers, office workers, and bus drivers. Local politicians liked to boast that it was the city's most successfully integrated community.

Jackson flicked on the living room light, kicked off his shoes, and threw his jacket into the hall closet. Loosening his tie, he picked up the remote control and switched on the TV. Not that there was anything he wanted to watch; he just needed to hear the sound of human voices.

He strode into the bathroom and took a long piss. After washing his hands, he squeezed a few drops of baby oil onto his palm and massaged it into his scalp, which tended to get dry and itchy when he sat in an air-conditioned room for too long. He'd shaved off the last of his hair two years earlier because he decided a bald dome would be more intimidating than the medieval monk look.

Entering the kitchen, he grabbed a Coors and gulped down half the can before returning to the living room. The TV was tuned to CNN. For Jackson, it was either that or ESPN. Turning up the volume, he lit a cigarette and plunked down on the recliner — a gift from his wife. It vibrated and had an electric heating pad, for his bad back.

On the tube, Larry King and some wild-eyed lawyer whose hands were busier than an Italian pizza maker's were talking about the latest misadventures of O.J. Simpson.

Jackson shook his head. He began to wonder if the media would ever get over its obsession with the Simpson case — all because white America couldn't handle the possibility that a black man had beaten the system. Precious few ever did. Meanwhile, in the South, there were hundreds of old white codgers who, as young men, had participated in beatings and lynchings of innocent blacks and had never even been brought to trial. You didn't hear too many white folks complaining about *that* miscarriage of justice.

Disgusted, he switched to a middleweight boxing match on ESPN. He watched the bout for about ten minutes, but couldn't get involved. A cold, damp indifference had settled on his mind like an autumn mist. He turned off the TV and guzzled the rest of his beer. What now? He didn't feel tired enough for bed, but was too dozy to do any reading. A little music, maybe.

Walking over to the record player, which sat on the floor because he hadn't yet gotten around to buying a stand, he put on an old Nina Simone album, and then stretched out on the sofa. He closed his eyes, took a deep breath, and tried to relax.

At first, the music soothed him. Then, like it had almost every night for the past year, the memory of the incident that had ruptured his life wedged itself into his brain the way an old-time vacuum cleaner salesman used to wedge his foot in the doorway, insisting on being heard.

It was one of those bizarre twists of fate you read about in the papers, but never imagined could happen to you. A cold, dreary afternoon in February, the South Bronx. A New York City police detective, working out of the 41st Precinct, parks his car to buy a pack of smokes. Turning a corner, he glances across the street and spots a pair of do-rag-wearing characters in heavy overcoats acting strangely in front of a bank. They huddle and chatter excitedly for a moment, then rush inside. The cop decides to check it out.

Staying low and out of sight, he approaches the bank and sees the two men waving weapons and screaming out threats. He runs to his car and calls for back up. Then he makes his first mistake. Instead of waiting for the robbers to come out, he enters the bank, pretending to be a customer. He figures he can do more good on the inside, either by talking the perps down or taking them out if the situation threatens to get out of hand.

The robbers, who turn out to be a couple of teenage Latinos, no more than 17 or 18 years old, immediately herd him into a corner with the other hostages and force him to lie down on the floor. One of them is armed with an Uzi, the other with a handgun. They're both high — crack, it was later determined — and extremely agitated. A dangerous combination.

That's when the cop makes his second mistake. He listens to his heart instead of his brain. Twice he's presented with a narrow window of opportunity to take the perps out, but is deterred by his concern for the hostages — who are actually outside the probable line of fire — and the youthfulness of the robbers — a fact the cop doesn't mention during the subsequent inquiry.

Within minutes, the bank is surrounded by a phalanx of patrol cars and dozens of heavily armed uniforms. A member of the Hostage Negotiation Unit grabs a megaphone and prattles on about the hopelessness of the situation. What happens next comes right out of left field. The kid armed with the handgun grabs a male hostage, drags him to the front door, pushes him onto the sidewalk, and pumps three rounds into the back of his head. BOOM! BOOM! BOOM! Then he screams he'll kill another unless he gets an armored car in 15 minutes.

A million things flash through the cop's mind, making him feel like he's got snakes squirming around in his skull. What are his chances of taking the perps out? One's standing to his left, about eight yards away. The other's a dozen yards to his right. When he qualified at those distances, how accurate was he? If he hits them, will it stop them cold? Because if it doesn't, hostages are going to get shot. Ultimately, he decides it's too risky; he needs to get close enough to aim for their vitals.

Because of human error, the armored car doesn't show on time. True to his word, the kid grabs an elderly woman by the hair and drags her toward the front door. The cop realizes he's run out of options; he has to act, now. He pulls out his ankle gun and fires. He manages to disable the kid with a shoulder shot, and then all hell breaks loose. The hostages panic. The room is filled with screams and people running for cover. The cop's view of the second robber is momentarily obscured. Before he finally gets a bead on him, the whacked-out little bastard fires his Uzi and kills seven people.

Then comes part two of the ordeal, courtesy of Internal Affairs and the brass at One Police Plaza. Although the cop is eventually absolved of any negligence, his friends and fellow officers begin to treat him differently. Not with open hostility, mind you, but with a chill that makes him feel like crud on the bottom of someone's shoe. Meanwhile, guilt and endless second-guessing plague the cop. He becomes surly, defensive. The fights with his wife turn nastier and occur more often. He begins to alienate his kids. In short, his life turns to shit.

Four months later, the cop's wife takes the kids and moves back to her parents' place in Chicago. The divorce papers are filed. Around the same time, the cop's superiors decide that a change of scenery would be best for all concerned. After briefly toying with the idea of blowing his brains out — a not uncommon notion for veteran homicide detectives — the cop accepts the transfer.

Jackson sighed heavily and sat up. The record player had switched off and the apartment was silent except for the faint hum of the refrigerator. Ah, what the hell, he reasoned, trying to put a positive spin on the direction his life had taken, at least it had gotten him out of the South Bronx. In the last decade, the drug trade had turned the place into a hellhole. Once the stuff got a foothold in a community it spread like the Ebola virus, leaving destruction and ruined lives in its path. And turned kids into killers. Jackson wanted nothing more to do with drugs. Or with the South Bronx.

Yawning, he switched off the light and went to bed.

Chapter 4 — Wednesday, June 18

Rachel Curran sucked on a breath mint as she wiggled into a white, pleated cotton skirt with matching top, the last of several tennis outfits she'd been hired to model for a sporting goods flyer. Hovering nearby, overseeing the fitting, was the company's advertising director, a squat, stern-looking man with tufts of hair sprouting out of his ears and a high forehead, creased with worry. He scrutinized her for a few seconds, nodded his approval, then left the dressing room.

Rachel stripped down to her bra and panties and sat in front of the illuminated vanity mirror. The hairstylist, Gwen, a young black woman with long braids and a gold ring in her left nostril, gave her a blunt trim while the makeup artist, a slim Cuban expatriate named Armando, touched up her face.

Armando, who'd introduced himself by proudly proclaiming he'd been plying his trade for almost 25 years, liked to babble while he worked, and had done so incessantly since his arrival. He'd already exhausted a number of topics, including the newest lipsticks, movies, Broadway musicals, and the New York spring collections — he *loved* Todd Oldham's beaded top and pinstriped trousers; *hated* Isaac Mizrahi's fur-trimmed leopard, cheetah, and tiger patches; was *blown away* by Cesar Galindo's use of Playboy playmates to introduce his new line — and was now dispensing the latest dirt about one of the city's more notorious models.

"—by nine o'clock she was so high she started to do a striptease on the pool table. People were freaking! Later, she ended up fucking some agent's brains out in the bathroom. Can you imagine? But you got to hand it to the lady. The next morning she was in the studio for an eight o'clock shoot. That is what you call a real pro."

Rachel arched an eyebrow.

"Still," continued Armando, a wistful smile playing on his lips, "things today are tame compared to the way they were back in the seventies. Studio Fifty-Four was rocking. Warhol was hosting the most amazing parties in the Village. Sex was still safe. And there was more coke on the street than snow in December.

"And Milano was even wilder. The agencies used to put their new models into these two hotels that insiders called the Fuck Palace and the Principessa Clitoris. The girls would get off the plane and there would be a fleet of Rolls-Royces driven by these slick dago playboys with roses in one hand and a bag of nose candy in the other. We are talking total excess. If a girl did not have her shit together, she could get messed up real good."

"A lot of them still do," added Gwen. "Hundreds of wannabes pour into this town every month, lookin' for glamor and fast money. They don't realize how competitive it is, and that only a few ever reach the top. Which means it can get real crowded at the bottom. The girls who are too dumb to understand what they're up against end up as prey for the bottom feeders." She moved around to face Rachel. "How long you been in the biz, honey?"

"About six years, but mostly part-time while I was going to school."

"Here in New York?"

"No, Buffalo. I moved here about seven months ago."

"Well let me give you a bit of sisterly advice. The models that survive in this town are the ones who know how to treat it like a business. Watch your money. Stay away from drugs. And don't sleep around — especially with agents or photographers."

"What about makeup artists?" asked Armando, grinning.

"Most of the ones I know aren't into chicks," replied Gwen.

"Oh, I don't mind a little pussy every now and then."

"I'll make sure to keep my cat off the street."

"Oooo, very wittay. If I—"

Just then the door opened and the photographer, Byron Clark, a gaunt redhead sporting a pair of khaki shorts, a yellow T-shirt with the phrase 'Models Give Good Face' stenciled across the front, and a Rod Stewart haircut, entered the dressing room and positioned himself behind Rachel. Peering into the mirror, he studied her face in silence, his eyes hidden behind a pair of blue-tinted oval sunglasses.

"How much longer, Armando?"

"Almost done, compadre."

Clark nodded. "Bring her out as soon as you're ready. I'm all set up." Then he spun around and returned to the studio.

Finally, just before 1:00 p.m., Rachel stepped before the camera for the first time. It was a simple set, consisting of half a dozen fake marble columns, staggered in height from left to right, and arrayed in an arc in front of a pale blue backdrop. Atop each column sat an upright tennis racquet. Someone turned on a CD player and the room was filled with the strains of U2's *Discotheque.* Rachel took a number of deep breaths to help her relax. She reminded herself not to think about what she was wearing, but to go with the flow and *feel* the outfit. Her job was to make the ordinary extraordinary.

Clark shot a couple of Polaroids, and then had Armando soften Rachel's makeup while he walked away to study his compositions.

Twenty minutes later, he returned and had his assistant switch on a fan. Picking up his camera, he began to prowl around the set, snapping away from several angles. The assistant hovered in the background, along with Armando and Gwen, each of them ready to jump in as required, to load a camera, adjust a spotlight, or fix Rachel's hair, clothing, or makeup.

"Go with it, baby," urged Clark. "That's right. Put you hands in your hair...very sexy. Now raise your chin a bit...good, good. John, move that reflector a couple of inches to the right. Okay. Rachel, turn your head toward me slightly and place your hands on your hips. That's it...very nice. All right, we need a good cleavage shot. Bend forward a bit and look right into the camera. Excellent. You're the best, sweetheart."

What a jerk, thought Rachel. Why did every hack photographer in the business have to carry on like he was Richard Avedon?

*****

The shoot ended at 3:45. Rachel, now dressed in white Bermuda shorts, a baggy T-shirt, and a pair of sandals, walked out of the East 48th Street studio and strolled toward Park Avenue. She had a squash court booked for 4:30, which left plenty of time since the YMCA was located just down the block. Hopefully, Sally wouldn't get caught in rush hour traffic again.

It was a gorgeous afternoon. Warm, but not too humid. Clear sky. A slight breeze. Rachel took a deep breath and soaked up the sights, sounds, and smells of Manhattan. She still found it hard to believe she was living and working in the Big Apple — even if she wasn't exactly setting the place on fire.

The situation did have a certain irony. As a kid, she had often dreamed of conquering New York — but as a concert pianist, not a model. She might have accomplished her original goal, too, if her steady climb up the musical ladder had not been interrupted on that day in 1989 when a photographer 'discovered' her during a high school recital and insisted she had potential. Shy by nature, she'd reacted with skepticism, but not enough to dampen her intrigue. A family conference and several phone calls from the photographer ensued. Finally, her parents agreed to a test.

For the next few months she tested with several local photographers and eventually put together a decent portfolio and a composite. Her mother, who had been most opposed to her involvement, did a complete about turn. She began to buy her new clothes and to offer suggestions about hair and makeup.

Soon, Rachel began to earn back her mother's investment by modeling after school for $60 an hour. She also began to fantasize about being a supermodel — gracing the covers of *Glamour* and *Cosmopolitan* and *Vogue*, earning a million dollars a year, and dating a cool, devilishly handsome, hotel-room-smashing rock star.

She continued to model while attending the University of Buffalo, where she studied drama and music. Again, she worked after school, primarily for a local department store. By this time, her fee had jumped to $100 an hour.

Rachel's newfound success as a model turned out to be a fortuitous twist of fate because, halfway through her second term, she realized that she lacked both the discipline and, more to the point, the desire to be a concert pianist. But instead of wallowing in self-pity, she decided to devote her energy and resources to becoming a top model.

Her first big break came a few months later, when a photographer friend suggested she should enter a local beauty pageant, claiming it was a great way to garner free publicity — especially if she won. Rachel demurred at first, because she didn't consider herself beautiful enough. She had small breasts, a moderate overbite, and a slight bump on the bridge of her nose that could be touched up in a photograph but would be glaringly visible on a brightly lit stage.

However, her desire to succeed soon prevailed over her lack of confidence — especially when she realized there were ways to correct her physical shortcomings. That summer, after another heated family debate — with her father providing the main opposition this time — she had her nose altered and her breasts enlarged. But she decided against correcting her overbite, believing it gave her face character and originality.

The following September, she qualified as an entrant in the *Miss Pride of Buffalo* pageant and, to her surprise — and with the help of her piano skills — had won. Not only did she carry off a number of prizes and a modest scholarship, but more importantly, the victory led to dozens of new modeling opportunities.

The road seemed clear and the future, promising — until fate threw yet another monkey wrench into her plans. By the time she graduated, in the spring of 1996, with degrees in music and theater arts, her interest in becoming a career mannequin had been supplanted by a passion for acting. This turn of events surprised her almost as much as it did her family. Yet there was nothing to be done about it; she was hooked.

Rachel's next decision proved to be one of the toughest of her young life. Over both her parents' protestations, she announced her intention of moving to New York City. She had it all worked out. She would enroll in an acting class and support herself with the money she earned from modeling. Modeling would also provide her with another advantage: it would keep her in the public spotlight. If she became well known enough, it could even lead to commercials or minor acting jobs.

But all of that was still in the future. First she had to generate a little seed money. She also needed to update her portfolio. So, for the next six months she pushed herself to the limit, taking on as many modeling assignments as she could squeeze into a 14-hour day. She also entered — and won — the *Miss Erie County* pageant.

Finally, on a cold, snowy day in late November — after wrapping up her local modeling contracts — she gathered up her portfolio, her copy of the *Madison Avenue Handbook*, a map, and a single suitcase, and took the train to Manhattan.

Talk about a rude awakening. Despite having a photogenic face — hazel eyes, high cheekbones, a slim jaw line, and short brown hair — and the right figure — five feet, eight inches tall, 124 pounds, medium frame — it took almost a month of knocking on doors before she found an agency that would represent her. Even then, no one would mistake Peerless Models, which operated out of a three-room suite above an East 62nd Street printing shop, as a major player, like Ford, Wilhelmina, or Elite.

Six and a half months later, Rachel was still perched precariously on the agency's 'junior board,' an industry euphemism for being on probation. If she didn't make the grade soon she'd be dropped. Most newcomers were usually given six months; the only reason she was still hanging on was because of her good relationship with the owner. But in the end, her continuing employment would depend entirely on the bottom line.

At first, she couldn't comprehend her lack of success. But now she realized that she'd been pigeonholed as a girl-next-door type, a situation that had frozen her out of the high-paying glamor and cover girl jobs and had relegated her to the secondary market of catalog and retail advertising. She augmented these assignments with runway work for local department stores, as well as the occasional trade show.

It was a dizzying, unbelievable grind. Every day she and her booker would make appointments with advertising agencies, photographers, magazine editors — often as many as a dozen a day. She'd get a nibble here, a minor assignment there. If it weren't for her perfect size eight figure, which kept her in demand for fittings, and her part-time waitressing job, she'd probably be back in Buffalo.

The problem wasn't just Manhattan's astronomical cost of living and the steep fees she had to pay for her acting lessons; she also had more expenses than the average person, for business related items like modeling cards, clothing, makeup, and transportation.

Age was another sore point. Rachel had turned 24 in March. That was considered old for a model. Even in the secondary markets, there was always someone younger and better-looking competing for the same jobs. And since she had no acting experience, which made it unlikely she'd be able to earn a living in that profession, she knew she needed some kind of miracle. Soon.

*****

Sally Schuster, a raven-haired 26-year-old who bristled with the potential energy of a coiled spring, sat waiting in the YMCA members' lounge, sipping on a Perrier while ogling the men who wandered about in tank tops and skin-tight Speedos.

Sally was the only real friend Rachel had in New York. They'd met at the Rusty Nail, a Greenwich Village pub where Sally tended bar full-time and Rachel worked weekends waiting on tables. When Sally split up with her boyfriend, the two women moved into a two-bedroom apartment together, primarily for financial reasons, but also because Sally figured having a roommate would make it easier to blow off unwanted suitors.

Rachel smiled and waved at her friend, then bought a cup of plain yogurt before joining her.

"How'd the shoot go?" asked Sally.

"Okay, until I made the mistake of offering the photographer a suggestion about the lighting. You'd think I'd made a rude crack about his mother the way he started jumping and hollering."

"You're kidding."

"I wish."

"Are all photographers that thin-skinned?"

"The good ones know their stuff, so you seldom have anything to complain about. And if you do, most of them will usually hear you out as long as you're tactful. But God spare me from the hacks. It's so weird. It seems the more incompetent the photographer, the more he hates getting suggestions."

"Isn't there some way of doing it so the guy thinks it's his idea?"

"I suppose, if you're willing to make the effort. But I have a hard time getting past the attitude."

Sally patted her on the hand.

"Fortunately," added Rachel, lowering her voice, "there is an upside — besides the cash, I mean."

"What's that?"

"At least the creep didn't hit on me."

Sally smiled and drained the last of her Perrier. "Speaking of getting hit on, the other night I met a guy who would be *perfect* for you."

Rachel groaned. Sally made matches as regularly — and as methodically — as she mixed drinks.

"I'm serious. He's a hunk, and very, very bright — I think he's an associate editor with some computer magazine. He likes the theater. And, he's a vegetarian."

"Sounds like my dream man, all right, but I'm still not interested."

"Why, for heaven's sake?"

"Because, as I've explained a gazillion times, I'm trying to earn enough to pay my bills *and* launch an acting career. I don't have the time, or the energy, for a relationship."

"Who's talking about a relationship? I just want you to have some fun."

"There'll be plenty of time for fun later."

"Don't count on it, kiddo. You're only young once."

Sally narrowed her eyes and scrutinized Rachel's face. "Hey, you're not still pining over that Fred guy from college, are you?"

"Of course not!" replied Rachel, defensively. Although she had convinced herself that her career *was* the reason she'd been avoiding emotional entanglements, she still found it difficult to meet her friend's accusing gaze.

She had dated Fred Emerson for almost two years. They'd even talked about marriage. Then, just before graduation, he took her for a walk in Delaware Park, mumbled something about how their needs didn't match up, and broke off the relationship. No warning. No further explanation. And although Rachel wanted to believe she had gotten over him, the memory of their time together still had the power to wound. Maybe, on a subliminal level, the breakup had also affected her ability to trust men.

"Listen," said Sally, "take some advice from a pro. The best way to get over a man is to get *under* another. The sooner, the better."

Rachel laughed. "I appreciate the advice, but the truth is, I've never been very good at playing the field. When the time comes, I'll be looking for something permanent. In the meantime—"

"I know, I know. Your damned career."

"Right."

"Okay, kiddo, but don't say I never tried."

Sally glanced at the clock. "We'd better get going before we lose our court."

Rachel spooned up the last of her yogurt and threw the container into a nearby trashcan. "Sal? I've got something to tell you."

Sally's eyes widened.

"I've decided to enter the Miss Empire State pageant in July."

"Really? Just like that?"

"Of course not, silly. It's only open to women who've won a sanctioned local competition. At first I wasn't interested, but now I think it might be a good idea."

"You never told me you'd won a beauty pageant."

"I never considered it a big deal."

"That's your problem, Rach. You're too damned modest. There's nothing wrong with blowing your own horn every now and then, especially in your line of work."

"Thank you, Dale Carnegie."

Sally grinned. "So, out with it, which pageant did you win?"

"You're looking at the current Miss Erie County," replied Rachel, striking an exaggerated runway pose.

"All right!"

"I know it's a long shot, but if I were to win the state title, I'd qualify for the national competition, and that could get me all kinds of modeling work."

"No kidding."

"Then, if I became famous enough, it would be the perfect springboard to an acting career. There are dozens of models who took that route. Sigourney Weaver, Jessica Lange, Anjelica Huston. And even if I didn't win, at least I'd pick up a nice chunk of prize money."

"I think your chances are excellent, Rach. You're a fox. There's not a guy who comes into the bar who doesn't get a woody every time your cute little ass bounces by."

"Don't be gross."

"I'm serious!"

"Listen, this state is full of gorgeous women, many of them a lot more beautiful than I am."

"Well," replied Sally, jokingly, "there's always plastic surgery, to help smooth out the rough spots. Maybe a touch of collagen for your lips."

"Oh, no. I've already gone that route and have no intention of doing it again."

"What! You're a real bundle of surprises today, aren't you?"

"Nothing major. Just a minor nose job and breast implants."

"Nothing major, she says."

"Well, not when compared to what some women do to their faces. They look as pasty and expressionless as that robot guy on Star Trek."

Sally chuckled. "Anyway," she said, "beauty pageants have changed in the last twenty years, haven't they? They're not just about looking good in a bathing suit any more, right?"

"No, but—"

"So your chances are *still* excellent, because you're bright, you have great poise, and you play a mean piano."

"And you," said Rachel, throwing an arm around her friend's shoulder, "have a tongue that would charm the frock off a Franciscan monk."

"You mean a rabbi. I'm Jewish, remember."

Laughing, the two women picked up their racquets and hurried toward the squash courts.

Chapter 5 — Friday, June 20

Robert Molinaro set his cigar in the ashtray, slid his earphones over his head, and took a sip from a monogrammed mug containing one part Colombian coffee and two parts Chivas Regal. The proportions varied from night to night, depending on his mood, which at the moment hovered between bitterness and resignation. His latest job application had been rejected by yet another local television station and he was beginning to think he'd be stuck in small-time radio indefinitely — unless management fired his ass first. Or unless he could change his wife's mind about leaving New York. The odds were heavily stacked in favor of scenario number one.

Molinaro had been with WSNY for six years, jumping aboard shortly after graduating from the Columbia School of Journalism. He'd started out as a proofreader in the news department, then moved up to copy editor, reporter, news announcer and, finally, host of his own talk show. Most people would have been satisfied with that track record, but Molinaro never intended to spend his life in radio. It was supposed to have been a proving ground, a jumping off point for a lucrative, high profile job in network television.

What was that old saying about best-laid plans?

It wouldn't be so bad if his show were more successful; say, rated among the top five in the tri-state area (he had no illusions about being number one, not with Howard Stern ruling the roost with his vacuous, yet incomprehensibly popular shock-talk routine). Instead, *Molinaro on N.Y. 99* had been stuck near the middle of the pack for the entire year and a half it had been on the air. Management had tinkered with the program's length, format, subject mix — they'd even saddled him with a female co-host for a few months — but none of the changes had improved the ratings. Through it all, he'd ignored the backroom whispers and dutifully put in his time, his enthusiasm seeping away like motor oil past a worn gasket.

Molinaro took another sip from his mug and wiped his mustache with a napkin. Any day now he'd probably be replaced by some psychic, crystal-worshipping, smart-drug popping, reincarnated New Age astrologist.

A crackle in his earphones. "Five seconds, Bob."

Molinaro glanced at Sid Crouse, his producer, sitting in the control room. Sid raised his hand and began the count down with his fingers.

Molinaro cleared his throat and switched on the microphone. "Hell-o New York, and welcome to Molinaro on N.Y. Ninety-Nine, the voice of the Big Apple. If you've got an opinion about politics, current events, or the arts, we're here to listen. And make sure you stick around for the second half of the program. Tonight's guest is former mayor Ed Koch, who, I'm sure, will have a few provocative things to say. All right, then. Let's get to our first call."

Sid fed him a name, which he then repeated on air: "Here's Muriel, from Staten Island."

"Bob?"

"What's on your mind, Muriel?"

"I'd like to talk about a film I saw the other night."

"Which one?"

"The People Versus Larry Flynt."

Molinaro rolled his eyes at the prospect of yet another feminist rant against the evils of pornography. "For those listeners who haven't seen the film, which was up for last year's best picture Oscar, it chronicles the life of Larry Flynt, the publisher of Hustler magazine. It was directed by Milos Foreman and stars Woody Harrelson and Courtney Love. What did you think of the film, Muriel?"

"I found its moral dishonesty pretty hard to stomach. I mean, I can accept that Flynt's fight against the religious fundamentalists who wanted to suppress his magazine was intended as a metaphor for all battles over freedom of speech, but the film ignores the female point of view. And that completely undermines its intended purpose.

"First of all, the film whitewashes Larry Flynt. If you look at the record, the man is nothing like the charming hick we see on the screen, and his magazine has been far more disgusting than the filmmakers let on. Take the movie's most important scene, for example. There's Flynt standing on a stage draped with American flags, presenting a slide show contrasting bloody images from the Vietnam War with fairly tame pictures of naked women. Meanwhile, he's yelling that wars, not vaginas, are the real obscenity."

"Do you disagree with that?"

"Of course not. Any sane person would say the same thing. The problem is, the scene ignores the fact that most women in the audience know the truth about Hustler magazine. If the filmmakers had been honest, they would've alluded to the violent, degrading images of women often found in its pages. Instead, they decided to censor those images to enhance their message about freedom of speech. How does that differ from attempts by fundamentalists to censor images in the name of God?"

"Your point is well taken, Muriel. But let's face it; films are not the most suitable medium for tackling serious issues. Any time you try to cram a message into a two-hour time slot, the result is going to be simplistic and superficial."

"True, but unfortunately, many people form their opinions from the quote, unquote, facts they get from movies and television. And that can be dangerous when you have a filmmaker who has an agenda."

"Watch it, you're wading into the turbulent waters of free speech."

"Believe me, I'm a strong supporter of the first amendment. I just think that filmmakers need to be more responsible when they set out to make a moral or political statement — no matter how laudable their intent."

"I wouldn't hold my breath, Muriel. Thanks for your call."

Sid fed him another name. "Here's George, from Brooklyn Heights."

"Hi, Bob. Listen, I see here where O.J. Simpson—"

"Sorry, George. That horse is not only dead, it's beginning to stink." Molinaro motioned to Sid to patch in another caller. "Here's Ray, from Hell's Kitchen."

"Evening, Bob. I just want to say that I think the country's turning into a nation of crackpots."

"Can you be more specific?"

"Look around, for God's sake. We've got children shooting each other over drugs; militia goons blowing up innocent women and children because they hate the government; secessionist movements popping up all over the place; a growing number of cults, including those yahoos who just committed mass suicide so they could climb aboard a spaceship and follow some comet to paradise; bigots and racists using quotations from the bible to justify the destruction of their enemies; tabloid television polluting the airwaves with a never-ending parade of freaks, deviants, and exhibitionists. And you want to know what's most disturbing about all of this? It's become routine, part of the daily fabric of American life. Hell, there are even people making jokes about this stuff on late night T.V."

"I agree it's a bleak picture, but that's the price you pay for living in a democracy."

"There must be something we can do."

"Like what? Throw all non-conformists into jail?"

"No, but—"

"Listen. There's always going to be a certain amount of mayhem in this country. But there'd be a lot less if people minded their own damn business. And that goes for the government, too. Instead, we've got all these public wars raging over issues that are a matter of personal choice. Abortion, suicide, euthanasia, sexual orientation. Even drugs. You want to end the violence associated with drugs? Treat narcotics the same as alcohol. Legalize the stuff, then restrict its sale to minors and provide information about its dangers. If people become addicted, or end up killing themselves, so be it. That's their choice."

"But you can't just allow people to do whatever they want. There have to be some rules about public conduct."

"Of course. But they should only apply if a person's actions infringe on the rights of others. If not, butt out."

"I'm not sure I agree with you."

"That's your prerogative. Thanks for your call."

"Frank's on the line, Bob."

Molinaro turned to Sid and nodded. Frank was a regular who had some truly weird ideas. Nevertheless, he was more diverting — and more eloquent, in a cold, detached way — than the average caller. His comments were always inflammatory and usually triggered a heated response from other listeners. For this reason, Molinaro had provided him with access to a private phone line reserved for a select group of similar provocateurs.

"Here's Frank, from the upper east side."

"How are you tonight, Robert?"

Molinaro immediately recognized the voice, a slow, modulated bass, reminiscent of Orson Welles.

"Fine, Frank. What's on your mind?"

"I wish to enlarge on the statement made by the previous caller. The country *is* in trouble, but not for the reasons he indicated. The real cause is the disintegration of the family. The statistics are appalling. Divorces are at an all-time high, the birth rate among unwed mothers is soaring, and the streets are swarming with abused and unwanted children."

"Why do you think these things are happening, Frank?"

"Women are to blame."

"You can't be serious."

"I am always serious, Robert."

"But why target women? It takes both parents to create a functional family."

"My point exactly. But that paradigm is in jeopardy, because too many women have strayed from the path that nature created for them. Look at animals in the wild. The male is the guardian and the provider while the female propagates the species, nurtures the young, and tends to the nest. But many women have relinquished this role and instead, are trying to usurp that of the male. In the process, they are emasculating their mates and abandoning their children."

"What about women who don't want to have a family, or men who like the idea of staying home to take care of the children?"

"Mere statistical blips."

"So what you're saying is that women must choose between raising a family or having a career. Is that right?"

"Yes."

"You don't believe a woman can do both?"

"Not without putting the welfare of her children at risk."

"That's a pretty extreme view, Frank."

"Opinions have nothing to do with it. There is only one natural law and it is immutable."

Molinaro took a drag on his cigar and winked at Sid. It was time to tighten the screws a bit. "Tell me something, Frank. You don't like the idea of women in the workplace, do you?"

"That is not the point. As I have just explained—"

"Never mind the child-rearing angle. I'm talking about working women in general."

"I do have some difficulty with the idea, yes."

"Why?"

"For two reasons. One, because they take away jobs that should be going to men, which contributes to higher male unemployment. As a result, many men have lost their self-esteem and are confused about their role in society. Two, because most women are hired for their looks rather than for their skills."

"Oh, come on."

"You have eyes, Robert. Look at the women who earn the most money: models, actresses, media personalities. Do you believe they got where they are because of their brains?"

"Maybe not all of the jobs you mention call for a PhD, but they do require certain skills. Besides, being attractive is a prerequisite in the entertainment industry. That's what the public wants."

"The public is an ass."

Molinaro was inclined to agree with him, but held his tongue. "What about handsome men? Don't they have the same advantages as beautiful women?"

"It is not the same thing."

"Why not?"

"Because regardless of their looks, men are judged primarily by their actions. In every arena, a man must outperform his opponents in order to surpass them."

"Nonsense. There are just as many men who get to become news anchors, actors, and top models because of their looks, as there are women."

Frank didn't respond right away and Molinaro wondered if he'd lost him. But no, he could hear his shallow breathing.

"A woman who trades on her physical assets for money is no better than a whore."

Molinaro pumped his fist into the air.

"Models are the worst offenders," continued Frank. "They are a blight on society. Everywhere you look you see their leering, half-naked images flogging some product or service. Have you been to a fashion show lately? They rival strip clubs for their lewdness. The models slither up and down the runway to the rhythms of suggestive rock music, exposing their breasts, their buttocks — sometimes even the outline of their vulvas. If that does not describe the behavior of a whore, what does?"

"Jeez, Frank. Lighten up. The ladies are just trying to make a living."

"Prostitutes use the same justification. But at least society recognizes them for what they are and duly condemns their behavior. Models, however, do even more damage but yet are treated like royalty."

"What damage?"

"By being held up as the feminine ideal, they create a gulf between fantasy and reality. In desiring them, men lose sight of the fact that true beauty resides in the woman who stays home to raise her children and care for her mate. And in trying to compete with them, other females are made to feel inferior."

"But isn't your criticism misplaced? After all, a model is nothing more than a marketing tool."

"These women have a choice, Robert. No one is holding a gun to their heads. They are either part of the problem or part of the solution."

"The problem being...?"

Frank sighed. "The breakdown of the American family, of course. By heaping money and prestige on models and females in similar vulgar occupations, we are sending out the wrong message, one that is luring more and more women away from their natural role of wife and mother. It has got to stop. Somehow, we must get back to our traditional family values."

This goombah's logic is loopier than a Slinky, thought Molinaro, swallowing the rest of his drink. "It's not going to happen, Frank. Not as long as a woman can earn a six-figure salary just by strutting her stuff. They don't call America the land of opportunity for nothing. Besides, if some women do choose to sell their bodies or their looks for money, it's men who do most of the buying."

"Only because their natural instincts are being perverted by these witches!"

"Oh, come on."

"You are just as blind as the others, Robert. Well, so be it. Great causes are often those one must fight alone."

"If you say so."

"Scoff if you must, but the day of reckoning is at hand."

"What's that supposed to mean?"

"You will know soon enough," replied Frank, and hung up.

Molinaro looked over at Sid. The producer had both of his thumbs up, his way of indicating that the switchboard was flashing like an Atlantic City slot machine.

"Here's Erica, from Greenwich Village."

"Hi, Bob. Listen, I'm a model and I've got a couple of things to say to that creep who just got off the air. First of all, being beautiful is no guarantee of anything in this life, other than being hit on by every self-styled Don Juan within sniffing distance. As for those of us who choose to exploit our God-given looks to earn a living, all I can say is that modeling is bloody hard work. It involves long hours, a lot of early morning calls, demanding travel schedules, putting up with the antics of egomaniacal designers, editors, and photographers, and constant rejection.

"On top of which, we've got to exercise regularly, watch what we eat, and constantly fret over our make-up, hair, and clothing. And as soon as we're considered too old, we're tossed onto the scrap heap. I'd like to see Frank try to handle that kind of stress. He'd probably curl up in the fetal position and cry for his mommy."

"What about the argument that models make too much money?"

"Why should we be singled out for that? What about athletes or actors or rock stars? Besides, it's only a select few who make the really big bucks. For the rest of us, it's a constant struggle to make ends meet, especially if you're just starting out. Did you know that for the first year or so in the business, a model's expenses run to more than five thousand dollars?"

"Is that right?"

"The truth is, for the number of hours we put in, most models live quite modestly."

"What about agencies? Is it true that it's virtually impossible to get work if a girl is not affiliated with an agency?"

"In New York it is."

"What's the fee situation?"

"The agency receives a commission, generally between fifteen to twenty percent of a model's earnings. In all cases, the client pays the agency, then the agency deducts its commission and pays the model."

"Do you think it's a fair arrangement?"

"Absolutely, if you're with a good agency."

"One last question, Erica. How to you respond to the criticism that models are nothing more than mindless clotheshorses?"

"Honey, I don't care whether people think of me only as a face, a body, or a lifeless mannequin, as long as it brings in more work and lots of cash."

*****

Night had fallen on Manhattan. Robert Molinaro hurried through the WSNY parking lot and climbed into his red 1993 BMW. Lighting a cigar, he pulled out onto East 62nd Street and settled back for the long drive to his split-level home in New Rochelle.

Luckily, his show's time slot allowed him to avoid rush hour, otherwise he probably would've gone nuts ages ago. He'd begged his wife to move to the city; they could certainly afford to. But no, she needed to be near her family, in a safe community, in a house with a verandah and a back yard. Like he ever had any time to appreciate those things.

Thank God it's Friday, he thought, as he steered the car onto FDR Drive and headed north toward the Triborough Bridge. Sighing, he wedged his cigar between his teeth and shoved a Marvin Gaye cassette into the tape deck, hoping it would lessen the tedium. He turned up the volume, pressed down on the accelerator, and sped toward the horizon.

A short time later, the wailing of an ambulance siren startled him out of his hazy reverie. It wasn't the first time he'd slipped into automatic pilot while commuting. He had made the trip so often there were times he'd get home and wouldn't be able to recollect a single detail of the drive.

Rubbing his neck, he glanced to his left and saw he was passing through his old neighborhood, the South Bronx, a dense, hilly landscape of tangled streets, vacant lots, scrub parks, abandoned factories, schools that had been turned into armed compounds, and block after block of graffiti-covered tenement buildings, many of them in various stages of disrepair.

Wisely, his parents — along with most of their other Italian neighbors — had moved out of the area while he was still an infant, before it turned into a war zone. He couldn't even begin to imagine growing up in such a place. Drugs. Guns. Gangs. Who knows? He might've ended up working for the mob, a regular wise guy. On the other hand, maybe that wouldn't have been so bad. There were plenty of people he wouldn't mind whacking.

The Molinaros had resettled in the northeastern part of the borough, close to Mount Vernon. Up there, on the other side of Gun Hill Road, the Bronx was a different world, an oasis of parks and well-ordered neighborhoods. The area still contained stands of the original forest that once covered the entire archipelago: oaks, cedars, and poplars as old as the first Dutch settlements. Farther west, on the banks of the Hudson and in the hills above it, one could find some of the most impressive Tudor and Palladian mansions in the state, all with a view across the river to the Palisades and the suburbs of New Jersey.

Of course, the house his parents moved into was no mansion. But it was roomy enough, and comfortable, and it was situated in a safe, quiet community where he and his two older sisters had been allowed to run rampant. More importantly, the house had what every Italian immigrant yearned for: a huge back yard. Every summer the old man would grow enough produce to feed a small army. The stuff that wasn't eaten right away was frozen, preserved, or given to the neighbors. Now the surplus was given to the children, since none of them had gardens of their own, his sisters because they both lived in apartments and he because he had neither the time nor the inclination to rut around in the dirt.

Whenever Molinaro reminisced about his childhood, the central image was one of food. Besides the produce his parents grew, they also made their own sausages, various cured meats, fruit preserves, tomato sauce, and gallons of home-made red wine, all kept in the *cantina* the old man had constructed under the verandah. The children always had to participate, either by picking fruit and vegetables, cranking the wine press, or guiding ground meat into sausage skins.

Instinctively, Molinaro glanced at his truncated right index finger, a memento of the time he was careless while pressing a handful of pork into the mouth of a meat grinder. His father had smacked him in the head for being a clumsy oaf. It took Molinaro years to realize that the blow was triggered by his old man's panic, not anger over having his sausage spoiled.

Smiling wistfully, he crushed out his cigar and shoved another cassette into the tape deck.

*****

To his surprise, Anna was still up when he got home. She was leaning over the kitchen sink, rinsing out her best espresso cups.

"It's pretty late, honey. How come you're not in bed yet?"

"Lena and Carmen were over. We watched a couple of videos."

Molinaro walked up behind her and gently massaged her distended belly. "Were they any good?"

"Okay," she replied, wriggling out of his grasp. She dried her hands and slowly hunkered down onto a chair. "Are you hungry? Lena brought over a dozen ricotta cannoli — a dozen, can you beat that? Like I don't already look like a cow."

"No, thanks. And you don't look like a cow. You look like a beautiful woman who's seven months pregnant."

"Yeah, right." Sighing, she brushed aside a loose strand of auburn hair that had fallen across her brow. "Listen, did you pick up that yarn I asked for?"

Molinaro cringed. "Shit! Sorry, hon. I forgot."

"God, Bobby. I reminded you three times before you left this afternoon."

"What can I say? I had a bad day, what with that goddamn job application being rejected and all the bloody rumors whirling around down at the station."

"Oh, and you think my day was a picnic?"

"Don't put words in my mouth."

"What else am I supposed to think? This is your baby, too, remember? But I'm the only one who ever seems to want to take any responsibility."

"Don't start with me, Anna. I'm tired and I'm not in the mood."

"You're never in the mood! Just once I'd like to see you do something for me without my having to ask first. It's like you don't even see me any more."

"That's bullshit."

"No it's not. You're completely self-absorbed. You spend ten hours a day at work, then when you come home you disappear up your own asshole."

"Maybe if you'd let us move to Manhattan, or let me look for a job in another city, I wouldn't have to work so hard or drive so fucking far every day."

"I told you a million times. I'm not moving."

"Then get off my back!"

"God, Bobby, I can't understand why you're so miserable. You've got a good job. You make good money. We have a nice home. Why isn't that enough?"

"Because in my business you either move up the ladder or you fade away. And being a non-entity is not part of my life plan."

"Do you really believe that becoming a big shot is going to make you happy?"

"Damn right. And I intend to do everything in my power to make it happen, with or without your help."

"What's that supposed to mean?"

"You figure it out."

She glared at him, but did not reply. An uneasy silence filled the space between them while Molinaro struggled to find words that would at least put them back in neutral corners. But none came. At least none that he hadn't already used on a dozen different occasions.

Turning away, he rushed upstairs to the bedroom and quickly changed into a pair of white cotton slacks, a blue silk shirt, and a pair of clean socks. He then slapped on some cologne and went back downstairs.

"Anna!" He waited until she stuck her head into the kitchen doorway. "I'm going out for a beer."

Her shoulders sagged. "Suit yourself."

Molinaro hesitated, then drew a deep breath and pulled open the front door.

Outside, the moon hung fat and low on the horizon and a westerly breeze ruffled the branches of the oak tree that stood in front of the house. But the wind did little to diminish the humidity.

Goddammit! thought Molinaro, lighting a cigar with trembling fingers. Lately, all his conversations with Anna seemed to degenerate into arguments. It was like treading through a mine field. Not that the marriage had ever been a romp in the park — given that they were both as obstinate as mules — but their differences had multiplied tenfold since the onset of Anna's pregnancy.

Molinaro had wanted to put off starting a family for a few more years, at least until his career was on track. But Anna, worried about her ticking biological clock and obsessed by the fact that all her friends had children, hounded him mercilessly. He finally relented, hoping the prospect of a baby would at least improve their relationship. Instead, she had become even more sullen and querulous. She'd even lost interest in sex, the one thing they'd always done well together.

What in the name of Christ had compelled him to get married in the first place? The world was teeming with beautiful women, all just sitting there, waiting to be plucked from the branch like so many ripe cherries.

Molinaro glanced at his watch. It was 12:25. Linda's shift at the Shady Meadow Home For the Aged ended in a few minutes. If he hurried, he could still catch her. Linda Febiger, a nurse's aide whom he'd met at a local bar, was a bit on the plump side and not the brightest of women, but she was a terrific listener, loved to dance, and always welcomed him into her bed.

Chapter 6 — Saturday, June 21

Frank Ryman stood in front of his living room window and watched the sun, swollen and blood red, dip below the Manhattan skyline. Within minutes, the city was shrouded in darkness. He closed the curtains, collapsed onto the easy chair, and began to nervously drum his fingers on the armrests.

A week had passed since the Tanya Holt incident, and although he'd kept his vow about avoiding women, it had been a struggle. To make matters worse, his fantasies had been occurring more frequently — even when he wasn't in a state of arousal. It was like being wired into a movie projector that couldn't be shut off. The resulting sexual agitation had his brain squirming like a swarm of hungry maggots.

He had tried to sublimate his carnal cravings by extending his daily swims to the point of exhaustion, and by throwing himself into his work and his puzzles, but it didn't help. Neither did masturbation, an activity that always left him feeling dirty and dissatisfied.

Curiously, his avoidance of women had also produced a positive effect: there'd been no more visits from the she-devil who resided in his head. He wondered if the two things were related.

Sighing, he slung his legs onto the footstool and switched on the TV, hoping it would help him relax — and allow him to forget it was Saturday night, his favorite time for prowling. The screen flickered to life. A baseball game. *Ugh.* He pressed the skip-search button on the remote and watched as a succession of vapid, dislocated images flashed before his eyes. Wait! What was that? A woman in a red bikini, lying on a lounge chair beside a swimming pool.

Back-tracking, he discovered it was an infomercial for one of those 1-900 chat lines. The image faded, to be replaced by that of yet another scantily clad female, this time walking along a secluded beach. The only thing that differentiated the two women was their hair color. Otherwise, they both had the same pout, the same taunting manner, and the same gargantuan breasts, so pumped with silicon it was a wonder they didn't topple over.

"Are you looking for that special someone?" she crooned, above the repetitive beat of an electronic soundtrack, while the camera zoomed in on her cleavage. "Give me a call. I like hiking, travel, and candle-lit dinners" — *and if you're willing to pay through the nose for the privilege, I'll let you say filthy things to me for as long as you like. Then I'll arouse you with pornographic word pictures...while you stare at the ceiling and masturbate, faster and faster until you spill your seed down the front of your pants.*

Stinking slime, thought Ryman, with mounting rage. Sluts like that should have their heads shaved as a mark of their depravity, like those French women who were accused of sleeping with German soldiers during the Nazi occupation.

No, humiliation wasn't enough. They needed to be eradicated, like vermin. He pictured the woman lying motionless in the sea foam, crabs picking at her gray, decomposing flesh. Ryman's grin dissolved into a frown. The image was pleasing enough, but left him feeling cheated. A true artist derived satisfaction from the act of creation, not from the finished work. He needed to participate, to handle the material. Switching off the TV, he closed his eyes and pictured himself using a variety of carving tools to mold the woman's body into a series of interesting shapes.

A disturbing sensation, like an icy hand clutching at his heart, caused his eyes to pop open. He had the feeling someone else was in the room. Gulping, he leaned forward and stared into the surrounding gloom. It was so quiet he could hear his breath whistling through his flared nostrils.

Suddenly, his fear evaporated. He felt light-headed, yet energized. Rising, he grabbed his wallet and a jacket, and strode toward the front door. He had no idea where he was going; only that momentous events were about to unfold.

*****

Ryman gagged. Something large and wet was slithering around in his mouth and a heavy weight was pressing down on his chest, pinning him where he lay. Shuddering, he slowly opened his eyes, terrified by what he might find. But it was too dark to see. He heard a moan, and then felt something soft and fibrous brush against his face.

Panicking, he freed his hands and grabbed at the thing, pushing it away with all his strength.

"Hey! That hurt! What the hell's the matter with you!" Fumbling sounds, a click, illumination.

A series of flashbulbs went off in Ryman's head, producing a succession of fleeting snapshots. An oriental rug. His sports jacket, lying on the floor. A lamp. A brown cloth couch. A walnut coffee table on top of which sat a bronze Buddha. A young woman. She was grimacing and her blouse was undone.

Ryman sat up, blinked a couple of times, and gaped at the woman. Only then did he realize he was sitting next to her on the couch. But before he had a chance to figure out how he got there, a jolt of pain exploded inside his skull, causing him to clutch his head in anguished rage.

Picking up the Buddha, he sprang at the terrified woman and smashed her in the jaw with a vicious straight-arm. She made a gurgling sound as her head flew back, rebounded, then lolled to the left, eventually dragging her torso sideways onto the couch. Her eyelids fluttered a moment, and closed.

Ryman's pain evaporated. It was replaced by the light-headed feeling he'd experienced earlier at his apartment. Setting down the Buddha, he sat down stiffly and stared at the floor, like a marionette waiting to have its strings pulled.

Dear, dear Frankie. I do hope you finally understand. I am and always will be the only woman in your life, just like mamma wanted. All those other females you've consorted with — like that tramp lying there beside you — why, they cared nothing for you. They just wanted your manhood. I am the only one who truly loves you, because we are opposite sides of the same coin. With my help, you are going to fulfill your glorious destiny. So come on, now. Your first subject is waiting. Make me proud.

Ryman turned toward the woman. Sliding one hand under her legs and the other under her shoulders, he picked her up and laid her face down on the hardwood floor. After undressing her, he braided her nylon stockings together, placed his right knee in the hollow between her shoulder blades, wrapped the makeshift garrote around her neck, and pulled on the two ends until her breathing stopped. Then he shoved the stockings into his pocket and flipped the woman onto her back.

Rising, he cocked his head to admire his handiwork. The texture and color were fine, but the composition was all wrong. He leaned over, grabbed the woman's ankles, and spread her legs apart, frog-like. He then cupped her left hand around her right breast and placed her right hand between her legs. To ensure the critics didn't misinterpret his intent, he took a dollar bill out of his wallet, rolled it into a tight tube and inserted it into the woman's vagina.

Something was still missing. Ah, yes. His signature. Grabbing a knife and a pair of yellow rubber gloves from the kitchen, he knelt down beside the woman's head and carefully sliced off her lips. From a distance, the gap would look like a large, comical grin. And people said he had no sense of humor.

After washing the knife and the bronze Buddha with soap and water, he dried them with paper towels and returned each item to its proper place. He then used Windex and another paper towel to wipe down every surface he may have touched, including all the doorknobs. Finally, he picked up the severed lips and flushed them down the toilet, along with the soiled paper towels.

He returned to the living room and stared at his creation. Satisfied, he folded the rubber gloves and placed them in his jacket pocket. It would be safer to discard them, since he couldn't be sure that washing would remove all the interior fingerprints.

That left one final task. Pulling the woman's stockings out of his pocket, he smoothed them out and laid them on the sofa. He took off his pants, sat down, and slowly slid the stockings over his naked legs, relishing the way they felt against his skin. Exhilaration surged through his body. He felt natural, confident, and powerful, like a jungle cat.

Once the waves of emotion had subsided, he pulled his pants on over the stockings, grabbed his jacket, and walked to the front door. Using a paper towel to grasp the knob, he pushed the door open slightly and peered into the corridor. It was deserted. Ryman took a deep breath and stepped out into a new world, one that no longer seemed intimidating and chaotic.

Chapter 7 — Sunday, June 22

Detective Sergeant Lionel Jackson broke off a piece of toast and mopped up the last of the egg yolk clinging to his plate. He washed it down with some coffee and reached for his cigarettes. Being on his own, he'd gotten out of the habit of eating a full breakfast. But that morning, loud noises from the next apartment — tenants moving out — had awakened him at 6:15. Unable to get back to sleep, he decided to treat himself to a feast of fried eggs, ham, and baked beans.

He looked at his watch. His shift didn't start for another hour and a half, which meant he even had time to put a small dent in his magazine backlog. He enjoyed reading, but seldom had the time. The few leisure hours he did manage to scrape together were usually spent working on his bonsai collection. A Japanese colleague at the 41st Precinct had introduced him to the hobby in the late 1980s and he'd taken to it like a bear to honey.

The phone rang. Lieutenant Hawthorne.

"Don't bother coming in, Lionel. We've got a homicide, right in your own backyard. Lewicki's on his way to pick you up."

Jackson groaned as he hung up the phone. Detective Ed Lewicki was a dour, opinionated, barrel-chested Pole who preferred action to words. He could bench press 420 pounds and had a pair of International Practical Shooting Competition championships under his belt. In his last win at Rodman's Neck, the NYPD's practice range in the Bronx, he'd put nine rounds into the ten ring at 50 yards in under six seconds. Like everyone else on the Task Force, Jackson found him more than just a little intimidating.

Crushing out his cigarette, he picked up the dirty dishes and placed them in the sink. He had barely finished rinsing when the intercom buzzed to announce Lewicki's arrival. Jackson grabbed his jacket and gun and rushed out of the apartment.

Half an hour later, their car pulled up outside a low-rise apartment building on West 74th Street, not far from Amsterdam Avenue. Three RMPs were parked out front. Two bored-looking male uniforms, one white, one black, were leaning against the nearest patrol car, drinking coffee from Styrofoam cups. They both straightened up when Jackson flashed his badge.

"Third floor, Sarge," said the white uniform, a middle-aged Italian with a neatly trimmed mustache and an expanding waistline. "Apartment three-fourteen."

After writing the officers' names and badge numbers in his notebook, Jackson ordered them to set up a command post in the lobby and stock it with plenty of coffee. He also told them to barricade the front entrance and reroute tenants to other exits, to keep the press out of the building, and to get the superintendent to shut down the elevators until the Crime Scene Unit had a chance to examine them.

Jackson eyeballed the white uniform. "Spinetti, I'm making you Recorder. I'll need you to keep on top of all the comings and goings."

Spinetti frowned, with good reason. Being a crime scene Recorder was no picnic. He'd have to work overtime, carry an increased workload, pay attention to every detail, and eventually go to court or deal with the District Attorney's office, all of which provided ample opportunity to commit a major fuck-up.

"How many officers we got at the scene?" asked Jackson.

"Two, sir," replied Spinetti, inflecting the "sir" just enough to suggest insubordination. But Jackson let it pass. He and Lewicki entered the apartment building.

Jackson felt a sense of urgency as he hurried up the staircase. In every murder investigation, the most critical period was the last 24 hours in the victim's life and the first 24 hours after the body was discovered. Before the start of that 48-hour cycle, the circumstances that led to the killing were too hard to pin down; afterwards, forensic evidence began to deteriorate, witnesses began to suffer memory loss, weapons and clothing were being destroyed, and alibis were being concocted.

Entering the third floor corridor, Jackson and Lewicki approached apartment 314 and identified themselves to the uniform who was guarding the door.

"Are you first officer?" asked Jackson.

"That'd be Rodriguez, sir," replied the uniform, pointing inside.

Jackson pushed open the door and almost crashed into a dazed-looking policewoman with the olive skin and black doe eyes of a South American. She couldn't have been older than 22. Probably recruited from Spanish Harlem or the

Lower East Side and still a little stunned by the frenetic razzle-dazzle of midtown Manhattan.

"Rodriguez?"

She nodded.

"What's your first name?"

"Adelina, Sir."

"Let's take it from the top, Adelina."

"Central got the call at zero-eight-thirty-five, from the victim's cleaning woman, a middle-aged Filipino who works for the Dainty Dolly maid service. She's sitting in the kitchen."

"So we've got a positive ID?"

"Yes, sir. The victim is a twenty-five-year-old single Caucasian female named Sandra Geddes."

"Any roommates?"

"Not to my knowledge."

"Have you checked the body for vital signs?"

"Yes," she replied, swallowing. "It shows signs of rigor and lividity."

"Did you call the medical examiner? The crime scene unit?"

"Yes, sir. They're on their way."

"Okay, let's go see what we've got."

Rodriguez turned and led Jackson and Lewicki to the body, which was lying on the living room floor.

"Aw, Christ," muttered Lewicki, grimacing.

Jackson stepped to the foot of the body and made a cursory examination. The victim's lips had been cut off and her blanched, naked body was posed in a ritualistic position. A dark pool of blood from the mouth wound had collected on the floor. There was a large bruise on the jaw and a narrow mottled band around the neck, which suggested ligature strangulation. A white silk blouse, a black leather skirt, a bra, and a pair of white lace panties were neatly piled nearby. No stockings. That could be significant. No sign of the blade used to sever the lips, either. The victim was wearing a Swatch watch on the right wrist, a gold necklace, and a sapphire ring on the left index finger, all of which seemed to rule out a botched robbery attempt.

Although Jackson had learned to keep his feelings hidden, murders of this type always filled him with shame for his gender, for there was little doubt in his mind that the killer was a man. Female murderers rarely mutilated their victims.

As he stepped around the body, he noticed the stricken expression on Rodriguez's face. Most likely it was her first murder. He wanted to say something soothing, profound, but the best he could do was trot out the old adage that homicide cops had been using to delude themselves since time immemorial.

"I know it's little consolation, Adelina. But believe me, she was already dead when the guy cut her. She didn't feel a thing. Now go back to your post. I'll get the rest of your report in a minute."

"Looks like we've got a goddamn sex maniac on our hands," said Lewicki as soon as Rodriguez was out of earshot.

"A killer can act like a maniac and still know exactly what he's doing," replied Jackson. "In any case, I suggest we wait for the Crime Scene Unit before we start throwing theories around, okay?"

Lewicki's jaw muscles tightened. "Whatever you say, Sarge."

"I'm going to write out my report. In the meantime I want you to interview the cleaning lady, then do a preliminary canvass of the adjacent apartments."

He'd organize a more thorough canvass later that evening, when most of the building's tenants would be at home. Experience had taught him that people were more inclined to talk after a good meal. Besides, he'd have the Medical Examiner's report by then, and enough of a handle on the situation to be able to give his canvassers a proper briefing.

Jackson took out his pen and notepad and began to write, starting with the time of Hawthorne's call and the date. Next came the First Officer's report. After jotting down what Rodriguez had already told him, he went to the kitchen to get the rest. She was leaning against the sink, watching Lewicki interview the cleaning woman. Jackson caught her eye and waved her over.

"Okay, Adelina. I need you to tell me exactly what happened from the time you first approached the body."

She pulled out her memo book and studied it for a moment. "I placed two fingers on her chest, in the hollow where the ribs meet the breastbone. I felt no movement. I then tried to raise her wrist and found that it was slightly stiff, indicating that rigor was setting in. I concluded that the victim was dead and called for assistance. Communications relayed the call to the precinct desk officer, who dispatched another patrol car to help secure the crime scene."

"Did anybody touch anything?"

"The cleaning woman says she discovered the body as soon as she opened the door and immediately ran downstairs to the superintendent's office. The super instructed her to call nine-one-one while he came up to investigate. They both claim they touched nothing but the doorknob."

"Okay, go on."

"I noted that neither the victim's lips nor the blade used to cut them appeared to be near the body and that there were no signs of a struggle, or any obvious signs of a break-in."

Jackson continued to question Rodriguez until he was satisfied there were no holes in her report. The chain of evidence started from the moment the First Officer arrived at the crime scene, and a case could easily be lost if the evidential chain or sequence of events was broken by sloppy observations.

But in this case, Rodriguez had done well. She'd even marked down her path to and from the body. Having a clean crime scene would make his job that much easier. Jackson could recall instances where he'd arrived at a murder site to find people passing evidence around like a bowl of nachos at a Super Bowl party. The Jonbenet Ramsey debacle in Colorado was a perfect example of what could happen when a crime scene was compromised.

Dismissing Rodriguez, he put away his notepad and returned to the body. This was where he earned his pay. While Hollywood made a fortune romanticizing the exploits of countless fictional detectives, movies often trivialized the fact that every homicide investigation involved the body of a real human being. Someone's wife or husband. Son or daughter. Brother or sister. It was Jackson's job to confront that body; to crawl under its skin and uncover its secrets; to become intimate with it, yet remain detached.

He slipped on the thin plastic gloves he always carried in his jacket pocket and crouched down beside the victim's head, wincing slightly as the coppery smell of blood reached his nostrils. The first thing he needed to do was estimate the time of death.

He placed his right hand on the chest and noted that the skin felt cool. Roughly speaking, the adult human body maintained its normal temperature for the first hour or two after death and then began to cool at a rate of about 2.5° F an hour, becoming cold to the touch after 12 hours. But there were other variables to consider. The victim was thin, and thin people cooled faster than fat ones. Also, a body that was stretched out cooled more rapidly than one curled up or hunched against a wall.

Shifting his weight, Jackson pressed a finger against the victim's jaw, then against the left cheek. The muscles were taut, indicating advanced *rigor mortis*. He then carefully lifted the body a few inches to check for lividity, port-wine-colored areas on the skin — pooled blood — caused by dilation of blood vessels and the effect of gravity after the heart stopped pumping. In average room temperature, post-mortem lividity became fixed about eight hours after death. Sure enough, there were dark blotches on each of the victim's buttocks and on her back, between the shoulder blades.

His guess was that the woman had been dead somewhere between 10 and 14 hours.

Jackson stood up and recorded his observations. He had a female victim, Caucasion, 25 years old, large bruise on the jaw, mottled markings on the neck, lips cut off with a sharp instrument. Both the lips and the blade unaccounted for. Body posed in ritualistic position. No visible defense marks on the hands or other signs of a struggle. Body temperature, post-mortem lividity, and degree of rigor suggested a probable time of death somewhere between 2200 and 0200 hours.

"Sergeant?"

Jackson turned. It was Officer Rodriguez. With her was a stout, elderly man dressed in an ill-fitting blue suit that looked slept in, a gray fedora, and a pair of rimless eyeglasses. He was a carrying a black valise.

"This is the assistant medical examiner, Sam Goldenberg."

Jackson peeled off his gloves and extended his right hand. "Glad to meet you, Doc. Lionel Jackson."

"Please, call me Sam. Doc makes me sound like a character in a cowboy movie."

"I'm afraid you're going to have to cool your heels for a few minutes, Sam. We're still waiting for the Crime Scene Unit. Why don't you go down to the lobby and grab yourself a cup of coffee."

Goldenberg took off his hat and ran a hand through his thick white hair. "I've already had three this morning, but I guess one more won't kill me."

The Crime Scene Unit arrived ten minutes later, led by a redheaded buzzsaw with wide shoulders and a sallow, angular face, who breathlessly introduced himself as Sean Murphy. His team included a photographer, a fingerprint specialist, and a pair of technicians whose job it was to take measurements, create the formal sketches, collect all objects, hairs, dust, and fibers found on or around the body, search for secretions and bloodstains that might belong to the murderer, and look for signs of forcible entry.

It was Jackson's job to direct them to evidence that could be of special significance, based on his intuition and on his observations of the crime scene.

Jackson knew it would take Murphy and his team a while to set up, so he decided to go downstairs for some coffee. A break would also give him a chance to mull over the more disturbing aspects of the crime, especially the ritualistic positioning of the body, the way the victim's clothes were carefully folded and placed in a neat pile and, most perplexing of all, the severed lips. Mutilations were usually random and messy, the product of rage or sexual frenzy. But this killer had targeted a specific part of the victim's body and the incision itself had been made with surgical precision. In fact, everything about the crime smacked of neatness and order. This suggested intelligence, someone who had a game plan.

Not surprisingly, the lobby was now bustling with activity. Things were livelier outside, as well. A small crowd of reporters and curious onlookers — kept in check by half a dozen uniforms — had assembled in front of the building's front entrance. Pouring himself a cup of coffee, Jackson sought out the assistant medical examiner and spotted him seated in the corner, reading the *Times*.

"How's the news this morning?"

Goldenberg peered up at him over the top of his glasses. "That's a loaded question when you're reading the obits. The bad news is that many people have died; the good is that none are friends or relatives."

Grinning, Jackson set his cup down and pulled out his cigarettes.

"You're new around her, Jackson. Transferee?"

"Yeah, from the 41st in the South Bronx."

"Fort Apache? Now there's a neighborhood that must keep its M.E. on his toes."

"No kidding."

"How long have you been in homicide?"

"Nine years. How long you been an M.E.?"

"Too long."

They continued to exchange small talk until Sean Murphy burst through the door, brandishing a handful of rough sketches for Jackson to sign.

"How much longer?" asked Goldenberg.

"You can go up now, Sam."

Goldenberg carefully folded the newspaper, shoved it back into his valise, and stood up with an audible creak. He tossed his empty coffee cup into a nearby wastebasket and shuffled toward the stairwell.

"I gotta tell ya," said Murphy, while Jackson studied the sketches, "whoever did that broad kept his head together. The place is spotless. There are a number of prints on the front doorknob, but I don't think they're going to be of any use. Everything else is clean: light fixtures, the coffee table, the kitchen sink, the kitchen cabinets, and all the washroom fixtures. The perp even wiped down that little statuette sitting on the coffee table."

"The Buddha?"

"Yeah."

"Make sure you bag it for me."

"I'm way ahead of you. Anyway, we did lift a few fresh prints in other parts of the apartment, but I'm pretty sure they belong to the victim."

Jackson knew he was probably right. So far, everything pointed to a perp who was in complete control. In any event, elimination prints taken from the corpse, the superintendent, and the cleaning woman would soon clarify the situation. Pulling out his pen, he signed Murphy's sketches and returned them.

"Oh, I almost forgot. Is your fingerprint guy trained in the Kromekote technique?"

Murphy arched an eyebrow and gaped at him like he'd just sprouted a third eye.

"Then make sure he looks for any latent prints on the body, especially around the neck, the wrists, and the inner thighs."

Most people didn't realize that human skin sometimes retained fingerprints or that those found on a victim were as conclusive as an eyewitness and could nail a suspect once he was caught.

"He knows his job," snapped Murphy, spinning on his heels and rushing toward the stairwell.

Jackson smiled. He'd take a surly professional over a good-natured incompetent every time. Draining the last of his coffee, he dropped his cigarette butt into the dregs, tossed the cup into the wastebasket, and followed Murphy back up to the crime scene.

Goldenberg was hunched over the corpse, poking, prodding, lifting, and tweaking. Turning the body onto its side, he inserted a thermometer into the rectum and left it there for a few seconds. Then he withdrew it and peered at the calibrated markings.

"What's the verdict, Sam?"

"I'd say she's been dead about twelve hours."

"And the cause? Ligature strangulation or blunt-force trauma to the head?"

"I'm almost certain it was strangulation."

"When will you be sure?"

Goldenberg looked at his watch. "It's eleven forty-five. I think I can set the autopsy for around two. Will you attend, or are you going to send Lewicki?"

The law required that one of the detectives investigating a homicide had to witness the autopsy, in order to provide the evidential chain and to request fluid or tissue samples that might be considered pertinent to the case.

"I'm the new kid on the block," replied Jackson, "so I'll do the honors. Besides, I want to see how you work."

"I'm flattered," said Goldenberg, stripping off his gloves and rising to his feet. "Okay, I'm done. I suggest you cover the body before the district attorney arrives and uses it for a photo op."

"It wouldn't be the first time," said Jackson.

Goldenberg nodded a couple of times and headed for the door. "See you at two, Sergeant."

"Okay, Sam. And thanks."

When Assistant District Attorney Connie Maraino finally did show up — on the heels of the 20th Precinct's Duty Captain — she stayed just long enough to warn Jackson to catch the killer "or else" and to make a terse, self-serving statement to the press.

As soon as Maraino left, Jackson released the body to the Medical Examiner's attendants, made sure that every piece of evidence was properly bagged, and checked the Recording Officer's notebook against his own record. He and a pair of uniforms then undertook a grid search of the crime scene perimeter — the hallway, the stairwell, both elevators, and all the building's exits — but found nothing.

It was now 1:15, which left him with 45 minutes to call Lieutenant Hawthorne with an update, then make his way to the Medical Examiner's office on the east side. He'd need the car for that, so he tracked down Lewicki and told him to hitch a ride with one of the RMPs. He also gave him the unpleasant task of notifying Sandra Geddes' family.

*****

Four hours later, Jackson walked through the front door of the 15th Precinct station house with the results of Sandra Geddes' autopsy. It was dinner time, so the lobby was packed with drunks, pickpockets, drug pushers, whores, and a horde of other scuzzbuckets who'd been picked up along 42nd Street and the area surrounding Columbus Circle. The noise and commotion rivaled Grand Central Station at rush hour.

Still, despite appearances, the situation *was* improving, thanks in large part to the determination of Rudolph Giuliani. One of his first acts as mayor was to challenge the NYPD to achieve a dramatic decline in crime. The department responded by adopting six crime control strategies dealing with guns, youth violence, drugs, domestic violence, public disorder, and auto-related thefts. Each strategy was designed to provide a comprehensive analysis of how the department could best marshal its resources to have a real and lasting impact on crime and disorder.

At the time, many people — including Jackson and a lot of other cops — blew it off as just more political posturing. But the results spoke for themselves. In the first four years of the Giuliani administration there'd been a 44 percent decline in the seven major felonies, including an astounding 63 percent drop in homicides and a 50 percent decrease in rapes and robberies.

Nor were the improvements restricted to crime prevention. Notoriously sleazy Times Square had been given a makeover by the Disney corporation, most of the porno theaters and arcades had been driven off 42nd Street, and the subway system had been given a major facelift: clean platforms; graffiti-free cars, currently being fitted with air conditioning; and a major drop in hawkers, panhandlers, and sermon-spouting prophets. There were even rumors that a growing number of token-sellers were learning to be courteous.

A clean, polite New York City. It sounded strange. No doubt the new image was doing wonders for tourism, but residents were having a more difficult time getting used to the idea. Some didn't like it at all. They claimed that without its edge, New York would become as bland and bereft of personality as Los Angeles. Others disliked Giuliani's anti-crime initiatives for a different reason. They argued that his administration was focusing on the effects of the problem — which wasn't one of crime, but of social justice — rather than the cause, and that as a result, the main targets of the crackdown were young blacks and Latinos. Jackson figured the truth lay somewhere in between.

Loosening his tie, he strode past the portraits of President Clinton, Governor Pataki, Mayor Giuliani, Commissioner Blundell, and various deputy chiefs in their blue and gold uniforms, to the Patrol Supervisor's office. After getting the P.S. to agree to release a few of his people for that night's canvass of the Geddes neighborhood, he walked up the stairs to the squad room.

Lewicki was at his desk doing a two-finger tap on his typewriter. Two members of the afternoon shift — Dan McDougall, a raw-boned Long Islander with a boxer's nose and a severe brush cut, and Jimmy Choi, a squat, powerful bear of a man with huge hands and no discernible neck — were leaning against the bars of the holding cell, chatting up a prisoner.

Jackson sat down at his desk and stared at the mole behind McDougall's right ear. His head was shaved almost bald at the temples, tapering to a curly tuft at the nape of his neck. Jackson knew the man disliked him, but he couldn't tell yet if it was a racial thing or just resentment about the hostage incident. In any event, he thought it best to stay clear of him until he had a better handle on what revved his engine.

"Hey, Jimmy. Come here for a minute."

Choi turned and walked over to Jackson's desk.

"I need you to organize a canvass for me, beginning around seven-thirty. I've already talked to the patrol supervisor about lending us some of his people to help out. I'll give you the details as soon as the lieutenant arrives."

As if on cue, Hawthorne barged into the room and planted himself on the edge of Jackson's desk. "So, what did the autopsy turn up?"

Jackson pulled out his notebook. The formal autopsy report wouldn't be ready until the next morning. "We've got confirmation that the cause of death was ligature strangulation, and that the murder weapon was probably one or both of the victim's stockings, which were missing from the crime scene. A bruise found between the shoulder blades suggests the killer knelt on her back while he strangled her. We also learned that her jaw was fractured, suggesting she was knocked unconscious, then strangled, and that her lips were severed after death by a very sharp, non-serrated blade."

They would need to find the missing lips if they hoped to determine the shape and pitch of the cutting edge. The FBI's Firearms and Toolmarks Unit could not provide that information unless it had both sides of the cut.

"The pathologist found quite a bit of alcohol in the victim's system," he continued, "but since there's no evidence that any drinking took place at the crime scene, I'd say she'd been in a bar, either with someone she knew or someone she picked up."

"So you're certain we're not dealing with a break-in situation?"

"Positive. There's only one viable entrance to the apartment and it was intact, and nothing of value seemed to be missing. Besides, there were no defense wounds on her hands, skin fragments under her fingernails, or any other evidence of a struggle. The killer was definitely invited in."

"That's my opinion, too," said Lewicki. "The woman who lives in the next apartment said she heard the victim talking to a man sometime between nine and ten p.m. She claims it sounded like a normal conversation; nothing loud and no strange noises."

"That's settled, then," said Hawthorne. "Back to the autopsy. Was the victim sexually assaulted?"

"That's the part that puzzles me," replied Jackson. "There was no trace of semen on her body or her clothes."

"So much for DNA typing," mumbled Hawthorne.

"In fact," continued Jackson, "there was no evidence of penetration, period. Nor of any other kind of sexual activity. But we did find something else. A rolled-up dollar bill inside the victim's vagina. I had it sent for prints."

"Good," said Hawthorne, rubbing his hands together. "That could be our case-breaker. It's also the one piece of evidence that only we and the killer know about, so let's keep it that way."

No further elaboration was necessary. Every cop in the room knew that the department routinely kept critical details of murders and other major crimes hidden from the media. This made it easier to dismiss the many false confessions that often plagued investigations and to cross-check any leads supplied by informers.

Hawthorne popped a stick of gum into his mouth, chewed on it for a few seconds, and leaned against a filing cabinet. "Well, gentlemen. Judging by the pathologist's findings and the presence of ritual, I'd say we've got a psychopath on our hands. I suggest you get busy."

Jackson finished briefing Jimmy Choi, and then began to type out his Investigation Summary. Although Lewicki had already assembled most of the paperwork required by the day's efforts, they still had to organize and document all the evidence from Sean Murphy's Crime Scene Unit, write up a Response Report — a precise chronological list of all the officials who'd had an impact on the case so far — and create a Homicide Investigation Index, consisting of three-by-five cards with specific details about the case.

Paperwork, mused Jackson, frowning. The bane of every cop on every police force on planet Earth.

Chapter 8 — Monday, June 23

Eleven detectives were on hand for Hawthorne's 4:00 p.m. conference on the Sandra Geddes case. They were scattered throughout the squad room, nursing cigarettes, coffees, sodas; staring out the windows, leaning on filing cabinets, talking shop. Lionel Jackson and Ed Lewicki stood hunched over a desk, studying the crime scene photos. Jackson had received the photos and a forensics update earlier that afternoon, along with the official autopsy report. The lab results would take a more few days.

The purpose of the conference was to evaluate the evidence and look for the stressor in the recent life of Sandra Geddes: some anomaly that might connect her with her killer — a large debt; a new acquaintance; a fight with a lover, relative, or friend; the loss of a job; a take-out delivery made to her apartment. This was standard procedure after every homicide. Hawthorne also held regular weekly conferences — involving all the shifts in the Task Force — to review how cases were progressing. He would then make whatever alterations in duty assignments he deemed necessary.

"Okay, people," said Hawthorne, moving to the center of the room. "Let's get this thing done. Lionel, why don't you start by going over the autopsy report again, for the benefit of those who weren't here last night."

Jackson did so, with the addition of one new piece of information. Sam Goldenberg had confirmed that the victim's jaw had been broken with the bronze Buddha. But as Sean Murphy already reported, the statue had been wiped clean.

"The only hard evidence we've got so far are three strands of short, sandy-colored hair found on the victim's clothing," he added. "They've been sent to the lab for analysis."

Forensic technicians could determine a person's race, sex, diet, state of health, and approximate age from hair, as well as what part of the body it originated from and whether or not it fell out naturally or was ripped out during a struggle. And if any root cells were still attached, they could also match its DNA against a blood sample taken from a suspect, thereby proving he was at the crime scene.

"Unfortunately," continued Jackson, "it's been determined that none of the fingerprints lifted from the apartment belonged to the killer. But forensics did find a number of partials on the dollar bill they removed from the victim's vagina. I've already asked the F.B.I. to run a match against those of all known sex offenders and violent felons residing in the five boroughs."

Jackson knew it would be a daunting task. There were more than 200,000 prints representing more than 68,000,000 people on file in the FBI's Criminal Justice Information Services Division. These prints were accessed by a computer system known as FINDER. But in order to initiate a search, FINDER first needed to know which finger or fingers made a particular latent print. And so far, that determination had not been made. The computer's effectiveness would further be hampered by the lack of physiological information about the suspect — like height or race. Without such details, you were dealing with the proverbial needle in a haystack.

Jackson slipped a cigarette into his mouth. "That's all the forensics info we've got for now."

"Okay," said Hawthorne, "let's talk about the night of the murder. What did the canvass turn up?"

"Not much," said Jimmy Choi, flipping open his notebook. "We interviewed three hundred and thirty-eight people in the area, including a dozen or so who knew the victim, and none of them saw anyone matching her description on Saturday night. None of her immediate neighbors heard anything, either, except for that woman Lewicki talked to yesterday. She's the only one who can place a man at the crime scene on the night of the murder."

"What about the victim's lifestyle?" asked Hawthorne.

"We did have some luck there," said Choi. "It seems Miss Geddes spent a lot of nights at bars. Her neighbors said she often had men over, seldom the same ones."

"Her sister said the same thing," added Jackson. "It turns out the victim's fiancé was killed in a car accident two years ago. Apparently, she's been having a real hard time coping. She stopped seeing her family and friends and has been drowning her grief with booze and a string of one-night stands."

Hawthorne sat on the edge of a desk and folded his arms. "So I guess we can assume she invited the killer to her place for sex, even though none actually took place."

"Maybe the guy snapped because he couldn't get it up," said Lewicki.

"I don't think so," replied Jackson. "Individuals who kill in a rage usually panic once they realize what they've done. And even if this guy had the presence of mind to clean up after himself, it doesn't explain why he messed with the body."

"Maybe it's window dressing," said Lewicki, "ritualistic mumbo-jumbo intended to throw us off the scent."

"No way," said Jackson. "Your average perp might go as far as posing the body...maybe even that business with the dollar bill, but the mutilation, and the fact that the victim's lips *and* the stockings used to commit the murder were taken from the crime scene, points to someone who had an agenda. I think our man *intended* to kill."

"I agree," said Hawthorne. "What we need to do now is determine whether the guy was a stranger or someone who knew the victim."

In most cases, the odds favored the latter since, statistically, people were seldom murdered by strangers. But based on the evidence and on what he'd seen at the crime scene, Jackson had his doubts.

"Lieutenant? You might want to consider calling in a mindhunter for this one. I think we may have a repeater on our hands."

A 'mindhunter' was a member of the FBI's Investigative Support Unit, an elite group of psychological profilers and crime scene specialists who targeted violent offenders. Over the course of several years the Unit had interviewed dozens of assassins, mass murderers, and serial killers — people like James Earl Ray, Sirhan Sirhan, Richard Speck, John Wayne Gacy, David Berkowitz (the Son of Sam), and Charles Manson — to understand the method behind their madness.

The unit subsequently used this knowledge to help various police departments track down some of America's most notorious killers, including Ted Bundy, David Carpenter (San Francisco's Trailside Killer), Wayne Williams (the Atlanta child murderer), and the Tylenol poisoner.

"The thought's crossed my mind, too," replied Hawthorne. "But so far, we're dealing with an isolated incident. There's no way I'm going to be able to persuade the department to put in an official request. You know what the brass are like when it comes to dealing with other agencies."

Who didn't, thought Jackson. When it came to matters of jurisdiction, New York City resembled a WWF free-for-all. There were at least half a dozen law enforcement agencies in the area, each jealously guarding its turf, regularly stealing each other's witnesses and, on occasion, even protecting a felon wanted for one crime because he or she was needed to help crack another.

"For now," continued Hawthorne, "I want you to find out all you can about the last week of Sandra Geddes' life and talk to everybody she might've come into contact with. If our killer *is* a repeater, let's make sure he doesn't get the chance."

*****

That night, in the WSNY broadcast booth, Robert Molinaro stifled a yawn as he listened to a male caller drone on about "the disturbing increase" in youth crime, concluding his diatribe with a demand for more police and harsher sentences.

"How old are you, Carl?"

"Forty-six."

"So you grew up during the sixties?"

"Uh...yeah."

"Were you into that counter-culture thing?"

"Absolutely. I smoked a little pot, had long hair, demonstrated against the war — the whole nine yards."

"You were a hippie, then?"

"That's right."

"If I'm not mistaken," said Molinaro, "you guys hated the establishment, especially cops, right? I believe you used to call them pigs."

Carl hesitated. "Yeah, but—"

"So how come now, all you ex-hippies want to see more police rooting around in your neighborhoods?"

"The situation's different. We were into love and peace, not muggings and gang warfare."

"And that's what you think today's kids are about?"

"Not all of them, but quite a few."

"Based on what authority?"

"Statistics."

"Can you quote the source?"

"Not right now, but all you gotta do is watch the news."

"Listen, Carl, maybe the media *is* helping to create this perception of rampant youth violence — which, by the way, is a myth, and I *can* cite the statistics to prove it — but I think part of the problem is the hostility that people like you have toward kids. One would have thought that your generation would be willing to cut young people some slack. After all, you're the ones who used to claim you couldn't trust anyone over thirty. Now, you freak out every time you see a kid dressed in baggy pants, a hooded sweatshirt, and a backward baseball cap. You've turned into a bunch of hypocrites. So the next time you begin to wonder what's wrong with kids today, look in a mirror. Thanks for your call."

Sid Crouse fed him another name. "Here's Karen, from Queens."

"Hello, Bob."

"What's on your mind, Karen?"

"I'm just calling to voice my support for the Timothy McVeigh death sentence."

"So you believe in an eye for an eye, then?"

"I certainly do, especially in this case. The man not only butchered a hundred and sixty-eight souls, most of them women and children, but his cowardly act also sounded the death knell for American innocence."

"Innocence?"

"Certainly. The Oklahoma City bombing was the first serious act of home-grown terrorism, and it took place in the American heartland."

"As opposed to the South Bronx or some other hellish inner-city neighborhood, you mean?"

"Well...yes."

"Karen, the history of Oklahoma makes the South Bronx look like Disneyland. After the Civil War, it was the most violent and lawless region in the country. And the violence continued even after a semblance of order was finally imposed. The citizens had a particular affinity for lynching black people. But I guess none of that matters, because Oklahoma is part of the American *heartland*, which according to conventional wisdom, is supposed to represent the essence of innocence.

"Well, I'm sorry to disillusion you, but American innocence is just another myth, and a bloody one at that. All you have to do is examine our history. This country stands for many fine things, but there's no escaping the fact that its past is also steeped in war and violence.

"I'll give you an example. A while back, Ronald Reagan referred to his growing up in a small Illinois town as 'one of those rare Huck Finn-Tom Sawyer idylls.' Well, as it happens, the novels he was referring to — especially Huckleberry Finn — deal with a time and place that was rife with crime and racism. As for Reagan's home town, a writer named Garry Wills dug up some old issues of the local newspaper and discovered that three black men were brutally lynched a few months after the Reagan's moved there. So I guess you can say that Reagan's idyll was someone else's nightmare. Thanks for your call."

Sid Crouse's voice crackled in his earphones. "Frank's on the line, Bob."

Molinaro stroked his mustache. He was hesitant about putting Frank on the air at this point because the show seemed to be going well enough without him. On the other hand, most of the calls so far had been fairly tame. Shifting in his chair, he turned to Sid and gave him the thumb's up. "Here's Frank, from the upper east side."

"Good evening, Robert. I am very busy working on plans for an important project so I will keep my comments brief. Do you recall the statement I made last Friday, when we were discussing how a certain class of women were responsible for the destruction of the American family?"

"Not really," replied Molinaro, rolling his eyes. "Why don't you refresh my memory."

"I said that the day of reckoning was nigh."

"So you did. What about it?"

"The reckoning has began," said Frank, and hung up.

Molinaro glanced at Sid, who peered back with a perplexed expression on his face. Shrugging, Molinaro lit a cigar and motioned for another call to be put through.

Chapter 9 — Tuesday, June 24

Rachel Curran sat in the Lotus position on the floor of her cramped apartment, imagining she was a log gently floating on a cool mountain stream. Modeling — especially in New York City — was a high-stress occupation; it was important to find some way to cope. She had already tried Shiatsu, polarity therapy, aromatherapy, and hypnotherapy, with unsatisfactory results. So now she was experimenting with that old standby, yoga.

Rachel made it a point to meditate for at least an hour every day, usually before the start of her acting class or her shift at the Rusty Nail. Today, however, the cancellation of a morning runway assignment had left her with some free time so she'd begun her breathing exercises a few hours earlier than usual. She'd already taken a stroll in Hudson Park and later planned to do a little reading. She preferred self-help books and biographies, especially those of powerful women.

Idleness was not a luxury she got to enjoy very often. On the flip side, free time was anathema to a model because it meant a loss of earnings. Actually, a local photographer who wanted her to pose for a number of 'art' studies had offered her a job, but she declined. There were serious pitfalls to undressing for the camera, especially for a beginner who aspired to be a serious actress some day. Vanessa Williams and Suzanne Sommers both posed for provocative nude shots when they were starting out and the photos came back to haunt them.

Rachel uncrossed her legs and stood up. After kneading out her kinks, she went into the kitchen, poured herself a glass of freshly made apple juice and grabbed a handful of shelled, unsalted pumpkin seeds. She was a committed naturopath — no meat and only organic fruits and vegetables — who augmented her diet with a daily fix of vitamin and mineral supplements. The regimen provided a level of nutrition sufficient to sustain energy, yet low enough in calories to prevent weight gain — a model's worst enemy. There were other benefits as well. She slept soundly and seldom got sick.

Overall, Rachel considered herself to be a good custodian of her physical self. But she also appreciated the importance of her spiritual side, a trait she'd picked up from her mother, Rebecca, who was fond of saying that a life steeped in self-absorption was only half a life; you needed to make time for others, as well. And this wasn't just idle chatter. Back in Buffalo, she did volunteer work for at least half a dozen charitable organizations.

Her mom's motivation had nothing to do with religion, either — she had an Anglican background, her dad, Roman Catholic, yet they'd always encouraged Rachel to follow her own heart — but from a deep-rooted belief that humankind was a work in progress that needed to be tended and nurtured in order to reach its full potential.

At present, Rachel's down time was stretched pretty thin, but she still managed to volunteer at the Daily Bread food bank most Thursday afternoons and to give piano recitals at a local senior's center the first Sunday of each month.

The phone rang and Rachel rushed into the living room to pick up the receiver. It was Charlie, her booker.

"Hi, Rach. I'm surprised to find you home on such a gorgeous afternoon."

"I was out earlier, and now I'm just taking it easy."

"Must be nice."

"What's up?"

"Good news. Montgomery Ward's art director liked your headsheet photo and I think we may be able to get you a booking for their Christmas catalog. I've scheduled a go-see for tomorrow morning at nine."

"That's terrific," she replied. True, it was another catalog shoot, but this was a major player with national distribution. "Maybe I can finally get off the junior board."

"Let's hope so. You know I'm your biggest fan. By the way, I hear you've decided to enter the Miss Empire State pageant. I think it's a good career move."

"My thoughts exactly."

"Where's the pageant being held this year?"

"Right here in town, at Radio City."

"Fabulous. Have you got someone to work with you?"

"A couple of people from the Miss Erie County organization will be here during pageant week and my roommate's volunteered to act as my coach until then."

"Have you decided on your platform subject yet?"

"Naturopathy as an alternative to conventional medicine."

"That figures. Well, the best of luck, hon. And don't forget to get me a couple of tickets for the final."

"I won't."

Rachel hung up the phone and stretched out on the sofa with a hint of a smile on her lips. Maybe her luck had finally changed.

*****

Lionel Jackson shielded his eyes from the setting sun as he stepped out onto his balcony carrying a watering pail and a pair of pruning shears. He wasn't due at his brother-in-law's for another hour or so, which gave him a welcome opportunity to work on his modest bonsai collection.

He preferred trees to shrubs and currently had eight varieties, a gingko, a variegated juniper, a Norway spruce, a Tamarack pine, a mountain cherry, a Japanese maple, a bird's nest cypress, and an Irish yew. Ranging in age from four months to seven years, the plants were spread out on a laminated card table, each in its own brown, unglazed pot.

Although considered a Japanese invention, the art of dwarfing plants in small containers actually originated in ancient China and crossed the East China Sea to Japan sometime before the thirteenth century, along with Buddhism and the Kanji characters that composed the Japanese alphabet.

Traditional bonsai technique was slow, tedious, and called for great delicacy and skill, yet it was one of the most rewarding activities Jackson had ever known. The idea was to create a genuine landscape in miniature. This was done by restricting the plant's root growth, carefully pinching leaves, pruning stems, and 'training' the shape of the trunk with wire — while always striving to achieve a natural appearance. You could then enhance the effect by adding other materials, like moss, grass, figurines, pieces of driftwood, or unusual rocks.

Jackson had taken a lot of ribbing about his hobby, most of it good-natured. Cops weren't supposed to be artsy-fartsy. But growing bonsai had become a lot more than just an outlet for his creativity; it grounded him, kept him sane.

As he began to tend his plants, his thoughts turned to Sandra Geddes. That morning, he'd learned that the forensic lab's toxicology and serology tests had failed to turn up any new evidence and that the FBI's computer had been unable to find a match for any of the partial fingerprints he'd sent them. If nothing else, at least he had the satisfaction of knowing that once they nabbed the son-of-a-bitch, those prints would put him away.

The only real lead he had was the lab's analysis of the hair found on the victim's clothing, which indicated the suspect was a healthy male Caucasion with sandy-blond hair, 22 to 28 years old. Unfortunately, none of the strands had its root attached, so there'd be no DNA trace. But the lab did find high levels of chlorine. That suggested the suspect was a serious swimmer. Maybe even a competitor. Which made sense. It took a tremendous amount of upper body strength to strangle someone.

Lieutenant Hawthorne had formed a detail to check out all the swim clubs and public pools in the city. If that didn't pan out, they'd be stuck with the more daunting task of tracking down all the residential pools.

The description provided by the lab's hair analysis jibed with the information Jackson and Lewicki had gathered from their interviews with the victim's family and acquaintances, who claimed she rarely dated older men or men of color.

What the interviews didn't turn up, however, was a possible stressor. It appeared the last week of Sandra Geddes' sad life had been no different than those that preceded it — uneventful days in the midtown bank where she worked as a teller; desperate nights trolling through the frantic world of singles bars.

This discovery strengthened Jackson's belief that a stranger had killed her. After a lot of digging, he and Lewicki had discovered Sandra's favorite bars. Detectives Choi and McDougall were checking them out that evening, armed with her photograph and a very sketchy description of the suspect. Maybe someone would remember seeing them together on Saturday night.

✶✶✶✶✶

An hour later, Jackson climbed behind the wheel of his '95 Chevy Impala and made his way to Central Park West for the short drive to his brother-in-law's place in Harlem. As usual, the street was a bumper-to-bumper tangle of cabs, trucks, vans, limos, cyclists, and pushcart peddlers.

Stopping for a red light at West 77th Street, opposite the American Museum of Natural History, he was bombarded by a wave of odors: flowers, freshly cut grass, diesel fumes, horse manure, dead leaves, popcorn, pretzels, sizzling hot dogs — the rich, close smell of a New York summer evening.

As he approached 96th Street, he caught a whiff of a different kind of aroma: money. Here the sidewalks broadened and the apartment buildings came with uniformed doormen, entrances made of carved wood and smoked glass, canopies, and large bronze street numbers coated in verdigris. One out of every four pedestrians seemed to be an elegantly dressed matron tugging at the leash of a tiny yapping dog.

Beyond 110th Street, the traffic thinned and the number of white faces on the sidewalks began to diminish rapidly. Jackson turned right onto 126th Street and continued east. A wistful smile played on his lips as he drove past Sylvia's, Harlem's best-known soul food restaurant. He and his wife had often gone there for Sunday brunch, always served with some of the finest gospel singing east of the Mississippi.

Jackson sighed. Harlem had changed a lot in the last few years. Not long ago it had been home to more than a million blacks. Now there were barely half a million. Politicians attributed the exodus to new housing programs and the improvement in living standards. Social activists claimed the poor had been forced out by the increasing dilapidation of their neighborhoods. Looking at the ruined landscape, Jackson had to agree.

A few minutes later, with the sun now well below the horizon, he pulled up in front of a brown and red row house. Lester Ellison, a skinny forty-two-year-old with a broad, slightly flat nose, prematurely gray hair, and a mustache so thin you couldn't see it unless you stood right up to his face, was waiting for him on the front stoop with a six-pack of Coors and a jumbo bag of pretzels.

"What's up, Lester?"

"Same old, same old," replied his brother-in-law, climbing into the car.

"Where do you feel like hanging out?"

"Someplace with a view."

Jackson knew just the spot, a hilly area near the corner of Park Avenue and 125th Street. From there, you could see much of lower Manhattan, including the white pinnacle of the Citicorp Center Tower to the east, the arcs and bars of the Chrysler Building straight ahead, and the illuminated steppes of the empire State Building to the west.

As soon as they'd found a secluded parking spot, the two men lowered their seat backs and cracked open their beers.

"So," said Lester, "how's life in the new precinct?"

"Better than I thought it'd be," replied Jackson, taking out his cigarettes. "The C.O.'s a good man, and sharp as a razor. Most of the other detectives seem okay."

"Nobody's tried to hassle you?"

"I get the occasional stare, and there's a couple of guys who treat me like I'm invisible, but it's nothing I can't handle. I'm there to work, not win a popularity contest."

Nodding, Lester ripped open the bag of pretzels and offered it to Jackson, who declined.

"They got you working on anything special?"

Jackson blew a smoke ring. "Yeah, a real nasty murder on the Upper West Side."

"The white woman who had her lips cut off?" said Lester, grimacing.

"That's the one."

"Man, what's up with that shit?"

"Tell me about it."

"You got any leads yet?"

"A few, but nothing solid. Listen, Lester. I really don't want to talk about the case. It's all I've been thinking about for the past three days."

"You got it, my brother."

The two men spent the next few minutes drinking beer in silence, waiting for the right moment to bring up the real reason behind Jackson's visit.

"You heard from Alyssa lately?"

"On Sunday," replied Lester. "She and the kids are just fine."

"Did she ask about me?" The look on his brother-in-law's face provided all the answer he needed.

"Shit, Lionel. You know what that damned woman's like. She's as hard-nosed as a dago loan shark. Her and me fought all the time when we was kids. Still do, come to think of it. But that don't mean she's given up on you. Let her cool off for a while, then you can get together and talk things out without tearing into each other."

"I don't see that happening, Lester. This wasn't our first fight. The marriage was in trouble long before the hostage thing went down. And it's mostly my fault. I was hardly ever around while the kids were growing up. And even when I did spend time at home, I was so obsessed by my work that Alyssa must've felt like a single parent. She had to cook and clean, pay the bills, get the kids to school, make sure they did their homework, all the while trying to hold down her own job."

"But she knew the score when she married you."

"Maybe she was ready to deal with my not being around, but not with the head games."

"I don't get ya."

"You see a lot of ugly shit in this job, Lester, and every homicide cop has to find a way to deal with it. Sometimes, you bury your feelings so deep down in your guts you don't even realize that you're coming off like a cold-hearted motherfucker. Alyssa and the kids must've felt like they were living with some damned iceman.

"I can still remember the time Cassie fell off the swing we had in the backyard and skinned her knee. Alyssa came running into the kitchen yelling loud enough to make a body think the child had broken her neck. Man, I was so stressed out at the time that instead of trying to calm her down or offer my support, I snapped. I started screaming that a scraped knee was nothing compared to the brutal shit I saw being done to kids every day. Can you imagine what the woman must've felt like?"

"Shit, everybody gets pissed off some time. Besides, you both have a handle on the problem now. And that's half the battle."

"Man, the only way Alyssa and I would ever be able to live together again was if we were both given a lobotomy and planted next to each other in the same vegetable patch."

Lester chuckled. "At least you ain't lost your sense of humor."

Jackson took a last drag on his cigarette and flicked it onto the road. "The worst part is not having the kids around. I miss them so much it aches."

"When you gonna see 'em?"

"That's hard to say with this case hanging over my head. If we're lucky, we'll wrap it up in the next couple of days. Otherwise, I'm probably looking at the fourth of July weekend."

"That ain't too far off," said Lester, handing him another beer.

"I guess not."

Chapter 10 — Wednesday, June 25

Frank Ryman sat at his office desk, staring blankly at the spreadsheet on his computer monitor. Normally, he loved his work; he believed that mathematics exhibited a natural eloquence that was both deeply beautiful and profound. Not only did it keep track of outlays and receipts — an accountant's bread and butter — but also unraveled the complexities of the natural world.

Today, however, he found it hard to concentrate on the long rows of numbers, which kept shifting in and out of focus like birds circling in a fog. Oh, well, he thought, leaning back in his chair, perhaps it was only natural that a man who had discovered his true calling would find his regular work dull by comparison.

He'd spent the last four days in a state of near ecstasy. No anger. No confusion. No bad dreams. Just a wonderful sense of fulfillment, mingled with a yearning to repeat the experience. Now the wait was finally over; he was ready to seek out the raw material for his next masterpiece. But this time he intended to choose carefully because he wanted to create a work that would not only express his artistic vision but also make a profound political statement. Till now, society had ignored his views; no doubt it would pay more attention to his actions.

He looked at his watch. It was almost noon. Plenty of time. The fashion show at Chez Monique, a trendy clothing boutique located in the shopping complex of the Hanover Building on nearby Broad Street, was scheduled to begin at 1:30.

Ryman saved the spreadsheet program and logged off the computer. He then closed the volumes of Tax Code that were on his desk and replaced them in their alphabetical slots on the shelf. Putting on his jacket, he paused a moment to check his tools: a knife and a pair of black latex gloves in the right pocket; a length of twine and a fake security badge in the other. He was especially proud of the badge, which he'd created with his computer and a clip-on name tag holder left over from a recent conference. He'd even personalized it for effect, using the name Tim Flannery.

Taking a few calming breaths, he left his office and walked toward the foyer at a slow, deliberate pace. He knew he had to maintain his usual demeanor if he hoped to avoid undue attention.

The receptionist looked up as he approached her desk. "Going to lunch, Mr. Ryman?"

"Yes. And I have some business to attend to afterwards. I expect to be back by four or so."

"Okay. See you then."

Ryman smiled and stepped into a waiting elevator.

*****

There were about 40 people in the tiny auditorium, most of them women. Ryman, his eyes concealed behind a pair of reflective sunglasses, sat alone in the back row, in an aisle seat next to the entrance. The fashion show had just ended and the hostess was calling the half dozen young models onto the stage for the finale.

Using the audience's applause as a screen, he stood up and quietly slipped out of the room. He waited in the shadows until the auditorium had emptied and the lights had been switched off, then removed his sunglasses and stepped back inside. He quickly made his way to the rear exit and pushed the door open just enough to get a glimpse of the corridor. It was empty. Better yet, the dressing room was less than five feet away.

Ryman took the fake security badge out of his pocket and clipped it to his lapel. The web was ready. All he needed now was an obliging fly.

After a long, torturous wait, the dressing room door finally burst open. But instead of emerging one by one, as he had hoped, three of the models walked out together. They linked arms and strode toward the stairwell. Ryman ground his teeth in anger. Having reconnoitered the building earlier, he knew those stairs led directly down to the street. Sighing, he shifted his weight and leaned his damp forehead against the door jamb.

A moment later, the dressing room door opened again. Ryman held his breath. When he saw the three remaining models also emerge together, the air rushed out of his body in one long whoosh, like a slashed tire. Enraged by the thought that his scheme had been thwarted, he grabbed his knife and reached for the door knob. He would slash the hateful creatures to ribbons right there and then.

But something held him back...a voice, soothing yet insistent. Ryman closed his eyes and listened.

Calm yourself, honey. It's unbecoming of a Southern gentleman to go flying off the handle. Any ordinary man can behave like a butcher. But only a select few can call themselves true artists. Great things are waiting for you, Frankie, so don't lose sight of your purpose.

A different voice, of external origin, snapped Ryman out of his trance. For some reason the three models were lingering in the corridor. He placed his ear next to the door.

"...hated Cats. If I hear *Memories* one more time my head will explode."

"I thought it was fun. And touching, too."

"I guess there's no accounting for taste."

"Listen, why don't we go for a drink? I know a place uptown with a fabulous patio. We can be there in fifteen minutes by cab."

"I'm in."

"How about you, Carol?"

"Thanks, but I can't. My boyfriend's waiting for me."

"Can we give you lift then?"

"I've got a car."

"In that case, I guess this is goodbye. It was great meeting you."

"Yeah. Me, too. I hope we get to work together again some time."

"I'd like that."

"Ciao."

Two sets of footsteps hurried toward the stairwell, while a third proceeded at a more leisurely pace toward the elevator at the opposite end of the corridor. Ryman pulled a handkerchief out of his pocket and wiped his brow. It was time to create. Assuming his most charming smile, he opened the door and stepped into the corridor.

"Excuse me, miss?" he said, mimicking the slow, reassuring speech pattern of the young Henry Fonda. The hours spent watching old movies had made him adept at imitating the voices of his favorite actors.

The woman turned. She was a scrawny brunette, younger than he had expected. If it became necessary, he could snap her in two like a dry twig.

"Good afternoon," he added, walking forward with authority, "my name's Tim Flannery, building security. I've been asked to escort you to your car."

The brunette's eyes flitted from his face to his badge, then back to his face. "Is that really necessary?"

"I'm afraid so. We had an incident in the garage last week. And at the risk of being politically incorrect, you *are* a very attractive young woman."

Her smile, conditioned by years of practice, held a hint of boredom. Holding the elevator door open with his arm, Ryman ushered the woman inside, then stepped in after her. The door closed and they rode down to the garage in silence.

"I'm just down here to the right," she said, exiting the elevator.

Ryman leaned out and scanned the area. It was deserted. His next obstacle was the security camera, which was mounted in the ceiling to the left of the elevator, about 15 feet away. He exited at a diagonal, keeping his head down and cocked to one side.

The remaining cameras posed little problem because they were few in number and were rigged to provide wide-angle surveillance, primarily of the driving lanes, rather than blanket coverage. Also, as in most indoor garages, the lighting was woefully inadequate. Ryman found it ludicrous that companies would spend a small fortune to install a security system, then not bother to put in more powerful lights.

"That's it," said the brunette, pointing to a blue Toyota. She turned to glance at him, then continued toward her car.

Ryman slipped his gloves on and placed his hands behind his back.

The brunette stopped in front of the Toyota and fumbled in her shoulder bag for the keys. Licking his lips, Ryman locked his fingers together and moved toward her.

A burst of shrill female laughter erupted nearby, setting off a series of diminishing echoes. He turned and saw an elderly couple climbing out of a station wagon, apparently in no particular hurry.

By now, the brunette had her key out and was inserting it in the lock. Ryman's jaw tensed in frustration as he glanced at the receding couple. They were still too close for him to make his move. He turned back to his prey. She had the car door open and was settling in behind the wheel.

"Thanks for walking with me," she said, reaching for the door handle.

"No problem," muttered Ryman, struggling to contain his growing fury. As he watched her place the key in the ignition, his mind scrambled for some way to prevent her escape.

The Toyota's engine roared to life.

Ryman stepped back, feeling powerless and defeated. He began to turn away, then froze in mid-stride. He had an idea. Feigning a look of concern, he stepped in front of the car and waved his arms. The brunette lowered the window.

"What is it?"

"I think you've got a problem with your right rear tire."

"Oh?" She shifted into park and climbed out of the car. "What kind of problem?"

"It looks like you've got a nail embedded in the tread," he replied, backing away.

"Really?" she said, frowning. She walked past him to the rear of the car and crouched down to investigate. "Where?"

Ryman balled his hands together and smashed the woman between the shoulder blades, sending her sprawling face first to the pavement. Using his knee to pin her down, he wrapped the twine around her neck and pulled at the ends until the veins in his forehead bulged with the effort.

When he was certain she was dead, he stood up and scanned the area. Not a soul around. He took the keys out of the ignition, opened the trunk, and carefully placed the body inside. Putting on his sunglasses, he climbed in behind the wheel and collected his thoughts.

He had to find the parking ticket. No problem. It was on the dashboard. What else? Take off the gloves. He did so and put them in his pocket. He also reminded himself to keep his face hidden when he stopped to pay. How should he handle that? Give the attendant the ticket and a $20-bill and tell him to keep the change? No, that would just attract attention. The normal thing would be to hold his palm out for the change and slowly drive away.

Ryman felt a familiar presence insinuating itself into his thoughts. Instinctively, he glanced up at the rearview mirror. Francine's blue eyes, clear and steady and wide with delight, gazed back at him.

I am so proud of you, Frankie. You've taken to your new vocation like a baby to its mother's milk. I am simply shivering with anticipation to see the end result of your latest endeavor. Shall we go?

Ryman started the car and drove toward the exit.

*****

In the Task Force squad room, Lionel Jackson lit a cigarette and stood up to stretch his back. It always bothered him when he sat too long. He had to be careful because it seized up from time to time, prompting a painful trip to the chiropractor. He'd incurred the injury in the winter of 1989, while pursuing a perp who had beaten his wife to death with a baseball bat. He'd lost his footing on an icy fire escape ladder and fell backward some eight feet, landing spread-eagled on the pavement. Luckily, his partner had been there to call an ambulance. And make the collar.

Grimacing, he massaged his lower spine and walked over to the nearest window. Outside, the sky was darkening. He glanced at his watch. It was almost six. Although his shift ended two hours ago, he'd stayed behind to discuss the Sandra Geddes case with Detectives Choi and McDougall.

Their canvass of the bars she frequented had drawn a blank. A number of people remembered Sandra Geddes but none of them could recall whether or not they'd seen her on the Saturday night in question. As for the suspect, his description proved too vague to be of any real value.

Nevertheless, the two detectives had questioned every sandy-haired patron under the age of 30. Half-a-dozen men admitted they'd known Sandra Geddes. Jackson was more interested in those who claimed they didn't — even though he knew there was little chance the killer would be stupid enough to return to the bar where he'd met his victim. But a homicide cop could not afford to take anything for granted. That's why Choi and McDougall were at their desks, poring through their notes in the hopes of finding a weak link — a possible motive, a time that didn't cross-check, a shaky alibi.

Jackson took a drag on his cigarette and rested his forehead against the cool glass. On the street below, the cars were jammed together like a colony of sea lions, honking and jostling as they maneuvered for position. Rush hour in Manhattan. By now, both river drives would be engorged by an endless stream of cars, trucks, and motorcycles, lining up at the white-tiled entrances of the city's tunnels and crawling across its bridges.

It seemed like half of the people down there had a cell phone glued to their ears. Jackson found that disquieting. There was nowhere left to hide. Cell phones, fax machines, and home computers were radically altering the accepted notion of privacy. Why worry about Big Brother when the population was willing to plug into the network voluntarily?

"Listen up, people!"

Jackson turned. Lieutenant Hawthorne was standing outside his office with his arms crossed and a grim expression on his face.

"A couple of teenagers just found a female body in East River Park." He paused a moment, then looked directly at Jackson. "Her lips were cut off."

*****

"Can you believe the balls on the cocksucker who did this thing?" snapped Hawthorne, pacing back and forth in the twilight like a caged tiger. "Bringing her to a public park in the middle of the goddamn afternoon!"

"The son-of-a-bitch is motivated," replied Jackson, "no doubt about it."

They were standing under an elm tree inside the band of yellow ribbon that marked the southern perimeter of the crime scene, located in a wooded area of the park, just north of the Williamsburg Bridge. A crowd had gathered and a dozen uniforms had their hands full trying to keep them at bay.

Jackson had already viewed the body — which had been left naked on the hood of a blue Toyota — and was waiting for the medical examiner to finish up. The woman had been dead for less than five hours. The M.O. was the same as in the Geddes case: ligature strangulation, severed lips, a bruise on the small of the back, ritualistic positioning of the body, neatly piled clothing, and the detail that proved conclusively that this was the work of the same freak and not a copy cat, a dollar bill shoved inside the vagina.

The only variation was a second bruise just below the back of the head, no doubt caused by the blow that disabled the poor wretch.

Jackson was disturbed by the fact that the killer hadn't taken any steps to conceal the woman's identity. He'd left her purse, containing a driver's license and other I.D., in plain sight next to her clothing. This was no sloppy mistake; either he was thumbing his nose at the authorities or he *wanted* the victim to be identified.

Hawthorne stopped pacing and motioned to the head of the Crime Scene Unit, a bearded ex-football player named Ross Blackwell, who had just broken off his examination of the ground surrounding the Toyota to confer with one of his technicians.

"What's the story, Ross?"

"We've got a number of footprints around the car, all made with the same shoes, including one set that have a deeper indentation than the others, leading from the rear of the car to the hood, probably made when the perp was carrying the body."

"So you figure the victim was originally in the trunk?"

"It looks that way."

"That means he must've driven her here himself."

"There's no doubt about it. We found a set of the same footprints leading away from the area but none approaching."

Hawthorne turned to Jackson. "Do we know whether she was killed here or somewhere else?"

"Not enough time's elapsed to fix lividity, but I'd say she was dead when she got here. I think the guy likes to get the killing over quickly, so he's got time to play with the body."

Usually, provided a person had been dead long enough for the blood to thicken — about eight hours — the exact location of lividity could offer an important insight into the circumstances surrounding a murder. If the body was moved after this time, lividity would appear in the wrong places, indicating that the corpse had been tampered with.

"What about fingerprints?" asked Hawthorne.

"Nothing on the car," said Blackwell, absent-mindedly stroking his beard. "We won't know about the body or the dollar bill until later."

Hawthorne shoved a stick of gum into his mouth and patted Blackwell on the arm. "Thanks, Ross."

Blackwell nodded and rejoined his team.

Jackson and Hawthorne watched him go in silence. Neither seemed willing to acknowledge the inescapable fact that crept into their thoughts like a dark miasma rising out of the East River. A serial murderer was loose on the streets of New York City. Not some drooling maniac with an ice pick but a cool, intelligent killing machine.

"You look exhausted," said Hawthorne. "Go home and get some sleep. I'll get someone else to finish up here."

"You sure?"

"Absolutely. I need you fresh in the morning. We've got a shitload of important decisions to make."

Chapter 11 — Thursday, June 26

"The victim's name is Carol Linehan," said Lieutenant Hawthorne, starting off the morning briefing, "a model, aged twenty-two. The similarities between her death and the Sandra Geddes murder makes it pretty damn clear that we're dealing with a repeater."

He sipped his coffee and waited for the buzz to subside. "The only new information we have on this psycho is that he seems to have an underwear fetish. In the Geddes case, it was a pair of stockings. This time, he took the victim's panties. On the surface, he doesn't appear to be following any particular pattern in choosing his victims; the only obvious similarity between the two women is that they were both young and attractive.

"For now, our best chance of catching this guy is to find a witness. We seem to have hit a wall in the Geddes case but we might have better luck with this one because it appears the murder occurred in daylight in a public place.

"We know that Carol Linehan worked a fashion show yesterday afternoon at Chez Monique, a clothing store on Broad Street. We believe that's where the killer accosted her, probably as she was going to her car.

"Lionel, I want you to get over there and find out what time she left the building, where she parked her car, and who last saw her alive. Lewicki, as soon as you're done witnessing the autopsy I want you to take as many uniforms as patrol can spare and do a canvass of the area where the body was found. There must be someone who saw that Toyota in the park."

Hawthorne finished his coffee and tossed the cup into a wastebasket. "One last thing. Chief O'Ryan has made this case our number one priority. To that end, he's put me in charge of a special unit consisting of twenty-five detectives, five from each of the four precincts within our jurisdiction and five from the task force itself. That group will consist of Detectives Lewicki, Cordova, Choi and McDougall, and will be headed by Sergeant Jackson."

Someone grumbled.

"You got something to say, Greg?" asked Hawthorne.

Sergeant Gregory Carter, a compact 52-year-old with sloping shoulders and a sharply hooked nose, stood up and crossed his arms.

"Yeah, I do. With all due respect to Sergeant Jackson, I've got seniority and a sizeable edge in experience; I'm the one who should be in charge of our group."

"I agree," said someone from the back of the room, a night shifter who Jackson didn't recognize, "and not just for those reasons. I want to go on record as saying I've got no confidence in Sergeant Jackson. Everybody in this room knows he made serious errors in judgment during that hostage situation in the Bronx."

Hawthorne's jaw muscles tensed. "That matter is closed, mister!"

"But sir, his failure to follow procedure caused the deaths of eight innocent people. How do we know he isn't going to screw up again?"

"That's right," added Dan McDougall. "He shouldn't even be on the damned force any more. The only reason they didn't nail his hide to the wall was because of his color. The brass didn't want a political situation on its hands."

"You cracker son-of-a-bitch!" yelled Jackson, leaping to his feet. "I've *forgotten* more than you know about being a cop!"

"Is that why they kicked your ass out of the Bronx?"

Jackson felt all eyes turn expectantly in his direction, including Hawthorne's. He hesitated, and in that instant, despite his desire to rip McDougall's head off and drop kick it into the Hudson, he realized he was standing at the edge of an abyss. If he snapped, he'd be playing right into the hands of every detective in that room who considered him a loose cannon. It would destroy any chance he had of ever being accepted.

Taking a deep breath, he glared at McDougall and sat down.

"All right, people," said Hawthorne, taking Jackson's cue. "We're all under a lot of pressure here and maybe it's good to blow off a little steam. But let me make one thing clear. My decision stands. If any of you have a problem with that — for *whatever* reason — you've got two options. You can resign, or you can put in for a transfer. And that's the last word I'm going to say on the subject. Is that understood?"

Nobody took up the challenge.

"Okay, then. Let's get to work. Lionel, you're with me."

Jackson avoided looking at the others as he stood up and followed the lieutenant into his office.

"Close the door," said Hawthorne, sitting down behind his desk, which was littered with papers, folders, reports, a display case containing a baseball autographed by Don Mattingly, and a brass-framed family portrait. A battered couch stood against the right wall; a file cabinet and a metal stand holding a 20-inch TV and a VCR stood against the other. Jackson sat down in one of the two armchairs facing the desk.

"Listen," continued Hawthorne, "I put you in charge because I believe you're the best man for the job, period. Carter's a fine cop, but he's not a kid any more and I need someone with stamina and moxie. Having said that, I'll understand if you want to take a pass."

Jackson thought it over as he lit a cigarette. True, he'd probably score a few points with his peers if he deferred to Carter, but at what cost to his self-respect? It was hard enough being a black cop, with everyone's eyes on you all the time, second-guessing your every decision, watching your every move — especially in cases where race was involved — without compounding the problem by being perceived as someone who shirked responsibility.

No, the only way to win his colleagues' respect was by jumping into the frying pan, not by simmering on the sidelines. Besides, nailing the killer would go a long way toward putting that damned hostage incident behind him once and for all.

"I want the job, Lieutenant."

"Good man."

Jackson stood up to leave.

"Before you go, just a word about McDougall. I know he's got a big mouth, but he's a good cop."

"He's not the first racist I've had to deal with, and I *know* he won't be the last."

"It's not as simple as that. Cop racism seldom is — on either side of the color line. More often than not, it's based on personal experience...some real or imagined act of injustice that distorts a person's ability to think straight."

"Lieutenant, please. I've heard it all before. The excuses, the platitudes, the heartfelt pleas for understanding. Words are cheap. I'm only interested in a person's actions."

Jackson placed his hands on the edge of the desk and leaned closer. "Let me tell you something. That day Rodney King went on TV and made his 'why can't we all just get along' speech, I wanted to put my fist through the screen. Not because I disagreed with his sentiments. It's just that getting along is all my people have been trying to do for more than three hundred goddamn years! But it's never going to happen as long as this country continues to churn out ignorant yahoos like Dan McDougall!"

"Look," said Hawthorne, rubbing his neck, "I'm not trying to make excuses for the man. All I'm saying is that his behavior out there was not indicative of his character. And since you're going to be working with him, maybe for quite some time, it would help if you knew the facts."

Jackson took a deep drag on his cigarette and sat back down. "You're the boss."

"McDougall's old man was also a homicide detective, a good one, down in the ninth precinct. I think he retired last year. Anyway, sometime in nineteen eighty-six, he decided to take the sergeant's exam. Passed it, too, with flying colors. But the Guardians — remember them?"

Jackson nodded. The Guardians were a group of brothers who had sued the city back in the mid-1980s — around the time he joined the force — over the number of black officers who had failed to pass the NYPD sergeant's exam.

"They delayed his promotion for almost three years," continued Hawthorne. "Understandably, McDougall was bitter as hell, and some of that bitterness spilled over to Dan. He's had a grudge against black cops ever since — especially sergeants."

Jackson recalled that the controversy was triggered by a 1980 federal court decision that claimed the city intentionally discriminated against minorities. The court decreed that one out of every three new police recruits would have to be a member of a minority group, and that all subsequent promotions would have to reflect that quota.

But by the mid-eighties, it became clear this wasn't happening. So the Guardians, along with the Commissioner's office and the mayor, decided the testing procedure was to blame. As a result, they lowered the standards.

That's when the shit really hit the proverbial fan. Most experienced cops, including many blacks and Latinos who had made their way through the ranks on merit, opposed the move. They argued that police work required specific skills and basic standards; that it was madness to hire someone who lacked the size, education, or character to handle the job.

Most of the organizations representing minorities, on the other hand, argued it was precisely that kind of self-serving attitude that had created the problem in the first place. And as part of their protest, they deliberately set out to block the promotions of white officers.

The controversy led to years of bad blood and racial unrest in the department. Jackson, for one, thought the issue had finally been laid to rest.

"Okay," he said, "so maybe McDougall does have a legitimate beef. Then again, so did the Guardians. The point is, shit that happened to his old man ten years ago doesn't give him the right to disrespect me. If he gets in my face again, I'll plant my foot so far up his ass it'll make his tonsils spin."

"That's one option," replied Hawthorne, leaning back in his chair. "Or, you can make him see that he's wrong about you."

Frowning, Jackson crushed out his cigarette and headed for the door. What was there to say in the face of such maddening logic?

*****

Seven hours later, he was back in Hawthorne's office, staring bleary-eyed at the third of five video cassettes that had been turned over by the Hanover building's security personnel. Taken by the cameras in the parking garage, the grainy black and white recordings covered the period between 2:00 and 4:00 p.m. on the day of Carol Linehan's murder.

Jackson had learned that the fashion show ended at 2:30 p.m. and that Carol Linehan's Toyota checked out of the garage at 3:07. The attendant remembered her arrival, "because she was a real fox," but claimed not to have noticed the car. As a result, he had no recollection of it leaving the lot.

Jackson had also tracked down the two models who'd last seen the victim alive. But neither remembered spotting anyone who matched the suspect's description, either during the fashion show or lurking around the dressing room area afterwards. They claimed that when they left Carol Linehan, she was heading toward the service elevator, alone. Which meant the killer must've accosted her either while she was—

"Hold it!" he cried. "There she is!"

Hawthorne pressed the 'pause' button on the remote, rewound the tape, then began to advance the image one frame at a time.

The two men watched Carol Linehan step out of the elevator. She stopped, glanced back briefly, then turned to the right, away from the camera. A moment later, another figure, a man dressed in a dark suit, stepped into view. Keeping his head down, he hurried out of the elevator at an angle that made it impossible to see his face. But they did catch a glimpse of his hair. It was blond, the same color as the strands found at Sandra Geddes' apartment and in Carol Linehan's car.

"The son-of-bitch knew about the camera," said Hawthorne.

"That doesn't surprise me," replied Jackson. "This guy's not throwing darts at a map. He's got a plan."

The suspect took a position about three feet behind Carol Linehan's right shoulder. Surely she had to know he was there, thought Jackson. Why wasn't she reacting? Suddenly, she stopped and pointed at something off screen, probably her car. Then she turned to the suspect and smiled!

"Jesus Christ," said Hawthorne, freezing the frame. "Do you think she knew the guy?"

"I suppose it's possible," replied Jackson, trying to cling to his crumbling preconceptions. "Either that or he was able to gain her confidence in the few seconds they were on that elevator together."

Hawthorne rewound the tape and played the last section over again. "If the bastard did know her, he probably knew Sandra Geddes as well. That could be a huge break for us."

Jackson felt a twinge in his gut. It was all wrong. Serial killers — especially those with intelligence — seldom targeted people they knew. It was too risky and offered little challenge. There had to be another explanation.

Glancing up at the screen, he watched as the two figures proceeded to walk away from the camera for another ten yards or so before making a right turn and disappearing from view. The time display read 2:55. Sometime during the next 12 minutes, Carol Linehan had breathed her last.

"Why don't we take a break," said Jackson, rubbing his eyes. "I don't think we're going to see any more of the suspect — unless one of the other cameras managed to catch him while he was driving out of the garage. I'll look at the rest of the tapes later."

Hawthorne switched off the set and stood up to stretch his arms. "At least we've got a better handle on the bastard's body type. Which reminds me. When you're done, send that last tape to the photo unit. Ask them to isolate the elevator sequence and see if they can clean it up a bit. I want copies and stills sent to every television station in the area. Let's see if we can pressure the cocksucker into making a mistake."

Jackson picked up his cigarettes and headed for the door. "Listen, I don't want to keep bugging you about this, but I really think we need to get permission to bring in the FBI's Investigative Support Unit. We don't have the experience or resources to deal with this kind of psychopath."

"It's already been taken care of," replied Hawthorne. I'm seeing the profile co-coordinator at the Bureau's New York field office at four."

*****

Frank Ryman climbed out of a cab on the Park Avenue ramp, under the watchful eyes of Mercury, Hercules, and Minerva, the three mythological characters who welcomed travelers to Grand Central Station from their perch high atop its colonnaded facade.

He entered the terminal and made his way down to the main concourse with its magnificent vaulted ceiling. Inspired by a medieval manuscript, its zodiac design contained more than 2,500 stars, including all the major constellations, each delineated by tiny pinpoints of light. He could gaze at its transcendent beauty for hours at a time, imagining he was a comet, blazing majestically through the cold, empty vastness of space.

But right now he had more important things to do. He glanced up at the clock atop the information kiosk and noted that it was 7:50 p.m. Perfect. Only ten minutes to go before *Molinaro on N.Y. 99* went on the air. Hurrying across the concourse, he ducked into an alcove and found an empty phone booth. At precisely 7:55, he placed a quarter in the slot and dialed.

"W.S.N.Y."

"Good evening, Sidney," said Ryman, mimicking the voice of Orson Welles. He had chosen Welles' voice because of the actor's stature as one of the great pioneers of radio drama. His legendary, 1938 *War of the Worlds* broadcast still gave him goose bumps.

"Is that you, Frank?"

"Yes."

"How are you?"

"Better than ever, thank you. Sidney, would it be possible for me to lead off tonight's show? I have something very important to say."

"I'll have to clear it with Bob, first."

"Please do, and tell him I will make it well worth his while."

There was a clicking sound, followed by an abrupt cut to a recording of Mozart's *Eine Kleine Nachtmusik*. Ryman propped the receiver under his chin and leaned against the side of the booth. Despite the gratifying new twist his crusade against female turpitude had taken, he fully intended to continue expressing his views on Molinaro's program. Of course, now that he was becoming a celebrity, he'd no longer be making any calls from home.

The phone clicked again. "Frank?"

"Yes?"

"Bob says it's all right. We're just running the intro so I'll patch you through in about thirty seconds."

"Thank you, Sidney."

Ryman spent the time enjoying Mozart.

"Hello, Frank," said Molinaro. "I'm glad you called. I've been thinking about that remark you made the last time we spoke. What exactly did you mean by 'the reckoning has begun'? What reckoning, and for whom?"

"I thought you might have figured it out by now, especially after what happened last night."

"This is New York, pal. What *didn't* happen last night."

"True. But then again, puzzles are no fun unless you solve them yourself."

"I'm a talk show host, Frank, not a cryptographer."

"All it requires is a little deductive reasoning. When you have a moment, read today's *Times*. You'll find a news item similar to a piece that appeared in last Sunday's edition. Then, think about the concerns I have been expressing on your program for the past number of months. On the one hand you have a cause, on the other, multiple effects."

"I've got to be honest with you, Frank. You may find this stuff entertaining but it makes for lousy radio. Unless you're ready to talk turkey, I'm afraid I'll have to—"

"Solve the puzzle, Robert. I guarantee that by this time next week, your ratings will be higher than you ever imagined."

Ryman hung up and smiled. He was extremely pleased by the moderation he'd shown. No boasts. No histrionics. Just enough information to drive Robert Molinaro to distraction for the next few days.

Now it was time for supper. Exiting the alcove, he walked across the concourse and descended to the lower level. His destination was the Oyster Bar & Restaurant, a seafood eatery located at the south end of the terminal.

Ryman licked his lips — but not solely in anticipation of satisfying his hunger. His creative juices were beginning to bubble again. It was time to start thinking about where to seek the raw material for his next masterpiece.

Chapter 12 — Friday, June 27

Lieutenant Hawthorne began the morning briefing of the special unit by screening the Hanover Building surveillance tape. Afterwards, he had Jackson distribute a set of grainy stills provided by the photo lab: a close-up of the suspect leaving the elevator, a tight medium shot of him walking alone, and a long shot of him trailing Carol Linehan.

"As you can see," said Jackson," none of the photos provides a clear view of the suspect's face. But they do show us his build. Taken together with our other evidence, we now know that he's a fit Caucasion male, twenty-two to twenty-eight years old. He's about six feet tall, weighs between one-eighty and two hundred pounds, and wears a size nine and a half shoe. He's got straight, sandy-blond hair with a square-back cut. The tailoring of his suit suggests a professional man. We can also be reasonably sure that he's good-looking, articulate, and highly intelligent. He also spends a lot of time in the pool. You'll find all of this information printed on the back of each photo."

"Thank you, Sergeant," said Hawthorne, standing up. "As soon as we're finished here I want the East River Park detail to take a set of these shots and the one of Carol Linehan's car back to the crime scene for another canvass. Maybe we'll have better luck than we had yesterday. Ditto for the swimming pool detail.

"I want a third detail to start checking with psychiatrists and mental hospitals in the area. It's possible the suspect spent time in an institution. Finally, I want a fourth detail to show these photographs to *everybody* who had *anything* to do with Carol Linehan — family, friends, coworkers, casual acquaintances, her doctor, her dentist, her druggist, her grocer, even her priest, if she had one."

Hawthorne paused to shove a stick of gum in his mouth. "The funeral's tomorrow morning at ten. Choi, McDougall, I want you there. Bring along a photographer but make sure he keeps his distance. And get there early so you can ask a few of the victim's relatives to act as spotters. When you're done, sequester the guest book and have R and I compare it with the one we got from the Geddes' funeral. Lewicki, what did the autopsy turn up?"

Ed Lewicki set down his coffee cup and opened his notepad. "The M.E. says the victim was strangled with some kind of cord, and that the blade used to sever her lips was different than the one used on Sandra Geddes. Again, he found no evidence of sexual molestation. He also confirms that she was disabled by a blow to the back of the neck, a fist, probably."

"Okay," said Hawthorne. "Lionel, you've got the floor."

Jackson picked up a file from his desk and walked to the front of the room. "Based on what forensics turned up," he said, flipping open the file, "it looks like our boy is getting smarter. None of his prints were found in Carol Linehan's car, on her person, or on the dollar bill. No hair, either. The Crime Scene Unit did get casts of his footprints, however. Let's hope the son-of-a-bitch didn't think to get rid of his shoes. They also found strands of the victim's hair in the trunk of the car, so we can be reasonably sure she was killed in the parking garage, then driven to East River Park."

Jackson set the file down and lit a cigarette. "Our problem isn't a lack of evidence; we have enough from the Geddes case alone to put the bastard behind bars for the rest of his life. But we've got to catch him first. And right now, the only clues we have to his identity are some grainy photographs of his backside and a description that probably fits half a million men in the tri-state area. We need an eyewitness and we need one fast, because this guy is going to kill again."

"Excuse me, Sergeant." It was Ira Kaufman, the public relations hack assigned to the unit by the Commissioner's office. "I know we've already released these photos and a description of the suspect to the media, but isn't there more we can be doing to show people that we're on top of the situation ...to calm their fears a little?"

"Like what?" muttered Lewicki. "We're dealing with a psycho who chooses his victims at random."

"From what I know about serial killers," said Jackson, "they rarely select their victims at random. In this case, the suspect chose these women because of who they were or what they did or what they looked like. But until we know for sure, we have no way of identifying his intended target group. So the best we can do is advise *all* women to stay alert."

A black detective near the back of the room raised his hand. "What about the possibility that the perp knew the victims?"

"The evidence seems to suggest otherwise."

"But your report claims he was a guest in Sandra Geddes' apartment, and that videotape shows Carol Linehan *smiling* at the guy."

"That tells me women like him, either because of his looks or because of his charm, probably both. That's why he's so dangerous."

"What confuses me," said Jimmy Choi, "is the guy's M.O. I mean, he doesn't seem to be interested in sex, yet he chooses attractive victims and poses their bodies in a sexually suggestive way. On top of that, he likes to shove dollar bills into their twa— vaginas, and take their underwear as a souvenir."

"My guess is that he's either sexually dysfunctional or his actions are meant to be symbolic," replied Jackson, not wanting to admit he was in over his head. This was the kind of psychological swamp he was hoping the FBI mindhunter would be able to navigate.

"What about his need to mutilate?" asked Choi. "Why the lips, and not the sex organs?"

"Maybe the senoritas said something to peess him off," said Octavio Cordova, a squat Puerto Rican whose quick wit, mischievous grin, and boundless energy had earned him the nickname, 'Latin Leprechaun'.

"That's it," said McDougall. "He's probably a flasher who didn't appreciate their cracks about the size of his dick."

Jackson grinned. Humor, like cynicism, was a defense mechanism; a way for homicide cops to deal with the pressures and horrors of the job.

"Okay, okay," said Hawthorne, "enough with the bullshit. You've all got your assignments, so hit the road."

When the room had cleared, Jackson sat down and tried to imagine what would drive a man to kill and mutilate two innocent young women. Generally, most murders were depressingly mundane. People got stabbed for their watches in underground parking garages or for their wallets on some deserted street. Others were shot over a woman or a gram of crack. Domestic disputes, bar fights, mob hits, teenage gang wars — all produced their share of corpses in the rivers, streets, alleys, and parks of New York City.

Homicide cops reacted to such killings with a certain degree of professional dispassion. But there were others that got under your skin: the killing of a child or a fellow officer, and atrocities like the ritualistic slaying of Sandra Geddes and Carol Linehan.

Whenever such a case came along, the mood in the squad room, usually informal and marked by spurts of horseplay, changed to one of grim determination. Cooperation became the buzzword. Off-duty detectives reported in without being asked; others took on extra duties.

Jackson stood up and headed for the door. He had an appointment downtown, to see if he could get any assistance from CATCH, the department's Computer-Assisted Terminal Criminal Hunt system, a microfilm-based program containing mug shots of every person ever formally photographed during an in-state booking process.

Although the system's search engine was name-driven — including possible variations such as aliases, nicknames, legally altered names, and typical abbreviations — it could also be programmed to search for specific types of charges. In this case, violence against women, sexual deviation, and criminal fetishism. The fact that Jackson could also provide the suspect's race, hair color, and probable age would help narrow the search parameters even further.

If the madman who killed Sandra Geddes and Carol Linehan had ever been arrested in New York state, his photo would be on file.

*****

At 12:15 p.m. Jackson walked into Brannigan's, a steak house on 34th Street, just west of Herald Square. Lieutenant Hawthorne was waiting for him in a booth at the rear of the restaurant. He was already digging into his lunch, a thick T-bone and a baked potato stuffed with sour cream and chives.

"How'd the chief's meeting with the D.A. go?" asked Jackson, sliding onto the opposite bench.

Hawthorne frowned. "Take a guess."

"Damned lawyers. They think we're fucking magicians."

"He's just doing what he's paid to do," said Hawthorne, "like the rest of us. Except he's higher up on the totem pole."

"And we're at the bottom."

Hawthorne fished a piece of gristle out of his mouth. "What can I say? Everybody's feeling the heat, right down the line — the mayor, the D.A., the commissioner, the chief. That's why we've got to see some movement on this case. Soon."

"We're doing everything we can."

"Did you have any luck downtown?"

"The CATCH attendant came up with a number of guys in the area who fit the general description but it's going to take some time to track them all down."

"I'll get you all the help you need. What happened with Carol Linehan's boyfriend?"

"Lewicki talked to him this morning. The kid's got an airtight alibi. Besides, he's five-nine and has brown hair."

A pony-tailed waiter appeared and Jackson ordered a cheeseburger, well done, with mustard, pickle, and fried onions, and a small Caesar salad.

"Anything to drink?"

"Just water, with lots of ice."

Jackson reached for his cigarettes but was stopped by a sign indicating he was in a no-smoking section. "By the way," he said, running a hand across his scalp in exasperation, "any word on when we can expect to see that FBI profiler?"

"Tonight," replied Hawthorne, wiping his mouth. "Speaking of which, did you know I was involved in the very first collaboration between the N.Y.P.D. and the Investigative Support Unit, back in seventy-nine?"

"No kidding."

"I pulled the file last night, to refresh my memory. The case involved a particularly brutal murder of a young woman named Francine Elveson. She was a tiny thing, less than five feet tall, about ninety pounds. Lived with her parents in an apartment in the Bronx and taught handicapped children at a day-care center. Got along real well with them, too, because she was mildly handicapped herself.

"On the morning of the murder, a boy who lived in Francine's building found her wallet on the stairwell. He was late for school, so he took the wallet with him and waited until he came home for lunch before giving it to his old man. The father returned the wallet to Mrs. Elveson, who immediately called the day-care center to let her daughter know her wallet had been found. When she was told Francine hadn't been in that day, she got worried and decided to search the building, along with her other daughter and a neighbor.

"They found Francine's nude and severely beaten body spread-eagled on the landing at the top of the stairwell, tied up with her own belt and stockings, and with her underwear pulled over her head to cover her face. Her nipples had been cut off and she had bite marks on her thighs and knees, and several shallow cuts on her body, made by a small penknife. The killer had also forced an umbrella and a pen into her vagina, after using the pen to scrawl 'You can't stop me' and 'Fuck you' on her skin. As if that wasn't enough, the sick son-of-a-bitch took a shit near the body and covered it with some of Francine's clothes."

"Christ almighty," said Jackson, grimacing.

"The only consolation for the mother was the M.E.'s determination that the mutilation occurred after Francine's death."

"Some consolation. What was the cause?"

"Ligature strangulation, with the strap of her pocketbook."

"Had she been sexually molested?"

"The M.E. found traces of semen on her body, but he subsequently ruled out rape. There were no defense wounds on her hands or skin fragments under her fingernails, either, which suggested there'd been no struggle. The investigating detectives figured she was battered unconscious as she walked down the stairs, then carried up to the landing."

"Any other forensic evidence?"

"A single hair found on the body during the autopsy, identified as belonging to a black male."

"Not much to go on."

"Exactly. But that didn't stop the public and the media from clamoring for an immediate arrest. The pressure was unbelievable. I was one of twenty-six detectives eventually assigned to the case. We must've questioned more than two thousand potential witnesses and suspects and checked out every goddamn sex offender in New York county. But a month later, we still didn't have a suspect.

"That's when the Investigative Support Unit was called in. The agent assigned to the case was no other than the head honcho himself, John Douglas. I assume you've heard of the man?"

Jackson nodded. Douglas was retired now, but while on the job he was considered one of the leading experts on criminal personality profiling.

"He shows up," continued Hawthorne, "examines the evidence, the autopsy protocols, and the crime scene photos, and a few days later he comes back and blithely announces that we should be looking for a disheveled white male, between the ages of twenty-five and thirty-five—"

"What about the hair found on the body?" asked Jackson.

"He dismissed it. Claimed that crimes of that type rarely crossed racial lines, and that when they did, there was usually other substantiating evidence — of which there was none in the Elveson case. He also said he'd seldom seen that kind of mutilation from a black perp.

"Anyway, he tells us our suspect is unemployed, likes to prowl around at night, lives within half a mile of the Elveson building with his parents or an older female relative, is an unmarried loner who can't have relationships with women, is a high school or college dropout with no military experience, and has no car or driver's license."

"Jesus Christ."

"There's more. He also says the guy has low self-esteem, has spent time in a mental institution and takes medication for his problem, has attempted suicide by strangulation or asphyxia, shuns narcotics and alcohol, and likes to collect bondage and S and M pornography. He ends his little speech by claiming that we'd probably already interviewed the suspect and his family.

"Man, you could've heard a pin drop in that room. Don't forget, no one knew shit about profiling back then. Most of us thought Douglas was off his rocker. And a lot of officers said so. I guess he'd gotten that kind of reaction before, because he patiently took us through the process, explaining how he'd come up with every one of his impressions and recommendations. I'm not going to repeat what he said — you can read the report yourself if you're interested — but let's just say that his insights blew me away."

"Did the brass buy it?"

"What choice did they have? We took Douglas's profile and went back over our suspect and interview list until we had it pared down to twenty-two names. Of these, one individual fit the profile like a glove.

"The guy's name was Carmine Calabro, a white, thirty-six-year-old high school dropout who lived off and on with his widowed father in the Elveson's building. On the same floor, in fact. He was unemployed, single, and had trouble maintaining relationships with women. No car, no license, no military experience. He also had a history of suicide attempts by hanging and asphyxia, both before and after Francine's murder. And here's the kicker: when we searched his room, we found a ton of bondage and S and M pornography."

"Unbelievable," said Jackson, shaking his head.

"That's what I thought at the time. Only problem was, the guy had an alibi. Like Douglas said, we'd already interviewed the father during our canvass of the building. The old man had told us that Carmine suffered from severe depression and was an in-patient resident at a local mental hospital. That's why we'd ruled him out as a possible suspect.

"But now that we had the profile, we immediately went back to work on him. Within days we were able to establish conclusively that he'd slipped out of the institution unobserved the night before Francine's murder.

"It had taken thirteen bloody months but Carmine Calabro was finally arrested. A few days later, we got three forensic dentists to confirm that his teeth matched the bite marks on Francine's body. That was the end of the line for Mister Calabro. He was convicted of murder and got twenty-five to life."

"You still haven't explained the Negroid hair found at the scene," said Jackson.

"Talk about your classic screw-up. It turned out the bag used to transport Francine to the morgue had previously contained the body of a black male and hadn't been properly cleaned."

"So Douglas's instincts were right about that, too," said Jackson, awestruck.

Hawthorne chuckled. "After the conviction came down, one of the investigators said it was a wonder Douglas hadn't given them Calabro's phone number on top of everything else."

*****

Seventeen detectives were in the squad room when Lieutenant Hawthorne walked in at 5:15 p.m., accompanied by a balding, bespectacled beanpole of a man who carried himself with the dignity and casual ease of a tenured university professor.

"Listen up," said Hawthorne, escorting the newcomer to the front of the room. "This is FBI Special Agent Raymond Carmichael. He's here to try and help us catch our repeater."

Just in time, too, thought Jackson, pushing his chair back and locking his hands behind his head. The day's canvass blitz had turned up one solitary lead. An old Jewish shopkeeper on Delancy Street had seen a tall blond man dressed like the figure in the surveillance photos walking out of East River Park on Wednesday afternoon. The suspect was heading west, carrying a plastic bag.

When asked what made him notice this individual, the old man said it was unusual to see someone dressed in a suit and tie strolling in East River Park in the middle of the afternoon. Besides which, he said the guy had the look and carriage of an SS officer.

Hawthorne had ordered a detail to scour both sides of Delancy from the park to the Essex Street subway station, paying particular attention to alleyways and garbage bins, in case the suspect had discarded evidence. As yet, nothing had been reported.

"Some of you may not be that familiar with what the Investigative Support Unit does," continued Hawthorne, "so Mr. Carmichael has agreed to provide a brief overview. Ray."

Carmichael cleared his throat, spread his legs, and slipped his right hand into his pocket. "Basically, we examine the crime scene and related forensic evidence in order to create a behavioral profile of the perpetrator, describing his habits and trying to predict his next move. Our philosophy is simple. If you want to understand a great painter, you study his art. If you want to understand a criminal's personality, you study his crime.

"In some ways, serial offenders are all the same. But it's their differences and the clues they leave to their individual personalities that are the key to a successful profile. Our research shows that no matter how hard a serial offender tries, much of what he does after committing his crime is beyond his conscious control. This behavior is what we call his signature. It defines what he is and what he needs to do to find fulfillment. A signature is static; it doesn't change. It differs from the perpetrator's M.O., which is learned behavior and *can* change.

"When we're called in on a case, the first thing we do is ask ourselves the following questions: Why did the perpetrator select this particular victim? Is there anything behaviorally significant about the crime? Why did it go down the way it did? For example, was there mutilation after death? Was anything of value taken, either from the victim or from the crime scene? If so, why? Was there forced entry? If not, why?

"What we're trying to do is come up with a reason for every behaviorally significant factor. We then try to figure out who would have committed the crime for those particular reasons."

"I got a question," said Dan McDougall, craning his bull neck like a turtle that's just smelled food. "You say that part of your job is trying to predict a perp's next move. How do you do that, exactly?"

Carmichael adjusted his glasses. "We've learned that it's the thrill of the hunt that excites most serial killers. So we try to think like a hunter. Once we've identified the perpetrator's target prey, we try to figure out which individual in that group is most vulnerable, the one most likely to be the next victim. We do this by studying behavior, lifestyle, dress, non-verbal cues, and a number of other factors.

"We also try to put ourselves in the victim's place; to understand what she went through from the time she was abducted to the moment of her death. Most profilers do this by recalling the fear they felt when their own lives were on the line."

Octavio Cordova raised his hand. "What happens when you can't nail down a perp's target group? It eess one thing when a killer goes after hookers, but in theess case one of thee victims was a blonde bank teller, the other a brown-haired model. Where eess thee pattern?"

"I can't answer that question until I've had a chance to examine the evidence. But I'm confident we'll find a link."

"Okay," said Hawthorne, stepping in front of Carmichael, "that's enough for now. It's getting late and Ray's got a lot of work to do." He caught Jackson's eye and waved him over. He introduced the two men, then dashed into his office to make a phone call.

"So," said Jackson, leading Carmichael to his desk, "what's number one on the agenda?"

"I'll need to look at the autopsy protocols for both victims, including serology and toxicology. Then I'll need to see the preliminary police reports, the forensic reports, and the crime scene photos. I'll also want to examine the actual sites at some point."

"Just let me know when you're ready and I'll take you there myself," said Jackson, pulling up an empty chair. "By the way, did the lieutenant tell you we have the suspect on tape?"

"He did, but I don't want to see it until I've examined the physical evidence first. It might prejudice my analysis."

*****

Nightfall, Greenwich Village. Inside the cramped, dark, and noisy confines of the Rusty Nail Pub, Rachel Curran cradled a tray under her arm and walked back to the curved oak bar to place another order. Her throat itched and she was beginning to develop a slight headache, both the result of second-hand smoke inhalation. For some reason, Friday night crowds always produced the heaviest billows of the vile stuff.

Picking up the plastic tumbler she'd left at the end of the bar, she stirred its contents with a straw and took a long drink. The tumbler contained the juice of five oranges, one lemon, half a grapefruit, and four carrots, mixed with a quarter cup of wheat germ. One of her naturopathy books claimed that regular doses of beta-carotene and vitamins C and E helped to clean the lungs and wash away pollutants.

Rachel wiped her mouth with a napkin and returned the tumbler to its nook. A few feet away, her roommate-cum-bartender, Sally Schuster, was chatting up a customer — a muscular, long-haired hunk dressed in Nikes, denim shorts, and a pale blue T-shirt. Sally ended the exchange by handing the guy a book of matches she took from her private stash, which she kept in an ashtray behind the bar. Each had her phone number written inside.

Rachel shook her head. "You're incorrigible, you know that."

"Listen, kiddo, you've got to give and take as much love as you can, while you can, because in a very short time you'll be old and ugly and no man will want to touch you."

"That's got to be the most original justification for promiscuity I've ever heard."

"God, you're such a prude. Are you sure you haven't got some Quaker in you?"

"I happen to like oats."

"Very funny. Now tell me what you want before I come over there and give you a wedgie."

"Two Buds, one Bloody Mary, and one Dewar's, straight up."

When Sally had finished filling the order, Rachel leaned across the bar and gripped her friend's hand. "Seriously, Sal. Be careful about who you flirt with, okay? There's a maniac on the loose out there."

"Not to worry, kiddo. I won't be dating any six-foot Teutons any time soon. Besides, the creep seems to go for the bombshell type and I'm just a mousy little—" Her eyes widened. "*You're* the one who has to be careful, Rach. Don't forget, one of the women he killed was a model."

"Believe me," replied Rachel, picking up her tray, "I'm well aware of that."

She cradled the tray on her palm and began to weave her way through a maze of tables, chairs, and drunken revelers. The truth was, since hearing about the murder of Carol Linehan, she'd grown suspicious of every man who ogled her — an irritating and not uncommon occurrence for someone with her looks.

There was one now, sitting alone in the corner, nervously picking at the label of his beer bottle, a cigarette drooping from the corner of his slack mouth. Sure, his hair was dark. But how did she know it wasn't dyed? He certainly looked like a predator. Then again, most horny men had that intense, hungry look. And therein lay the dilemma. How was *any* woman expected to tell if a man had more on his mind than just a quick romp in the hay?

A shudder ran through her as she recalled the last time a serial killer had haunted her imagination. It happened when she was a teenager in Buffalo and the monster's name was Arthur J. Shawcross.

Shawcross first attained notoriety in 1973, the year he was convicted of murdering and sexually assaulting two children in Watertown, a sleepy community in upstate New York. He ended up serving an unconscionably mere 14 years, just enough time to heat his bloodlust to the boiling point. Shortly after his release, in April of 1987, he began the worst killing spree in the history of New York State. By the time the police finally caught him in January of 1990, he'd murdered 11 women, prostitutes mainly, in and around the city of Rochester.

Although at the time Rachel was too young to understand what a prostitute was, it didn't diminish the horror she'd felt at the pain and suffering inflicted on those poor women. She'd had nightmares for months. It was at that point when she first began to suspect that the true monsters lurking in the shadows were human.

The Shawcross case also prompted Rachel's father, an avid hunter and target shooter, to enroll her and her three older brothers in his gun club. In time, she became so adept that she won several sharp-shooting competitions for her age group. She'd been a registered handgun owner ever since.

Spooked by the morbid turn her thoughts had taken, Rachel forced herself to think of more pleasant matters, like the fact that she'd gotten the Montgomery Ward Christmas catalog assignment, which was scheduled to start shooting in early September. There were also a ton of things to do in preparation for the upcoming pageant. She had to update and submit her fact sheet, get some flattering photos taken for the pageant program and judges' workbook, practice the piano composition she would be performing — Chopin's *Sonata #3* — and select her competition wardrobe, including shoes, a sexy yet sensible swimsuit, and a couple of gowns.

Rachel smiled. Nothing cheered a woman up like the anticipation of shopping for new clothes.

Chapter 13 — Saturday, June 28

Robert Molinaro chewed on the end of his cigar as he read an article in *Talkers Magazine*, an industry trade publication. The scuttlebutt was that Rush Limbaugh, the so-called 'Elvis Presley of talk radio' and the current king of the loudmouths, was beginning to lose his grip on the crown.

As evidence, the article cited two factors: Limbaugh's abandonment of his syndicated television broadcast and a survey conducted by the Pew Research Center for the People and the Press which claimed that his listenership had plummeted from 20 percent to 11 percent in just two years, while the number of people who never listened to his program had risen from 61 percent to 70 percent.

Molinaro tossed the magazine on his desk and smiled. He always enjoyed seeing a competitor hit the skids, especially one who got under his skin.

Still, he grudgingly had to admit that men like Limbaugh and Howard Stern had made it possible for small fry like himself to get into the game. By pushing the talk show envelope, they had helped the format attain phenomenal popularity. In 1989, the year after Limbaugh's show went to syndication, there were 308 news-talk stations nationwide. By 1992, the number had doubled, and the ratings placed news-talk just behind adult music as the most popular AM format. Now there were an estimated 1,272 news-talk stations, with the highest combined audience share of any format.

What a weird and wonderful racket, thought Molinaro, flicking a sliver of ash off his shirt. Considering how much New Yorkers loved to chew the fat, it was no surprise that talk radio had its birth in Manhattan — although no one could accurately pinpoint the father. Some credited Barry Gray, who hosted a show from a night club for WMCA in the 1940s, with being the first to incorporate phone calls into his program (his first on-air caller was big-band leader Woody Herman). Others harkened back to the *Goodwill Hour* on the Mutual Broadcasting System, hosted by John J. Anthony during the 1930s, whose listeners phoned in for household advice.

Other early notables included WOR's Alexander Woolcott, who dispensed *New Yorker*-style gossip about what he'd heard around town, and 'Long John' Nebel, a one-time salesman who further developed the format's 'live participation' aspect.

Then came the next generation and the gradual move from substance to vitriolic showmanship; men like 'Mean' Joe Pyne — the first radio talker to take his act to television — Don Imus, Morton Downey Jr., Howard Stern, and Rush Limbaugh, who liked to rile as well as inform.

Molinaro felt the bile rising in his throat. Every time he mused about the giants of his profession, it reminded him that he was never going to be in their league. As for making the switch to television, that possibility seemed dead in the water. Every station within commuting distance had now rejected him, and with Anna's continuing intransigence about moving to another city — which he expected to become entrenched once the baby arrived — there was nothing left to do but hang on until management decided to cut him loose.

A knock on the door.

"What is it?" he yelled.

The door opened and Sid Crouse stuck his large, balding head into the room. "Yoko's here."

Yoko Ono was the guest on that afternoon's program, principally to talk about her new exhibition at the Guggenheim. "I'll be out in a second," said Molinaro.

"One other thing," added Sid. "You know how Mister Nichols has been a judge at the Miss Empire State beauty pageant for the last umpteen years. Well, he can't make it this time around and he wants you to take his place."

Walter Nichols was the station's owner.

"Why me?"

"Because you're our best-known celebrity, and the fact that your show deals with contemporary culture makes you more qualified than our other on-air personalities."

"But I don't know squat about judging a beauty pageant."

"The organizers will send you an instructional video and sometime in early July you'll be invited to a seminar. Then, at the beginning of pageant week, you and the other panelists will attend an orientation session."

"Christ, it sounds like a fucking ordeal."

"Mister Nichols says it *can* be pretty nerve-wracking."

"Great. When does the damn thing take place?"

"From Sunday, July thirteenth to Saturday, July nineteenth, at Radio City. And don't worry about the show. We'll get someone to fill in."

I bet you will, thought Molinaro, glancing at his calendar. "Anna's not due until late August, so that shouldn't be a problem. Seeing as I don't have a choice, I guess I'm in."

"Excellent," said Sid, turning to leave. "I'll inform Mister Nichols."

"Wait. I just had a thought. Why don't we get a couple of the contestants to appear on the show. It'll be good publicity for the pageant and it might just stir up a little controversy for us. A lot of people think that beauty pageants are politically incorrect relics of the past."

"Nice idea. I'll get right on it."

"Just make sure they don't send us a couple of airheads. I want women who can speak eloquently about themselves and the pageant. Oh, and Sid. If that guy Frank calls today, don't put him through. He's been useless lately."

"Sure thing," said Sid, shutting the door.

Molinaro angrily puffed on his cigar at the thought of all the time he'd wasted trying to decipher Frank's cryptic message. As instructed, he'd read those two editions of the *Times* and found nothing in either that had the slightest connection with any of the man's bizarre views.

Deductive reasoning my ass, he thought, rising to his feet. He crushed out his cigar, sprayed a blast of Binaca into his mouth, and walked out of the office to relay his regards to Miz Ono.

*****

Frank Ryman's breathing deepened as he watched his ghostly video image follow the scrawny model he had transformed. Every news program on every television station in the city had been showing the clip continuously since Friday evening. A lot of good it would do, though. The man on the screen could be anyone.

Of more pressing concern was the police description that accompanied the video. Although it was too sketchy to pose any real danger, it most likely had placed every model in New York on the alert. He'd no longer be able to approach his subjects directly. Instead, he would have to rely on strategy and stealth. To that end, he'd resigned from his job — claiming a desire to move back to Louisiana — and would now be able to devote all his time and energy to his new avocation.

Ryman, naked in his easy chair except for Sandra Geddes' stockings and Carol Linehan's panties — which were a little too snug for his liking — switched off the TV and dug his fingers into the armrests. Viewing the video clip was enjoyable, but not as much as the actual act of creation. He leaned back and closed his eyes. In the last few days, his life's purpose had become much clearer. True, he was gaining skill as an artist. But that was of peripheral importance. His main objective — and sacred duty — was to guide womankind back onto the one true path; to eliminate the weeds so that the flowers would grow straight and tall and strong, the way nature had intended.

Beware ye of questionable virtue, for thy doom approaches. I am The Guardian, avatar of Shiva, the destroyer and the creator. I annihilate in order to preserve. Change thy wicked ways or prepare to face my terrible wrath. Run and hide as ye may, but like Shiva with her third eye, The Guardian sees all.

Taking a deep, restorative breath, he stood up and walked into the bedroom to dress and to pack his disguise: a policeman's uniform he'd stolen earlier that day from a wardrobe trailer in Central Park, along with a night stick and a hat, to conceal his hair. He'd stumbled upon the trailer by chance, while passing a film crew shooting a scene near the Bow Bridge. Someone had obligingly left the door open.

The prospect of playing the role of a policeman excited him. He'd been practicing his Pat O'Brien imitation all afternoon, modifying the actor's thick Irish brogue to give it a more contemporary inflection. The performance would be taking place outside the Superstudio Industria, a fashion photo studio in Greenwich Village. He'd read somewhere that dozens of models could be found working there at any given time.

Chapter 14 — Sunday, June 29

The squad room crackled with anticipation as FBI agent Raymond Carmichael set his briefcase on the floor and trained his placid brown eyes on the assembled members of the special unit. An exhausted Lionel Jackson loosened his tie and took a seat near the front.

"Good morning," said Carmichael, adjusting his glasses. "I'd like to begin by making a few observations about the first victim, Sandra Geddes. From the evidence, I'd say her murder was spontaneous, a crime of opportunity. If the killer had gone after her with intent he would've taken precautions, like wearing gloves rather than relying on cleaning the crime scene. And he certainly wouldn't have taken the victim back to her own apartment, where he risked being seen. It's also doubtful he was carrying the knife he used to sever her lips, which means he must've gotten one from the kitchen. I suspect it's still there.

"Something happened to anger this individual, traumatic enough to cause him to fracture the victim's jaw. His decision to kill came later. The young woman's promiscuous lifestyle suggests we can probably rule out rejection as the cause of his rage.

"Whatever the psychological stressor was, it unleashed the perpetrator's deep-rooted hatred of women. Our research shows that most serial killers are angry misfits who feel that life has given them a raw deal. More often than not, they focus this anger on women, initially by engaging in violent fantasies. Their first kill provides a tremendous emotional release. It also emboldens them and fills them with the need to repeat the experience.

"Which leads us to Carol Linehan. There's no doubt her murder was planned, though I'm still not certain why the killer chose her in particular. In any event, we do know that he accosted her after the fashion show — my guess is that he was in the audience — and somehow gained her confidence. Again, this indicates an individual who is charming and articulate.

"The perpetrator's presence at an obscure fashion show and the remoteness of the area where Carol Linehan's body was found suggests he's familiar with lower Manhattan. There's a good chance he lives or works there."

Carmichael took a handkerchief out of his pocket and blew his nose. "I'd now like to examine the sexual overtones of these crimes," he continued. "Although both bodies were arranged in a sexual position, there was no actual intercourse. This is a classic indicator that the individual you're looking for is insecure and sexually immature. And even though he appears to be at ease with women, he's actually intimidated by them, which is why he tries to render his victims powerless as quickly as possible. The killing and mutilation are his way of depersonalizing these women.

"On the other hand, there's no evidence that he abused or tortured his victims *before* he killed them, which suggests someone who does not derive sexual satisfaction from inflicting pain. That means the mutilations are fetishistic rather than sadistic and have more to do with the possession part of his fantasy than with a need to dominate and control.

"Also, posing a victim's body in a degrading, ritualistic position usually indicates that the killer has little remorse about his crime. In this case, the fact that both victims were posed masturbating also indicates his disdain for them, maybe even his moral superiority. Leaving a dollar bill in their bodies is probably his way of labeling them as whores — cheap ones at that."

"Can you explain why he only mutilates his victims' mouths?" asked Jimmy Choi.

"Not really, though I suspect there's some symbolic significance. Perhaps he suffered verbal abuse as a child, either at the hands of his mother or some other female."

"But why would he take the lips with him?"

"Many serial killers take souvenirs from their victims, including body parts, usually to keep as a fetishistic memento; something to help them relive the experience. Jeffrey Dahmer would be the most extreme example."

"Is that why he also takes their underwear?"

"It would appear so," replied Carmichael, walking over to the water cooler.

Jackson heard a muffled snigger from Octavio Cordova, who was sitting just behind him. Peering over his shoulder, he saw the detective lean toward Choi and whisper, "Maybe thee freak likes to wear women's clothes, like old J. Edgar Hoover used to do, eh?"

Jackson placed a hand over his mouth to hide his grin. Then he shot a quick, anxious glance at Carmichael. Fortunately, the FBI man was hunkered over the water cooler, which was conveniently emitting a series of loud gurgles.

"The absence of sexual frenzy in these crimes," continued Carmichael, walking back to the front of the room with a paper cup in his hand, "and the care shown in the positioning of the bodies and the handling of the victims' clothes, suggests a rigid, controlled personality type."

He swallowed some water, then leaned against the edge of a desk. "The man you're looking for is methodical, well-organized, and obsessively neat; a conservative in both dress and lifestyle. He probably drives a dark-colored sedan. He's a single, nocturnal loner with a college education. He's very good with figures, diagrams, puzzles, things of that sort. He could be an architect or an engineer. Or perhaps an accountant or bookkeeper. Maybe even a bank clerk. He has no criminal record and has never served in the military. He probably spent time in a mental institution."

Carmichael finished drinking his water and crumbled the cup in his hand. "Obviously, he has a pathological hatred of women. But not all women. It's no coincidence that both his victims were young and beautiful."

"How can you be so sure just by reading forensics reports and looking at crime scene photos?" asked a female detective leaning against the far wall.

Jackson smiled. He could tell by the FBI man's expression that he'd answered that question more times than he cared to.

"Experience and research, mostly," said Carmichael. "And the fact that we're trained to be visual rather than cerebral. We see where others think."

"Anything else we should know about this guy, Ray?" asked Lieutenant Hawthorne.

Carmichael leaned over and dropped his crumpled cup into a wastebasket. "Often, serial killers have an abnormal interest in police procedure and will try to insinuate themselves in their own cases, even to the point of hanging around cop bars and station houses. I suggest you inform your colleagues to be especially vigilant.

"Also, it's important to remember that most serial killers are legally sane. Their mental disorders are a product of their individual sexual deviances and dysfunctional characters. They know what they're doing, know it's wrong, but choose to do it anyway. There's no question that they're responsible for their actions. Which means they're capable of reacting to outside stimuli. Some can even experience feelings of remorse. On the flip side, they can be easily angered. For that reason, it's important that you don't provoke this individual by belittling or reviling him in public."

"The media are already doing that," replied Hawthorne.

"Then get them to stop. Ask them to concentrate on the victims, to do everything they can to personalize these two young women. They should be writing and talking about their innocence and their suffering, and the suffering of their families and friends, things like that."

"I'll see what I can do," said Hawthorne.

Just then, the door burst open and a frazzled looking patrol sergeant rushed into the room. "Sorry, Lieutenant, but this can't wait. Another lipless body just turned up in Chinatown."

*****

The victim was a young black woman. Jackson, Lewicki, and Special Agent Carmichael — who'd asked permission to accompany them to the crime scene — found her in an alley off Doyers Street, near Chatham Square, lying naked in that all-too-familiar pose amid piles of wooden crates, overturned trash bins, and the remnants of decaying produce. Her clothes and a small leather backpack were neatly piled next to her head.

After ordering Lewicki to examine the body, with Carmichael observing, Jackson dragged the First Officer away from a loud, toothless, and wildly gesticulating Chinese old-timer and led him to a nearby doorway. "What've we got, son?"

"I found some ID in the victim's backpack, sir. Her name's Jasmine Taylor. Twenty-three-years old. Lives on East Eighty-Third."

"That's high-rent territory."

"Sure is, sir. Could be she was a fancy call girl."

Jackson scowled. "Just because an attractive woman's got money don't mean she's a whore."

"No, sir. Sorry, sir."

"When was the body found?"

"Central got the call at zero-nine-zero-five hours, from the old guy I was just talking to."

"Did you check the body for signs?"

"Rigor and lividity are both present. I also called for the medical examiner and a crime scene unit."

"Fine. Now take that old man inside before he brings the whole damn neighborhood down on our necks."

Jackson finished writing in his notebook and walked over to the body. "What's the story, Ed?"

Lewicki stood up and peeled off his gloves. "I'd say she's been dead for between twelve to sixteen hours. Except for a large gash above the right eye, the M.O. fits to a tee. Same pose. Ligature markings on the neck. Bruise on the back, between the shoulder blades. Lips cut off cleanly with a sharp instrument. No sign of the lips or the knife. No visible defense marks on the hands or other signs of a struggle."

Jackson moved closer, to avoid being overheard. "What about the dollar bill?"

"It's there."

"Any underwear missing?"

"A bra, assuming she was wearing one."

Jackson let out a long sigh, then turned to Carmichael. "Does anything you've seen here change your profile, Ray?"

Without hesitation, the FBI man shook his head.

"What the hell do we have to do to nail this mother?"

"It's not going to be easy. An intelligent psychopath is hard to catch, for several reasons. There's no traceable motive. He knows enough about police procedure to leave a clean crime scene. And you won't get any help from informants because most of these guys are loners who seldom talk about their murders. All you can do is examine the evidence and extrapolate. Try to reconstruct his thinking. Find the patterns."

"But the only patterns I see are that his victims are young and beautiful and that the killings have all taken place in Manhattan. Are there others we haven't noticed?"

"A few," replied Carmichael, taking off his glasses to rub his eyes. "For one thing, the individual you're looking for is not an ambusher. He gets off on winning his victims' confidence, making them feel at ease. And it's not enough for him just to kill; he needs to leave his mark.

"Also, besides being young and beautiful, his first two victims were single and self-supporting. Judging by the absence of a wedding ring and the quality of the jewelry and clothes *this* victim was wearing, I'd say the same applies to her. Yet the killer feels the need to label these women as cheap whores. Why? Because there's something he finds deeply disturbing about strong, independent females. If he was simply a pathological misogynist, he'd probably be going after the most vulnerable prey he could get his hands on, regardless of age or any other consideration."

Carmichael looked down at the body. "The fact that this victim is black only strengthens my contention."

"Why's that?" asked Jackson.

"Because it's very unusual to see crimes of this nature cross racial lines."

*****

Jasmine Taylor's autopsy revealed little of value other than that the cut above her eye was caused by a heavy piece of curved hardwood. Afterwards, Jackson drove to Brooklyn to notify the victim's family. He then brought the father back to the Medical Examiner's office to identify the body. Without a doubt, this was the hardest part of being a homicide detective.

Formal identifications were usually conducted in a special viewing area because few people had the strength to remain in the same room with a loved one who'd met with violence — especially when mutilation was involved.

Isaac Taylor, his face swollen from crying, was a short, pudgy man with even white teeth and mild brown eyes. His head, bald except for a few thin curls at the nape of the neck, was covered with age spots. He was sitting on a bench with his soft fat hands pressed together between his knees, staring blankly through the window of the elevator room, waiting for the attendant downstairs to finish preparing his daughter's corpse. His glasses kept misting over, causing him to continually wipe them with a handkerchief he kept in the inside pocket of his suit jacket.

Finally, the elevator motor sprang to life with a loud whine. A few seconds later, Jasmine Taylor's body rose into view. Thankfully, the attendant had covered her mouth with a piece of gauze.

Isaac Taylor stood up and approached the window. Leaning his forehead on the glass, he silently stared at his daughter, his face a mask of stunned immobility. His lips trembled and he looked at Jackson with slightly protruding eyes.

"Why did he do this thing to my baby, Sergeant? Why? She never hurt nobody. She was my little angel...a blessing to everyone who knew her."

Jackson couldn't meet his gaze. "Some men don't need a reason, Mister Taylor. Crimes like this are the product of a sick and evil mind. And although I know it's little comfort, I swear to you, we *will* make him pay for what he did to your daughter."

*****

Robert Molinaro, a glass of Chivas Regal clutched in his hand, sat slumped on his living room couch, trying to pay attention to the six o'clock news. His nerves were frayed as a result of yet another argument with Anna, this time over his unwillingness to attend a birthday party for the brat of one of her old college cronies. She ended up going on her own.

As he took a sip of his drink, a photograph of a stunning young black woman flashed onto the screen. Molinaro picked up the remote and turned up the volume.

"...The twenty-three-year-old model was last seen alive around ten o'clock last night, leaving the Superstudio Industria, a fashion photo studio located in Greenwich Village. The police have confirmed that she is the latest victim of the serial killer who has taken the lives of two other young women during the past week.

"The first victim was a twenty-five-year-old bank teller named Sandra Geddes, while the second, twenty-two-year-old Carol Linehan, also was a model. At this time, there's been no..."

Models, thought Molinaro, trying to grasp a seemingly significant idea floating at the edge of his subconscious.

"...the investigation. The police advise all persons connected with New York's fashion and advertising industries to be on the lookout for..."

Molinaro shifted position and rubbed his forehead. Why was this news story bugging him so much?

The description of the suspect was accompanied by a video that purported to show him trailing Carol Linehan moments before she was killed. This was followed by three black and white still photographs taken from the same video, none of which were very revealing — except for the fact that the individual pictured certainly looked calm, and imposing, like the angel of death himself.

"Jesus Christ!" yelled Molinaro, sloshing scotch down the front of his shirt. "The reckoning! Frank's goddamn reckoning!" *That's* what the wacko was trying to tell him. The *Times* stories he'd alluded to were the accounts of the first two murders. A cause and multiple effects. The son-of-a-bitch was killing working girls so people would pay attention to his rantings!

Jumping to his feet, he ran to the credenza on the far side of the room, grabbed a pen and a scrap of paper out of a drawer, and jotted down the police hot line number that was flashing on the screen. But by the time he got to the phone, he was having second thoughts. Did he really want the hassle of being involved in a murder investigation? It would probably mean numerous visits to the police station, cops hanging around the broadcasting booth, maybe even a court appearance once they caught the guy. Besides, what if Frank found out about his involvement?

On the other hand, helping the police reel in a serial killer was worth its weight in gold in terms of publicity, not only for his radio show, but also for his personal prestige. He could even play with it a bit. Maybe manipulate Frank into talking about the killings on air. Get a dialogue going between him, the police, and the audience. The ratings would go through the roof! It could be just what he needed to put him on the fast track to that network TV job he'd been dreaming about.

Molinaro picked up the phone and dialed the hot line number. A tired-sounding female answered.

"Yeah, hi," he said, "I want to talk to someone in authority about that model who was killed last night."

"Can I have your name?"

"Never mind my name. Just put me through to someone in authority."

"One moment please."

There was a clicking sound, followed by two rings. "South-Central Detective Area Task Force. Lewicki speaking."

"Are you in charge of the serial killer case?"

There was a pause. "That'd be Lieutenant Hawthorne, but he's not here right now. Is there—"

"I prefer to speak to someone in authority."

Another pause. "Hang on."

Molinaro wondered if they were tracing the call. The prospect was kind of exciting.

"Sergeant Jackson here. Is there something I can do for you?"

"No, but there's something I can do for you," said Molinaro.

"I'm listening."

"My name's Robert Molinaro. I'm the host of a talk show on W.S.N.Y. radio. Molinaro on N.Y. Ninety-Nine. Ever heard of it?"

"Can't say I have."

"No?" replied Molinaro, annoyed. "Anyway, I'm almost certain the serial killer you're looking for is one of my regular callers. He recently made a statement that sounded a lot like a confession of guilt."

Molinaro described the reasons for his suspicion, including Frank's cryptic allusions to the first two murders and his professed loathing for working women, especially models.

"What else can you tell me about this guy?" asked Jackson.

"His name's Frank—"

"Do you think that's his real name?"

"He's been a regular for quite some time, since well before the killings began, so I see no reason why he'd be using a pseudonym."

"Go on."

"He says he lives on the upper east side. Sounds a little like Orson Welles. He's articulate, chooses his words carefully, and never loses his cool. But you can tell that there's this hysteria lurking just below the surface."

"When's the last time he called?"

Molinaro thought a moment. "That'd be Thursday."

"The day after the second murder?"

"Exactly. He specifically referred to something that happened the previous night and challenged me to figure it out, by analyzing what he said on the show."

"Has he called since then?"

"No." Molinaro decided not to mention his decision to block Frank's calls. But he was certain the creep would try again.

"How often does he usually call?" asked Jackson.

"A couple of times a week."

"When's your next show?"

"Tomorrow night, at eight."

"Tell you what. I'd like to hear this guy for myself before taking any further action. We'll monitor your show for the next couple of nights and see what happens. Oh, one last thing. If Frank does call, don't antagonize him. Encourage him to talk, especially if he alludes to any of the killings, and keep him on the air as long as possible."

You bet your sweet ass I will, thought Molinaro. After he and the sergeant exchanged phone numbers, he walked over to the bar and fixed himself another drink. "Move over Rush and get out of my way Howard," he crowed, raising his glass in salute. "Molinaro on N.Y. Ninety-Nine is about to blast its way into the big time!"

Chapter 15 — Monday, June 30

Lionel Jackson entered the squad room clutching a copy of the *New York Post* under his arm and headed straight for Hawthorne's office. He took a deep breath and knocked.

"Come in!"

Jackson opened the door and entered. The lieutenant, who was hunkered over a batch of paperwork, looked the way Jackson felt: tired and haggard. The lack of progress on the case was taking a heavy toll on everyone involved.

"I thought you said that radio program didn't start till eight," said Hawthorne, looking at his watch.

"It doesn't. I've got some news about Jasmine Taylor."

Hawthorne set down his pen and leaned back in his chair. "Shoot."

"Another model who was working with her on Saturday night has come forward with a lead. Turns out she was around the corner buying cigarettes about the same time the victim was getting ready to leave the studio. When she returned from the store, she saw Jasmine Taylor walking down the street with a, uh, cop."

"A cop!"

"Yeah. It ties in with a citywide we got from patrol yesterday morning. On the day of the murder, a police uniform was stolen from a film crew shooting in Central Park."

"That's just fucking dandy," said Hawthorne. "So now this psycho is walking around dressed as a goddamn cop! Did your witness at least get a good look at the guy?"

Jackson shook his head. "He was too far away. All she can say for sure is that he was tall and lean."

"That's a big fucking help. You'd better get P.R. to issue another warning...remind women who are accosted by a cop to ask for I.D. And make sure they show what a real badge looks like. Christ, I can just imagine the reception our uniforms are going to be getting from here on in, especially if they're tall and blond. Someone's liable to get shot."

Hawthorne shoved a stick of gum into his mouth and started chewing with savage fury. "Did the Greenwich Village or Chinatown canvasses turn up anything yet?"

Jackson shook his head, wishing he had something positive to report. He considered mentioning the other initiatives that were still under way — the screenings being conducted by the swimming pool and psych details, the tracking down of individuals whose names were spewed out by CATCH, and the re-evaluation of the suspect and interview lists to see if anybody fit Special Agent Carmichael's profile — but he didn't think it would do much good.

Hawthorne ran his hands through his hair and sighed. "Man, I sure hope this Molinaro guy's onto something. I'm at the end of my rope."

"I've asked Doctor Liebrandt to monitor the show for us," said Jackson. "Maybe he can tell us something about the suspect that we don't already know."

Anton Liebrandt was a noted forensics psychiatrist who'd assisted the NYPD a number of times in the past.

"We're drowning here, Lionel. I'm ready to clutch at any straw thrown my way."

"I hear you," said Jackson. "By the way," he added, tossing his newspaper on the desk, "the Post has given our killer a nickname."

"I wonder what took them so long," replied Hawthorne, picking up the paper. "I assume it's suitably witty." His brow furrowed as he read the headline. "Mister Sardonicus? What the hell is that supposed to mean?"

"It's a character in an old 'B' movie of the same name, about this recluse whose face has been disfigured in an accident, leaving him with a permanent hideous grin. Just like *our* boy's victims."

Hawthorne shook his head in disgust. "Leave it to the fucking Post."

*****

Uptown, on East 54th Street, Rachel Curran stood in the doorway of the Neighborhood Playhouse Theater School and peered nervously into the surrounding gloom. A warm gust of wind rose up, sending paper and other debris swirling into the night. Rachel gripped her shoulder bag and stepped onto the sidewalk, comforted somewhat by the presence of the Browning automatic — a twenty-first birthday gift from her father — tucked inside her bag.

Usually, she walked to the Third Avenue subway station after class. But that was before a madman with a penchant for butchering young models had made the night a time of terror. From now on, she'd be taking cabs — even if it did put a further strain on her already overextended budget. The wardrobe and photographs she'd purchased for the Miss Empire State Pageant had already taken a large bite out of her savings account.

"Hey, Rach."

She turned toward the doorway. It was Tom Brennan, a 27-year-old transplanted Bostonian with reddish-brown hair, brown eyes, and an impish smile that seemed permanently fixed on his strong, well-made face. They'd enrolled in the program at the same time and had developed a casual friendship, though it was obvious *his* interest was far from platonic.

"What gives?" he said, slinging an old cloth backpack over his shoulder. "I've never seen you so out of sync."

They'd been rehearsing the 'gentleman caller' scene from The Glass Menagerie and she had flubbed her lines four times. "It *was* a disaster, wasn't it?" she replied, frowning. "Too much on my mind, I guess." She didn't want to admit that fear was the reason for her poor performance.

"Anything I can help with?" asked Tom.

"I've just been working too hard, that's all. It'll pass."

"You need to relax. You're so damned intense all the time."

"I can't help it. That's the way I am. Just like you're always good-natured."

"Right," he said, shoving his hands into his Levis. "I guess I see your point."

He shuffled his feet, keeping his eyes glued to the pavement. "Feel like some coffee?"

"I can't, Tom. I've got a photo shoot first thing in the morning."

"It's only ten-fifteen. Come on, one tiny cup."

"Really, I can't. Maybe some other time."

"I don't mean to be pushy, Rach, but that's what you've said the last three times I asked."

Rachel reddened.

"Look," he continued, "I like you, okay. I want to get to know you better. If I'm stepping out of line, just say so and I won't bother you any more. But please, stop giving me polite brush-offs like I'm some kind of half-wit."

"Oh, God. I know, I know, and you're absolutely right. I like you, too, Tom. It's just that I'm not in a position to get involved with anyone right now. But I do want us to continue being friends."

"Then have some coffee with me, for Pete's sake. I promise I'll have you home by eleven. Eleven-thirty, tops."

Rachel shifted position, fidgeted with her bracelet, and finally allowed herself a tiny smile. "Oh, all right."

"Terrific. There's a cozy little café just down the road."

Taking her arm, he led her across the street, then east, toward First Avenue.

As they neared the intersection, a fleshy black arm flopped out of a doorway, its hand cupped in supplication. "Spare some change?" muttered a barely audible voice.

Startled, Rachel peered at the panhandler, who was sitting cross-legged on a torn plaid blanket. The woman — who appeared to be in her fifties — was well-scrubbed and wore clothes that were shabby, but clean.

"Hey, Charlene," said Tom, causing Rachel to look at him with surprise. "How are you tonight?"

"Just fine, honey. How's yourself?"

"Okay, I guess," he replied, digging a handful of coins out of his pocket and gently laying them on the woman's palm. "This is Rachel, a friend of mine."

"That's a very pretty name, like that lady in the bible."

"Thanks," replied Rachel, smiling. She reached into her purse and handed the woman a five-dollar-bill.

"Thank you, miss. God bless."

"You, too."

"Isn't it late for you to be out here, Charlene?" asked Tom.

"It's been kinda slow today, so I figure on stayin' till eleven or so."

"In that case you be careful, okay?"

"I surely will."

Tom took Rachel's arm again and led her away. When they had reached the corner, Rachel, whose estimation of her friend had risen considerably as a result of his modest display of empathy, turned to him and asked, "How do you know that woman?"

"I ran into her after our first class."

"She sure doesn't look like a typical panhandler."

"Looks can be deceiving. Charlene's a widow, with no children. Her relatives live in Georgia. Four years ago she spent her life savings to pay for triple bypass surgery. Her disability pension is four hundred and fifty-seven bucks a month and her rent is four hundred and forty. The woman's got to eat, right?"

Nodding in agreement, Rachel studied Tom's face as if she was seeing him for the first time. Up to now she'd dismissed him as the emotional equivalent of fast food: an attractive package containing little substance. Obviously, she'd have to revisit that assumption.

*****

Lionel Jackson stood outside an all-night deli near the corner of West 47th and Broadway, mechanically chewing on a pastrami-on-rye as he listened to the pinging caused by the cooling of his car's engine. He felt flat, disoriented, like an old bloodhound that had lost the scent of its prey.

He had listened to the entire broadcast of *Molinaro on NY 99*, but Frank never called. A member of the special unit would continue to monitor the program, at least until week's end, but in the meantime, it was back to the proverbial drawing board.

Sipping his coffee, he thought about Special Agent Carmichael's statement on the night of Jasmine Taylor's murder, that serial killers were legally sane and therefore responsible for their actions. Later, on the way back to the station house, the FBI man had elaborated, claiming that true psychotics — those who had lost touch with reality — seldom committed serious crimes. And when they did, they were generally so disorganized and made such feeble attempts at avoiding detection that they were usually caught right away. No one disputed that these individuals needed medical help. Most serial killers, on the other hand, deserved to rot in jail for the rest of their lives.

Jackson heartily agreed with Carmichael's opinions. He just wished the legal system would do the same — especially all those bleeding heart shrinks and social workers who kept convincing parole boards to put these monsters back on the street halfway through their sentences so they could kill again, which most inevitably did.

Swallowing the last of his sandwich, he tossed the wrapper away and climbed back into his car for the drive home. Christ, he thought, starting the engine, it was obscene enough that serial killers were routinely sentenced to 25 years or less for their crimes; it was even harder to imagine *any* reason for giving the sons of bitches an early release.

The way he saw it, the decision to do so could only be based on two possible scenarios: one, that despite the repeater's dysfunctional personality he finds prison life so uplifting that he resolves to become a law-abiding citizen; or two, that despite his entrenched impulse to murder and maim he finds life in the can so horrific that he resolves to do whatever it takes to avoid going back.

Anybody with half a brain would have a hard time accepting either of those premises, yet many therapists routinely did just that, without once stopping to consider that most repeaters are hard-wired to kill again.

What these so-called professionals didn't understand was that repeaters were themselves experts at assessing and manipulating people, and that the ones seeking an early release were going to say exactly what a therapist wanted to hear. That's why Jackson believed parole boards needed to base their decisions on a single factor: the repeater's perceived threat to society. Better to keep a high-risk killer in jail forever than risk the death of one more innocent victim.

Jackson lit a cigarette as he swung onto Columbus Circle. As usual, the monument was surrounded by a motley mix of anxious tourists, panhandlers, drunks, small-time dope peddlers, homeless teenagers who looked like exiles from another planet and, most probably, one or two undercover cops from the Street Crime Unit. A lot of shit went down in the triangle formed by the intersection of Eighth Avenue, Broadway and Central Park South.

As he motored north along Eighth Avenue, he leaned back and thought about his wife. Even though Alyssa had just turned 33, she was still an impressive-looking woman. Auburn eyes framed by long, delicately curved lashes, short, glossy black hair, a narrow waist above shapely hips, and strong, muscular legs. A great ass, too, and firm breasts with nipples the size of thimbles. With a painfully evocative jolt, he remembered how she looked after they'd made love, her soft, smooth skin glistening in the dark and her warm breath caressing his neck.

God, he needed a woman, and not just because he hadn't had one in a while. He always got horny when he was involved in a particularly gruesome murder case. Most homicide cops did. Jackson figured it was a procreative thing, nature's way of thumbing its nose at the grim reaper.

He considered picking up a hooker, but quickly brushed the idea aside. It didn't seem to be worth the time and effort. Besides, he was exhausted. He'd probably fall asleep the moment he got his pants down.

Chapter 16 — Tuesday, July 1

Prior to the start of his broadcast, Robert Molinaro sat in his office watching the video he'd received from the *Miss Empire State* organization, spelling out the pageant's judging system. The accompanying letter indicated the training seminar he was expected to attend would be held on Thursday, July 10th. At that time he'd be given a copy of the judges' workbook, containing resumes and photos of each contestant.

Molinaro hated the idea of giving up so much of his free time to such nonsense, but he was in no position to argue with the boss. Then again, there were worse things in life than hanging out with a bevy of babes for a couple of days. He smoothed his mustache and turned his attention back to the television screen.

"The Miss Empire State judging system has been designed to promote individuality, diversity and overall achievement among our lovely and accomplished contestants," intoned the narrator, while the camera panned past a group of nervous young women waiting to hear which of them had grabbed the brass ring. "The woman you help to choose as our winner should be a role model, a vital, thinking individual with values, opinions, and ambitions — a true woman of the nineties."

Molinaro chuckled at the narrator's solemnity. One would think he was talking about the Nobel Prize.

"As one of our judges, you will be asked to score individual contestants immediately following each phase of the competition, based on a one-to-ten point scale, in whole numbers.

"During the preliminary round, the weighting of scores awarded per category will be distributed as follows: talent, forty percent; private interview, thirty percent; on-stage personality in evening wear, fifteen percent; physical fitness in a swimsuit, fifteen percent. The contestants receiving the ten highest composite attribute scores will advance to the final, taking their composite scores with them.

"On Saturday night, you will be asked to assess the top ten contestants in order to determine the final ranking. The weighting of scores for this phase of the competition will be as follows: composite attributes, forty percent; talent, thirty percent; on-stage personality in evening wear, fifteen percent; physical fitness in a swimsuit, fifteen percent.

"At this point, the ballots will be collected and given to the auditors. As soon as they have tabulated and double-checked the results, the ten finalists will return to the stage for the grand finale. A few moments later the quest for the crown will end with a flourish as the emcee reaches for the auditor's envelope and announces the names of the four runners-up and, after a dramatic pause, the new Miss Empire State!

"We will now show you a number of highlights from each phase of last year's competition, accompanied by an in-depth analysis by Dick Herbert, chairman of our judging committee. Dick will describe the qualities you will be looking for in—"

Stifling a yawn, Molinaro switched off the VCR and looked at his watch. Ten minutes to air.

*****

"Let's get to our first call. Here's Phil, from Queens. What's on your mind, Phil?"

"Violence, Bob. Specifically, the kind associated with hand guns. I guess you heard about that schoolyard shooting we had down here the other day."

"I did, yes. How old were those kids again?"

"The shooter was eleven, the victim, nine."

"Man."

"You want to know what really disturbs me? How people reacted. You had these shocked, tear-stained citizens on TV, all saying the same things. 'Oh, what a tragedy.' 'He seemed like such a good little boy.' 'How could something like this happen?' Well, I'll tell you how it happened. An eleven-year-old kid got his hands on a gun. Say what you want about the erosion of family values or the glorification of violence in movies and TV; that little boy would not have died if his killer hadn't gotten his hands on that gun. And it's a scenario that's being repeated somewhere in this country every single day.

"Did you know that in 1985, three thousand, two hundred and eighty children under the age of eighteen were murdered with guns? And that four hundred and forty died in accidental shootings? Or that some fifteen hundred committed suicide with guns? But I heard few people mention the proliferation of guns as a possible cause of the tragedy."

"You know what they say, Phil. Guns don't kill people; people kill people."

"Yeah, right. I challenge *anybody* to prove there wouldn't be fewer murders or accidental deaths if guns weren't so easily available. Let's get real here." He paused. "What *is* it with guns in this country? Our love affair with the damn things borders on the pathological."

"Guns are an integral part of our history, Phil; a facet of our national character."

"Then maybe it's time we took a long, hard long at ourselves. God, how many more people have to die before we do something about the problem?"

"Whoa. I can just see Charlton Heston and his N.R.A. cronies reaching for their phones."

"Screw 'em. Look, I've got no problem with hunters, but you don't need a hand gun or an Uzi to kill a deer."

"What about collectors or target shooters?"

"Let them take up another hobby. I hear stamp collecting is fun. Seriously, though. As far as I'm concerned, hand guns and automatic weapons have no purpose other than to take human life. The damned things should be banned outright."

"Dream on, pal. You're talking about changing the constitution and that's never going to happen."

"That's because the gun lobby is distorting the truth. When the constitution refers to a citizen's right to bear arms, it's not talking about individuals but about the maintenance of an effective militia, as a defense against outside aggression. But you're right. No administration would have the balls to bring in serious gun control legislation."

"We're locked in a vicious circle, Phil. People are frightened by the violent crime they see in the media, so they run out and buy a gun. Some of those same guns end up being used in a violent crime and the story ends up in the media, creating more fear. Until we wipe out crime, the cycle will continue. Thanks for your call."

Instead of spitting out another name, Molinaro's headphones remained silent. Frowning, he glanced at the control booth. Sid Crouse had a strange expression on his face, like he'd just bitten into a wormy apple.

"It's him, Bob."

Molinaro muted the microphone. "Put him through, then call that number I gave you and make sure the police are listening." He took a deep breath and licked his lips. "Here's Frank, from the upper east side."

"Good evening, Robert."

"Frank. We, uh, haven't heard from you in a while."

"I have been quite busy."

"I know."

"Do you?"

"I think so, yes."

"Then I imagine you have already notified the police."

Molinaro's heart jumped. "What? Not at all. I—"

"Come now, Robert. Don't take me for a fool. They are probably listening as we speak. Well, in case they doubt that I am who I say I am — which is likely since the police are such skeptical creatures — I will give them proof, by way of a riddle. What is green, worth a dollar, and occasionally found in damp, dark places? They will understand my meaning."

"What about the rest of us?"

"That information is not for public consumption." He paused. "You know, it is better this way, with everyone's cards on the table. It makes for a more interesting game. It also gives me the opportunity to explain my motives — something the media has not being doing well at all. Not only does their use of that ridiculous 'Mister Sardonicus' moniker trivialize my work, but their reports make it appear that I am some kind of sadistic monster, which is a blatant lie."

"But you killed three young women, Frank."

"Not killed, Robert. Weeded out, for the betterment of the species. The females in question were unclean...sybarites bent on perverting the feminine ideal. I am simply trying to coax womankind back onto the high moral ground from which it has plummeted. Natural women have nothing to fear from me."

"Murder is murder, Frank, regardless of semantics."

"Extreme crises call for extreme measures."

"Seriously? You really expect people to buy this idea of yours that women who use their looks to make a living are responsible for most of society's ills?"

"Ah, Robert. It is clear the enemy has clouded your judgment. Open your eyes, man. Try to see beyond the physical facade these creatures hide behind. Think with your brain, not your libido. We are in the midst of a war between good and evil. In such a high-stakes conflict, the ends justify the means. Of course there will be casualties. There are in every war. This country would not exist if our forefathers had not been willing to destroy those who threatened our way of life. And we have continued that tradition ever since."

"No rational person is going to see what you're doing in that light, Frank."

"Perhaps not. But then, every revolutionary and striver after truth has his detractors."

"Most revolutions are built around a just cause. What you're doing is criminal."

"That is a matter of opinion. But I will say this about criminals. At least they have the courage of their convictions in a world where most people live in a gray void and have to wear masks in order to be considered normal."

"Yes, but—"

"Enough! This is not a debate. There can be no compromise. Having failed to sway the enemy with words, it is time for action. Now, you must excuse me. I have a pressing engagement."

"When can I expect to hear from you again?"

"When the spirit moves me."

"Wait! Can I ask you one last question?"

"For you, Robert, anything."

"Why do you cut off your victims' lips?"

"To reveal their true nature, of course. That *is* what succubae do, is it not? Flash a false smile in order to steal a man's soul?"

*****

An uncomfortable silence prevailed in Lieutenant Hawthorne's office as half a dozen stunned detectives digested Frank's chilling diatribe. The blatant transparency of his riddle left no doubt they had just heard the voice of Mister Sardonicus.

Lionel Jackson, who'd been so engrossed that he burned his bottom lip with his cigarette, glanced at Hawthorne. The lieutenant's expression reminded him of someone who had just smelled dog shit, but couldn't quite figure out where it was coming from.

"Christ," said Hawthorne, rubbing his neck, "as if this case wasn't squirmy enough. Now it turns out we've got a fucking true believer on our hands. I can tell you from experience, a murderer with a cause — especially one with brains — is more dangerous than ten ordinary killers strung together."

"What spooks *me* is how calm he sounds," said Ed Lewicki. "Like he's talking about killing cockroaches instead of people."

Dan McDougall stood up and stretched his legs. "I still can't figure why he's targeting models. With all his holy roller crap about natural women and the moral high ground, you'd think he'd be going after whores or strippers. All models do is slink around and show a little tit from time to time."

"Maybe he went out with one who did him dirt," said Jackson. "Or it could be he's obsessed with that ice queen image models project. A lot of guys have a problem with beautiful women who come off as being superior or inaccessible."

"You might be onto something," said Hawthorne. "In the morning, form a detail to track down every model in town and make sure they've seen the suspect's photograph. Whatever his motivation is for going after these women, he obviously spends a lot of time hanging around the places they frequent. Even if no one recognizes the bastard, at least they'll have his description seared into their brains. It might just save some lives."

"We should also advise them to listen to Molinaro's show," said Jackson. "Maybe someone will recognize the voice."

"Better yet," added Hawthorne, "let's get a tape of tonight's program and send copies to the media. And make sure you get tapes of all his previous appearances and see if there's anything in them we can use."

"I'll call the station," said McDougall, heading for the door.

After a brief lull, Lewicki cleared his throat and said, "What do you think happened to turn this Frank guy into such a raving psycho?"

"According to an FBI study a few years back," said Jackson, "most serial killers come from dysfunctional families and suffered some kind of abuse as children."

"I have a hard time buying into that," replied Lewicki. "A lot of people had fucked-up childhoods, but few turn into goddamn maniacs."

"I'm not talking about being yelled at or getting an occasional slap on the ass. I've read about what some of these guys endured as children and believe me, it turned my stomach. Not that I'm not trying to excuse what they've done. No one has the right to kill another human being, whatever his reasons. I'm just giving you a possible explanation."

Lewicki grunted.

"Mira," said Octavio Cordova, his dark eyes darting from face to face, "maybe when Frank was a kid, heess mamma locked heem in a closet for playing with heess pecker too much, eh?"

"Let the shrinks worry about his state of mind," snapped Hawthorne, cutting short any further attempt at humor. "Our job is to catch the son-of-a-bitch. Starting tomorrow morning, I want every detail working this investigation to focus its attention on the upper east side. If that's where Sardonicus lives, I want to make it so hot he begins to think he's already in hell."

"At least he's got one trait that works in our favor," said Jackson. "He likes to talk. We might be able to get a trace."

"Believe me," replied Hawthorne, "he won't be as talkative the next time. He probably knew we wouldn't be able to get authorization for a trace based on an unsubstantiated suspicion — especially at a radio station. Besides, I think he's too sharp to be calling from his home. But," he added, rising to his feet, "I guess it's still worth a shot."

The others took the hint and filed out of the office. The mention of shrinks reminded Jackson to call Anton Liebrandt. Walking over to his desk, he picked up the phone and dialed the doctor's home number. As he waited through a series of rings, he recalled Special Agent Carmichael's comment that psychiatrists relied on personality to infer a person's behavior while profilers relied on behavior to infer personality. It was the most concise explanation he'd heard yet about the way the two professions approached the criminal mind.

"Hello?"

"Doctor Liebrandt? Lionel Jackson. Were you listening?"

"Yes."

"And?"

"If you're asking me if I think Frank is legally insane, the answer's no. He sounds like an extremely focused individual who knows exactly what he's doing and firmly believes he's acting in the public interest. I would venture to say his disorder stems from a deep-rooted need to strike back at an abusive female from his past, most probably his mother. This is reinforced by his use of expressions like 'the feminine ideal,' and 'natural women,' and by his desire to coax womankind back onto the high moral ground from which he feels it has plummeted."

"What's revealing is that his antipathy is directed at beautiful young models instead of so-called 'loose' women. Perhaps this means his mother was also a model or held some similar occupation at the time the abuse took place. I'm puzzled, however, by his calm demeanor and by the control he exhibits when he kills. Usually, murderers who believe they are exacting retribution against an abusive parent display tremendous savagery."

"That bothers me, too," said Jackson. "One last question. How stable is this guy?"

"He's not suicidal, if that's what you mean. I doubt he's lost a moment's sleep over what he's done. However, I do believe he is willing to sacrifice himself for his cause if it comes to that. And although his behavior so far suggests he has no interest in harming anyone other than his target group, that pattern is unlikely to hold if he's cornered. I suggest you remind your fellow officers to keep that in mind. This man is extremely dangerous. He will keep on killing until he is stopped."

Chapter 17 — Wednesday, July 2

Although it was mid-afternoon, the drenching rain and heavy gray clouds draped across the Manhattan skyline made it seem like dusk. But for Robert Molinaro, who couldn't stop grinning as he steered his BMW south along FDR Drive to the strains of Frank Sinatra's *My Way*, it was the sunniest day of the year. And why not? His name was on the front page of every major newspaper in New York City. And in the 18 hours since Mister Sardonicus's appearance on his show, he'd been interviewed by every radio and TV station in the tri-state area. By week's end, the entire country would know who he was — including all those network executives who'd given him the finger.

Talk about being in the catbird seat. His show's numbers for the next ratings period were going to be awesome. It didn't even matter if Sardonicus called again or not. The possibility alone was enough to make people tune in, and keep them coming back until the police finally caught the freak — but not too soon, hopefully. Molinaro figured he needed to remain in the public spotlight for at least another week or so in order to show the networks what he could do.

As he approached the 63rd Street off-ramp, a heavy gust of wind buffeted the car and a blinding flash of lightning split the sky almost directly overhead, searing its after-image into his retinas. Molinaro gripped the steering wheel and blinked several times in rapid succession. He hadn't been paying much attention to the storm but now became instantly aware of its intensity.

To his right, the city's brightly lit skyscrapers, their tops obscured by clouds, eerily shimmered through the thick, diaphanous curtain of slashing rain. To his left, the East River was a tumult of black water, rhythmically sending sheets of white foam crashing against the piles. Up ahead, the lights of the Queensborough Bridge reflected off the oily water, making it look like a grounded ghost ship.

Molinaro ejected the Sinatra tape and frowned. The storm reminded him that there was at least one person who wasn't impressed by his newfound notoriety. Anna violently disapproved of his plan to string Mister Sardonicus along in order to further his career. She'd spent the morning following him around the house, insisting, in that whiney voice she used when feeling particularly self-righteous, that it was morally reprehensible.

Morally reprehensible! Christ, he'd notified the police, hadn't he? There was a good chance his call would turn out to be instrumental in catching the guy. In the meantime, what was wrong with getting some mileage out of the situation? If *he* didn't, the station would replace him with someone who would. Sardonicus had put WSNY on the map. Management wasn't about to kill their golden goose just because a host's wife had a few misguided qualms.

That had shut her up — for about 15 seconds. Then she played the 'danger' card, suggesting he was liable to say something to anger Sardonicus, causing him to drive out to New Rochelle some night and slit both their throats while they slept. That's when he put an end to the discussion by slamming the front door in her face.

God almighty, he thought, easing the BMW onto the turn lane, either the pregnancy was messing with the woman's hormones or she was losing her mind. Either way, he was beginning to wonder what in hell he'd ever seen in the crazy cow. She seemed incapable of pragmatic thinking, especially when it concerned his career. He was brought up believing a wife was supposed to support her husband, but all Anna ever thought about was her own comfort.

Tensing his jaw, he shoved the Sinatra tape back into the cassette deck and turned up the volume. Maybe it was time to start thinking about a divorce. Anna could keep the baby, keep the house, and bury herself in the expansive bosom of her ever-loving family. That seemed to be all she ever wanted anyway.

*****

Frank Ryman loved electrical storms but was glad this one was losing steam. Otherwise, it would've threatened his planned sortie. Drawing the living room drapes, he finished his tea and went to the bedroom to get dressed. Regrettably, he had to destroy the policeman's uniform because he'd been seen in it, prompting the authorities to issue yet another public warning.

Ryman chuckled. As if public warnings were of any use. The only way the enemy would be safe was if they all locked themselves inside a steel cell and never emerged. But everyone had to go out sometime, even succubae. Besides, the creatures were too dim-witted to heed the warnings.

It was funny how people rarely saw themselves as potential victims. Instead, they clung to the belief that bad things only happened to others. That made his job ridiculously easy — especially since he never appeared in the guise the enemy expected.

He opened the dresser drawer and carefully removed his underwear collection. He liked to put the items on in the order in which they were acquired. First came Sandra Geddes' stockings, then Carol Linehan's panties, and finally, Jasmine Taylor's gingham bra, which, mercifully, was the kind that clasped in front. After flattening the bra against his chest, he pulled open the closet door and began rummaging for a pair of slacks.

Suddenly, he experienced that familiar sense of psychic displacement that had been plaguing him of late. Dropping his arms to his sides, he blinked twice and walked over to the mirror. There she was, appraising him with the calm, imperious detachment of a preening cat.

Hello, Frankie, honey. How's my little man? I thought I'd drop in to commend you on the wonderful job you're doing. I must say, you've exceeded my wildest expectations. Everybody's talking about your work. It's made me so proud I can barely contain myself.

Ryman's right hand moved mechanically up to the bra and began to trace its way along the upper edge.

My oh my, but that little niggra hussy sure had delicate taste in underthings. This brassiere is simply heavenly. It certainly is thoughtful of you to bring back such lovely gifts for li'l ole me. And don't go thinking your generosity isn't appreciated. Some day, soon, I'll show you just how much.

Ryman hooked his thumbs into the waistband of the panties and gave it a tug.

I don't mean to carp, honey, but these panties are a tad tight. Maybe tonight you can find me a pair that are a little larger. Okay, sugar? Well, I guess I'd best be on my way so you can finish getting dressed. I know how anxious you are to get on with your work. I'll be seeing you.

*****

Ten minutes later, in the privacy of his Volvo, Ryman put on the brown wig, matching mustache, and green-tinted contact lenses he'd purchased at a theatrical prop shop. He'd felt no anxiety about arousing the suspicion of the sales staff or the other customers. That was the beauty of living in New York; no one ever looked at you that closely or paid the slightest attention to what you were doing.

Starting the car, he exited the garage and made his way down Fifth Avenue to East 47th Street. His destination was The Modeling Boutique, a store he'd read about in the *Madison Avenue Handbook*, one of the many reference manuals he'd collected to assist him with his correspondence.

He felt confident his looks would allow him to easily pass as a member of the tribe. As for character, he intended to mimic the voice and 'aw-shucks' Montana mannerisms of the late, great Gary Cooper.

After parking the car, he inspected his face in the rearview mirror, grabbed the satchel containing his 'tools,' and stepped out onto the sidewalk. The rain had stopped but thick billows of dark clouds continued to hang oppressively low over the city.

Ryman strode into the store and quickly sized up its layout. Half a dozen customers were milling around in the aisles, examining the racks and shelves of books and magazines, instruction videos, exercise equipment, cosmetics, soaps and shampoos, curling irons and hair dryers, nutrition and diet products, and an absurd variety of portfolio cases. He nodded at the cashier and headed for the nearest aisle.

It didn't take him long to find a suitable prospect, a tanned, busty brunette who was standing alone in front of the magazine section, leafing through the latest issue of *Mademoiselle*. Stopping just behind her, he reached for a copy of *Vanity Fair* and intentionally brushed her arm.

"I beg your pardon, ma'am," he said, flashing a toothy smile.

"That's all right," she replied.

Ryman held her gaze. "Say, I know you. You just did a Calvin Klein spread in Cosmo, right?"

"I wish."

"You mean that wasn't you?"

"Most definitely not. My agency's still got me doing trade shows and advertising flyers."

"That's a doggone shame. You've got the kind of face that just cries out to be on a magazine cover."

"I'm glad somebody thinks so."

"Aw, don't you fret about it now. I reckon it's gonna happen real soon."

"Sure," she replied, rolling her eyes.

"If you don't mind my askin', how long you been in the business?"

"About a year. You?"

"I'm just startin' out, arrived from Montana about a month ago."

"Montana. That's quite the journey."

"In more ways than you think," said Ryman, chuckling.

"Have you found an agent yet?"

"Uh-uh, but I ain't done lookin'."

"Well, I hope it works out," she said, turning to go. "It was nice meeting you."

"Likewise."

Ryman waited until she turned the corner, then followed after her. He paused behind a sunglass display at the end of the aisle and watched as she paid for her magazine, shoved it into her purse, and walked out of the store.

Ryman lingered a few seconds before stepping through the door in pursuit. To his dismay, the woman was standing on the curb, trying to flag a passing taxi. He'd counted on her being on foot or having her own car. Now he'd have to start all over again. He clenched his fists and turned to re-enter the store. But as he reached for the door handle, he had an idea. Composing himself, he rushed up to the woman and tapped her on the shoulder.

"Hi, again," he said, grinning.

"Hi yourself," she replied, warily.

"Listen," he continued, "I realize you don't know me from Adam and that it ain't polite to be pesterin' ladies in the middle of the street like this, but I was wonderin' if you'd like to share a cab."

The woman's brow furrowed.

"Don't get me wrong, now. It's not like I'm tryin' to pick you up or ask for a reference or anything like that. The truth is, I ain't exactly rich and as you probably know, money don't go very far in this town."

"Tell me about it," she said, scrutinizing his face. "Which way are you headed?"

The question, thought Ryman, was where did *she* live? Her earlier comments about her career ruled out any of the high-rent neighborhoods uptown. Judging by her unruly short hair and Bohemian clothes, he figured her to be a denizen of one of the trendy downtown communities favored by actors, artists, and musicians — the kind of people models liked to fraternize with in an attempt to legitimize their superfluous and exploitative profession.

"South," he replied. "I'm stayin' with relatives at Battery Park City."

After a moment's consideration, she smiled and said, "Sure, why not."

"Thank you, ma'am," said Ryman, gently moving her out of the way so he could take her place on the curb.

When he finally got a cab to stop, he pulled open the back door, helped the woman inside, and climbed in after her.

"Where to?" asked the black driver through a mouthful of wasted teeth.

"Tribeca," said the woman, "Washington Street." She turned to Ryman. "I'll get out first since I'm closest."

"Anything you say, ma'am."

"It sounds weird to hear myself called 'ma'am'. My name's Rosa."

"Glad to make your acquaintance, Rosa," said Ryman, extending his hand. "I'm...Gary."

*****

By the time the cab pulled up in front of an apartment building near the south end of Washington Street, dusk had settled over lower Manhattan. The other factor in Ryman's favor was the area's relative seclusion. There was little traffic and few pedestrians.

"Well," said the woman, reaching into her purse, "this is the end of the line for me."

An apt choice of words, thought Ryman, glancing at the driver. The man had his head cocked and was busy scouring out his ear with the end of his right pinkie. Ryman quickly reached into his satchel, pulled out a stun gun, and pressed it against the back of the driver's neck. The man squealed like a stuck pig and bounced about a foot in the air before collapsing back onto his seat in a disheveled heap.

Ryman turned to the woman. She sat frozen in the corner like a deer caught in a car's headlights, mouth slack, eyes wide with terror. A funny simpering sound emanated from somewhere deep in her throat. Ryman winked and pressed the stun gun to her abdomen.

As soon as she stopped twitching, he put on his gloves, grabbed her by the ankles, and pulled her forward until her body was stretched out lengthwise on the floor. Reaching back into his satchel, he took out a roll of duct tape and tore off enough strips to cover her mouth and bind her ankles and wrists. He then climbed out of the cab, pulled open the front passenger door, and pushed the seat as far back as it would go. After trussing up the driver, he hauled his bulky carcass up and over the gearshift and dumped him onto the floor in front of the passenger seat.

So far, so good, he thought, settling in behind the wheel. Now he had to find a secluded place to dump the driver so he couldn't do any mischief. Then it was off to the east side 'gallery' he'd chosen to display his latest masterpiece. Strapping on his seat belt, Ryman started the car and slowly pulled away from the curb.

Chapter 18 — Thursday, July 3

"What's the fucking point of issuing public warnings if nobody listens!" snarled Lieutenant Hawthorne as he watched a pair of attendants cart away the body of 25-year-old Rosa Sandrelli, Sardonicus's latest victim. "So what if he was wearing a wig or dyed his goddamn hair! The guy was a stranger! Why in God's name would she get into a cab with a stranger?"

"Some people have trusting natures," said Jackson, rolling a fragment of brick back and forth under his foot. "They've never experienced evil."

Hawthorne shook his head. "I hate to say it, Lionel, but this guy's got me spooked. He's always one step ahead. It's like he's toying with us. Hell, we finally get a witness who sees him up close and the bastard's wearing another goddamn disguise. It's just a big fucking game to him. My gut tells me that unless he makes a stupid mistake *real* soon we're going to be up to our necks in corpses."

Jackson took a drag on his cigarette and slowly released the smoke through his nostrils. "I think I've figured out when he intends to kill again."

Hawthorne spun around and brought his hand up to shield his eyes from the morning sun. "Say what?"

"Remember what Carmichael said when he gave us Sardonicus's profile, about his being methodical and well-organized?"

"Yeah?"

"He was right. The guy's on a time-table. His killed his first victim on a Saturday. The next on a Wednesday. Then Saturday again. And yesterday was—"

"Wednesday! I'll be damned."

"Unless we're dealing with a remarkable coincidence, he's going to be on the prowl again the day after tomorrow."

"Then we've got to set up some kind of trap. I'm going downtown to talk to the chief. You get back to the station and have another chat with our friend Jenkins. Maybe his cobwebs have cleared up by now."

Samuel Jenkins was the cab driver who'd last seen Rosa Sandrelli alive. His dispatcher had reported him missing at 9:45 p.m. A patrol car found his cab at 10:20, near Tompkins Square Park in Alphabet City, a residential area encompassing Avenues A, B, C, and D on the Lower East Side. Jenkins himself wasn't found until 7:10 a.m., in an alley not far from the victim's apartment building, by a shopkeeper who heard his muffled whimpers while putting out the garbage.

Jenkins' subsequent statement triggered an immediate and massive manhunt that led to the discovery of Rosa Sandrelli's body less than an hour later, splayed out amid the rubble of a demolition site half a block from where the police had found the cab. Somehow, the uniforms had missed her during their search for Jenkins.

Jackson wanted desperately to believe otherwise, but there seemed to be only one explanation for their sloppiness. Heavy cloud cover had made it a darker night than usual; the demolition site was treacherous; and Samuel Jenkins was a middle-aged black man. The uniforms probably figured he wasn't worth the bother.

Scowling, Jackson flicked his cigarette butt into a muddy pothole, signaled Ed Lewicki to let him know he was leaving, and walked toward his car.

*****

By the time he got to the station house, every radio and television station in town was abuzz with the story of Sardonicus's latest murder. That meant the hot line would soon be jammed with another flurry of questionable prowler and stalker calls from jittery citizens, more useless tips in the squad room's 'In' basket, and another bunch of screwballs crawling out of the woodwork claiming to be the killer. Additional crap to further muddy an already murky investigation.

Jackson walked upstairs to the interview room, a bland, closet-sized box equipped with a desk, a couple of chairs, a bench, and a two-way mirror. Samuel Jenkins was in there with the precinct's sketch artist, trying to come up with a computer composite of Sardonicus's face. The cab driver's eyes were half-closed and he had his chin propped on the palm of his hand. His exhaustion was understandable, given his ordeal and the fact he'd spent the morning being interviewed and plowing through a pile of mug shots.

"Hey, Sarge."

Jackson turned to face Jimmy Choi.

"Good news. We got the okay to run a trace at W.S.N.Y."

"It's about bloody time. Get over there with a technician as soon as you can and start setting up. There's a good chance Sardonicus will call tonight to gloat about his latest kill."

"You got it. Oh, one other thing. Forensics called to confirm that the brown hairs they found on the back seat of the cab *were* synthetic."

"I didn't think our man would be stupid enough to draw attention to himself by dying his hair. I'll put out an F.A.T.N. advising the other precincts to add a brown wig to the list of items to search for if they're involved in the collar."

"Don't forget to mention the duct tape."

"Right. Thanks, Jimmy."

If Sardonicus still had the roll of tape in his possession when he was caught, and hadn't used it again, forensics would be able to match the tear pattern to one of the strips used to bind Samuel Jenkins.

After issuing the advisory, Jackson poured two cups of coffee and entered the interview room. He greeted the sketch artist, smiled at Jenkins, and handed him one of the cups. "Feeling any better?"

"Not really," replied the cabbie, shifting his weight.

"Well, hang in there. We're almost done."

"Man, I hope so. I gotta get me some sleep. My head feels like a bowling ball."

Jackson leaned forward to examine the face the sketch artist had created on his laptop computer. Although its accuracy was questionable — Jenkins had proved to be a less-than-observant witness — its features were clean and well-proportioned, like one of those Greek statues in the Metropolitan Museum. No wonder women were drawn to the guy.

"Think you'll be much longer, Tom? I need to talk to Mister Jenkins for a few minutes."

"He's all yours. I'm just cleaning up the chin a bit."

"When you're done, I'll need hard copies with and without the mustache."

"What about the hair? Do you want just the blond, or should I print him up as a brunette as well?"

"Just the blond for now. If anybody's going to recognize this freak, it'll be with his natural hair color. I'd appreciate it if you could get copies out to the newspapers in time for their afternoon editions."

"Not a problem."

Jackson placed his hand on the cabby's shoulder. "Let's go to my desk, Mister Jenkins. We'll be more comfortable. Don't forget your coffee."

Groaning, Jenkins stood and followed him into the squad room.

"Whaddaya want now?" he asked, plopping heavily onto the padded armchair Jackson had snatched from behind another desk.

"I need you to go over your statement again."

"Shit, man. I already told you. The cat had short, straight brown hair, a brown mustache, and he talked with a twang. He was wearin' a plain, light blue shirt and a dark blue sports jacket. I didn't catch the color of his pants. I picked him and the woman up on East Forty-Seventh and took them to an apartment building on Washington Street in Tribeca. After dropping the woman off, I was supposed to take the guy to Battery Park City. But the sucker knocked me out while I was waitin' to get paid. When I woke up I was lyin' in an alley trussed up like some goddamn turkey. End of story."

"You say he spoke with a twang. Can you place it at all?"

"Shit, no. I never been farther west than New Jersey. All I can tell ya is that he sounded like one of those country hicks on T.N.N."

"What about distinguishing features? Did he have a mole, a scar, a tattoo...anything out of the ordinary?"

"Like I said before, none that I seen."

"You said you didn't notice the color of his eyes. Are you sure of that? Think real hard now. It's very important."

"Man, I can think about it till my face turns purple and it ain't gonna make no difference. It was dark and the cat never looked right at me."

Jackson lit a cigarette. "Did he say anything that might tip us off about where he'd been before he got into your cab?"

"I wasn't payin' attention, but it seems to me the woman was the one doin' most of the talkin'."

"And you're sure they'd just met?"

"I ain't *positive*, but that's how it sounded when they got in the cab."

Jackson took a deep breath. "Okay, Mister Jenkins. You might as well go on home. We'll call if we need you."

"Hallelujah and pass the peanut butter," he replied, rising to his feet with a wobble. "Listen, you guys figured out what that sucker hit me with yet? It was the god*damndest* sensation I ever felt."

"Based on the paramedic's report, we think it might've been a stun gun."

"Man, that's some nasty piece of work."

"I hear ya. Want me to walk you down to the front door?"

"I can manage," he replied, and waddled toward the exit.

Seconds later, Hawthorne strode into the squad room, grabbed Jackson by the elbow, and guided him into his office.

"It's all set," he said, settling into his chair. "Come Saturday night, Mister Sardonicus is going to get a little surprise."

Jackson leaned forward expectantly.

"We're going to recruit a local designer to help us stage a benefit fashion show for the victims. Publicize it like crazy. We're going to use the old Tivoli Theater on West Forty-Fifth. It's self-contained, easy to secure, and available. We'll have undercover officers working backstage, in the foyer, and in the audience. The commissioner has already set the wheels in motion."

"Do you think Sardonicus will bite? At this point, he's going to be expecting us at *any* fashion show, never mind a benefit."

"Of course he'll be suspicious, but I'm counting on his being unable to resist the challenge — especially if we can convince a couple of big-name models to participate."

"Good luck."

"Some of these ladies are pretty ballsy. Besides, it's an opportunity to help us take this guy out. No model in this city is going to be safe until that happens."

"Yeah, but if some supermodel gets killed we're going to find ourselves in the middle of a major shit storm."

"Not a chance. There'll be two detectives assigned to each model who agrees to participate. They'll be escorted to and from the theater and will never be left alone backstage. Don't forget, Sardonicus is a con man, not an assassin. They only way he's going to hurt one of these women is if he can get her alone and lure her out of the theater. And that's not going to happen."

*****

At WSNY that evening, Jackson was surprised to discover that Robert Molinaro was taller than expected, given the Napoleonic ego the talk show host displayed on air.

"Sure you won't join me?" asked Molinaro as he fixed himself a drink.

Jackson looked at his watch. "No thanks."

"So," added Molinaro, leaning against his desk, "how is this tracing business going to work?"

"It'll all be taken care of from the control booth. All we need you to do is keep Frank talking for at least a minute."

"Is that all it takes?"

"If the call comes through all-electronic switching. A bit longer if it doesn't. The fact you've got him using a private line that bypasses the main switchboard gives us a bit of an edge."

Molinaro took a sip of scotch and peered over the top of his glass like a fox examining a plump chicken. "If you don't mind my asking, Sergeant, how close are you guys to catching this psycho?"

"We'll get him tonight if the trace works."

That's not what I meant."

"You know I can't discuss that."

"Come on. You wouldn't have this chance if it wasn't for me. Can't you just give me a rough idea?"

"Sorry."

"So much for being a responsible citizen."

Jackson had to check an impulse to chortle. If Robert Molinaro had any sense of responsibility, it was primarily to himself. His link with Sardonicus had made him a local celebrity and he was milking it for all it was worth. But if Jackson was any judge of talent and character, Molinaro and his talk show would sink back into obscurity the instant his 15 minutes were up.

Jackson looked at his watch again. "It's almost time. I'd better go check with my technician."

"I'll be out in a few minutes."

Jackson strode down the hall, turned left past a large rectangular window that looked in on the broadcast booth, and entered the control room. He shook hands with Sid Crouse, then walked over to the makeshift workstation that the technician, a 38-year-old Brooklynite with the stern demeanor of a high school gym teacher, had set up in the corner.

"Ready to roll, Alice?"

She glanced at her equipment and nodded. The tools of her trade included a voiceprint spectrograph, a device that transcribed the human voice into a graphic image that could be used as a forensic means of identification; a psychological stress-evaluator, a device that picked up sub-audible tremors in speech and provided a hard printout similar to a polygraph; two tape recorders; and a special phone, wired into Frank's line, that was linked directly to Bell's Electronic Switching Center.

"Mister Crouse," said Jackson, placing his hand on the producer's shoulder. "I know Alice has already gone over the procedure, but let's review it once more. The indicator on Frank's line lights up. The call is transferred to Alice's phone. The circuit is completed and Bell begins the trace, but we keep the tone generator switched on so he doesn't know we've picked up. How many rings do you figure we can get away with, Alice?"

"Four, max."

"Okay," said Jackson, turning back to Crouse, "at three seconds a ring, that gives us a twelve-second head start. You pick up after the fourth ring and try to stall him for as long as you can. Is that a problem?"

"I don't think so. Bob's usually got somebody on whenever Frank calls so he's used to waiting."

"Good. The key is to sound natural. He mustn't suspect that this call is any different than his previous ones."

Just then, Molinaro entered the broadcast booth and waved. Jackson grabbed a headset from the technician and sat down beside her. After a short count-down, Sid Crouse punched a button on his console, initiating the program's recorded intro. Molinaro puffed on a cigar while he waited for the intro to end, then switched on his microphone.

"Hell-o New York, and welcome to Molinaro on N.Y. Ninety-Nine, the voice of the Big Apple. As usual, we're here to listen to your opinions about politics, current events, and the arts. And make sure you stay tuned for the second half of tonight's program because we've got a special treat in store. Veteran stage and screen actor Tony Randall is here and he's ready to talk candidly about his remarkable and multifaceted career.

"But before we start taking calls, I'd like to say a few words about the murders that have cast such a dark pall over our fair city. Four young lives have been snuffed out, all because of one man's twisted views about feminine beauty. In light of this terrible tragedy, some of you may be questioning the relevancy of carrying on with programs like this one. That's understandable. But ask yourselves this. Do we not all become victims if we allow this man to hold our minds hostage? Are we to cower in the dark and give him the run of the city? We here at W.S.N.Y. believe not. And we're confidant that most New Yorkers feel the same."

He paused a moment for effect. "Now, let's get to our first call."

Jackson glanced at the indicator light on the private line. It remained dark.

Sid Crouse pressed a button to accept a call, then relayed the individual's name into the microphone suspended around his neck.

"Here's Steve, from the Bronx," repeated Molinaro. "What's on your mind, Steve?"

"Yeah, um, about this Frank guy who claims he's Mister Sardonicus. Do you think he's telling the truth?"

"The police seem to think so. Why?"

"I don't want to sound like I condone his actions, but if you listen to his words, the guy does have a point. Beautiful women usually *do* get whatever they want handed to them on a silver platter. I also agree with his opinion about models. They're treated like royalty and are given tons of money even though they don't actually do anything that has any real social value."

"Maybe so, Steve, but like I've said before, are they to blame for that? We're the ones who've placed them on that pedestal. Examine your own behavior for a moment. Do you treat a beautiful woman the same way you treat one who's plain? I doubt it."

"I'm not saying I blame them for *being* beautiful, but for exploiting the fact."

"Now you're being a hypocrite. You might as well scorn a baseball player for exploiting his ability to hit home runs. It's human nature to take advantage of the skills, talents, or physical attributes we've been given. That's life. So instead of getting your nose bent out of shape by someone else's success, I suggest you work on maximizing your own potential. Thanks for your call."

Sid Crouse uttered another name into the microphone.

"Here's Patricia," said Molinaro, "from Jersey City."

"Hi, Bob. I'd like to respond to what Steve just said. I'll admit that in a superficial sense, he's right. A beautiful woman can usually get what she wants. But in the larger scheme of things, it's still a man's world. I won't get into the inequities of the workplace because that's been done to death. Instead, let's look at relationships. I think you'll agree that a man of virtually any age is free to chase after any woman he wants. The world is teeming with forty- and fifty-year-olds who are dating women in their early twenties and no one bats an eye.

But if a woman in her forties is seen with a man of thirty, she's treated like some kind of freak."

"Your point is well taken, Patricia."

"Age bias is just one part of the problem. Another is the actual way the two sexes approach a relationship. A woman usually places stability, trust, and faithfulness ahead of looks. Men, on the other hand, are usually stopped in their tracks by a woman's beauty. They could care less about her education or professional accomplishments. In fact, the more gains a woman makes in the business world, the harder it is for her to have a successful relationship. Men who haven't reached the same level are likely to feel uncomfortable, while those who *are* successful often prefer a partner who does so-called women's work...something that won't interfere with his own social or professional aspirations."

"So what are you implying, that most men are still chauvinist pigs?"

"You said it, not me."

"Thanks for your call. Here's Angela, from the upper west side."

"Mister Molinaro. I found your opening remarks offensive and self-serving. Where do you get off lecturing the rest of us about doing the right thing when you continue to allow that monster to spout his venomous views on your show? All you're interested in is ratings."

"That's not true," replied Molinaro. "We allow him on the air because we believe it's important to keep the lines of communication open. That way, we can try and make him understand that what he's doing is wrong and that there are people who can help him."

Turning to the technician, Jackson stuck a finger in his mouth and pretended to gag. In the same instant, the control room reverberated with the sound of a phone being slammed down.

"I guess I failed to convince her," said Molinaro, shifting his weight. "Oh well, you can't win 'em all. Here's Ellen, from Brooklyn."

"Hi, Bob. Listen, I agree with Steve's criticism of models. Not because they're beautiful, per se, but because they're presented as the feminine ideal. They make the rest of feel inadequate. I'll give you an example. Did you know that the top modeling agencies won't even consider a woman unless she's at least five feet, eight inches tall? How realistic is that? The only place in the world you'll find women that tall is in the W.N.B.A."

"I appreciate your point, Ellen, but you're making the same mistake that many of our other callers have made. You're blaming models when the real culprits are the decision-makers in the advertising and fashion industries."

"Uh-uh. It's the models who agree to have their surgically altered, heavily made-up faces plastered on magazine covers and who flirt with anorexia in order to squeeze into impossibly skimpy bikinis for *Sports Illustrated*. And the only reason they do it is for the money. They could care less about the message they're sending to all the impressionable young women out there."

"Fair enough, but even if a model felt the way you did, what could she do about it, quit the business?"

"Maybe that's not such a bad idea. Let's face it, if the modeling profession disappeared tomorrow, who'd miss it?"

"That's ridiculous. There's only one way women are going to get the advertising, cosmetics, and fashion industries to change the way they're depicted and that's by boycotting their products and the magazines that carry their message. How about you, Ellen? Do you wear make-up? Do you own a pair of Gucci shoes or a Perry Ellis sweater? Do you subscribe to *Vogue* or *Cosmopolitan* or—?"

Again, the sound of a phone being slammed down.

Molinaro grinned and sucked on his cigar. "Here's Catherine, from SoHo."

"Hi, Bob. I just want to say that I take great exception to all this trash talk about beautiful women. First of all, beauty *is* in the eye of the beholder. Secondly, physical beauty is an accident of birth...the result of random genetic fusion. A beautiful woman can no more *not* be beautiful than a black person not be black. Thirdly, if beautiful women *are* treated differently than those who aren't, it's because human beings are biased in favor of beautiful things, be it a woman, a painting, a sunset, or a Michael Jordan slam dunk."

"Not to mention a Wayne Gretzky breakaway."

"I prefer Mario Lemieux, but we can save that argument for another day. Anyway, now there's evidence that this bias we have toward physical beauty — like beauty itself — may be genetically determined. A couple of months ago, I saw a TV program where a group of kindergarten children were asked to listen to two female teachers reading from a storybook. One of the teachers was attractive, the other plain. The two women read in exactly the same way, in a flat monotone with no gestures or facial expressions.

"Later, each child was asked to vote for which of the two women was the better teacher. Almost all of them chose the attractive one. So, all you people out there in radio land, to paraphrase that shampoo commercial, don't hate a woman just because she's beautiful. If she's treated better than the rest of us, blame it on D.N.A."

"An interesting new twist, Catherine. Thanks for your call. Here's Ron, from Staten Island."

"Hey, Bob. I'm going to keep it short and sweet. Women — and I mean *all* women, regardless of their looks, their shapes, or their color — are the backbone of a civilized society. If it wasn't for their influence men would be even greedier and more violent than they already are. I say, God bless them all."

"Well put, Ron. Thanks for your call. Okay, folks. I think Ron's comment is a fitting end to our discussion of this particular subject. Let's move on to something else."

Jackson felt the same way. It disturbed him to hear people having a serious discussion based on the ramblings of a murderous madman. They didn't realize that by legitimizing Sardonicus's views, they were sending him a message that they approved of his actions.

He lit a cigarette and glanced at his watch. An hour and forty-five minutes to go, plus the Randall interview, just in case. He blew out a thin stream of smoke and glared at the private line's indicator light. Come on, you bastard, he thought, tapping his fingers on the armrest. Call!

*****

Disappointment creeping into his brain like an unwanted memory, Jackson exited the WSNY building and headed for his car. Sardonicus's non-appearance meant he'd have to supervise another trace attempt the following evening — which just happened to be the eve of the Fourth of July weekend. And with his presence required at Saturday night's benefit fashion show, his planned trip to Chicago to visit his kids was dead in the water. His hatred of Sardonicus was becoming personal.

Jackson climbed into his car, folded his arms across the steering wheel, and leaned forward to rest his head. Homicide cop. What a life; a seemingly endless journey through a dark and desolate psychological landscape, most of it spent looking under rocks in search of human monsters. And the longer you kept your hand in, the further you receded from the light. The things that others strove for, like love, marriage, family, began to take on the appearance of fantasy, like episodes of the old Cosby Show.

What a bitter irony. In police circles, homicide work was considered the top of the ladder. But Jackson was beginning to discover just how much it cost to stay perched up there. Eventually, if you didn't self-destruct or get yourself killed, you either lost your nerve and landed in a desk job or you turned to stone.

Sighing, he started the car and pulled out onto 62nd Street. It was hard for a man — especially one approaching his thirty-sixth birthday — to face up to the fact he was stuck in a rut of his own making. Other than a brief stint as a grocery clerk at a D'Agostino's supermarket and an even briefer one as a counter man at a Brooklyn rib joint, he'd been a cop his entire adult life. It was all he knew.

Only once did he ever seriously consider leaving the force — to enter politics of all things, during the 1989 municipal elections. At the time, he was a lapsed Democrat, a result of his conviction that the party had lost touch with reality; that it no longer served the best interests of the individual or of the African-American community. He had come to believe that government handouts and programs like affirmative action had engendered dependency rather than self-sufficiency.

Not that he believed the Republican platform to be much of an improvement. In fact, he felt that neither party was doing enough to address the needs of his people, be it the eradication of racism and poverty, urban renewal, youth unemployment, or the recognition of the African-American experience in the school curriculum. The result was a deeply ingrained cynicism that had limited his involvement in politics to the voting booth.

So when his wife, an activist since her college days, asked him to join her in supporting the David Dinkins mayoralty campaign, he flatly declined. But she and a number of her fellow volunteers kept badgering him until he finally relented, on condition that his involvement be confined to putting up placards and distributing leaflets.

The experience transformed him. He became absorbed in the political process and soon took on more and more responsibilities. In the end, when Dinkins actually won, becoming New York City's first black mayor, he was euphoric. It renewed his belief that the system could work. He even began to explore ways in which he could continue his involvement.

But as the months wore on, and the wheels of party politics began to once again assert their numbing effect, Jackson realized the status quo was in no danger of collapsing. His interest began to wane. Within a year, he had settled back into his old cynicism.

Now, for better or worse, it was time to accept the fact he was a career cop — and to prove he was a damn good one. Catching Sardonicus would be an excellent start.

*****

At his apartment, Jackson changed into a sweat suit and cracked open a Coors. He then went into the living room, flopped onto the easy chair, and placed a long distance call to Chicago. His mother-in-law answered the phone.

"Hey, Emma. It's Lionel."

"Lionel. How are you, son?"

"Fine. How 'bout you."

"Can't complain, I guess. Except for the heat. The temperature's been in the nineties all week. They're even talkin' about rationing the water."

"You don't say."

"I guess you want to talk to 'lyssa."

"Is she there?"

"She's in the living room watching TV with the girls."

"I hope they haven't been giving you too much trouble."

"Those two? Not one tiny bit."

"That's good."

There was a pause. "I'll go get 'lyssa."

A few seconds later, his wife picked up the phone.

"How've you been, 'lyssa?"

"Okay. You?"

"The usual."

Silence.

"Listen, something's come up on that case I was telling you about and, uh, I'm not going to be able to get up there this weekend."

"Why doesn't that surprise me."

"Look, we're dealing with the worst killing spree this city's seen since Son of Sam, so don't start with me, okay?"

"You're the one who started it, Lionel, by putting your job ahead of your family. Let me ask you something. When you were told you'd have to work this weekend, did you put up any kind of fight? Did you tell your precious lieutenant how much this trip meant to your children?"

"For God's sake, woman. We've gone through all this before. I'm tired of fighting the same battle. Just tell the kids I'm sorry and that I'll see them as soon as the case is wrapped."

"Uh-uh. No sir! I'm not gonna do your dirty work. You can tell them yourself. Cassie! Janet! Get over here. Your daddy's got something to say to you!"

"Aw, man. Come on 'lyssa, gimme a break."

He heard the receiver being set down, followed by the sound of running feet.

"Daddy, daddy!"

It was his youngest, Cassie. "Hi, precious. How's my little girl?"

"What time are you coming tomorrow?"

Jackson felt like crawling under the rug. "Listen, sweetie. I'm afraid I won't be able to make it. Me and the other policemen are chasing a really bad man right now and we can't stop until we catch him."

"But you promised."

"I know, but there's nothing I can do about it."

"Give me the phone." It was Janet, his 13-year-old.

"Hi, dad."

"Janet, honey. I know you're disappointed, but I really need your support on this. You're almost a young woman now. You need to appreciate the fact that life isn't always fair...that some responsibilities can't be put off. But that doesn't mean I don't love you."

"I know. It's just that we haven't seen you in such a long time."

"I won't disappoint you again. I swear. So please, be strong for me, and for your baby sister. Will you do that?"

"Okay, dad."

"Thanks, honey. I love you."

Jackson cradled the phone and swallowed the rest of his beer. Then he went into the kitchen for something stronger. Something that would help him get good and stinking drunk.

Chapter 19 — Friday, July 4

Morning sunlight streamed in through Rachel Curran's bedroom window, warming her back as she bent over to fasten the clasps of a small suitcase. In two hours she'd be on the train to Buffalo, to spend the holiday weekend with her parents.

She was glad to be getting out of town, to be leaving behind the mayhem wrought by Mister Sardonicus, if only for a few days. His murderous reign of terror had brought the city's fashion and advertising industries to a virtual standstill. Out-of-town models were reluctant to work in New York while those who lived there were afraid to leave their homes. The ones who did continue to work, when it was available, were being extremely selective: no evening gigs; no shoots with unknown photographers; no shoots at remote locations; no go-sees unless the client had been screened in advance. Many of the girls had also taken to traveling in pairs. And if taxis were used, they were booked through a dispatcher, not flagged down on the street.

Rachel herself had turned down two jobs and had lost another when the client, a shampoo manufacturer, decided to move the shoot to Hartford.

Just then, Sally Schuster stuck her head in the doorway. "Tea's ready, kiddo. How's it coming?"

"All done."

"I still can't understand why you're only going for the weekend. You should stay with your folks until they catch the creep."

"Who knows how long that'll take. In the meantime, what happens to my position at the agency?"

"Oh, please. Like I'm sure they'd drop you for trying to stay safe."

"It's not just that. There's the preparations for the pageant, my acting classes...oh, and something I haven't told you about yet. I've been asked to appear on a radio talk show next week."

"Oh, yeah?"

"They want me and one of the other contestants to answer questions about the pageant."

"Whose show? Not Howard Stern's, I hope."

"Good God, no. Do I look like I have a bull's-eye stenciled on my forehead? It's called Molinaro on N.Y. Ninety-Nine."

Sally's eyes widened. "Isn't that the one—?"

"The same. Ironic, huh?"

"Christ, I hope they don't intend to tell the world you're a model. That psycho might be listening."

"Believe me, I've already thought about that. The producer assured me there'll be no mention of my occupation. And if I'm asked by a caller, I'll say I'm an aspiring musician."

"Good plan. So, how come they chose you for this dubious honor?"

"The other half dozen contestants who were already in town copped out."

"Have you ever done this sort of thing before?"

"I've been interviewed by reporters, but I've never been on a talk show. It'll be a good experience."

"Don't be so sure. People who are into that scene can be pretty rough sometimes."

"I'm an actress, remember? Criticism comes with the territory."

"Are you sure you're not just a closet masochist?" asked Sally, picking up the suitcase.

"Not at all," replied Rachel, laughing as she followed her friend into the living room. "Acting teaches you discipline and does wonders for your confidence."

After setting the suitcase down near the front door, Sally walked over to the couch, sat down, and started pouring the tea. "Is that what turned you on to acting?"

"Partly. But it's also about expressing yourself, and moving people in the process. That's the same reason I wanted to be a concert pianist."

"What about fame?"

Rachel grinned. "I wouldn't turn it down. I mean, besides bringing in buckets of cash and the chance to work in exotic locations, being a star gets you the best tables in restaurants...invitations to great parties packed with handsome actors and interesting people...tickets to the Oscars and the Emmys ...trips to Cannes and Venice and all those other fabulous film festivals."

"What about the down side?"

"Like what?"

"For one thing, not knowing who's there for you and who's just there for the ride. You know as well as I do that famous people always attract a string of hangers-on. Not to mention obsessive fans. This country is full of morons who can't tell the difference between an actor and his or her screen image. And don't forget the stalkers. Just ask Jodie Foster and Theresa Saldana what it's like to have someone like that on your case. Or what about that poor Rebecca Schaeffer. She lost her life because of some freak's twisted obsession."

"You're talking about a tiny minority. Crazoids like that are an occupational hazard."

"What about privacy then? Right now you can come and go as you please. But once you're famous, you won't be able to take a pee without some paparazzi hanging over the stall, or go to a restaurant without being pestered for an autograph. Even worse, you'll be fair game for the tabloids. They'll try to bribe your friends and they'll have people sifting through your garbage, and if they can't find any real dirt, they'll just make it up."

"I think I'll be able to handle that stuff."

"Listen, kiddo. You're a human being, and that means you're going to screw up. And when you do, they'll be on you like vultures on a rotting carcass. The list of actors who've been raked over the coals for not having their halos on straight could fill volumes. Rob Lowe, George Michael, Hugh Grant, Eddie Murphy, Pee Wee Herman—"

"All men, of course. And that's because they have a hard time keeping their pants on."

"Good point," replied Sally, grinning.

"Look," continued Rachel, "I know what you're saying. But life is risky, no matter what you do. Planes fall out of the sky; cars mount curbs; people get shot during robberies. God, just look at what's happening in this city right now. There's no such thing as absolute safety and because of that, we're left with two choices. Live like a recluse, in constant fear of the unknown, in which case you might as well be dead anyway, or get out there and do your thing."

"I believe that, too — up to a point. Hell, I wouldn't have a sex life otherwise. But being in the spotlight changes the rules. It brings out the worst in people."

"So what are you saying? That I should give up acting?"

"Of course not. I'm just pointing out some of the pitfalls."

****

Lionel Jackson lurched up the stairs of the station house, trying to shake off the effects of a nasty hangover. His eyelids refused to stay open and his head felt like it was encased in slow-drying cement. Weaving down the corridor toward the squad room, he crashed into Jimmy Choi, who was just emerging from the closet in which the precinct's homicide case folders were stored.

"Sorry, Sarge," said Choi, squatting to pick up the folder he'd dropped. "Didn't see you coming."

"My fault, Jimmy. My eyes are so goddamn bloodshot I feel like I'm wading through tomato juice."

Choi grinned. "I know where you're coming from."

Jackson entered the squad room and made a bee line for the coffee machine. A moment later, he sensed someone standing behind him. It was Dan McDougall.

"Can I buy you a coffee, Dan?"

"Thanks, but I've already got one at my desk. I just came over to run something by you."

Jackson took a sip of coffee. "I'm listening."

"Got a call from the *Times* this morning. One of their op-ed editors. Says he used to get letters from some guy calling himself 'The Guardian' who liked to bitch about the same things as our friend Sardonicus. You know, natural women, the use of half-naked models in advertising, shit like that."

"Does he still have the letters?"

"Yep, and the envelopes, too. No return address, but the postmark does prove they were mailed from the Upper East Side. The guy's sending them over by courier."

"Good. Have them checked for prints first, then send the envelopes to the lab for DNA analysis." Often, saliva used to moisten stamps and envelope flaps contained enough DNA to provide a positive match. "Were the letters typed or hand-written?"

"That I can't tell ya."

"If they're hand-written, send copies to the FBI's document section for analysis."

McDougall nodded, but didn't leave.

"Is there something else?" asked Jackson.

"I was just thinking. If Sardonicus wrote to the *Times*, there's a good chance he wrote to other newspapers, too. Maybe even to a few magazines."

"Good point. Check it out."

Jackson took another sip of coffee and walked over to the nearest window. A gray haze hung over the city. On the street below, a bicycle courier and a cab driver were screaming at each other. A businessman wearing in-line skates and earphones whizzed past them, lost in his own electronic dome of silence. And somewhere out there, a madman was planning his next murder.

Jackson recalled FBI Special Agent Carmichael's comment that Sardonicus was one of an estimated 250 serial killers who were currently stalking the highways and byways of America. It was a sobering thought.

*****

That night, Jackson was back in the WSNY control room, listening to more inane ramblings by Robert Molinaro and his callers. He'd been hunkered over the tracing equipment for some 40 minutes, worrying, chain-smoking, and clinging to the hope that Sardonicus was waiting for the interview portion of the program, in order to confront Rudy Miceli, the prominent New York fashion designer who had agreed to stage Saturday night's benefit. The brass had arranged for Miceli to appear as Molinaro's guest, believing it was the best way to ensure Sardonicus heard about the event. And maybe provoke him into calling.

Kicking off his right shoe, Jackson leaned over and massaged his aching foot. He and a group of fellow officers had spent the day pounding the sidewalks in search of witnesses, beginning with people who lived near the demolition site where Rosa Sandrelli's body was found, then moving uptown to talk to shopkeepers in the area around the Modeling Boutique. No new leads had been uncovered.

In the meantime, a more comprehensive canvass was under way in the Upper East Side. A large contingent of plainclothes detectives, armed with the photos taken from the surveillance video and the computer composite of Sardonicus's face, had begun a door-to-door search of every house and apartment in the area bound by 57th Street to the south, 110th Street to the north, Fifth Avenue to the west, and FDR Drive to the east. It would be a laborious and time-consuming effort, but if a tall, blond man named Frank did live in the area, it was only a matter of time before he was found. The tricky part would be tightening the dragnet without tipping him off.

Jackson was about to kick off his other shoe when he was alerted by Sid Crouse's low whistle. He looked up. The producer's eyes were fixed on the control console. Jackson followed his gaze. The indicator light for the private line was flashing!

Alice switched the call to her phone and activated the tone generator to initiate the trace. Four rings. Alice deactivated the tone generator and Crouse picked up the phone.

"Molinaro on N.Y. Ninety-Nine."

"Hiya, Sid. Any chance of getting on?"

Crouse shook his head. "Sorry, Stan. Not tonight." He hung up and turned to Jackson. "That was one of our other regulars."

"How many do you have?"

"About half a dozen."

Jackson put his shoe back on and stood up to grab a coffee. Monitoring a phone trace, a task that combined equal measures of boredom and anxiety, always left him feeling a little spaced out. He sat back down and lit another cigarette.

A few seconds later, he was distracted by a metallic rattling sound. He glanced to his left. Alice was nervously fingering her charm bracelet. She stopped as soon as she noticed his expression. Back at the control console, Sid Crouse cleared his throat as he keyed in a commercial. Jackson sipped his coffee. The commercial ended and Crouse fed Molinaro the name of the next caller. But his hand froze in midair before he had a chance to punch the call through.

The indicator light was flashing again.

Alice quickly set the trace in motion and pointed at Crouse.

"Molinaro on N.Y. Ninety-Nine," he said.

"Hello, Sidney. How are you this fine evening?"

Crouse's thumb shot into the air. Molinaro, who was anxiously watching from inside the broadcast booth, nodded, and dismissed his current caller.

Jackson's heart was thumping in his chest. Eighteen seconds had elapsed. Realizing he had a death grip on his armrests, he took a deep breath and rolled his chair closer to Alice's.

"Hi, Frank," said Crouse, glancing nervously at the wall clock.

"I need to speak to Robert."

"Sure. I'll let him know you're on the line."

"Tell him he has five seconds. Otherwise, I hang up."

Crouse looked at Jackson, who vigorously nodded his head. Crouse put the call through. Thirty-three seconds had elapsed.

"Here's Frank," said Molinaro, "from the upper east side."

"Happy Fourth of July, Robert. I am calling to congratulate you on the quality of last night's program. It is gratifying to see that my actions have initiated such a stimulating public dialogue."

"That's not surprising. You're a very bright and provocative guy. Too bad you have this compulsion to hurt people. You might've done something of real value with your life."

"Robert, Robert, Robert. How can I make you understand that I *am* doing something of value. Something that will be remembered and appreciated long after most of my contemporaries have been consigned to history's scrap heap."

Jackson looked at his watch. Sixty-three seconds had elapsed. Alice tapped him on the arm. He spun around and saw that she was scribbling something on a pad. It read, "Phone booth. Penn Station. RMPs scrambling."

Jackson made a fist. Don't hang up, you son-of-a-bitch. Keep talking!

"...ready to resume battle," continued Frank. "I think even you will appreciate the ingenuity of my next project, not only for its execution — pardon the pun — but also for its style. You can give me your critique the next time I call."

The line went dead.

"Shit!" snapped Jackson, slamming his right fist into the palm of his other hand.

"There's still a chance they got there on time," said Alice, with more hope than conviction in her voice.

An anxious silence settled over the control room as they waited for the news from Penn Station. Sid Crouse even forgot to punch through another caller, until Molinaro loudly reminded him that they were still on air.

A few minutes later, Ed Lewicki called to report that half a dozen officers had rushed the phone booth, but found it empty. He added that several patrolmen were being stationed at every exit and that a search of the building was underway.

Jackson's shoulders sagged. "Keep me posted."

Handing the receiver back to Alice, he patted her on the shoulder, stood up, and stepped out into the corridor. Thankfully, the air was less stifling. He leaned against the wall and rubbed his tired eyes. He felt used up, deflated. There was only one thought bouncing around inside his skull. Sardonicus had outfoxed them yet again. That didn't bode well for the scheme the D.A. and the brass at One Police Plaza had cooked up for Saturday night.

Chapter 20 — Saturday, July 5

Rachel Curran woke up in her old bedroom and stretched her arms in a languorous yawn. Propping her pillow against the headboard, she sat up and absorbed the familiar surroundings: the N'Sync, Janet Jackson and Johnny Depp posters, the numerous high school scholastic awards, including the ones she snared for winning her age group's spelling bee three years running, the plaques for her musical accomplishments, and her sharp-shooting trophies.

Not that her teenage years had been all sunshine and roses; like most of her peers, she'd had her fair share of bumps along the way, including the inevitable boy troubles. But overall, her parents had kept her grounded and had given her the tools to deal with whatever drama life threw her way.

Rachel tossed aside her comforter, slid off the bed and ambled to the closet for her robe. She suddenly noticed how quiet the house seemed. During high school, she and her three older brothers had conspired to make Saturday mornings more rambunctious than the monkey house at the zoo. Now her parents were empty nesters. One by one, her brothers had graduated from college, gotten married, and moved away to start families of their own.

After a quick shower, Rachel put on a pair of shorts and a sweatshirt and hurried downstairs to the kitchen. She experienced a nostalgic pang when she spotted her mother, Rebecca, standing in front of the sink in her faded floral print apron, brushing aside a sprig of hair that kept sliding down across her eyes. Rachel rushed over and kissed her on the cheek.

"Morning, mom."

"Morning, dear. There's fresh orange juice on the table. And I've made your favorite: waffles with homemade blueberry sauce."

"Sounds wonderful. Can I help with anything?"

"Nope. You just dig right in."

"Where's dad?"

"Oh, he's out watering his vegetable garden. You know how the man fusses over his little patch. He should be here any moment."

"God," said Rachel as she sat down and reached for the orange juice, "it feels so good to be home."

Her mother smiled. "We missed you, too, sweetheart."

"When is the rest of the gang arriving?"

"Not until this evening." She poured herself a cup of coffee and sat down across from Rachel. "Your brothers are beginning to realize that planning and pulling off a family trip is as complicated as a military campaign."

Rachel laughed and started in on her waffles.

"So," added her mother, peering intently over the rim of her cup, "how are things going with that boy in your acting class?"

"Jeez, mom" said Rachel, rolling her eyes, "like I said the *last* time you asked, Tom and I are keeping things casual for now. I mean, he's sweet and considerate and maybe someday we'll take it to the next level, but I'm just not in that place right now. We'll see how things stand once the pageant is over."

"I'm not trying to pester you, honey. I just don't like seeing you all alone in New York, especially with that Sardonicus creature roaming the streets."

"First of all, I'm not alone. Secondly, I'm being extremely careful about my movements."

"Don't you think those other girls were too? Yet he still managed to get to them."

"I know you're afraid for me, mom. I'm scared too. But trust me, I don't intend to let any strange man get anywhere near me. Besides," she added, feigning nonchalance, "what are the odds of my actually coming face to face with that creep?"

"I don't care if it's one in a million!" She took a deep breath and leaned forward. "Look, I know we've already talked about this, but seriously, why don't you stay with us until they catch that maniac?"

"I can't, mom. There's just too much going on right now. I risk everything I've been working for if I walk away. I need to find out if I actually have what it takes to make a living as an actress and this pageant is the best chance I have of getting noticed"

Just then the screen door sprang open and her father, Patrick, strode into the room carrying a handful of fresh-cut parsley. He made a beeline to the table and planted a kiss on Rachel's forehead.

"Morning, angel. How'd you sleep?"

"Like a baby."

"Smell these," he said, placing the bouquet of parsley under her nose. "Isn't that amazing?"

Rachel's mother grabbed his arm as he skirted past her on his way to the sink. "Patrick, will you tell your daughter it's not safe to go back to New York."

"Thanks in no small part to you," he replied, patting his wife's hand, "Rachel is a very capable young woman. She knows the risks and knows what to do to avoid them."

"Of course I do," said Rachel. "In fact, I still remember what you said to me when I was a child and was having nightmares about Arthur Shawcross. You said the world could be a dangerous place at times but that you should never let fear prevent you from living your life."

"Exactly," replied Patrick. "An unhealthy obsession with all the possible perils that life may toss your way can lead to social paralysis."

"Oh, please," snapped Rebecca. "That may be true if you're dealing with the possibility of a meteor landing on your head, but we're talking about a very real and palpable threat."

"Okay, okay," said Rachel, "let's not get into a free-for-all over this. I *am* going back to New York and I *will* be careful. So can we please just mellow out and enjoy each other's company for the next few days?"

Patrick winked at Rachel as we bent over to kiss his wife on the cheek. "That works for me," he said and walked over to the sink.

"Fine," said Rebecca, draining the last of her coffee. "I'll drop the subject but I still think you're both being naïve."

After rinsing the parsley and placing it in the refrigerator, Patrick sat next to Rachel and put an arm around her shoulder. "What say we head out to the gun club and get off a few rounds before lunch. They just installed a new moving target range that's proving to be one hell of a challenge."

Rachel glanced at her mother. "What are you going to do, mom?"

"Don't worry about me. I still have a few things to do upstairs before the horde arrives."

"Maybe I should stay and give you a hand."

"Don't be silly. Go and enjoy yourself."

"Excellent," said Patrick. "I'll get my gun." He paused in the doorway and flashed an impish grin. "And ladies, as we move into an uncertain future, remember the words of that wise old philosopher, Catastrophius: Don't sweat the petty things…and don't pet the sweaty things."

*****

Frank Ryman angrily chewed on a piece of toast as he re-read the news item he'd clipped out of Friday's *Times*, announcing that evening's fashion show at the Tivoli Theater. The idea that the creatures he had transformed merited a benefit was as provocative as a slap in the face. He was especially incensed by the use of the word 'victims'. How could anyone waste sympathy on such women? The real victims were the wives and mothers who were struggling to remain on the one true path.

So be it, he thought, wiping his mouth. If the authorities were intent on throwing down the gauntlet, he was more than happy to pick it up. The question was, how to crash the party? He couldn't just traipse into the theater and expect to go unnoticed. Too many people had seen the police photos and computer composite. Even a disguise was risky because it no longer carried the element of surprise. Besides, the place would undoubtedly be swarming with police. He needed a new angle.

Ryman finished his toast and washed it down with some tea. He then placed his breakfast things in the dishwasher and walked into the living room to work on his jigsaw puzzle. Accountancy had taught him to solve problems by extrapolating to outcomes and weighing the assets and liabilities. What better way to prepare his mind for this task than by working on a puzzle.

The middle section of the image, a reproduction of *Les Tresors de Satan* purchased at the same time as the print hanging on the wall behind him, was almost completed. Ryman picked up a piece but before he could fit it into place, a spasm swept through his body, causing his arms to flop to his sides and his eyes to roll up into their sockets. He felt his mind slipping away.

Frankie, honey. How many times must I remind you? Whenever you're suffering from a creative block you should discuss it with li'l ole Francine. Like the saying goes, two heads are better than one. Besides, a great artist like you shouldn't be wasting his time fretting over petty details. That's what I'm here for. As a matter of fact, I do believe I've already come up with the perfect solution to our little problem. Let's go into the bedroom. I'll explain while I shave my legs.

*****

New York City Chief of Detectives Patrick J. O'Ryan, a stocky redhead dressed in brown slacks and an NYPD windbreaker, strode to center stage and called for attention. The staff of the Tivoli Theater and most of the police personnel were seated in front while those involved with the fashion show itself stood in the wings.

"Right," said O'Ryan, crossing his arms behind his back, "it's four p.m. In three hours the front doors will open and people will start streaming into this theater. We've got exactly that much time to get our act together."

A murmur rippled through the auditorium.

"We've got a situation here for which there's absolutely no margin for error," he continued. "If Sardonicus shows up he'll be wearing a disguise and he'll be trying to get close to one of the models. Cracking his disguise will be the responsibility of the foyer and auditorium details; making sure no unauthorized person gets close to the models will be up to you people backstage. That means each of you needs to memorize the face of every person involved in this operation. If someone you don't recognize approaches the backstage area or the stage itself, take him down.

"Then again, we don't want to scare the bastard off. Police personnel in particular need to keep an extremely low profile. Observe, but don't be too damned obvious about it. And don't speak to each other or move from your posts unless it's absolutely necessary.

"One last thing. The profile we have on Sardonicus indicates he gets a kick out of winning his victims' confidence. But we can't be certain he'll stick to that M.O., especially if he smells trouble. So don't get complacent. Expect the unexpected. Any questions?"

There were none.

"Okay. I'll be upstairs in the command post with Lieutenant Hawthorne and Agent Carmichael. If any of you thinks he's spotted Sardonicus, activate your tracking device and we'll send reinforcements. That's all."

Lionel Jackson stifled a yawn as he rose from his front row seat and headed up the aisle. He and his fellow officers had been in the theater since just before dawn. They'd arrived in staggered groups of four, using unmarked cars. Everyone else arrived at noon.

He entered the lounge and ordered a large coffee. Despite the formidable police presence and the impressive logistics, he couldn't shake the uneasiness that had been dogging him all morning. Whatever the brass thought, he remained convinced that Sardonicus was too smart to fall for such an obvious ploy. And even if he did make a move, it would probably come out of left field.

Meanwhile, a dozen high-priced models and a theater full of dignitaries — including the deputy mayor, a number of famous fashion designers, photographers, magazine editors, and many of New York's most prominent philanthropists — were about to be lined up like ducks in a shooting gallery. Thankfully, the D.A had arranged for the families of the victims to issue a statement requesting that the media be excluded. The last thing anyone needed was a gang of camera-toting reporters cluttering up the place.

"Yo, Sarge." Jackson turned. It was Dan McDougall. "I got the lab results on those *Times* letters."

"And?"

"Negative on the D.N.A. but they found lots of prints. The letters were definitely sent by our boy. The lab says they were printed on an Apple LaserWriter, using twelve point courier type, and that the paper itself is Xerox twenty-pound white bond. A fairly common brand, unfortunately."

"Were you able to track down any more of his correspondence? There's always a chance he might've slipped up and included his return address."

"Nothing yet, but Jimmy's still working on it."

"Good. Give him a buzz and tell him to send copies of the letters we've got and any others he finds to Anton Liebrandt. Maybe the good doctor can find something useful."

McDougall nodded. "So whaddaya think? Is our boy gonna show?"

"Want to know something? Part of me hopes he doesn't."

*****

Down the block, on the opposite side of West 45th Street, the Bristol Club's stout, uniformed doorman smiled appreciatively as he ushered an attractive, leggy, and unescorted blonde into the vestibule.

"Thank you, sugar," she cooed, in a soft Southern accent. "It's encouraging to see that the age of chivalry is still alive on this side of the Mason-Dixon line."

The doorman's grin widened. Bowing slightly, he backed out of the vestibule and pulled the door shut behind him.

Francine paused to examine herself in a mirror. She was dressed in a white tank dress, a black silk blazer, a floral silk scarf, and black pumps. Satisfied with her appearance, she sauntered into the lounge — fully aware of the many male eyes that followed her progress — and took a seat at the bar.

She felt nervous, yet exhilarated. This was the first time she'd been out of doors in years. In the past, Frank had always resisted. But now he needed her. She intended to use that leverage to strengthen her position. In time, she'd destroy what was left of his pathetically weak will and once again assume her rightful place in the world.

"Can I help you?" asked the bartender.

Francine smiled and batted her long lashes. "A cranberry martini, please, with a twist of lemon."

The bartender nodded and walked away. Francine surveyed the room as she pulled a package of Winston's out of her shoulder bag. There were about 30 people in the place, mostly couples. She placed a cigarette in her mouth and reached for her lighter, but before she had a chance to strike it, a lit match appeared in front of her face. Placing the end of her cigarette into the flame, Francine took a puff and smiled at her benefactor, a slim, middle-aged lounge lizard with bluish skin and stiff, graying black hair combed straight back. He was dressed in a blue, double-breasted Armani suit, a cream-colored turtleneck, and black loafers.

"Thank you," she said, huskily.

"My pleasure," he replied, sliding onto the adjacent stool. "My name's Alex."

"Mine's Francine."

"Francine. That's very pretty."

She smiled as the bartender appeared with her drink. She placed her cigarette in the ashtray and reached into her purse.

"Please," said Alex, staying her hand, "let me."

"How gallant. It's nice to know a lady can still depend on the kindness of strangers."

Alex slapped a $10 bill on the counter and picked up his vodka tonic. "Here's to friendship."

They clinked glasses and took a sip of their drinks.

"By the way," he added, "you've got a delightful accent. What part of the south are you from?"

"New Orleans."

"Ah, the Big Easy. I know it well."

"Is that right?"

"Yes, ma'am. I haven't missed a Mardi Gras in the past fifteen years. I've got a drawer full of beads to prove it. Best party on the planet, bar none."

"I wouldn't know. I never got a chance to participate."

"Are you putting me on? You're from New Orleans and you've never taken part in Mardi Gras?"

"My mother, God rest her soul, was very strict. She went out of her way to protect me from harmful influences."

"That's a shame."

Francine shrugged and took another sip of her martini. Sensing that Alex was running his eyes up and down the length of her body, she arched her back and slowly shifted position. "Like what you see, sugar?"

"Forgive me. I didn't mean to stare. It's just that you're such a gorgeous woman and…so statuesque, besides."

"Does that intimidate you?"

"Not at all."

"I'm glad. My height makes a lot of men uncomfortable."

"The way I see it, there's more of you to hold on to."

"Are you being naughty?"

"I just meant—"

"Oh, I *know* what you meant."

Alex moved closer and lightly touched her arm. "Listen, why don't we go to one of the booths. We'll be more comfortable."

Wanting to make him squirm a bit, Francine brought her cigarette to her lips, took a long draw, and let the smoke slowly roll out of her slightly opened mouth. "Why not," she said, turning to him with half-closed eyes.

Alex grinned and waved to the bartender. "Another round," he said, pointing across the aisle, "over there." Then he took hold of Francine's elbow and led her to the booth.

"I don't want to sound corny," he said, once they'd settled in, "but what's a fine-looking woman like you doing all alone in a bar during the middle of the afternoon?"

"I'm going to the theater later this evening so I thought I'd come downtown to do a little window shopping beforehand, then have a light dinner."

"Will you be meeting someone?"

Francine shook her head.

"You mean you're planning to dine and go to the theater alone?"

"Why not? Don't you think a lady can enjoy a meal or appreciate the theater on her own?"

"Of course, but wouldn't it be nicer if you had some company?"

"Perhaps, but on this occasion I find myself alone."

"In that case, why don't you have dinner with me, right here? They've got an excellent kitchen."

"That's very sweet, but I couldn't impose on you like that. We just met."

"Believe me, it's no imposition. I find you very attractive and I'd like to get to know you better."

Feigning indecision, Francine lowered her eyes and fingered the stem of her glass. She made him stew for a full minute before accepting his offer.

"Great," he said with a broad grin. "I'll get the waiter to bring over a bottle of wine and a couple of menus."

*****

After the meal, Alex tried to coax Francine into sharing another bottle of wine. But she insisted on coffee. It was almost time to go and she didn't want alcohol to impair her judgment.

"So," said Alex, snuggling closer, "what time do you have to be at the theater?"

"Seven."

"Is there any way I can talk you out of going...maybe get you to stay here with me instead?"

"It's a tempting offer, sugar, but I had to go through hoops to get a ticket for this particular event."

"You could always exchange it for another performance."

Francine frowned. "Oh, I see. You think I'm going to a play."

"What then?"

"A benefit."

"What kind of benefit?"

"A fashion show in honor of those young models who were killed by that terrible Sardonicus person."

"Oh, yeah. I think I heard something about it on TV. Is there some special reason why you're going? You're not a model, are you? You've certainly got the looks."

Francine swept a lock of hair out of her eyes. "It's kind of you to say so, but no, I'm not. I just want to do my part to help, that's all. Mind you, my mother did a little modeling when I was a child, so perhaps a part of me does feel a special bond with those poor girls."

She took a sip of coffee. "It's so sad. What kind of monster would hurt a poor, defenseless model? They're such delicate, innocuous little creatures."

"The guy's obviously nuts."

"I suppose he must be."

Alex leaned closer. "You're intent on going, then?"

"I'm afraid so. I do hope you won't think ill of me for running off after letting you buy me dinner and all."

"That depends," he replied, tentatively placing his hand on her leg. Meeting no resistance, he gently began to stroke her thigh.

"On what?" asked Francine, rubbing up against his arm.

"On your seeing me again."

She smiled and ran her tongue along her upper lip. "Convince me."

Alex's breathing deepened as his hand slowly made it's way up her thigh. Francine placed her head on his shoulder and watched the carotid artery throbbing in his neck. His hand reached the frilly edge of her silk panties, inducing a low gasp. He lingered a moment, then pressed his fingertips firmly against her crotch.

A look of surprise flitted across his face. He probed with his fingers again, then jerked his hand away like he'd just touched a hot iron.

"What the fuck," he muttered under his breath, his eyes darting from side to side in embarrassed agitation.

"Why you nasty little pervert," said Francine, straightening her dress. "And here I thought you were a gentleman. I guess it was too much to expect from a damned Yankee."

Alex's face reddened and shook and puffed up so much that Francine thought his head was going to explode. Sliding out of the booth with a smirk, she flung her bag over her shoulder and strode toward the exit.

*****

As expected, the nabobs milling in front of the Tivoli Theater and spilling out of a continuous stream of black stretch limos represented the pinnacle of sartorial splendor. Every gown, suit, handbag, and pair of shoes on display shouted homage to the current gods of the fashion pantheon.

Slipping on a pair of white gloves, Francine joined the throng pushing its way through the bank of glass doors flanking the box office. She made a point of smiling sweetly at the two grim-looking police officers standing a few feet away. She noted that two others were stationed on the opposite side. She handed her ticket to an usher and proceeded to the rear of the foyer, where she received a program, as well as directions to her seat, which turned out to be on the left side of the auditorium, about 30 rows from the stage.

She knew she had walked into a trap even before she reached her seat. If the authorities were primarily concerned with securing the building, there would have been dozens of police officers on the scene. But so far, the only ones she'd seen were the four near the front entrance. However, there did seem to be a surplus of ushers and other theater staff. Undercover types, no doubt, with more probably sitting in the audience.

No problem, thought Francine, settling into her seat. She had prepared for such a contingency. For one thing, her purse contained a couple of items that would neutralize the police's numerical advantage. For another, she'd spent the morning doing some research and now knew the Tivoli's layout almost as well as that of her own apartment.

The 1200-seat theater, built in 1905 by Herts and Tallant — who also designed the Lyceum and many other prominent New York stages — was a Baroque, pastel-colored bandbox with more frills than an Italian wedding cake. Auditorium seating was comprised of three sections, partitioned by two aisles on the left and two on the right. There was one balcony, and three private boxes on either side of the stage. There were three other exits in addition to the front doors: one on each side of the auditorium, and one backstage. The dressing rooms were located behind the right side of the stage.

The house lights dimmed and a single spotlight blazed to life, projecting a broad white circle against the deep blue of the velvet curtain. A figure stepped out of the wings, accompanied by a smattering of applause, and strode toward center stage, stopping within the spotlight's beam. It was a woman, a short, ancient hag in a white dress and an absurdly large hat.

"Good evening," she said, sonorously, "and thank you for joining us here in this marvelous old theater as we pay tribute to Sandra Geddes, Carol Linehan, Jasmine Taylor, and Rosa Sandrelli, four very special young women whose lives were cut so tragically short.

"I'm Elaine Potter, editor of *Inside Fashion* magazine" — more applause — "and I have the privilege of being your host. If you'll look in your programs you'll see that the evening's entertainment will consist of two segments; first, a selection of music, poetry, and prose specially chosen for their celebration of the human spirit. Then, following a short intermission, there'll be a fashion show featuring the latest creations from some of New York's hottest designers. I hope you've all brought your checkbooks because afterwards, you'll be given the chance to bid on all of the items shown.

"And remember. Everyone appearing here this evening, and everyone who helped to organize this event, including the management of the Tivoli Theater, has done so voluntarily. All the money generated will be used to create a scholarship fund to help disadvantaged young women further their education. This was the wish of the victims' families."

The crowd roared its approval. "Now," she added, "before we begin with our first performance, I'd like to introduce a few of the wonderful people who helped to make this event possible. "I'll begin with—"

Cut the sanctimonious chatter and get on with it, fumed Francine, squirming in her narrow seat. She shuddered at the thought of sitting through an hour and a half of caterwauling, but had little choice, since her plan couldn't go into effect until after the intermission.

Tucking her program into her purse, she folded her hands on her lap, leaned back, and closed her eyes.

*****

Intermission. Francine stood up, stretched her arms to work out some of the stiffness, and stepped into the aisle. She slowly made her way to the lobby, then turned left and headed for the lounge. After an interminable wait, she ordered a cappuccino and gingerly carried it through the jostling crowd to a secluded corner.

Her nerves were tingling with anticipation. She imagined it was how a boxer felt just before stepping into the ring.

She barely had a chance to savor her cappuccino before the house lights began to flicker, signaling the end of the intermission. She waited for the lounge to empty, then walked over to one of the pay phones located at the end of the room. Setting down her cup, she dropped a quarter into the slot and dialed the number for the Tivoli's box office. It was time for the mayhem to begin.

"Tivoli Theater," chirped a female voice. "How may I help you?"

"Listen carefully, because I am not going to repeat myself. I have planted a bomb in the backstage area and it is scheduled to go off in *exactly* five minutes."

Francine drained the last of her cappuccino and strode across the corridor to the women's washroom. As soon as she had checked all the stalls, she reached into her purse and pulled out a taped bundle of powerful M-80 firecrackers, the kind guaranteed to go off with an impressive bang. The bundle was fitted with a two-minute fuse — providing plenty of time for her to get back to her seat.

She carefully placed the firecrackers on a bed of paper towels at the bottom of the wastebasket and lit the fuse. She then slipped out of the washroom, using her coffee cup to prop the door open slightly — to ensure the sound of the explosion reached the auditorium — and calmly walked back to her seat.

She arrived just as Elaine Potter lurched onto the stage with a stricken expression on her ashen face.

"Ladies and gentlemen, I have just been informed that we've encountered some kind of...problem that requires us to immediately vacate the theater. Please stand and *quickly* make your way to the nearest exit. And I implore you to stay calm. Everything will be just fine if we all proceed in an orderly—"

A loud, muffled roar from the rear of the auditorium, followed by a moment of breathless silence then a crescendo of agitated chatter, culminating with Elaine Potter's piercing shriek as she rushed off the stage. Taking her lead, people began to jump out of their seats and scramble toward the nearest aisle.

Francine, vastly amused by the sight of New York's elite shedding all pretense at dignity in a mad rush to save their skins, stood up and allowed herself to be swept along by the others. Reaching the aisle, she swung around and began to push her way against the oncoming mob, toward the stage.

A few seconds later, the fire alarm went off, turning anxiety into full-blown panic. Waves of rampaging humanity, elbows and knees pumping furiously for every inch of ground, surged toward the exits. Inevitably, this resulted in dozens of severe bottlenecks, which only served to further crank up the fear quotient. People were screaming, stumbling, and falling throughout the auditorium. Those too weak to get back up were trampled.

As Francine broke free of the crowd, she noticed that a number of people had begun to climb onto the stage in search of an alternative escape route. At first, half a dozen security personnel tried to turn them back but they were quickly outnumbered and forced to retreat backstage. By now, she had no trouble picking out the other undercover officers in the auditorium. They were the ones barking out orders in a futile attempt at crowd control. Francine smiled. Events were unfolding just as she had anticipated.

Hiking up her dress, she clambered onto the apron and followed a burly, bald-headed man to the backstage area, where she was gratified to see that it was just as riotous as the auditorium. Performers, models — most of them in various stages of undress — hair stylists, makeup artists, stage hands and, increasingly, members of the audience, were stampeding toward the rear exit.

Francine hid behind a stack of props to reconnoiter. She counted at least eleven undercover officers, each trying to stay close to a particular model while simultaneously scanning the crowd and barking into two-way radios. Meanwhile, more and more people continued to converge on the scene. It was time to set the second part of her plan in motion.

Pretending to be disoriented, she slowly made her way along the rear wall, past the stage manager's booth, to the lighting control console. She slipped on the night vision goggles she'd hidden in her purse and switched off all the lights. The screams that filled the air were enough to make one think the devil had let loose the hounds of hell.

Francine flung her purse over her shoulder and wandered back toward the exit. In the spectral twilight, people were shoving and clawing and climbing over each other. Stragglers stood motionless, arms extended, eyes wide with fear. The undercover officers, no longer able to see their charges, bullied their way through the crowd, screaming out models' names. But their words were lost amid the general cacophony.

Francine spotted her prey, a spiky-haired creature in bra and panties that had stumbled and now sat huddled against a scenery panel, mewling like an abandoned kitten. Francine leaned over and gently placed a hand on her shoulder. The creature cringed and uttered a high-pitched yelp.

"It's all right, honey," cooed Francine. "I'm here to help."

"How? It's pitch black in here!"

"Not to worry. I've got excellent night vision. You just follow me; I know another way out of this place."

"But I'm not supposed to leave my—"

"Listen," whispered Francine, firmly, "word is that someone's planted a bomb back here, so I suggest we save the chit-chat for later, shall we."

"Did you say a b-bomb?"

"That's right," she replied, helping the girl to her feet. She grabbed her hand and led her to a nearby doorway, beyond which lay the stairs leading to the basement.

"Hold on, honey. We're going down some steps."

"Are you sure you know what you're doing?"

"Absolutely. You just put your faith in li'l Francine. You see, child, my sainted mamma spent her life in the service of others, and I *am* my mother's daughter. Now come along."

Chapter 21 — April 17, 1969

Vacherie, Louisiana

Fifteen-year-old Chantal Bonnard put on her denim jacket, picked up her knapsack, and tip-toed out of her second-floor bedroom. She waited until her eyes adjusted to the dark then hurried down the stairs to the vestibule. Her heart was beating so loud she was afraid it would wake her parents — although it seemed highly unlikely, considering the amount of Jack Daniels they'd put away earlier that evening.

Easing open the front door, she stepped onto the veranda and quietly closed the door behind her. A warm wind was blowing, rustling the Spanish moss-laden branches of the cypress tree in the front yard. Chantal drew a ragged breath and hurried down the steps to the sidewalk, pausing only to take one last look at the dilapidated wood frame house in which she'd spent her miserable young life. Curling her hands into fists, she briefly considered burning the place to the ground, along with its occupants. But that would be too good for those two. Better that they wake up in the morning and realize that their beast of burden had escaped their clutches, leaving no one left to abuse except each other.

Instinctively, she touched the fresh bruise on her left cheek. The swelling had gone down but it still stung. Muttering a curse, she crossed the street and started out on the long trek to the highway, where she intended to kiss off Vacherie — which, in French, appropriately meant "a place where cows are kept" — and hitchhike south, along the Mississippi, to a new life in New Orleans.

*****

Chantal's first six months in the Big Easy were anything *but* easy. Rejected by prospective employers because of her youth and lack of skills, harassed by the police, and propositioned by sweaty old men in big cars, she spent her days panhandling in the French Quarter and most of her nights fitfully sleeping in a downtown youth shelter.

She usually managed to scrape together enough cash for at least one decent meal a day; the rest of the time, she stole packages of cheese and luncheon meat from grocery stores or skipped out of restaurants without paying the check.

One day, on a sunny afternoon in late October, she met a handsome 22-year-old named Eddie Talbot, in an arcade on Decatur Street. He had a neatly trimmed goatee and long, glossy brown hair pulled back in a pony tail, and was dressed in a pair of corduroy pants, a paisley shirt, and a buckskin jacket.

Lord, how that boy could talk. In a voice as mellow as Tupelo honey he spoke of love and peace and all the other sweet things that Chantal's lonely heart desired. Calling her his Cajun princess, he flattered and cajoled her for almost two hours, all the while supplying her with an endless stream of quarters for her favorite pinball games. When he invited her to accompany him to Jackson Square, to smoke a joint and check out the work of local sidewalk artists, she quickly agreed.

Afterwards, he took her to a seafood restaurant on Bourbon Street, where he bought her a crab dinner and continued to beguile her with his wit and gentility. It wasn't long before he had her pouring out her soul.

They stayed till midnight, dancing and listening to the blues. They then took a stroll along the river and smoked another joint. Chantal knew the youth shelter would be closed by now, but she didn't care. It wouldn't be the first time she'd slept under the stars.

A few minutes later, almost as if he'd read her thoughts, Eddie invited her back to his place — just to crash, he insisted, sweetening the offer by claiming he had an exceptionally comfortable pull-out sofa.

At first, Chantal hesitated. Life on the streets had taught her that people seldom did favors without expecting something in return. But she was lonely, and Eddie was so cute and had treated her so gently, that she relented. In truth, part of her hoped he *would* try to seduce her. She couldn't remain a virgin forever. Why give it up to some fumbling, pimple-faced boy when she could place herself in the hands of a handsome, experienced man?

Eddie's apartment was housed in an old low-rise brownstone on the eastern fringe of the French Quarter. He attacked her as soon as they were inside. Covering her mouth with his hand, he pulled a knife out of his belt, held it to her throat, and whispered that he'd gut her like a pig if she uttered a sound. Chantal nodded to acknowledge that she understood.

He dragged her into the kitchen and used duct tape to cover her mouth and bind her arms behind her back. Chantal was certain she was going to die. But Eddie had other plans. Tearing off her clothes, he carried her back to the living room, tossed her onto the couch, and raped her, repeatedly.

Afterwards, he bound her legs with another strip of duct tape and carried her into the bedroom. He left her lying in the dark, muttering something about how much money her ass was worth. As she listened to the distant sound of zydeco music filtering in through the closed window, Chantal understood. Surprisingly, she wasn't scared. Rather, she found it humorously ironic that Eddie had turned out to be just like her father. He, too, hid his violent nature behind a sweet smile. The two men differed only in age and occupation. Marcel Bonnard was an unemployed laborer; Eddie Talbot was a pimp.

Eddie returned a few minutes later, carrying a wooden cigar box. He sat down beside her, opened the box, and took out a syringe, a length of rubber tubing, a teaspoon, and a packet of grainy powder. Grabbing the piece of rubber tubing, he wrapped it tightly around her upper arm and tied it off. He then poured some of the powder onto the teaspoon and heated it with a lighter until it liquefied. After sucking the liquid into the syringe, he pushed the plunger just enough to allow a few drops to squirt out of the tip. Grinning, he tapped the syringe twice and injected it into Chantal's arm.

He waited a moment, then untied the rubber tubing. Chantal's eyes widened and her body was wracked by a violent shudder. Clenching her teeth, she curled up in the fetal position and waited for the spasms to subside. The sensation was unlike any she'd ever experienced, and it terrified her. But in the next instant, she was suffused with a feeling of such utter calm and bliss that she was certain she had died and gone to the sweet hereafter.

She glanced up at Eddie. He was watching her intently, like one of those hungry gators she used to stumble upon down near Fiddler's Bayou. He gave her an exaggerated wink, then placed his drug paraphernalia back into the cigar box and left the room. Chantal hugged her knees to her chest and stared at a crack in the ceiling until just before dawn, when sleep finally overtook her.

The rapes and heroin injections continued for the next two weeks, augmented by regular beatings with a wire coat hanger. Through it all Eddie kept repeating the same litany: "You're my property now; if you don't fuck when I tell you to, or try to run away, or try to rip me off, I'll slit your throat and dump you in the swamp. But if you behave and make me lots of money, I'll protect you, buy you nice clothes, put you up in a decent apartment, and give you all the smack your little heart desires."

Chantal had no doubt he would follow through on his threat, so she made the only decision she could under the circumstances. On a bleak and rainy November night, wearing a black tank top, a pair of tight pink shorts, and make-up lent to her by another member of Eddie's stable, she hit the streets. Her mind, which still belonged to a bewildered and frightened little girl, began to burrow inward, toward a place where nothing more could hurt her.

Within three months she was Eddie's biggest money-earner. The reason was simple. As long as she got her heroin fix, she didn't much care what the johns did, short of mutilation — although there was little chance of that because everyone knew Eddie had a penchant for slicing off the thumbs of any man who damaged one of his girls. As a result, Chantal cornered the market on johns who liked their sex rough and kinky.

Her life settled into a pattern that oscillated between periods of emotional numbness and smack-induced euphoria.

*****

The following summer, on an overcast Tuesday morning in early June, Chantal woke up feeling sore and nauseous. The sensations were similar to those brought on by withdrawal, but with less of the attendant pain. Throwing off her sweat-soaked sheets, she hauled herself out of bed and managed to get to the washroom just before her guts erupted.

She threw up again the next morning, and the one after that. Annoyed, and worried that her illness would keep her from earning her quota, she got dressed and walked the two blocks to the local free clinic, which she preferred because the staff was less prone to pester her about her lifestyle than their more officious counterparts at the hospital. She had to wait almost two hours before a doctor could see her, but when one finally did, it took him little time to deliver a diagnosis: she was pregnant.

The news hit her like a punch in the jaw. She had no idea how it had happened — most likely she'd forgotten to take her pill — or who was responsible. One john's face was pretty much the same as any other. Regardless, she knew she'd have to get an abortion. Eddie would insist on it. No doubt he'd also give her a severe beating for being careless. So she decided not to tell him. Instead, she got the name of a reputable abortionist from one of the clinic's counselors, with the intent of undergoing the procedure before anyone was the wiser.

But an odd thing happened on the way back to her apartment; the idea of having a baby, albeit devoid of practical considerations like feeding and changing diapers and providing a suitable home, began to penetrate the crust that had formed around Chantal's heart. Life's possibilities, long dormant, came creeping back into her consciousness.

Intoxicated by these new sensations, and believing there was no harm in waiting a few days longer, she decided to postpone her appointment with the abortionist. She even thought about easing up on the smack, in order to better appreciate the strange and wonderful changes that were taking place inside her body. In her excited state, she forgot that when it came to feeding her drug habit, Eddie did the catering…that heroin was the whip he used to keep her and his other girls in line.

By week's end, Chantal's childlike fascination with motherhood had become an obsession. A reservoir of unexpected strength had bubbled up from somewhere deep inside, producing a sense of determination stronger even than her fear of Eddie. She saw there was only one way she'd be able to have her baby. She would have to run away.

Early that following Sunday, she packed her few meager belongings, took the money she'd earned the previous night, along with a few thousand dollars she had managed to squirrel away without Eddie's knowledge, and took a cab to the bus terminal.

That's when she realized she had nowhere to go. There were no friends or relatives who could take her in and, as far as she was concerned, her parents were dead. She was utterly and irrevocably alone. This realization scared her profoundly. She toyed with the idea of calling the whole thing off. But after taking a couple of deep breaths, she walked up to the nearest wicket and asked for a one-way ticket to the bus company's most southerly destination. It turned out to be a small town named Venice — a good omen, she thought — nestled deep in the verdant swamps of the Mississippi delta.

Chantal managed to find a cheap room in a dilapidated boarding house run by a fat, genial widow named Maisie Hackleberry. She told her new landlady about her condition, but prudently left out the parts about Eddie and her life as a hooker. Maisie didn't bat an eye. She simply asked for the first and last month's rent and escorted Chantal up a creaking spiral staircase to her cramped, sparsely furnished room.

The first few months proved to be a living hell as she struggled to cope with the constant physical and mental anguish of heroin withdrawal. The only reason she was able to persevere was her single-minded obsession with the baby that was slowly growing inside of her. She was determined to provide her child — there was no doubt in her mind it was a girl — with all the love and devotion that she herself had been denied.

Eventually, the pain subsided and Chantal settled into a languid existence marked by long walks, the knitting of baby clothes — a skill she learned from Maisie, who began to take an increasingly maternal interest in her welfare — and plenty of naps. Only one thing kept her from being utterly contented: a shortage of cash. She figured she had enough left to see her through the remainder of her pregnancy, and perhaps a few months beyond. After that, she would need to find a job.

She decided to discuss her problem with Maisie. To her surprise, the old woman provided an unexpected solution. It turned out her maid, a timid 24-year-old named Lureene Watley, was getting married the following spring. And since she and her new husband planned to move to Baton Rouge, Maisie would need someone to take her place. Dumbfounded by her friend's generosity, a trait she'd had little experience with, Chantal allowed herself to hope that the years of pain and disappointment were finally coming to an end.

*****

Chantal went into labor just before noon on January 18, 1971. Still suspicious of the authorities, she told Maisie she didn't want to be taken to the medical center in nearby Buras. Instead, they'd made prior arrangements with a local midwife, a spry, elderly, black fortune teller named Sister Bonalee, who had a gold tooth on each side of her upper jaw, like fangs.

After phoning to say they were on their way, Maisie bundled Chantal into her 15-year-old Chevrolet station wagon and drove her to Sister Bonalee's shack, which was nestled among a clump of mangroves on the outskirts of town. The rickety wooden structure was built on pilings to keep the Mississippi from lapping up onto its brightly painted porch. It was hidden from view by a tangled profusion of honeysuckles, morning glories, and rose-vines.

Inside, the place smelled of incense and cat piss. Its walls were festooned with a mindboggling assortment of weird objects, including chicken bones, feathers, beads, shells, crude crosses fashioned from dry twigs, and pieces of phallus-shaped driftwood. There was also a large cabinet containing dozens of jars and vials filled with different-colored mojo philters.

Chantal was taken to the bedroom, undressed, and eased onto her back. Six hours later, she gave birth to a nine pound, four ounce, blue-eyed boy. Like all babies born to a heroin addict, he was a screamer.

Chantal was bitterly disappointed she didn't get the girl she'd been praying for. She had no place in her heart for a boy child. Boys eventually became men and all men were brutish pigs. The last thing she wanted was to add one more to the population. As she drifted off to sleep, she thought about placing the mewling creature in a garbage bag and dropping it into the river.

The next morning, during the drive back to the boarding house, Maisie noticed Chantal's coolness toward her new son and asked if there was a problem. Chantal shrugged and calmly announced she had no intention of keeping the child. Thunderstruck, Maisie promptly launched into a lengthy sermon about maternal responsibility and the divine miracle of birth, peppered with numerous homilies, some taken from the bible, the rest probably from some paperback or magazine she'd read. She claimed her passion for children was due to her inability to have any of her own, and concluded by offering to be the child's surrogate mother.

Frightened of losing the old woman's patronage, Chantal grudgingly agreed to hang on to the kid — for a while, anyway. Maisie immediately began to pester her about coming up with a name. Chantal claimed it made no difference to her. Maisie suggested Frank, after her late husband. Chantal reckoned it was as good as any.

As they pulled into the driveway, Chantal realized she'd also have to decide on a surname — which wasn't as easy as it sounded. She didn't know who'd knocked her up and had no intention of naming the kid after any of the other men in her life, least of all her own wretch of a father.

Feeling too weak and exhausted to wrestle with the problem just then, she left the baby with Maisie and went up to her room for a nap.

By the time she woke up, eleven hours later, she had a solution. She'd name the kid after one of the regulars she used to screw back in New Orleans, a middle-aged encyclopedia salesman from Natchez. He was one of the few johns who ever treated her kindly. He even slipped her a few extra bucks from time to time. The guy never actually mentioned his last name, but Chantal remembered he used to pull a flask of rye whiskey out of his briefcase every time they got together. As a result, she came to know him as the 'Rye Man'. Her little bastard's surname, then, would be Ryman. Frank Ryman. She had no intention, however, of actually registering the birth. That way, if the baby became too much of a bother, she could dump him, leave Venice, and no one would ever be the wiser.

Chantal's efforts to adapt to a life of placid domesticity didn't last long. With Maisie doing most of the child-rearing, she found herself with a lot of free time on her hands. It was one thing to kick back while pregnant, but now she craved a little stimulation. The situation improved somewhat in the spring, when, as agreed, she took over the maid duties from the departed Lureene Watley. But within a few months, her boredom and restlessness returned tenfold.

She began to drink in her room after she finished her chores. Then she began to sneak off to the local juke joint, a place called the Walker House. Not surprisingly — after all, she had a pretty face and her figure had returned to its original shape — she attracted plenty of horny men. She flirted readily enough, mostly so they'd buy her drinks, but she always left them drooling in their beer.

It was during one such visit that Chantal hooked up with a burly, tattooed specimen of Southern white trash named Bobby Joe Nugent. Unlike the other men she'd met in the bar, he made no attempt to seduce her with sweet talk. He simply took out a roll of hundred dollar bills, slapped a couple on the table, and told her they was hers for a fuck. Noticing the track marks on his arms, she made a counter-offer: a blowjob for a hit of smack, then the fuck. Bobby Joe shoved the money into her hand with a mirthless grin and led her out to his pick-up.

Their relationship continued throughout the summer and into the fall, by which time Chantal was once again a full-blown junkie. Maisie, a God-fearing woman who'd had little experience with the seedier side of life, noticed the change, but attributed it to nothing more serious than man trouble. On a more positive note, she was gratified to see that Chantal was finally beginning to show some interest in her son, who was developing into a happy, inquisitive toddler.

Since birth, little Frank had remained on the ground floor of the rooming house with Maisie, but in early August, Chantal insisted on moving his crib up to her room. Although it hurt Maisie to give the baby up, she knew it would be the best thing for him in the long run.

She had no way of knowing that Chantal's motive for reclaiming her son had nothing to do with a sudden flowering of maternal love. In fact, Chantal loathed the child more than ever. But he *was* hers and, in her drugged state, she'd grown to resent Maisie's interference, especially her sickeningly gleeful nurturing of the child's male instincts. There was another reason, as well: she had experienced an epiphany during one of her highs. Not only did it provide a solution to the problem of the kid's sex, but also promised to satisfy her unrequited need to experience the joys of motherhood.

The plan was perfect in its simplicity. She would transform little Frank into a girl. To that end, she began to lock him up in her room, where she dressed him in female clothing, made him play with dolls, and referred to him as Francine. She even curtailed his visits with Maisie, fearing that too much contact with the meddlesome old cow would make her task more difficult.

Although Maisie was disappointed by this decision, she assumed it was a temporary arrangement, necessitated by Chantal's need to bond with her child.

By late October, her mind ravaged by the effects of heroin and a lifetime of physical and emotional abuse, Chantal's obsession with little Frank's sexuality had become pathological. She began to believe her son *was* a girl.

Maisie suspected that something was wrong. But every time she tried to question Chantal, she was firmly but politely rebuffed. Fearing for the child's well-being, yet leery of being labeled an interfering old biddy, she struggled over whether or not to notify the authorities.

She never got the chance to decide. On October 23, 1971, Maisie Hackleberry suffered a massive stroke while raking leaves in the garden and died on the way to the medical center. Chantal, secretly pleased to be rid of the old woman, pretended to be too sick to attend the funeral.

Then came the reading of the will. To Chantal's bitter disappointment, Maisie didn't leave her or her child one red cent. The boarding house and some $85,000 in savings went to Maisie's sister, a dour, blue-haired spinster from Shreveport, who immediately announced her intention of selling the property to a retired Yankee couple who planned to turn it into a bed and breakfast. Chantal was given two weeks to vacate the premises. At about the same time, Bobby Joe Nugent was arrested for drug trafficking.

Once again, events had conspired to send Chantal Bonnard's life into a tailspin. If anything, her situation was more desperate than ever. Not only was she homeless, almost penniless, and saddled with a money-sucking heroin habit, she also had a ten-month old baby on her hands.

A stream of black thoughts oozed through Chantal's mind as she roamed the streets of Venice looking for work and a place to stay. But her reputation scared off the town's more respectable employers. For the first time in her life, she began to entertain thoughts of suicide. She might have done it, too, if she hadn't remembered the name of a bordello Bobby Joe used to talk about, a place called Chez Simone, located on the Bayou Lafitte side road, just north of Buras.

The next day, she got up early and went to the hairdresser's for a perm, a facial, and a manicure. She then returned to her room, carefully applied make-up to hide her blotchy skin, and put on her sexiest dress and a pair of stilettos. Bundling the baby in an old blanket, she borrowed the station wagon and drove to Chez Simone to present her credentials.

The bordello's proprietor turned out to be a fat, elegantly dressed relic who insisted on being called Madame Simone. Chantal, using the name 'Ryman' in order to remain incognito, aimed her pitch directly at her prospective employer's heart. Punctuating her performance with much sobbing and pleading, she laid all her cards on the table, including her taste for heroin and her baby.

After much hemming and hawing, Madame Simone decided to give her a chance — with a warning that she'd be fired immediately if her drug habit interfered with her work.

She even offered to provide a room for the baby, at least until the child reached school age. At that point, the risk of incurring the wrath of the state's child welfare authorities would necessitate other arrangements. Madame Simone explained that the room in question, which was adjoined to the suite slated to become Chantal's new home and whose entrance was hidden behind a moveable bookcase, had been built to store contraband liquor during prohibition. It was even soundproof, so there was no danger the child's crying would spook the customers. All it needed was a thorough cleaning.

Chantal returned home to pack her belongings. She moved into Chez Simone that very afternoon. Little Frank, whom she introduced as Francine, was an immediate hit, especially with Madame Simone, who coddled the infant in her arms and declared it to be the prettiest little girl she'd ever seen. Chantal giggled with appreciative delight.

*****

By age five, Francine had become Chez Simone's unofficial mascot. Although forbidden to leave the building, she was allowed to visit the kitchen and play in the drawing room for a while after each meal – unless her mother felt too ill to eat, in which case they remained in their room. She spent those happy moments frolicking with the dozen ladies who lived in the sprawling mansion. They all took turns reading to her, teaching her how to write the alphabet, and combing out her fine, pageboy-style blonde hair. But as soon as it was time for the ladies to resume their duties, Madame Simone would shoo her upstairs.

Although Francine was pleased to have so many adult playmates, she often wished she had friends her own age. She also would've liked to spend more time playing with her mommy. But Chantal spent most of her free time laid up in bed.

Francine didn't understand her mother's illness, which, besides getting her into constant trouble with Madame Simone, made her cranky and mean. She needed to take medicine every day, with a needle she kept in her night table. Afterwards, she'd feel better, at least for a while. Francine would take advantage of such moments by jumping onto her mother's bed and snuggling with her until it was time to leave the world of daylight and scuttle into her cramped, windowless prison.

Although these daily banishments continued to perplex her, she'd grown to accept them. Not that she had much choice. She had done everything in her power to convince her mother to let her stay, from throwing temper tantrums to pleading for sympathy, but Chantal's reaction never varied. She'd push aside the bookcase, open the door, point, and say: "If you don't go to your room, mommy will lose her job, and if mommy loses her job, we'll have no money and no place to stay. I'll have to give you to someone else. Is that what you want?" Banishment seemed the lesser evil.

At first, the long hours of loneliness had been unbearable. Francine spent most of her time curled up in bed, crying. But as the months passed, she began to get used to the solitude. Her biggest challenge was figuring out what do with all that free time. Her mommy wouldn't let her have a TV and, although there were plenty of dolls and games and coloring books to play with, she quickly got bored with them.

She began to invent other ways to amuse herself. One of her favorites was pretending her daddy was still alive (mommy claimed he was in a nice place called heaven). Francine enjoyed lying in the dark and having long, heartfelt conversations with him inside her head. He was the one she turned to when she was feeling sad because he never got mad and promised to love her no matter what. Unfortunately, there were no pictures of him so she had no way of knowing what he looked like. But she was sure he was tall and handsome and kind.

When she wanted to be with someone her own age, she played with her imaginary friend, Jack, named after the little boy in *Jack and the Beanstalk*. She felt lucky to have him — even if he was a troublemaker who was always encouraging her to be naughty — because he said he normally didn't hang around with girls. She didn't even mind when he teased her for peeing in bed.

In time, partly because of her mother's indifference and partly because the world in her head seemed more satisfying and less confusing than the one outside her door, Francine began to spend less and less time with her real friends. Some days, she didn't bother to leave her room at all, not even for food; the cook would send her meals up on the dumbwaiter. A place she'd once thought of as a prison began to assume the aspect of a sanctuary.

*****

One afternoon, a few days after her sixth birthday, Francine was sitting in front of the bay window in her mother's bedroom, blankly staring up at a gray, overcast sky. Her gaze had wandered only once during the past hour, to watch the cook's helper, a large, craggy-faced black woman with frizzy gray hair, peeling crawfish under the magnolia tree in the courtyard. Francine would've preferred to stay in her room, but her mother, who seemed especially sick that day, had dragged her out.

Francine knew the only reason her mommy wanted her company was to have someone to listen to her incomprehensible ravings. Since she neither understood nor cared about what was being said, Francine would fix her attention on some distant point and let her mind burrow inward until she was safely ensconced in her secret place.

"Francine!"

She turned to look at her mother, who sat slouched in front of the vanity mirror, applying red lipstick.

"Pay attention when I talk to you," she mumbled, nasally. "I need to start work now, so be a good little mole and crawl back into your hole."

Francine picked up her teddy bear and hurried into her room. She heard the door slam shut behind her, and waited for the sound of the lock being slid into place. But it never came. She began to tremble with nervous excitement. Maybe this was the opportunity she'd been waiting for, a chance to solve the mystery of what happened inside Madame Simone's house during working hours.

She tiptoed back to the door and hesitated, remembering her mother's stern warning about leaving her room without permission. But her natural curiosity, fanned by Jack's taunts inside her head, eventually wore down her resistance.

Switching off the light, she eased open the door and gently pushed the bookcase forward a couple of inches. She held her breath and placed an eye next to the opening. Her mommy was lying on the bed, still dressed in her underwear. She had a funny look on her face. A group of men — Francine couldn't see exactly how many — were taking pictures of her, filling the room with bright flashes, like a lightning storm. She half expected to hear the roar of thunder.

Her mommy laughed and took off her underwear. Spreading her legs, she began to slither around on the bed, facing the men one minute, turning her back to them the next. Francine's eyes widened as she caught a brief glimpse of her mommy's peepee. Maybe it was a trick of the light, or the angle, but it seemed different from her own — which didn't make sense, since Francine knew she and her mommy were both girls. Instinctively, she reached up under her dress and touched herself. Maybe a girl's peepee changed as she got older, she reasoned, turning her attention back to the strange scene taking place on the bed.

Her mommy was holding something that looked like a peeled banana. Wetting its tip with her tongue, she slid the object along her leg and rubbed it against her peepee. Francine found this very odd. The men, meanwhile, continued to take pictures from every conceivable angle.

Ruby, one of the four Negro ladies who lived in the house, stepped into view. She took off her underwear and climbed onto the bed. With the men cheering and shouting encouragement, the two women began to hug and kiss and roll around the bed together. Francine smiled wistfully. She, too, wanted to hug and kiss her mommy, but seldom got the opportunity anymore.

Sighing, she shifted position and leaned her shoulder against the back of the bookcase. Too late she realized her mistake. The bookcase swung out, causing her to lose her balance and collapse to the floor. She heard her mother scream. Then the room became very quiet. Turning, she saw that everyone was staring at her. One of the men grinned and said what a cute little girl.

That's when her mother jumped out of bed, roughly pulled her to her feet, and slapped her so hard she fell to the floor again. Francine let out a loud wail and began to crawl back toward her room. Blocking her way, her mother grabbed her by the hair and raised her hand to strike again. But Ruby stopped her.

By now, the commotion had attracted the attention of Madame Simone and a number of other people. Francine, tears streaming down her face, sat up and wrapped her arms around Ruby's leg. Madame Simone pushed her way through the crowd and lifted Francine into her arms. After apologizing for the ruckus, she politely asked the men who had cameras to follow Ruby to another salon and everyone else to get on with their business.

Placing Francine on the bed, Madame Simone turned to Chantal and scowled. "This is the last straw, missy. If the authorities get wind of the fact that I got me a youngster on these premises, they'll shut me down faster than the snap of a gator's jaw. I want both of you out of her by tomorrow."

"Both of us?"

"You heard me. It's your negligence that caused this mess. Besides, I told you I'd let the child stay here only until she was old enough to go to school. That time has come."

"Fine," said Chantal, wiping her nose. "I'll find someone to take care of the kid. But I need this job, Simone."

"What you need, missy, is medical attention. You're so hopped up most of the time you can barely move your sorry ass. Do you have any idea how many of my clients have complained about you? They say you show as much enthusiasm as an inflatable doll. Why in hell do you think I got you spending most of your time posing for the shutterbug crowd? The only reason I didn't toss you out months ago is 'cause I felt sorry for you. But now I got to think about my business.

"I'll tell you what, though. I got a furnished place a few miles west of here, on Bastian Bay. Used to belong to my brother, God rest his soul. It ain't much and it probably needs a good scrubbing, but you're welcome to stay there, at least until you get yourself together. I also set aside some of your earnings...about five thousand dollars, I reckon. Provided you don't spend it all on smack, it should be more than enough to buy some food and other necessaries."

Madame Simone grasped Chantal's shoulders. "It's time to take stock, missy. Maybe you don't give a damn about your own life, but you got a child here who needs her mamma. Do her and yourself a favor and get some help."

*****

The next day, after buying a week's supply of heroin and a used Volkswagen Beetle, Chantal dragged Francine out of her room and started out for Bastian Bay in the teeth of a bayou storm. The trip, along a bumpy and puddle-strewn dirt road, took just over an hour. She spent the entire time loudly blaming Francine for the loss of her job.

The rain stopped just as they arrived at their new home, a weather-beaten fisherman's shanty located at the end of a road made of dirt and crushed oyster shells, about a quarter mile from the nearest town. A shrimp net, stiff with salt, hung on one wall and dozens of crumbling crab traps were piled against the other. Chantal didn't care. The place had electricity, running water, and a good roof. Best of all, it wouldn't cost her a penny.

Parking the car in the shade of an ancient oak tree, she grabbed the three suitcases that contained the sum of her worldly possessions and hauled them onto the veranda. She had to pick her way carefully because the floor boards were badly rotted. Using the key Madame Simone had given her, she unlocked the front door and stepped into the living room. Francine followed, timidly clutching her teddy bear to her chest.

The house smelled of fish and mildew. Chantal walked over to the nearest window and pried it open as far as it would go. She then went into the kitchen to plug in the refrigerator and turn on the water. It took a full minute for the brown liquid to clarify.

Returning to the living room, she picked up the smallest of the three suitcases, grabbed Francine by the hand, dragged her to the rear of the house, and ushered her into the smaller of the two bedrooms. The ceiling was cracked and the walls were festooned with strips of peeling wallpaper, some curled upwards, some down. She ordered Francine to unpack while she drove into town to pick up some food and other supplies.

All Chantal could think about during the ride was her troublesome daughter. Whatever affection she'd once felt for the kid was long gone. She now thought of her only as a burden. A sullen, ungrateful one at that. She began to wonder if she'd be better off leaving the little brat on the steps of some church.

By the time she returned home, she had calmed down enough to realize there were advantages to keeping Francine around. For one thing, the kid did provide some company, even if she didn't talk much any more. For another, she was old enough to help with the household chores.

Mother and daughter spent the next several mornings sweeping, dusting, and scouring. Chantal kept the afternoons free for getting high. Her routine never varied. She'd lock Francine in her room with a peanut butter sandwich and a glass of milk, do a hit of smack, turn on the radio, and lie down on the living room sofa until evening. Then, if her stomach felt strong enough, she'd get up and prepare some supper. Otherwise, she'd take a couple of valiums and go straight to bed, forcing Francine to go hungry until the next morning.

Once the house had been made moderately livable again, Chantal turned her attention to the problem of money. She decided her best bet was to visit the bars in the area to find out which one offered the likeliest prospects. After a week of searching, she settled on a place called Elmo's Roadhouse. Located on the water's edge, it was popular with the tarpon and shrimp fishermen who plied their trade off the coast of nearby Grand Isle.

Most nights, she took her johns to a nearby motel. But if they balked at the expense, which many of them did, she brought them home. She always locked Francine in her room when she went out, with standing orders to stay quiet if she happened to bring home a 'guest'. She never had to enforce this rule because the kid never made a peep.

Chantal managed to turn five or six tricks a week. She would've taken on more but the area's economy — especially the fishing industry — was going through a flat spell. Meanwhile, her physical and mental condition continued to deteriorate. She began to neglect everything but heroin and her bodily functions. Increasingly, she treated Francine as little more than an afterthought, like part of the furniture. The child got little fresh air or exercise, seldom bathed, and often wore the same clothes for days on end.

*****

A muggy June night, 1979. Moonlight streamed in through Chantal's bedroom window, reflecting off the beads of sweat that ran down Reuben Palmeiro's rigid face as he strained toward his orgasm. He was having a tough time because Chantal was making him do all the work. Which wasn't unusual; the woman was anything but a sexual athlete. Tonight, however, she seemed as lifeless as a department store mannequin. Reuben often swore he'd stop using her services, but he always returned because she was cheap and convenient.

"Come on, muchacha," he whispered hoarsely, raising his head to look at her face, which resembled alabaster in the pale moonlight. "Move you bloody ass."

Chantal remained silent. Her eyes were closed and her head was lolling to one side.

Madre de Dios, thought Reuben, not knowing whether to be insulted or amused, the puta has passed out! As he raised his hand to give her a slap, he noticed a stream of foamy white spittle oozing from the corner of her mouth.

He jumped off the bed and hastily made the sign of the cross. Pressing up against the wall, he stared down at Chantal's prone body. His legs felt rubbery and his heart was pounding in his chest.

Once he'd calmed down a bit, he leaned over and gingerly felt Chantal's wrist. There was no pulse. He made another sign of the cross and got dressed. His first instinct was to get the hell out of there. But he realized it could be days before anyone discovered the body. He'd seen animal carcasses that had been left to the mercy of fly larvae and the Louisiana heat. No human being deserved that kind of indignity.

Reuben ran into the living room, located the telephone, and placed an anonymous call to the sheriff's office. Then he jumped into his car and sped off into the night.

*****

Sheriff Sam Sloan suppressed a yawn as he watched a couple of attendants lift the body into the back of the ambulance. It wasn't often someone died of a heroin overdose in Plaquemines parish, let alone a woman. It seemed such a God-awful waste.

His men had searched the shanty thoroughly but hadn't been able to find a single piece of ID. No birth certificate. No social security. No credit cards. Not even a license, despite the Volkswagen parked out front. That meant his staff would have to devote several valuable man-hours tracking down the deed to the house and canvassing the woman's neighbors.

"Hey, sheriff!"

Sloan turned. One of his deputies was standing in the doorway, holding the hand of a dirty, dull-eyed, emaciated little girl, about eight or nine years old. She was wearing smeared lipstick and had a teddy bear clutched in her other arm.

"Jesus H. Christ," mumbled Sloan, rubbing the back of his neck.

"We found her in the other bedroom," said the deputy, "curled up under the bed."

Sloan took off his hat and slowly approached the youngster, smiling. He expected her to be timid or frightened or both. Instead, she held her ground and looked right through him, like she was staring at something only she could see. Her face showed no sign of emotion.

"Hi, there," said Sloan, crouching so he could look her directly in the eye. "What's your name?"

"Francine," she replied, in a flat monotone.

"Francine. That's very pretty. And your last name?"

"Ryman."

"Tell me, Francine, what—"

"Where's my mommy?"

"She's, uh, not here right now. But, uh—"

"I have to go back to my room. Mommy doesn't like it if I come out when people are here."

"She won't mind this time. I promise."

Francine blinked twice and glanced over her shoulder.

"Tell me something," said Sloan, shifting position. "What's your mommy's name?"

"Chantal."

Sloan stood up and patted her on the head. "Thanks, sweetie. You're a very bright young lady."

He took the deputy aside and in a lowered voice said, "Get her to the hospital and have her examined. There doesn't seem to be much physically wrong with her, other than malnutrition. But I don't know if I can say the same about the state of her mind. If everything checks out, we'll hand her over to children's welfare in the morning. They can take care of her until we locate her next of kin."

Sloan placed his hand on Francine's shoulder. "Now you be a good girl and go along with this nice man. He'll make sure you get a hot bath and something to eat, okay?"

"What about my mommy?"

Chapter 22 — Tuesday, July 8, 1997

Lionel Jackson loosened his tie as he entered the alley that led to the rear of the Tivoli Theater. Although it was just before 10 a.m., waves of heat were already rising off the pavement. It was going to be a scorcher.

He arrived at the stage door and sat down on the stoop. The Crime Scene Unit was long gone but strips of yellow police tape remained stuck to the door and windows. Jackson sighed. Like every other cop on the Sardonicus case, he was still reeling from Saturday night's debacle.

They'd found the murdered girl, a 22-year-old blonde named Denise Mills, on the basement floor, posed like the others, except for one macabre difference. She was wearing a pair of night vision goggles. No one had yet figured out how Sardonicus got into the theater or how he lured the girl — who had been thoroughly briefed beforehand — to her death.

Most galling of all was the killer's subsequent performance on the Molinaro show, where he gloated at length about how he'd outwitted the entire NYPD. The call was eventually traced to an empty phone booth at the Port Authority bus terminal.

Jackson shielded his eyes to watch a pair of noisy pigeons preening themselves on the ledge of an upper window, then lit a cigarette.

As a result of the public outcry that followed the murder — fanned by an increasingly hostile media — the Sardonicus case was no longer an NYPD show. Representatives from half a dozen local, state, and national law enforcement agencies had joined the manhunt. This worried Jackson, who feared that despite the killer's eagerness to be in the spotlight, bringing an army of police into the city would only drive him underground.

Sighing again, he stood up and used his sleeve to wipe away the prickly beads of sweat that were trickling down his collar. Christ, he thought, dusting off the seat of his pants, what the hell am I doing here? He certainly didn't expect to find any new evidence. Maybe he was in the grip of the same impulse that compelled pilgrims to visit a martyr's shrine. Or maybe he just needed a suitable place to lick his wounds.

A loud beep shattered his morbid reverie. He took out his pager and saw that someone at south-central was trying to reach him. Returning to his car, he picked up the radio and called in for a patch to the squad room desk. Ed Lewicki answered, sounding like he had marbles in his mouth.

"Stuffing your face again, Lewicki."

"I'm still a growing boy, Sarge."

"What's up?"

"Doctor Liebrandt just called. He wants to talk to you about those letters you sent him."

"Was he phoning from his office?"

"Yeah."

"Okay, I'll see you later."

Jackson took his cell phone out of the glove compartment and dialed Liebrandt's number.

"Morning, doctor. It's Lionel Jackson. What've you got for me?"

"Unfortunately, the letters don't contain anything that your man hasn't already talked about on the radio. However, I did find his logo interesting. On the surface, the image of a knight shielding a child from a female-headed hydra suggests he wants people to see him as a protector of public morals, specifically the threat posed by what he calls 'unnatural' women. But subconsciously, I believe he sees himself as the child, not the knight, which supports the conclusion that he once suffered trauma at the hands of a woman. In his mind, he's a victim, and the killings are nothing more than symbolic retribution."

"I see your point, but how does that help us catch the bastard?"

"Taken together, these letters and his frequent appearances on the radio suggest he has a pathological need to justify his actions. The fact he took the trouble to design a logo and create this 'guardian' character shows that his efforts in this regard are very organized. I'd say there's an excellent chance he's not only written to the media, but also to modeling and advertising agencies. Perhaps he even signed his name to some of his earlier efforts. Also, since his letters were composed on a computer, he likely sent E-mail, as well."

"Thanks, doc. You've given us something concrete to shoot for. If you come up with anything else, you know where to find me."

Jackson called in for another patch to the squad room. McDougall answered. After briefing him, he ordered a phone canvass of every company in town connected with the modeling profession.

*****

Just before 11:00 a.m., Rachel Curran stepped out of a cab in SoHo, entered her building, and walked up the stairs to her second floor flat. She took out her key, but before she had a chance to place it in the lock, the door burst open and Sally Schuster rushed into the hallway with her arms extended.

"Hey!" she squealed, enfolding Rachel in a vigorous hug. "I missed you, kiddo!"

"I missed you, too, Sal," replied Rachel, stepping back to catch her breath.

"So," said Sally, bringing the suitcase inside, "how was Buffalo?"

"Pretty much the same."

"And your family?"

"Ditto."

"What, no squabbles, intrigues, emotional outbursts?"

"My mom kept pleading with me to stay in Buffalo until Sardonicus is caught, but that was pretty much it. We're not a very demonstrative family. I spent most of the weekend relaxing and catching up with my brothers and a few of my old friends."

"You'll have to visit *my* family, sometime. You'll need earplugs and a wetsuit to protect you from the flying spittle."

"Sounds charming."

Sally cocked an eyebrow. "Uh-huh."

"Anything interesting happen around here while I was gone?" asked Rachel, plopping onto the sofa.

"You mean besides Mister Sardonicus's reign of terror? You must've read about his latest murder."

"Yeah, on the train. You know, I actually thought about going to that benefit. Thank God my folks urged me to come home."

"I can't believe how long it's taking them to catch the creep. I mean, there must've been dozens of cops at the Tivoli that night. What the hell were they doing, chowing down on donuts in the alley?"

"Either that or ogling the models."

"Both, probably. Listen, do you want some tea or something? Or maybe you're hungry. I can make you a sandwich if you like."

"No thanks. I had a big breakfast before I left. But a cup of tea would be great."

Sally strode toward the kitchen. "Oh. I almost forgot. That guy from your acting class called just before you arrived."

"You mean Tom Brennan?"

"That's the one."

"What did he want?"

"Oh, I think we both know what he wants. What he *said* was that he just bought a car and wants to give you a lift to class this evening."

"Really? But he lives in Queens. It would take him forty minutes just to get here and then another forty to get uptown."

"I guess he's concerned about you."

"But I can't ask him to go out of his way like that."

"Why not? With that maniac on the loose, I think it's a great idea. Besides, you shouldn't shrug such a gesture off so easily. It's obvious this man wants to take care of you."

"It doesn't seem right."

"Lord almighty, girl. I know how much you value your independence, but sometimes you take it too far. He sounds like a really nice guy."

"He is, but that's not the point."

"Here we go again. Look, kiddo, it's obvious that Tommy boy has the hots for you. What don't you at least give him a fighting chance? You do like him, don't you?"

"I just had this bloody conversation with my mother. Why is everyone so preoccupied with my love life? Okay, this is going to be my last word on the subject. Yes, I do like Tom but I'm not ready for a relationship at this particular time."

"I understand that, but why deprive yourself of some good lovin' just because you're afraid of making a commitment?"

"I'm not afraid. It's a question of timing."

"Timing, schmiming. Buy some condoms and you go ride that cowboy. At the very least you'll get rid of some tension."

Rachel chuckled, despite herself. "To tell you the truth, the thought has crossed my mind."

"You're only human."

"And he *is* cute."

"Even better."

Rachel chuckled again. "Sexual attraction sure is a strange and mysterious thing, isn't it?"

"And pow-er-ful."

"I read an interesting article about it in *New Age* magazine not too long ago. There's an ancient Greek myth that suggests the first human beings were perfectly round with four arms, four legs, and one head that had two faces looking in opposite directions. They were so smart, elegant, and resourceful that the gods became jealous and cut them in half so they'd be less powerful. Ever since, the two halves have been striving to reunite. And when they finally do meet, they're so enchanted they never leave each other's sight."

"That's cute."

"Then there's the *Yin* and *Yang* concept found in some Eastern religions. *Yang* means 'banners waving in the sun' and is related to heaven, sky, brightness, and creativity. It's seen as a masculine principle. But by itself, the sun would eventually scorch the earth, so Yin, the feminine principle, is necessary to create balance. *Yin* means 'cloudy or overcast' and is related to the earth, darkness, and receptivity. The idea is that *Yin* and *Yang* are spiritual poles along which all life flows and that we each carry an image of the opposite to which we're attracted."

"I like the Greek story better."

"Me, too."

"Well, I guess I'd better let you get settled in. I'll go put on the kettle."

Rachel picked up her suitcase and carried it to the bedroom, which she'd organized according to the principles of *Feng Shui*, the Oriental art of managing the flow of energy, or *Chi*, to create a more harmonious atmosphere. Bubble-gum pink paint, full spectrum lighting, a vase of fresh flowers near her reading chair, wind chimes outside the window, lavender, eucalyptus and mint potpourri, a butterfly mobile, and a pair of rectangular landscape paintings facing each other across the room.

The gown she'd purchased for the Miss Empire State pageant stood in the corner, draped over a tailor's dummy she found at a Greenwich Village yard sale. She could scarcely believe there were only five days left before the start of the competition.

Usually, the days leading up to a pageant were nerve-wracking. But this time, she was grateful for the diversion. It would help keep her mind off the killings. And allow her to put her modeling career on the back burner for the next two weeks. Hopefully, by then, Sardonicus would either be dead or rotting in some prison cell.

Chapter 23 — Thursday, July 10

Lionel Jackson sat in the squad room, glumly nursing his fourth cup of coffee that morning. Like every other member of the special unit, he was anxiously waiting for a phone to ring with the news that someone had found the body of Sardonicus's Wednesday night victim.

Needing a distraction, especially one with a positive spin, he took a manila folder out of a drawer and spread it open on the desk. It contained a statement by a woman named Tanya Holt, obtained by Ed Lewicki the previous afternoon. She claimed that one week before Sardonicus's first killing she met a charming, well-dressed man named Frank whose face resembled the computer composite she'd seen on TV. His height, physique, and hair color also matched.

To that point, her statement seemed no different than scores of others taken during the course of the investigation. The hot line had received dozens of calls from people claiming to know a tall, blond man named Frank. None had panned out. Neither had any of the individuals spewed out by the CATCH computer nor those interviewed during the various canvasses, including the massive one that was still working its way through the Upper East Side.

It was only when Tanya Holt described the man's behavior as "weird and threatening" that Lewicki had alerted Jackson. By the time they finished questioning her, they were certain they had their first legitimate witness. She not only helped to flesh out the suspect's physical profile, including the vital fact that his eyes were blue, but also provided them with information that opened up a new avenue of investigation. She said he had claimed to be from New Orleans — although he didn't have an accent — and that he'd been living in New York for about five years. Also, that his voice was softer and less distinctive than the one he used on the radio.

Besides being a master of disguise, it appeared Sardonicus was also skilled at mimicking voices.

Immediately following the interview, Jackson had sent a revised description and computer composite to the media and to the other precinct commands. He also sent a copy of the Sardonicus file to the New Orleans Police Department, with instructions to check the killer's description and M.O. against all violent offenders known to have been in their jurisdiction prior to 1992, along with a request for the names of psychiatric patients released from area institutions between 1990 and 1992.

It was a long shot, but one he couldn't afford to overlook. Especially since his only other solid lead — the search for Sardonicus's 'Guardian' correspondence — was not panning out. Dan McDougall had discovered additional letters, but none bore the killer's signature or return address. He'd also tracked down a couple of modeling and advertising agencies that received E-mail, but none kept hard copies, so there was no way of knowing if Sardonicus had identified himself.

Just then, Hawthorne's office door swung open. Everyone turned to watch as the lieutenant strode into the room, his face set in a grim scowl.

"They found her," he said, placing his hands on his hips.

"Where?" asked Jackson.

"The East River, near Carl Shurz Park. Within spitting distance of Gracie Mansion, for chrissakes."

"That doesn't sound like our guy."

"Not *in* the river, *on* it. The son-of-a-bitch made a raft out of some old tires and lashed her to the goddamn thing. He even put her clothes in a zip-lock bag so they wouldn't get wet. Can you fucking believe that?"

Jackson's shoulders sagged. It was hard enough to fathom why any model would choose to remain in New York, let alone go off with a stranger. How could anyone be that stupid? Unless...was it possible Sardonicus had changed his M.O.? Given all the psychological evidence, it seemed unlikely. So what was he saying or doing to these women to win their trust? In 12 years as a cop, it was the most baffling and infuriating dilemma he'd ever faced.

He stood up and walked over to the map of Manhattan hanging on the far wall. Stuck to it were five yellow pins, each representing one of Sardonicus's murder sites. Below the map was a corkboard with photos of the victims, along with details about each crime. Jackson picked up a yellow pin and angrily stuck it onto the small green patch representing Carl Shurz Park. He hoped to God it would be the last.

*****

A few miles uptown, Frank Ryman paced in his living room, trying to reconstruct the events of the previous evening. He usually recalled his exploits in vivid detail, but the memories of his Tivoli Theater and East River forays were vague and murky, and had a strange, dream-like quality that left him feeling like he'd been both participant *and* observer. It was disconcerting.

Equally disturbing was the fact that neither venture had produced the kind of euphoria he'd experienced in the past. If anything, both had left him feeling decidedly ungratified. He'd been up most of the night wracking his brain and had finally figured out what was wrong. The work had become routine. His growth as an artist demanded a wider canvass. One large enough to make the entire world sit up and take notice. Only then would he be assured of his rightful place in history.

Ryman went to the window and looked out over the roofs of Manhattan. He had the city in the palm of his hand. Every man, woman, and child anxiously waited for him to create his next masterpiece. What other artist could claim such rapturous attention from his public? Loyalty of that caliber deserved to be rewarded with something spectacular; a work of art to rival the Sistine Chapel in its scope and profundity.

Such a project would require his complete attention. There was no point, therefore, in dissipating his creative juices on another routine piece. Instead, he would devote all his time to the formulation of a suitably grand design. Regrettably, his public would have to wait a little longer than usual for the unveiling. But they would not be disappointed.

Ryman smiled. There was also a mischievous side to his plan. His temporary sabbatical would cause a great deal of confusion and hand-wringing in the enemy camp. Perhaps even lull the authorities into a false sense of security. This gave him another idea. After a final statement to his public, he would make no more appearances on Robert Molinaro's radio show. Everyone would think he had fallen off the edge of the world.

He looked at his watch. Noon, time for the news. Settling into his easy chair, he picked up the converter and turned on the TV. As expected, the lead story dealt with the discovery of his East River piece. He was surprised to learn they found the raft near Carl Schurz Park. He thought the current would've carried it farther south. Unfortunately, they didn't show any film clips. But he did learn the creature he had transformed was named Carmen Perez. Ryman raised an eyebrow when the reporter said she was 24 years old. She had seemed much younger.

Suddenly, a new, more detailed computer composite of his face flashed onto the screen. It stayed there a moment, then shrank to a quarter of its original size and anchored itself to the top right corner. Behind it, the scene shifted back to Carl Schurz Park. A bald black man in a blue suit, whom Ryman recognized as Sergeant Lionel Jackson, one of the detectives in charge of the investigation, was standing near the river's edge, holding a microphone.

Ryman listened attentively until Jackson finished speaking, then switched the TV off and slumped back in his chair. Somehow, the police had discovered the color of his eyes. And the composite was more accurate than any of their previous efforts. Where could they have gotten this new information? Did they have a witness? More importantly, considering he hadn't watched much TV during the past few days, how long had they been airing it?

Beads of sweat began to form on his brow. Not that he was afraid of getting caught; his own life was unimportant. Only the cause mattered, and there was still much work to be done. Clasping his hands together, he took a deep breath and began to rhythmically rock back and forth in the easy chair, pondering his next move.

A spasm wracked his body. His eyeballs rolled up into their sockets. Slowly, his anxiety gave way to soothing tranquility.

Frankie, honey. I was afraid something like this would happen. I suppose I should have spoken up sooner, but I always have trouble getting through when your confidence is high. Well, like mamma used to say, no use crying over spilt bourbon.

The gig's up, sugar. Everyone knows your first name, what you look like, and the area where you live. It's just a matter of time before a neighbor or one of those imbeciles you used to work with puts two and two together and starts salivating over that reward the authorities are offering. Let's face it, chile. Most people would sell out their own mammies for the right sum, let alone a quirky and reclusive artiste like yourself. It's time we took our little show on the road.

****

Dusk in Manhattan, the shadows lengthening and lights blinking on like the awakening eyes of a myriad nocturnal beasts. Robert Molinaro turned away from his office window and picked up the workbook he'd been given at that morning's Miss Empire State judging seminar. It contained a summary of the scoring criteria, as well as a photo and résumé of each contestant.

The final phase of training, a trial run during which he and his fellow judges would score a mock pageant, was scheduled for Saturday night. Then it was on to the real thing. And not a moment too soon. With his ratings going through the roof, the last thing he needed was to be taken off the air for a week.

As if that wasn't aggravating enough, the show was also coming under increased scrutiny from the mayor's office. After the way the cops had botched the Tivoli Theater benefit, hizzoner was scrambling to deflect some of the heat. He'd made WSNY a prime scapegoat, claiming the station was guilty of "immorality" for allowing Sardonicus on the air. He wanted it stopped.

Fortunately, both the police department and the district attorney's office were against the idea, claiming it was important to keep Sardonicus talking.

There was a knock on the door.

"It's open," shouted Molinaro, swiveling around in his chair.

Sid Crouse entered, grinning like the Cheshire cat.

"Bob," he said, ushering a pair of beautiful women into the room, "this is Rachel Curran and Deborah Wong. They're the two pageant contestants who so kindly agreed to appear on the show this evening."

"Welcome, ladies," said Molinaro, leaping up to shake their hands. "I'm delighted you could join us."

Both women smiled and nodded, but Molinaro's gaze stayed focused on Rachel, whose twinkling eyes would undoubtedly melt a block of ice.

"I appreciate your reversing the sequence of the program in order to have us on first," said Deborah. "My parents' train gets in at ten-thirty and I wanted to make sure I had plenty of time to get to the station. They're old world people, and they're more than a little intimidated by New York."

"Happy to oblige," replied Molinaro, placing an arm around Sid's shoulder. "So, did Sid explain the format and go over all the technical stuff?"

More smiles and nods.

"All right, then. Unless you have any questions, we're ready to mamba. Sid'll take you to the broadcast booth and help you set up, and I'll be with you in a flash. Oh, just so you know. There's a police team in the control room. They've been here for the last couple of weeks, trying to trace the calls of that Sardonicus whacko, so don't be distracted if you notice any unusual activity."

Sid left with the women, pulling the door closed behind him. Molinaro sat down and slung his feet onto the desk. What a couple of babes, he thought, clasping his hands behind his head. The photos in the workbook didn't do either of them justice. Especially Rachel. Man, what a knockout, with those soft brown eyes and that adorable overbite — a trait that had turned him on since his first glimpse of Gene Tierney, in the film *Laura*. At the time, he thought she was the most beautiful woman he'd ever seen. Rachel Curran could've been her twin.

It had been a while since any woman had given him such a rush. The fact she was a contestant in a pageant only helped to fuel his passion, since he'd often fantasized about banging a beauty queen. Now, thanks to a weird and wonderful confluence of events, he was in an excellent position to make it happen.

Molinaro lowered his hand and glanced at his wedding ring. Hopefully, Rachel hadn't noticed. He tossed the ring into a drawer, stood up, checked his hair in the mirror, and left the office.

Striding into the broadcast booth, he nodded at Deborah Wong and offered Rachel Curran his most charming smile. She smiled back, briefly, politely, then turned away. Deflated somewhat, Molinaro took his seat and glanced at Sergeant Jackson in the control room. He was grimly pacing back and forth like a caged tiger. Every cop in New York wanted a piece of Sardonicus, but Jackson, who'd been showing up at the station after each murder, seemed obsessed with the case.

No skin off my nose, thought Molinaro, putting on his headphones. He poured himself a glass of Perrier and leaned back to wait for Sid's cue.

*****

"I think beauty pageants are an abomination," said Eileen, from Hoboken. "It's difficult enough for women to be taken seriously without a bunch of airheads prancing around in bathing suits."

"Well, ladies," said Molinaro, turning to his guests. "Which one of you wants to field that hot potato?"

"I will," said Rachel, leaning into the mike. "First of all, I resent being called an airhead. Deborah and I both have university degrees. I'm a classical pianist and she's a professional dancer. As for our prancing around in bathing suits, it's obvious you haven't seen a major pageant lately.

"Nowadays, the swimsuit competition is worth only fifteen percent of the final score. The private interview and talent competitions combined are worth *seventy* percent. Besides, it's not like we wear bikinis and do a lot of jiggling on stage. The swimsuit segment is about physical fitness...things like muscular development and tone, and whether you have the appropriate weight for your bone structure and height. It's also about grace, poise, posture, and self-confidence under pressure."

"Oh, please! Pageants are nothing more than demeaning flesh bazaars that objectify women. They should all be abolished."

"Most people don't agree with you. Pageants exist because the public enjoys watching them, and because a lot of young women appreciate the opportunities they provide."

"Really? Then why have so many countries dropped their national pageants? And what about the riots that broke out at this year's Miss World competition in India?"

"I'm afraid I have to interject," said Molinaro. "First of all, you can't expect my guests to answer for political decisions made in other jurisdictions. Secondly, beauty pageants are a western phenomenon. The Miss World organizers should've known better than to hold their pageant in a country where they were bound to offend cultural and religious sensibilities."

"I *would* like to say one thing," added Rachel, "especially since it was overlooked by the media in their frenzy to stir up controversy. The organizers of the Miss World pageant donated ten percent of their profits — close to one and a quarter million dollars, I think it was — to an Indian charity. If you're going to criticize pageants, you should at least recognize their positive contributions."

"Nonsense. There are better ways—"

"Sorry," said Molinaro, pressing the 'kill' button. "We have to move on to the next caller." Sid fed him another name. "Here's Denise, from Harlem."

"I agree with that lady who just got off the air. I think beauty pageants send the wrong message, especially to our kids. It tells them that looks are the only thing that matters. The worst are the ones that exploit children. I read somewhere that each year, more than one hundred thousand kids under the age of twelve compete in pageants. I mean, we're talking about babies, for God's sake, dolled up in lipstick, false eyelashes, mascara, and bleached hair, and forced to sashay down runways in feather boas, sequined gowns, and swimsuits.

"Did you see those photos of that little Jonbenet Ramsey girl? The poor child was only six years old and her parents had her competing in pageants dressed like a streetwalker. She was like the poster child for every pervert in the country."

"I agree there should be some kind of control over the way children's pageants are run," said Rachel, "because with kids, all the decisions are made by the parents and some parents can be obsessive about winning. I especially dislike the idea of dressing children up as adults."

"But you still think it's okay for kids to compete in these things?"

"Sure, if they're run properly. There's nothing particularly harmful about entering a child in a pageant, just as long as parents make sure the experience doesn't consume the kid's life."

"I'm sorry, but I think you're *dead* wrong."

"Thanks for your call," said Molinaro. "Here's Ron, from Brooklyn Heights."

"Hi, Bob, ladies. I, uh, just want to say that I enjoy watching beauty pageants, for obvious reasons. But I hear they can be pretty cutthroat, with lots of backstage politics and whatnot. Is that true?"

Molinaro looked at Deborah Wong. "Why don't you take this one, Deborah."

"Sure. I guess I've been in about a dozen pageants so far and I'll admit that I've run into a few contestants who've been aggressive or had their noses stuck up in the air. And every now and then an official will hit on you. But overall, I can honestly say that most of the people I've met have been friendly and supportive."

"The other girl mentioned that you're both university grads and accomplished performers," said Ron. "If that's the case, why do you still compete in beauty pageants?"

Deborah smiled. "For the prize money, of course. And for the exposure. Many contestants are aspiring performers. And since state and national pageants are usually televised, there's always the chance that an agent or producer will notice you."

"How are the prizes distributed? Does it work like some sporting events, where you don't get any money unless you finish in the top ten?"

"Something like that," replied Deborah, flipping open a booklet she had on her lap, "except that pageants spread it around more. Let's see. This year, the winner of the Miss Empire State crown gets thirty-five thousand dollars. The first runner-up gets twenty thousand, the second gets fourteen thousand, the third gets eleven thousand, and the fourth gets eight thousand. All the remaining contestants get six thousand dollars each. In addition, the winners of the talent, swimsuit, private interview, and evening gown segments get fifteen hundred dollars. There are also a number of prizes and scholarships offered by some of the corporate sponsors."

"Thanks for your call," said Molinaro. "Here's—" but Sid failed to feed him another name. Scowling, he spun around to glare at the producer.

"It's Frank," said Sid. "He wants to make a statement. Now."

Molinaro glanced at Jackson and waited for the signal. Then he took a deep breath and leaned into the mike.

"Hello, Frank. What's on your mind?"

"You already know how I feel about the public display of female flesh, Robert, so there is no point in repeating myself. Instead, I would like to address my comments to the police, those overworked, underpaid, misguided public servants who are attempting to disrupt my work. Specifically, the one named Lionel Jackson."

Molinaro glanced at the detective. His arms were crossed and his face was fixed in a rigid scowl.

"I saw you on television this afternoon, Sergeant," continued Frank, "and was gratified to discover that you are black. It is not often that Negroes are given positions of authority in this country. After all, along with the disintegration of the family, racism is one of our major problems.

"Since you decided to disrupt *my* life, Sergeant, I did a little research into yours. It turns out you were involved in an incident in the Bronx some years ago. Eight people died, I believe. A terrible tragedy — not your fault, of course. I am sure you did what you could. Still, such things do not reflect well on a police officer, do they? Especially a black police officer who is being watched, and judged, by so many people on both sides of the color line. I imagine you must be desperate for redemption, and for a chance to prove your worth...at my expense. But alas, dear sir, once a failure, always a failure.

"Do yourself a favor, Sergeant. Stop meddling in my affairs and go seek your salvation elsewhere. The priesthood, perhaps."

*****

Rachel Curran, still shaken by Sardonicus's chilling words, removed her headphones, stood up, and followed Robert Molinaro and Deborah Wong out of the broadcast booth. Her hands were trembling and she needed to pee, badly.

"Excuse me, Mister Molinaro, can you tell me where the washroom is?"

"Sure, just follow me. I'm heading that way myself. And please, call me Bob."

Deborah stepped forward and gave Rachel a quick hug. "I've got to be going, Rachel. My boyfriend's picking me up out front to take me to the train station."

"It was great meeting you, Deborah. I guess I'll see you on Sunday."

"You bet." She shook Molinaro's hand and left.

"God," said Rachel, as she followed Molinaro along the corridor, "that was the creepiest experience I've ever had. How in God's name can you stand talking to that monster?"

"It's my job. Besides, each time he calls it gives the police another chance to nab him. Though I admit it is a long shot. He always manages to get off the line just as the trace is made."

"I thought Detective Jackson was going to have a heart attack when his name was mentioned on the air."

"Yeah, well. The good sergeant is one intense dude. And between you and me, I think those comments hit pretty close to home."

"Really?"

"Oh, yeah." Molinaro stopped and turned to face her. "By the way, you handled yourself very well in there. Your answers were clear and concise, and you never got rattled. A pro couldn't have done better."

"Thanks."

"Maybe we can have you back sometime," he added, "after you win the title, perhaps."

Rachel cocked an eyebrow. "I appreciate the compliment, but I don't think it's appropriate, coming from one of the judges."

"In that case, let's just pretend it never happened."

They walked a few more yards, then Molinaro stopped again. "Here we are," he said, pointing to a nearby door. "I'll wait for you."

"You don't have to do that."

"I insist."

"Suit yourself."

As she turned away, Molinaro gently but firmly grabbed her by the shoulders. "Listen, I know you've probably heard every line in the book, so I hope you'll believe me when I say that you're magnificent. Bright. Beautiful. Eloquent. The complete package. I would consider it an honor if you would have a drink with me."

"Are you serious?" she replied, wriggling out of his grasp. "You know I can't do that. If somebody saw us together it would mean my disqualification. Not to mention a major scandal for you and your station."

"Believe me, I know places that are *very* discreet."

"That's not the point. It's unethical."

"Why? It's not like I'm trying to sell you my vote — though I *am* open to the possibility — just kidding! Seriously, all I'm interested in is a drink and a chance to get to know you better. What harm is there in that?"

"I can't believe we're even having this conversation."

"Come on, it'll be fun. I promise."

"I'm sorry," she said, pushing open the washroom door, "but no. And please don't bother waiting for me. I can find my own way out."

With her emotions in turmoil, Rachel stormed into the washroom and entered the nearest cubicle. She had a similar crisis every time a man came onto her in a work-related environment. She could never tell whether his interest was genuine or, like the slew of agents, photographers, and other so-called professionals she had turned down over the years, whether he just wanted sex in exchange for a promise to grease the wheels of her career.

Despite Molinaro's glib charm, or maybe because of it, she was almost certain he had just made a proposition, albeit one carefully couched in ambiguous language. What disturbed her most was the realization that she was tempted by his offer — if only for a moment. The question was, why? She'd never played that game before.

The answer appeared a moment later, in the hazy reflection staring back at her from the door of the cubicle: her face and body, which, her talents not withstanding, represented key components of her livelihood. And both were under attack by an enemy that always won in the end: time. Soon it would destroy her career as a model, render her ineligible for most pageants, and perhaps even jeopardize her chances for an acting career.

Which is where Robert Molinaro entered the picture, because he wielded more real influence than any man who'd ever sought her favors. As one of the five judges in the *Miss Empire State* pageant, he was in a position to boost her chances by a considerable degree. And Rachel understood, with stark clarity, that winning the title was as close to a guarantee of future success as was ever likely to come her way.

Slumping forward, she cradled her face in her hands and slowly shook her head. Why was doing the right thing always so damned difficult?

Chapter 24 — Friday, July 11

In the squad room, Lionel Jackson was on the phone with Lieutenant Hawthorne when Dan McDougall leaned into view and flagged his attention. Jackson scowled and motioned for him to take a seat.

"But it's sheer insanity!" he snapped into the receiver. "Every design house and clothing store in town has cancelled its fashion shows, nobody's shooting an ad within fifty miles of the place, and these idiots want to put on a fucking beauty pageant! We might as well take out a full-page ad telling Sardonicus to come in and help himself!"

"I know the timing is rotten," replied Hawthorne, "but it's a private event and the organizers have a ton of money tied up in venues, hotel rooms, TV rights, and all kinds of other crap. There's no way we can force them to cancel. Besides, it's a pageant, not a fashion show."

"Come on, lieutenant. Sardonicus isn't a fool. A number of the contestants are models or wannabes. With the level of fear out there on the streets, where else in this city is he going to so find so many potential targets? If those idiots downtown had half a brain they'd understand that, and send every one of those women packing. But it's the same old story. Money talks, bullshit walks."

"Take it easy, Lionel. I know you're still steamed about being baited by that maniac last night, but I need you to stay focused. I can't afford to have one of my top guys involved in a personal vendetta. If you can't keep your perspective I'll have you replaced. Do I make myself clear?"

Jackson crushed out his cigarette and leaned back in his chair. "Crystal."

"Right, then. I know the situation is far from ideal, but we're going to have to make the best of it. The pageant organizers already have a pretty good security set-up, including video surveillance, and they're going to be hiring extra staff. All the contestants and their chaperones will be staying in a block of rooms at the Plaza, on the same floor, and they'll be shunted back and forth from there to Radio City by bus. Police and security personnel will be with them every time they're on the move. We'll also provide perimeter security at the hotel and at Radio City, and whatever other backup we think is necessary."

"Yeah, well," said Jackson, "we also thought we had excellent security at the Tivoli."

"This'll be better. For one thing, they'll have guards posted outside each hotel room and at every door in Radio City, including washrooms and closets, and monitoring the theater's circuit boxes. No one will be allowed within ten yards of any contestant without first being thoroughly screened. Don't forget, even when Sardonicus had the opportunity to hurt a lot of people at the Tivoli, he stuck to his M.O. Assuming he'll even *try* to infiltrate the pageant, there's no reason to think that'll change."

"Unless there's no other way for him to stick to his timetable."

"Whaddaya mean?"

"Up to now, he's had no problem finding a victim. What happens if he can't this time?"

"I understand what you're saying, but I just don't see this guy suddenly turning into an assassin. I'm still convinced there's no satisfaction in it for him unless the victim comes to him willingly."

"Yeah, well, I think we might be putting a little too much faith in this profiling business. The only certainty is that Sardonicus will kill again. Everything else is speculation."

"You might want to stress that point when you meet with the pageant organizers on Sunday."

"Say what?"

"Chief O'Ryan wants us to make sure that all their people, including the contestants, are up to speed on Sardonicus's methods. And since you've been on the case since day one, I've elected you to conduct the briefing."

"When?" asked Jackson, picking up a pen.

"You're to meet their head of security, a guy named Lorne Dickson, at four p.m. at the Plaza's registration desk. He'll be wearing an ID badge."

"Where will the briefing take place?"

"At an orientation meeting they're holding for the contestants."

"Okay," said Jackson, jotting the information on a notepad. "Anything else?"

"Nope. I'll see you when I see you."

Jackson turned to Dan McDougall, who'd gotten up for a cup of coffee and was just now sliding back into his chair.

"What's up, Dan?"

McDougall took two sheets of paper out of a folder he'd left on the desk and handed them to Jackson.

"What's this?"

"Hard copies of Sardonicus's E-mail."

"Do they include a name or return address?"

McDougall shook his head. "The son-of-a-bitch knew what he was doing. He even erased his user ID code." A wry grin spread across his face. "But it may not matter."

"How's that?"

"I called up the FBI's document section. They said they can trace E-mail back to the originating computer as long as the service provider knows the date and the exact time the submission was sent. Lucky for us, the ad agency that gave me this letter keeps a log of every submission it receives."

"Goddamn!" said Jackson, slapping his hand on the desk. "We've finally got the bastard!"

"Yeah, but it's gonna take a while."

"How long?"

"Hard to say, exactly. But the section chief promised to make it a top priority."

Jackson took a deep breath and ran a hand across his scalp. He then stood up and patted McDougall's shoulder. "You did good, Dan. Real good."

"Thanks," he replied, placing the letters back in the folder. He averted his eyes and began to fidget with the top button of his sports jacket. "Listen, Sarge. About those things I said at the start of this case…it wasn't personal. I hope you know that. I had some issues."

"Shit, man, forget about it. I have."

*****

Rachel Curran sat at her kitchen table, basking in the warmth of the afternoon sun and sipping on a glass of freshly made carrot juice, sweetened with two slices of apple. Picking up the envelope she had just received, she slit open the flap and shook the contents onto the table. It was a copy of the pageant schedule. Rachel swung her legs onto the adjacent chair and leaned back to examine the document.

1997 Miss Empire State Pageant Schedule

Sunday, July 13
1:00-3:00   Plaza Hotel registration and check-in
4:00-5:30   Orientation
6:00-7:30   Dinner/cruise of New York Harbor
8:00-10:00   All contestants, production number rehearsals
Monday, July 14
8:30   Breakfast at Rockefeller Center
9:30-1:00   Rockefeller Center publicity photos/lunch
2:30-4:00   All contestants, interview rehearsals
5:45   Dinner at Chinese restaurant
8:00-10:00   Sponsors' reception

Tuesday, July 15
9:30-12:00   Breakfast at Trump Tower Atrium/autographs/photos
12:00   Lunch in Plaza banquet room
1:30-3:00   Group B interviews; Group A and C talent rehearsals
3:15-4:15   All contestants, production number rehearsals
4:45   Dinner at French restaurant
6:30-10:30   All contestants, evening gown rehearsals

Wednesday, July 16
7:30-8:00   Breakfast in Palm Court/Plaza Hotel
9:00-11:00   Group C interviews; Groups A & B talent rehearsals
11:00-11:30   All contestants, swimsuit rehearsals
11:30-12:30   All contestants, evening gown rehearsals
12:30   Catered-in lunch
1:30-4:00   Group A interviews; Groups B & C talent rehearsals
4:30   Dinner at seafood restaurant
7:00   Arrive at Radio City Music Hall
8:00   Curtain
After show   Visitation

Thursday, July 17
7:30-8:00   Breakfast in Palm Court/Plaza Hotel

9:00-12:30	All contestants, talent rehearsals
12:30-1:00	All contestants, swimsuit rehearsals
1:00-2:00	Catered-in lunch
2:00-4:00	All contestants, production number rehearsals
5:00	Dinner at steak restaurant
7:00	Arrive at Radio City Music Hall
8:00	Curtain
After show	Visitation

Friday, July 18

7:30-8:00	Breakfast in Palm Court/Plaza Hotel
9:00-12:30	Talent rehearsals
1:00-2:00	Catered-in lunch
2:00-3:00	All contestants, production/evening gown rehearsals
4:10	Dinner at Italian restaurant
7:00	Arrive at Radio City Music Hall
8:00	Curtain
After show	Visitation

Saturday, July 19

7:30-8:00	Continental breakfast in Plaza banquet room
9:00-11:00	Closed TV rehearsal, Radio City Music Hall
11:00	Catered-in lunch
12:00-5:00	Continue TV rehearsal
6:00	Call for final performance/voting for Miss Congeniality
6:30-6:50	Pre-show
7:00-9:00	The Pageant — statewide television coverage
9:30	Reception

Sunday, July 20

8:00	Check-out
8:00-2:00	Pageant photos
10:00-10:20	Miss Empire State Photos
11:00	Miss Empire State press conference

Rachel put down the schedule and frowned. It was going to be a grueling week. The nerve-wracking tension of the various competitions would be bad enough but what she dreaded most about any pageant was the production numbers. She was convinced she had as much rhythm as a one-legged chicken.

Draining the last of her juice, she went into the bedroom to put the finishing touches on her platform essay. Initiated by the *Miss America Organization*, the idea of having pageant contestants submit written essays on meaningful issues was gaining in popularity. It was meant to show the public that women who participated in pageants had a brain; that they weren't just a bunch of bimbos who rode around in parades and cut ribbons in car lots. Each winner was now expected to use her reign to champion the issue she had chosen as her platform.

Rachel supported the idea, but wasn't particularly keen about the extra work it entailed. It made her feel like she was back in college.

Sitting at her desk, she pulled the manuscript out of the top drawer, picked up a pencil, and began to read. Halfway down the page, the phone rang.

"Hello?"

"Hi. Is this Rachel Curran?"

"Who's asking?"

"It's me, Rachel. Bob Molinaro."

"How did you get my number?" she asked, after a moment's hesitation.

"Ever hear of a remarkable resource called the phone book?"

"What do you want?"

"First of all, I called to apologize for coming on so strong last night. I don't usually behave that way. Then again, it's been a long time since any woman moved me the way you do. I haven't been able to get you out of my mind."

"I already explained why we can't go out together."

"Yeah, I know. Because I'm judging the damned pageant. But is that the only reason? Would you have accepted if the circumstances were different?"

"I don't know."

"It's a simple question. Either you're attracted to someone or you're not."

"Maybe I do find you attractive, but in my profession, I've learned that looks, or words for that matter, reveal very little about a person's character."

"Fair enough. But how can you get a handle on my character if you refuse to see me?"

Rachel clenched her teeth in exasperation. His persistence was beginning to derail not only her train of thought but also her resolve.

"Wait," added Molinaro, after a lengthy silence, "I know. Is it because you're involved with someone else?"

Rachel thought about Tom Brennan. "Kind of."

"Is it serious?"

"That's none of your business."

"Look, Rachel. I'm just trying to figure out if I have a shot here, that's all. But I can't make my case, and you can't decide what kind of man I am, unless we spend some time together. All I want is one evening. I don't think that's asking too much. I promise, I'll make it worth your while."

"What's that supposed to mean?" she asked.

"You'll have to find that out in person."

"What about the risk of our being seen together?"

"I guarantee there will be no risk. I know this great little piano bar on West Fifty-ninth. It's dark, it's designed for privacy, and its regular customers are too self-absorbed to pay anyone else the slightest attention."

"I don't know...."

"Come on, Rachel. Life's too short as it is. Don't waste it by denying yourself a little adventure."

Rachel's mind was wracked by indecision. Any fool could see that Molinaro was bright, handsome, and successful. If his interest was genuine, one drink couldn't hurt — especially since there was always a chance he could turn out to be the man of her dreams. But what if he *was* just another sleazeball looking for some trophy sex? How badly did she want to win this pageant? Enough to sleep with a stranger? Then again, if someone recognized them it would be a moot point because they'd both be booted out of the pageant. The prudent thing to do was send him packing.

"Rachel? Are you still there?"

"Okay," she said. "I accept."

"Really? That's great! I'll be by at eleven-thirty, sharp."

"Isn't that kind of late?"

"I've got a show to do, remember. Besides, it's Friday night. Nothing starts happening in this town until eleven."

"Yeah, well. I've got a very busy day ahead of me so I can't stay out too late."

"Whatever you say."

Rachel gave him her address, hung up, and wiped her hands on the front of her denim shorts. Although she knew she was taking an enormous risk, she had to be sure of Molinaro's intentions. And even if he did turn out to be a phony, all was not lost. A smart woman could string a horny man along for a long, long time. So no matter how the evening went, one thing was certain: at the end of it she'd have one of the *Miss Empire State* judges firmly tucked inside her hip pocket.

Good God, she thought, grimacing. Where in hell did that come from? She had no idea she was capable of such cold-blooded calculation. And here she'd been harboring suspicions about Molinaro's motives. Maybe it was time for a character check.

*****

Robert Molinaro stepped through the rear door of the WSNY building and hastened across the parking lot toward his BMW. The air was moist and heavy and a smattering of stars twinkled feebly in the smoggy night sky.

He could barely contain his excitement at the prospect of seeing Rachel again. It also agitated him a little because he wasn't used to losing his head over a woman. He preferred to be in control; it made for fewer complications. And, considering his foundering marriage — Anna had freaked when he told her he'd be home late because of a last minute meeting with pageant organizers — and the imminent arrival of their baby, the last thing he needed was an emotional entanglement.

He pointed the remote at his car and unlocked the door. But instead of climbing in right away, he leaned against the fender, lit a cigar, and watched a smoke ring expand, then dissipate.

"Mister Molinaro?"

He spun around and spotted a man lurking in the shadow of a nearby van. He was wearing jeans, a white sleeveless T-shirt, and a Yankees baseball cap.

"Christ," said Molinaro, wedging his car key between his index and middle fingers so the tip stuck out. If necessary, it would make an effective weapon. "You shouldn't go sneaking up on people like that. What do you want?"

"Well, sir," said the stranger, sounding a bit like Burt Lancaster, "first of all, I'd like to apologize for button-holing you like this. I know I should've made an appointment, but—"

"Look, I'm in a real hurry right now," said Molinaro, backing toward the car door, "Why don't you call my office in the morning."

"I won't keep you long," said the stranger, taking a step forward. "I just wanted to tell you how much your show means to me. I know it sounds like a cliché, but I'm your biggest fan."

"Thanks, I appreciate it. Now if you'll excuse me."

The stranger took another step. "Yes, sir. I listen to your program every night. It not only informs, but also stimulates dialogue, and that's very important in these troubled times. People don't talk to each other any more. They're all caught up in the rat race."

"That's a good point," said Molinaro, furtively placing his hand on the door handle. "You should bring it up on the show some time."

"I'll leave that to the sociologists," said the stranger, emerging from the shadows. "I've got more important things to worry about."

"Like I said. I'd be happy to discuss them on the air."

"Oh, we have. Many times."

The stranger was now close enough for Molinaro to see the color of his eyes, a deep blue. He also caught a partial glimpse of a blond sideburn. Molinaro's eyes widened in fear. "Frank? Is that you?"

"How are you, Robert?" replied Ryman, switching to his radio voice.

"You sounded different."

"A trick I picked up from watching old movies."

Molinaro had known dread before — a near drowning experience at Coney Island when he was nine — but this was infinitely worse, like leaning over the edge of a cold, implacable abyss.

"Is something wrong, Robert? You seem uncomfortable."

"I'm just surprised to see you, that's all."

"Calm down, old friend. I mean you no harm."

Molinaro swallowed. "What are you doing here?"

"Balancing the books. After all the intimate moments we have shared on the air, I thought it was time we met each other face to face. I meant what I said about your show, Robert. I feel I owe you a debt a gratitude for allowing me to voice my opinions. Most other talk show hosts would not have had the courage. You not only listened, you did so politely, without condescension. Who knows? Perhaps deep down, you even agree with my views."

Molinaro remained silent. It seemed the safest route.

"In any event," added Ryman, "you have my gratitude. Now it is *my* turn to do something for you."

"That's not necessary."

"Oh, but it is. You see, I have been mired in a creative rut. My work has become repetitive and for an artist, that is catastrophic. So I have decided to devote all of my time planning my ultimate masterpiece, a work of such scope and daring that the world will gasp in astonishment."

"What have you got in mind?"

"You know me better than that. Where is the fun in simple revelation? No, my friend. You must earn your reward. I am going to recite a riddle. If you solve it, you may do what you wish with the information. Even pass it along to the authorities. Not that your decision will affect my plans. But the solution will at least give you something spectacular to use on your show. On a more personal level, it will give you the satisfaction of being the first to understand my purpose. Now then, are you ready? I will only say it once."

"Can I write it down?"

"Of course."

Molinaro took a pen and a notepad out of his jacket and waited for Ryman to begin.

"What is wireless, is located in a metropolis, and produces vibrations in an auditorium?"

Molinaro finished writing and looked up, perplexed. "I don't understand. Are you referring to a place, a person, or an event?"

"All three."

Molinaro placed the pen and notepad back in his pocket and shook his head.

"Come now, Robert. An intelligent man like you should have no problem coming up with the correct answer."

"Yeah, right."

"I will give you a hint. If the answer seems too obvious, discard it." Ryman backed away and removed his cap. "Well," he added, slipping back into his Burt Lancaster impersonation, complete with the trademark grin, "my work here is done. If you're ever in my cornfield, look me up."

"Wait."

Ryman turned and smiled, but his blue eyes remained as dead as a shark's.

"Can't you at least tell me when this...surprise of yours is going to take place?"

"Within the next ten days," he replied, slipping into the shadows.

Molinaro took a deep breath and climbed into his car. His hands were still trembling. He took a deep drag on his cigar and placed it in the ashtray. Once he'd calmed down, he began to weigh his options. The obvious thing to do was notify Detective Jackson. The police had access to trained code breakers. They'd probably be able to solve the riddle in no time.

On the other hand, he could take a crack at it himself. If he succeeded, and the information led to Sardonicus's capture, his face would be plastered on every newspaper, magazine cover, and television screen in the country. Sure he'd gotten tremendous mileage out of the fact that a notorious killer was using his show as a personal soapbox, but orchestrating the maniac's capture would make him more than just another celebrity. He'd be a hero. Network executives would be climbing over each other for the chance to sign him up.

Talk about a no-brainer.

*****

"I feel like a truant schoolgirl who's afraid of being caught by her parents," said Rachel, trying to make herself inconspicuous. She and Molinaro were sitting in a basement night club called the Purple Tide. The decor featured a pleasing mix of glass, brass, and mahogany.

"Relax," said Molinaro, sidling closer. "It's so dark in here your parents wouldn't even recognize you."

"You've got a point," she replied, glancing furtively at their nearest neighbors. The only illumination was provided by candles that burned in each of the eight booths that lined the adjacent walls and on the dozen small tables that occupied the space between them. There was also a candelabra atop the piano, which was being played by a handsome black man currently in the midst of a Gershwin medley. The piano was located at one end of the narrow room, the bar at the other.

"I can't believe how quiet it is," whispered Rachel. "The bar I work in usually sounds like a construction site."

"You work in a bar?"

"Part-time."

"You're just full of surprises, aren't you."

"A girl's got to make a living."

"I thought you were a model."

"I am, but it barely covers my expenses."

"A beautiful woman like you?"

"Believe me, in modeling the word beauty has a million connotations. It's more about having a particular look. And so far, mine hasn't made much of an impact on Madison Avenue. Not that it bothers me. My real passion is acting."

"Really?"

Rachel nodded. "I haven't actually been in anything yet, other than a couple of student productions at the Neighborhood Playhouse — that's were I'm studying — but I'm confident things will work out. In fact, one of the reasons I entered the pageant was for the exposure it can provide if I do well."

Rachel immediately regretted having made that comment. It sounded too much like a hint. Fortunately, their waitress arrived just as Molinaro was about to respond. The woman placed their drinks on the table and left.

Molinaro picked up his scotch and clinked it against Rachel's wine glass. "Here's to the pageant," he said, "and to your acting career. I have no doubt whatsoever that you'll be a smashing success in both."

Rachel took a sip of wine. "Listen, Bob, I'd rather not talk about the pageant, okay? We've already compromised ourselves as it is."

"Whatever you say," he replied, deftly slipping his arm around her shoulder. "But you need to lighten up a bit. We're here to have a good time, remember?"

Draining his glass, he motioned to the waitress for another round. "I'm not a man to mince words, Rachel," he said, stroking the back of her neck. "I find you incredibly attractive. It's all I can do to keep from grabbing you in my arms right here and now."

"Any grabbing should wait until we get to know each other better."

"Don't you believe in love at first sight?"

"Not really. Besides, I think you're confusing love with lust."

"What's wrong with lust?"

"Nothing, if it cuts both ways."

"You mean I don't turn you on?"

"I wouldn't say that. I just don't believe in sleeping with a man on the first date."

"Then what are you doing tomorrow night?"

"Very funny."

"Okay," he said, rubbing his knee against her thigh, "can I at least have a kiss?"

"No," she replied, backing away, "but if you behave yourself I might give you a peck on the cheek when you take me home."

Molinaro frowned and removed his arm from her shoulder. He then reached inside his jacket and pulled out a cigar.

"Please, Bob. It's already like a smoke house in here."

He shoved the cigar back in his pocket and crossed his arms. Rachel studied his face, which was almost feminine in its softness, and wondered what was coming. But he remained silent until their drinks arrived. He downed his in one swallow and leaned toward her again.

"Let me put my cards on the table, Rachel. I want you. Right now. And I'm willing to do whatever it takes to make it happen. Do you get my drift?"

Here comes the pitch, thought Rachel, with a pang of disappointment. She had continued to cling to the hope that he was interested in Rachel Curran the person. Instead, he was just another hustler looking to score. But she had no intention of letting him off easy. She wanted to hear the words.

"Look, Bob. I don't know you very well, but I'd like to think that underneath the flash you're a decent man with a lot to offer. And I do like you. In time, I could even see myself sleeping with you. But it's not going to happen tonight. I'm not interested in casual sex. If you care about me at all you'll cool your heels until after the pageant, then we can go on a few more dates and find out if we're compatible."

"No-no-no-no-no," he said, stringing the words together in a staccato burst. "You're not listening. Here's the deal. You sleep with me and I'll guarantee that you'll score well in the pageant. I can't promise you'll win, but with my vote, you've got one hell of a chance."

"And if I refuse?"

"You'll be lucky to win the Miss Congeniality award."

"You mean you would purposely ruin my chances?"

"Welcome to the real world, sweet cheeks."

"My God, I can't believe I'm hearing this."

"Oh, come on. I'm not asking you to poison your dog, for chrissakes. All I'm talking about is a little recreational sex. It's a win-win situation."

"What if I decide to tell the pageant organizers about this?"

"I'll say you're the one who approached *me* and are just trying to cover your tracks. But hey, why be foolish? I'm offering you a once-in-a-lifetime opportunity here. Don't be so quick to blow it off."

"You know something?" she replied, sliding out of the booth. "I'd rather get into bed with Mister Sardonicus."

Chapter 25 — Sunday, July 13

The partially clad woman in room 822 of the Alexander Hamilton, an aging midtown hotel on Broadway, lit a memorial candle and set it next to a copper incense burner she had placed on the coffee table. Clasping her hands together, she sat on the couch and bowed her head.

Goodbye, Frankie. I know we've had our differences, but I'm not so mean-spirited that I can't appreciate your skill and dedication to our cause. Your legacy is secure, sugar. And I solemnly promise, on our sainted mamma's grave, that our work will not only continue, but will scale such heights that the world will tremble at mention of our names.

Francine tossed her head back and gave vent to a fit of loud, triumphant laughter. Her dear 'brother' was finally gone, crushed by the weight of her superior personality. She imagined this was how a butterfly felt when it finally shed its caterpillar carcass and spread its wings in anticipation of first flight.

Stretching her arms, she stood up and hastened to the bedroom. She picked up a wallet that lay on the bed and flipped it open. Ignoring the credit cards and other pieces of ID, she turned to the driver's license and pulled it out of its sleeve. The photo depicted a 25-year-old blue-eyed blonde with pencil-thin eyebrows, a pert, upturned nose, and an oval face. The woman's name was Ingrid Holmgren. Francine wrinkled her nose. It was an atrocious name, but the woman was the closest match Frank had been able to find.

He'd spotted her on Thursday night — after nearly four hours of searching — in front of the American Museum of Natural History. He had disguised himself as an Hassidic Jew. The look on the woman's face when he snatched her purse and sprinted across the street into the darkness of Central Park would have done Candid Camera proud.

Francine sat in front of the dresser mirror and compared her face to the one in the photo. The mouth and nose were strikingly similar. Make-up, tweezers, and a wig had taken care of the rest. The license listed Ingrid Holmgren as being an inch and a half shorter than her, but the personnel director who interviewed her had been more interested in her Latex cleavage than her height.

In the end, she'd gotten the job, a position that would place her at the very heart of the enemy camp. She would blend into the background, like a praying mantis, and wait for the optimal moment to pounce on her prey. Unlike Frank, who used the subtle approach, Francine preferred a grand gesture.

Shivering with anticipation, she walked over to the closet to select an outfit. Something chic, yet practical, since her new job entailed a lot of running around. Although she wasn't required to be there until 7:30 p.m., she wanted to have everything ready. She rummaged through the clothes she'd purchased on Saturday — part of a $3500 shopping spree funded by the liquidation of Frank's stock and bond portfolio — and settled on a silk broadcloth shirt in soft strips of laurel green, khaki pleated gabardine trousers with cuffed ankles, and a pair of lace-up black oxfords.

She laid the items on the bed and smiled. Everything was falling into place. She was free and the police were looking for a man who no longer existed. In a few days they'd begin to assume that 'Mister Sardonicus' had moved on to greener pastures, leaving the field wide open for her to create her *piece de resistance*. Afterwards, she would leave the frenetic, dirty, and malodorous confines of New York and return to Louisiana to live the life of a southern belle, as her mamma had intended.

*****

A few blocks away, on the 14th floor of the Plaza Hotel, Rachel Curran was in her room unpacking. Sally Schuster had dropped her off in front of the lobby at 2:30. It was now 3:00, which meant that the other contestants had probably arrived as well. The orientation session was scheduled for 4:00. That would be her first opportunity to evaluate the women she would be competing against.

Rachel finished putting her clothes away and placed her suitcase and garment bag on the closet floor. Her gown and the outfits she'd need for the production numbers had been sent ahead to Radio City. She picked up her makeup kit and walked over to the dresser. Although she had fixed her face before leaving home, the mid-afternoon heat had caused her mascara to smudge.

She looked at herself in the mirror and sighed, relieved the waiting was finally over. Two days of rehearsals and social functions, then the competition would begin in earnest. Notwithstanding her confrontation with Molinaro, whose malignant presence lingered in her thoughts like a rotting egg, she felt relaxed and confident. She knew he was an opportunistic creep, but found it hard to believe he'd deliberately sabotage her chances.

Just then, the phone rang. Before it had a chance to ring again it was picked up in the other bedroom by her chaperone, a dour, 44-year-old Long Islander who'd be sticking to her like glue for the next week.

"It's for you, Rachel!"

"Thanks!" she yelled, picking up the extension.

"Hello?"

"Hi, Rachel." It was Molinaro.

"What the hell do you want?" she replied, closing the bedroom door with her foot.

"You know exactly what I want."

"And you should know you've got a better chance of sprouting horns and a tail."

"Very clever. You're not only beautiful and feisty, but witty, too. I like that in a woman."

"Fuck you."

"Oh, yes. Please."

"Bastard."

"Not at all. My parents are married and live happily in the Bronx. But enough small talk. I'm calling to offer you one last chance, Rachel. The first competition takes place on Tuesday, and I see here on my schedule that it's the private interview with the ladies of group B. Your group, I believe. Meet me tonight after your production number rehearsal and you'll be one step closer to the crown."

"You know something, Bob? I feel sorry for you. Do you always rely on extortion to get women into bed?"

Molinaro remained silent.

"Look," she added, "I've worked long and hard to prepare for this pageant. It's very important to me. If you have any decency at all you'll stop this cruel nonsense before it goes too far. All I want is to be treated fairly."

"You've got my number," he replied. "I expect to hear from you before eight."

*****

Later that afternoon, in the Plaza lobby, Lionel Jackson drummed his fingers on his knee as he listened to a detailed description of pageant security from Lorne Dickson, an ex-marine with ghost-gray eyes, a congenial but guarded smile, and a mustache that resembled a patch of hog's bristles. His bulbous nose was lined with a fine network of broken capillaries, like a road map. His speech had the clipped cadence of a drill instructor.

Jackson's impatience had nothing to do with Dickson's spiel. He couldn't concentrate because he was expecting his beeper to go off. It was almost 5:00 and no one had yet found the body of Sardonicus's Saturday night victim. This troubled him because the killer always took great pains to place the body where it would be easily discovered.

"Believe me, Sergeant," concluded Dickson, "unless this guy can make himself invisible, there's no way he's getting close to any of our ladies."

"With all due respect, your contestants are staying in a public hotel. Hundreds of people are in and out of here every day."

Dickson shifted position. "First of all, every person involved with this pageant has had Sardonicus's description seared into his brain. Secondly, the fourteenth floor has been declared off limits to everyone but contestants and staff. Anyone else attempting to breach the perimeter will be detained until their identify has been established."

"That's fine, but what about when the contestants leave the hotel? Hell, you've got them running all over town, to restaurants, tourist sites, back and forth to Radio City. Unless you plan to march them around in single file, flanked by a phalanx of security personnel, they'll be vulnerable."

"I don't agree. We've worked out a plan for every contingency. Besides, you said that Sardonicus only strikes on Wednesdays and Saturdays. My staff has been instructed to be especially vigilant on those days."

"That's been his pattern so far. But there's always a chance it could change."

Dickson looked at his watch. "It's almost five," he said, rising. "The ladies should be through with their orientation by now. You've got exactly fifteen minutes to make your pitch. And please, Sergeant, they've already got a lot on their minds so try not to scare them too much, okay?"

"It's good if they're scared. It'll keep them alert."

"Hell, man. Everybody knows Sardonicus has a hard-on for models. Working models. We're running a beauty pageant. I'd say the chances of his showing up here are pretty slim, especially since we've removed all references to modeling from the biographies contained in the program. So instead of dealing with a highly improbable worst-case scenario, why don't you explain what the police are doing to catch the guy."

Jackson finished his Pepsi and leaned forward to rise, triggering a piercing pain at the base of his spine. His back had been bothering him all day. That morning, it had taken him almost an hour to coddle it to the point where he was able to get out of bed.

"If you want warm and fuzzy," he said, struggling to his feet, "you've got the wrong man. I'm here to make sure these women understand what kind of monster we're dealing with. And don't talk to me about altering biographies. He'll know that some of the contestants are models and he'll do whatever is necessary to identify who they are."

"Maybe so, but like I said, we're prepared for every contingency."

"You'd better be, because if you take anything at all for granted, someone's going to die."

*****

Jackson seethed with frustration as he slipped out of the banquet room after the briefing. What was the use of warning people if they insisted on putting themselves in the line of fire? If these women were truly concerned for their safety, they would've remained at home. And stayed there until Sardonicus was either dead or behind bars. Shaking his head, he lit a cigarette and headed for the elevators.

"Sergeant!"

He turned and saw a young woman hurrying toward him. She seemed familiar.

"Hi," she said, extending her hand. "Rachel Curran. I saw you the other night at W.S.N.Y., in the control room."

"Oh, right," he said, sucking in his gut. "You were a guest on Molinaro's show."

He recalled how blown away he'd been by her beauty, but up close like this, dressed in denim cutoffs and a clinging blue silk blouse, she was stunning. Especially her eyes, which were as bright and probing as a pair of searchlights.

"I was impressed by the way you handled yourself," he added. "Some of those callers were pretty rough."

"I enjoy a good debate. It's an effective way to test your convictions. But I'm surprised you even noticed. You obviously weren't there to take in the show."

"No, ma'am, I wasn't."

"I'll tell you one thing. It sure felt spooky being on the air at the same time as Sardonicus. That is one creepy individual."

"He's also one of the smartest killers I've ever known."

"Are your trying to spook me even more than I already am? I've been walking on eggshells from the moment he began his reign of terror."

"Sorry. Cops aren't exactly known for their tactfulness."

She crossed her arms and studied his face. "Tell me, why do you think he taunted you the way he did? What's he got to gain?"

Jackson took a drag on his cigarette and blew the smoke out the side of his mouth. "It's an ego thing. But it's not his words I'm worried about, it's his actions."

Rachel nodded and shoved her hands in her pockets. "You don't really think he'd try to target the pageant, do you?"

"Probably not, but there's no point in taking chances. Like I said in my presentation, the important thing is to stay alert. Don't wander off on your own, and if a stranger approaches, notify security — immediately."

"I've got my own security. I carry a Browning automatic and I can shoot a hole through the heart of a nickel at twenty yards."

"I'm not keen about civilians walking around with guns, Miss Curran, but I guess I can't blame you. By the way, you do have a license, right?"

"Of course. My dad taught me how to handle a gun when I was fourteen years old and I've been licensed ever since. Wanna see it?"

"I believe you, but remember this. Sardonicus isn't some maniacal slasher who jumps out of dark alleys. None of his victims saw him coming. So don't let that gun give you a false sense of security. Your best defense is extreme caution."

"I'll keep that in mind," she replied, glancing at her watch. "I'd better get going. We're having dinner at six. Maybe I'll see you later in the week." She turned to leave. "Oh, and Sergeant. Those cigarettes are going to kill you."

Jackson grinned as he watched her jog back to the banquet room, then continued toward the elevators. Man, he thought, crushing out his cigarette in a nearby ashtray, what a stone cold fox. And sharp as a tack, too. It would sure be nice to run his hands along those sleek, firm—

Whoa, cried his inner self, realizing the absurdity of the situation. Here he was, a 35-year-old divorced, emotionally screwed-up black man with two children and a bad back, and he was lusting after some hard-bodied white princess who was at least fifteen years his junior. Either he was losing his mind or he needed to get laid even worse than he thought.

Chapter 26 — Tuesday, July 15

The setup inside the hotel room chosen for the pageant's private interview segment — which accounted for a hefty 30 percent of a contestant's score — reminded Robert Molinaro of a court-martial. He and the other four judges, two women and two men, sat behind a draped banquet table facing the front door, while the judging chairman and a senior official sat to their right. The contestants were ushered in one at a time, introduced, and seated in the center of the room.

Because the private interview was the first and most revealing phase of the competition, it offered the judges an opportunity to assess which contestant was best equipped to undertake the responsibilities that came with the crown. Scoring was based on overall first impression, appearance, personality, intelligence, communication skills, and general knowledge and understanding of current events. Unlike the other categories, the winner of the interview segment was not made public.

Molinaro stopped his doodling and glanced at the young woman perched on the hot seat. It was Rachel, and she was doing her best to avoid his gaze. A wry smile tugged at the corners of his lips. She'd seemed uncharacteristically nervous at first — no doubt because she'd stood him up on Sunday night and therefore expected retribution — but to her credit she'd settled down and was eloquently responding to a question posed by one of the other judges.

What a woman, thought Molinaro, turning back to his doodling. He'd shoved a blank sheet of paper in the middle of his judges' workbook and had scribbled Frank's riddle across the top: "What is wireless, is located in a metropolis, and produces vibrations in an auditorium?" He'd been wracking his brain for the past four days trying to decipher the damn thing, but all he'd gotten for his efforts was a serious case of cerebral gridlock.

He'd begun with the assumption he was looking for some kind of stringless musical instrument, which meant brass, woodwind, or percussion. And even though all sounds produced vibrations, the riddle specified those that were made in an auditorium, which again suggested music. On the other hand, he knew of no instrument that was found only in cities — unless that part of the riddle wasn't meant to be taken literally.

Eventually, he'd concluded the instrument in question represented the name of the place where Frank intended to strike. He'd spent a day and a half thumbing through the Yellow Pages for modeling agencies, advertising agencies, and photo studios named after a musical instrument. His search turned up zilch. That's when he remembered Frank's warning about ignoring the obvious. Since then, he'd been proceeding on the basis that the riddle was meant to be metaphorical. The problem was, he'd never been particularly adept at abstract thinking.

"Robert?"

Molinaro looked up. The judging chairman, a tall sack of a man with hooded eyes and a jutting jaw, was regarding him gravely.

"Do you have a question for Miss Curran?"

"Um, yes," he mumbled, closing his workbook and picking up the list of questions he'd formulated, "of course."

He looked at Rachel and smiled. To his surprise, she smiled right back, without a hint of insincerity. The woman had moxie. Now it was time to see just how well she could maintain her composure.

"Tell me, Miss Curran. With sexual harassment being such a hot button issue in the workplace, what would you deem to be inappropriate behavior on the part of a male colleague or employer?"

Rachel didn't flinch. "Physical contact—"

"Even a pat on the back?"

"I'm a human being, not a pet."

"What else?"

"Sexual innuendo, derogatory language, demeaning, non-job-related demands like fetching coffee or shopping for personal items. And of course," she added, leaning forward and fixing him with a steady gaze, "sexual extortion. Though I think only the worst kind of man would do something *that* despicable."

✱✱✱✱✱

Back in the squad room, Lionel Jackson was trying to catch up on his paperwork. But his brain refused to cooperate. It kept filling his head with soft-focus images of Rachel Curran...standing, lying down, naked, dressed, brushing her hair, putting on nylons. Despite his misgivings, he hadn't been able to get her out of his mind. In the process, he'd convinced himself that a spark — albeit a weak one — had been ignited. All he had to do now was summon up the courage to act.

The sound of the door being flung open jerked him back to reality. He looked up and saw Ed Lewicki striding into the room. The big detective hung up his jacket and took up a position near the water cooler. "Did you guys hear what happened?" he asked, between chews of a Mars bar. "Someone just shot and killed Gianni Versace outside his place in Miami."

"Who thee hell eess that?" asked Octavio Cordova.

"Only one of the world's most famous fashion designers, dumbo."

"Maybe I would understand better eef you did not talk weeth your mouth full." Cordova's eyes widened. "Madre de Dios. You don't theenk Sardonicus left town to go after beegger game, eh?"

"I wouldn't put it past the bastard," said Lewicki.

Jackson set his pen down and leaned back in his chair. Was it possible Sardonicus *had* changed both his M.O. and stomping ground? It would certainly explain why they hadn't found another body, and why he hadn't been on Molinaro's show since Thursday.

Usually, there were only two other possible explanations for a serial killer's sudden disappearance — aside from retirement: suicide, which was certainly true of some personality types but seemed unlikely in Sardonicus's case; or, he'd been picked up for another offense in a different jurisdiction and was anonymously serving time on the lesser charge.

Jackson's gut told him that Sardonicus was still alive. And the more he thought about it, the more he found it hard to accept the other possibilities. He was certain the killer was up to something. Still, he had to check it out.

"Ed, call Miami P.D. and see if they've got anything on Versace's killer. Then send a copy of Sardonicus's description to every jail in the tri-state area. If they've processed anybody in the last week who even comes close to a match, I want to known about it."

Lewicki nodded, swallowed the cup of water he was holding, and hustled over to his desk.

A phone rang. A moment later, Dan McDougall jumped to his feet and let out a loud whoop that brought Jim Hawthorne storming out of his office.

"What the hell's going on?" demanded the lieutenant.

McDougall balled his hands into fists. "The FBI just got a trace on those E-mails we sent them! A guy named Frank Ryman. Lives in an apartment on Lexington Avenue, near East Ninetieth."

Hawthorne turned to Jackson. "It's your collar, Lionel. Get up there and nail the bastard. I'll issue a citywide."

By the time Jackson's assault team was ready to roll, every precinct in the five boroughs had been notified. Ryman's name and description would be read out to every mustering platoon on every watch in 76 precincts. Special Ops, Traffic Control, Narcotics, and Auto Crime would also be notified, as would police departments in the surrounding counties, as well as New Jersey.

At precisely 3:45 p.m., a dozen unmarked police cars surrounded a luxury apartment building on the Upper East Side. After posting guards at all the exits, Jackson led Lewicki, McDougall, and three uniforms armed with a battering ram past the startled doorman who met them at the main entrance, through the lobby, and into an empty elevator. Jackson punched in the floor number and exchanged a glance with Lewicki. The only sound was the hum of shallow breathing.

The elevator door slid open on the 14th floor and Jackson poked his head into the corridor. Clear. He and the others drew their guns and quickly made their way to apartment 1422. Jackson placed his ear to the door. No sound. He stood aside and motioned for the uniforms to crash the door. It gave easily. Storming into the apartment, they quickly established that the living room was empty and rushed forward to secure the other rooms. A thorough search revealed the apartment was deserted.

"The place looks lived-in," said Lewicki. "He's probably still at work. You gotta figure the fucker's making big bucks to afford this neighborhood."

"I agree," said Jackson. "But if he comes home and sees the place surrounded by cops, we may lose him for good. Radio downstairs and tell the others to stay out of sight. They can let people in but nobody leaves the building. And make sure the tenants remain inside their apartments. We don't need a bunch of curiosity seekers hanging around the front lobby. When you're done, join the garage detail. If Ryman does show, he might be in a car."

Jackson motioned to McDougall. "Dan, you and the others check the apartment for evidence, especially women's underwear. Make sure you look in the fridge. If he's kept his victims' lips, that's where they'll be. Oh, and see if you can find any recent photographs that show us what this motherfucker's real face looks like."

Jackson took a handset radio off one of the uniforms and called in for a patch to Hawthorne.

"Well?" asked the lieutenant.

"No dice," said Jackson. "But it doesn't look like he's cleared out. We'll sit tight until he shows."

"I'll send more men."

"No need. And tell patrol not to send any RMPs into the area. I don't want to spook the guy."

"Anything else?"

"Yeah. Get someone to call the New Orleans P.D. and see what they can find on Ryman."

"You got it."

Jackson handed the radio back to its owner and headed for the kitchen to join McDougall.

"Sergeant?"

Jackson turned toward the front door. The uniform he'd posted in the corridor was restraining a stout man in a black jacket and striped trousers who was waving a stubby finger at the damaged door latch. The guy looked like a penguin, with jowls.

"Who are you?" asked Jackson.

"The manager," snapped the penguin, trying to do an end run around the uniform.

"You need to stay in the corridor," said Jackson.

The penguin's nostrils flared with indignation. "May I ask what you're doing here?"

"We're looking for Frank Ryman."

"I gathered that much. Why?"

"Do you know what time Mister Ryman usually gets home from work?"

"I do not. But even if I did, it wouldn't be of much help."

"Why's that?"

"I believe he's away just now."

"Oh?"

"His car hasn't been out of the garage since last Thursday and he hasn't been picking up his mail."

Jackson's shoulders sagged. "You're sure of that?"

"Absolutely."

"All right. I'll let you know if we need anything else."

"But—"

Jackson slammed the door and slumped against the wall. Was that it, then? A madman crawls out of the woodwork to butcher six women, spends almost a month spewing his hateful message over the public airwaves, thumbs his nose at the police, eludes one of the largest manhunts in U.S. history, then quietly vanishes into thin air? Was this God's idea of a joke?

*****

Rachel Curran's mouth was slack as she stood backstage at Radio City Music Hall with her fellow contestants, waiting for the start of the evening gown rehearsal. She could scarcely believe she was about to step onto the fabled Great Stage, reputed to be the most elaborate and best equipped in the world. As wide as a city block and some 66 feet deep, it was fitted with four hydraulic elevators, each capable of being lowered 27 feet or raised 13 feet.

Radio City stood as a symbol of an era when everything Americans did had to be bigger and better than everybody else. It still held a number of world records: largest indoor movie theater, with a seating capacity of over 6,000; largest Wurlitzer organ; largest chandeliers, a pair of immense cylinders of Lalique glass suspended above the 60-foot-high Grand Foyer. The elegance and history of the place draped itself around you like a physical presence.

Rachel swallowed nervously and patted down the front of her gown, an unadorned, long-sleeved creation of white lace with a modest, heart-shaped neckline. Thankfully, the trend in pageant wear had moved away from the gaudy, heavily beaded, figure-hugging monstrosities that were aptly known as 'walking chandeliers,' toward a renewed appreciation for simple elegance.

Individuality was the key to earning points in the evening gown competition, which counted for 15 percent of the final score. The last thing you wanted to do was imitate a previous titleholder or wear something that clashed with your personality. Woman and gown had to complement each other.

The competition was divided into two segments: a modeling phase and an onstage interview.

In the modeling phase, judges assessed each contestant's physical beauty, confidence, poise and grace of bearing, fluidity of movement, and the appropriateness of her gown as a statement of individuality.

The onstage interview — conducted by the emcee, who asked penetrating questions related to each contestant's platform issue — gave judges an opportunity to assess each woman's ability to think and speak clearly under pressure, and to observe the warmth, intelligence, and composure she projected in front of a large audience. They also gave marks for voice, vocabulary, personality, sincerity, and understanding of current events.

Rachel glanced at her watch. It was 6:20. The first competitor was scheduled to take the stage in ten minutes. This would be the only opportunity to work out any kinks in your presentation. If you were going to fall on your ass or fumble for words, now was the time to do so.

Closing her eyes, she began to clear her mind in order to reach the tranquil plane she inhabited during her yoga exercises. But before she could complete the journey, one of the backstage hostesses tapped her on the shoulder.

"Phone call, Rachel."

"Now? Who is it?"

"He wouldn't say. Only that it's important."

Frowning, Rachel lifted the hem of her gown and carefully followed the hostess through the throng of restless young women.

"The phone's in there," said the hostess, pointing to what looked like a closet. "Try not to be too long."

Rachel entered the room and picked up the receiver, which had been laid on its side atop a small metal desk. "Hello?"

"Hi, Rachel. It's Bob."

Stifling an impulse to scream out a choice profanity, she leaned against the edge of the desk and took a deep breath.

"Rachel? Are you still there?"

"What in God's name is wrong with you?" she snapped, struggling to keep her voice down. "There are lots of women out there who would probably be quite happy to jump into the sack with you. Why are you obsessing on me?"

"Biological imperative, I guess."

"Well get over it."

"I can't. Like the song says, I've got you under my skin."

"And you're making *mine* crawl."

"Be nice, now. I've got some good news."

Rachel remained silent.

"To prove I'm not a bad guy, I gave you a perfect ten for your interview. That means you still have time to change your mind about our little arrangement. Think carefully before you reply, Rachel. My patience is wearing thin."

"It's not going to happen, Bob, so do whatever the hell you feel you need to do. Just stop pestering me, okay?"

"You're making a big mistake. Soon I'm going to have my own national TV show, a best-selling book about my relationship with one of the most notorious serial killers in history, money to burn, and enough clout to get the lady in my life anything her little heart desires. You want to be an actress? I'll be able to introduce you to all the major players... agents, producers, sta—"

Rachel slammed the phone down and stormed back to the stage.

Chapter 27 — Thursday, July 17

The morning sun blazed in a cloudless sky but inside the squad room, the mood was funereal. Most of the members of the special unit were on hand for a meeting that had been called by Chief O'Ryan the previous evening. Speculation about its purpose was rampant. Was headquarters going to officially adopt the position that Sardonicus was no longer in New York? Were they going to suggest a different approach or some new initiative? Or was the case about to be handed over to the feds? The uncertainty was driving Lionel Jackson crazy.

A week had passed since the discovery of Sardonicus's last victim and his final appearance on Molinaro's show. There was always a chance the bodies were out there, rotting in some remote corner of the city, but Jackson wasn't about to bet the house on it. He was almost certain an obsessive egomaniac like Sardonicus would never be able to control his need to gloat for that long. The madman had stopped killing. The question was, why?

While the city held its breath, Jackson and his team continued to go through the motions. A 24-hour-a-day watch had been placed on Frank Ryman's apartment. Statements were being taken from everyone who knew him. Leads were being followed. Evidence was being collected. Canvasses were being conducted. The department was operating on momentum, laced with desperation.

A phone rang, and was picked up immediately.

"Sarge?"

Jackson looked up. Jimmy Choi was pointing in his direction. Jackson transferred the call to his line and picked up the receiver.

"Jackson here."

"Morning, Sergeant. This here's Lieutenant Travis Gillett, N.O.P.D. Got some info on that Ryman character you boys been chasing down. Your hunch about him was right. He did spend time in a psychiatric hospital. Most of his early years, in fact. Some kind of personality disorder. Seems his mamma was a junkie whore who raised him as a girl."

"Say what?"

"You heard right. When the child welfare authorities got hold of him after his mother died — heroin overdose — he was dressed and made up like a girl. Hell, he believed he *was* a girl. It took a long time to convince him otherwise."

"Man, that is fucked up."

"No kiddin'. Anyway, neither he nor his mother had papers, so they never did find his father or any of his relatives. The kid was alone. But he did eventually recover and was released in ninety-one. He left the state shortly thereafter."

"Can you tell me anything about his personality?"

"The doctor who treated him says he was an athletic kid...liked to swim a lot. Real bright, too. Had an exceptional I.Q. Seems he was always reading text books and watching educational programs on T.V. Even managed to get his M.B.A. over at L.S.U., although he continued to live in the hospital. But he wasn't very sociable. He apparently spent most of his time in his room, watching old movies and doing puzzles...sometimes right through the night."

"And he never exhibited any signs of violence?"

"Nope. By all accounts the boy was as docile as a lamb."

"I wonder what set him off."

"Your guess is as good as mine, partner."

"I appreciate your help, lieutenant."

"Any time. The file's on its way."

"Did you manage to find any photographs? There were none in his apartment."

"One, taken when he was about eighteen. But I doubt if he's changed that much."

"Thanks again — oh, one last thing. Ryman hasn't been heard from for a week now. If he *has* skipped town, New Orleans would be a logical destination."

"I'll send out an immediate alert."

Jackson hung up and lit a cigarette. He'd seen people do some weird shit in his day but a mother raising her son as a girl? Man, that was cold.

*****

A stiff breeze whipped through Rockefeller Plaza, stirring up debris and rattling the colorful café umbrellas dotting the square in front of the General Electric

Building. Francine clutched her newspaper more tightly and flattened it on the table, almost spilling her lemonade in the process.

Once the wind died down, she lifted the paper and finished reading a front page story filled with frenzied speculation about Sardonicus's apparent disappearance. It was the predominant topic of conversation on radio and TV, as well. The city's collective sense of relief was almost palpable. Many of its fine citizens were probably hoping he was on his way to Boston. What a hoot, thought Francine, sipping some lemonade and letting the ice rest against her lips for a moment. Were they in for a surprise.

She folded the newspaper under her arm and casually surveyed her surroundings. The café was packed, mostly with camera-toting tourists and bored-looking office workers. They were all huddled together under their respective umbrellas, trying to protect their heads from the blistering midday sun. Across the square, dozens more people were sheltering in the Channel Gardens, a shaded oasis of fountains and floral displays situated between the British Empire Building and La Maison Française.

Francine slowly turned her head in the opposite direction, toward the elevated statue of Prometheus that dominated the square. Even though she was wearing sunglasses, the reflected glare off the statue's golden sheen forced her to avert her eyes. In the same instant, she was gripped by a vague uneasiness that elicited a mild shudder.

It took a moment but she finally discerned the cause of her discomfort. The statue bore a striking similarity to the jigsaw puzzle Frank had been working on before she'd flung him into oblivion, a reproduction of a painting entitled *Les Trésors de Satan.* Seeing it must've awakened his dormant psyche. Francine could feel him struggling to push his way into her consciousness. She closed her eyes and focused her concentration. A fierce battle of wills ensued, but it was over quickly. Frank was gone. This time, for good.

Francine took a deep breath and swallowed the rest of her lemonade. It was time to return to work. She took her ID badge out of her purse and hung it around her neck. She then flipped it up to examine its face and frowned. The photograph was serviceable enough but she still hated her adopted name. Ingrid Holmgren. *Ugh.* Thankfully, she wouldn't be needing it much longer.

*****

Backstage at Radio City, contestants and staff were preparing for the start of the swimsuit competition. The scene inside the lower level dressing room — one of two normally used by the Rockettes — was bedlam as dozens of anxious young women darted in and out to change their outfits, fix their hair, and apply fresh makeup, all under the watchful eyes of a score of hostesses, hairdressers, cosmetologists, and seamstresses.

Rachel Curran, who was in the group competing in the swimsuit segment, wrung her hands and nervously glanced at her crotch to ensure no errant pubic hairs were peeking out from under her yellow, one-piece suit. It was just the kind of stupid detail that could ruin her chances.

Her anxiety, however, was more than just pre-show jitters. To her amazement — despite having played extremely well — she had won the previous evening's talent competition for her group, which was worth a whopping 40 percent of the final score. Either Molinaro had changed his mind about sabotaging her bid for the crown or the other judges had deemed her performance so superior that his score didn't hurt her. Whatever the reason, she was now well-positioned to take a serious run at the title.

This was the second of three nights of preliminaries. The routine was always the same. At 8:00 the curtain went up and the Master of Ceremonies, the reigning Miss Empire State, and the women vying for her crown took the stage for an opening production number. Each contestant then introduced herself and took a turn along the runway, followed by a ceremonial stroll by the reigning queen. Finally, the judges were introduced and the pageant began in earnest.

The first event was the swimsuit competition. As each of the 15 contestants in the group was introduced, she had to pause briefly and turn before the judges, walk down the runway, then leave the stage. Fortunately, the organizers had shortened the time each woman had to hold her pose and had eliminated the heels-together stance, which helped to de-emphasize the idea that judges were looking for the perfect body. At the conclusion of the segment, ballots were collected by the judging chairman and given to the auditors for tabulation.

The next group of 15 performed in the talent competition. Again, the ballots were collected and the stage was cleared for another production number.

The last event was the evening gown competition. After participating in the on-stage interview portion, each of the 15 contestants in this group had to model her gown before the judges, then walk the runway. But unlike the swimsuit and talent segments, the winner was not announced to the audience. This was done to save some suspense for the final.

At the conclusion of each night of competition, the 45 hopefuls gathered onstage for a closing production number and for the announcement of that evening's preliminary winners in talent and swimsuit.

By Friday, all 45 contestants will have competed in each event, their scores tabulated and double-checked, the six preliminary winners in the swimsuit and talent segments selected, and the ten finalists — whose composite scores were carried over — determined. The scene would be set for Saturday night's final, when the names of the ten women vying for the title would be announced in front of a state-wide television audience.

A number of red lights began to flash. Curtain call for the swimsuit competition. Rachel took a last peek in the mirror, wiped her hands with a tissue, and slid out of her chair to join the rest of her group for the long, lonely walk toward the stage. Clearing her mind of all extraneous thought, she reminded herself that in addition to overall physical fitness, the judges would be looking for grace, poise, posture, and confidence under pressure.

*****

"I can't believe you didn't win," squealed Sally Schuster, throwing her arms around Rachel's neck as she stepped into the Art Deco splendor of Radio City's Grand Lounge for the post-show reception. "You looked awesome up there!"

"I *knew* I should've shaved another quarter inch off my butt," joked Rachel, smiling.

Sally released her grip and stepped back with a look of concern on her face. "You're still in good shape, though, right? I mean, you did win the talent competition."

"Oh, sure," said Rachel, as an image of Robert Molinaro in the guise of Mephistopheles popped into her head, "the important thing is to be near the top of your group in all four segments. Even though I didn't win swimsuit tonight, I think my score was okay. And I'm pretty sure I did well in the private interview, too, so that just leaves tomorrow night's evening gown competition."

"God, you must be so nervous. I'd be climbing the walls by now."

"I *am* nervous. The key is not to show it. That's where my acting lessons come in *real* handy." She put an arm around Sally's shoulder. "So," she added, with a sweeping gesture, "what do you think of our little romper room?"

"Little! It could hold *two* Jewish weddings simultaneously. But I hate the decor. It looks like a set from one of those goofy Busby Berkeley musicals from the thirties."

"I think that was the idea."

"Whatever," said Sally, clasping Rachel's hand. "Come on, let's grab a drink."

"Excuse me, Miss Curran?"

Rachel turned. "Sergeant!" she said, her eyes widening in surprise. "What are you doing here?"

"I, uh, happened to be in the neighborhood and, uh—"

"Were you in the auditorium for the competition?"

"I was standing at the back. And if you don't mind my saying so, I thought you looked fine. Real fine."

"Thanks," she replied, scrutinizing his face.

Jackson shifted position and fidgeted with his tie.

"I'll go get those drinks," said Sally. "Can I get you anything Sergeant..."

"Oh, I'm sorry," said Rachel. "This is my roommate, Sally Schuster. Sally, this is Sergeant Lionel Jackson. He's working on the Sardonicus investigation."

"Oh, right," said Sally, extending her hand. "I thought I recognized your face. Any news yet?"

"I'm afraid not," replied Jackson.

"What do you suppose happened to the scumbag?" asked Rachel.

"I'd like to think he got run over by a truck," said Jackson, reaching for his cigarettes. Rachel's frown stopped him. "I suppose it's possible things got too hot for him here in New York. But that just places the problem on someone else's doorstep."

"What if he just decided to stop?" asked Sally.

"That's not the usual pattern with this kind of sicko. The case'll remain open until we know for certain that he's either dead or behind bars. At least now we've got a positive ID. In the meantime, the FBI is running the show and they've launched a nationwide manhunt."

"God," said Sally, feigning a shudder, "just talking about that monster gives me the willies. I'll get those drinks. What's your poison, Sergeant?"

"Nothing for me, thanks."

"Okay, then. I'll be back in a flash."

Jackson turned to Rachel. "Well, I'd better let you go. I don't want to keep you from your family and friends."

"Sally's the only person I know in this place, other than a couple of casual acquaintances."

"Really? What about your folks?"

"Other commitments back in Buffalo. They'll be here for the final on Saturday."

"It must be hard, not having them around to support you."

"Their company would be nice, but I can fend for myself."

"I just bet you can."

Rachel smiled.

"Anyway," added Jackson, "I got a million things to do. I, uh, just wanted to come by and wish you luck the rest of the way."

"I appreciate that."

Jackson shook her hand, held it a moment, and walked away.

"Sergeant?"

He turned.

"Are you going to be here for the final?"

"I wish I could, but I've got an awful lot on my plate just now and—"

"Not even as a personal favor? It would mean a lot to me."

"Really?"

She nodded.

Jackson held her gaze a moment. "I'll try."

Rachel watched him go, surprised by her uncharacteristic boldness. There was something about the man, a calm solidity that inspired confidence. More importantly, he listened when she spoke and looked her straight in the eye. Most men were so infatuated by her beauty that their attention wandered, usually to her cleavage. A few pretended to listen but were actually busy thinking of clever things to say to impress her.

Lionel Jackson was definitely an exception. As was Tom Brennan. But the trouble with Tom was his impracticality and his sometimes infuriating lack of ambition. He was a dreamer, which wasn't a bad thing, but she wasn't particularly keen about playing Sanchita Panza to his Don Quixote.

Besides, she'd never dated a black man and her curiosity had been aroused. Being a homicide cop, he'd certainly be more interesting than most of the other men she'd gone out with. Her parents would probably freak out at the idea — because of his profession, not his color — but then again, what was life for if not to seek out new experiences?

Smoothing back her hair, she turned and headed for the bar. But as she pushed her way through the sea of bodies, she had the eerie feeling that someone was watching her, with more than simple admiration. She stopped and scanned the crowd. She caught sight of the culprit's reflection in one of the mirrored columns. Robert Molinaro. He was leaning against a sculpture of a dancing girl, near the entrance to the washrooms. Rachel whirled around to glare at him. Their eyes remained locked for what seemed an eternity. Then he lifted the glass he was holding, cocked it in her direction, and flashed a humorless grin.

Chapter 28 — Saturday, July 19

Pageant Day. A packed Radio City Music Hall resonated with the sound of chattering voices and the tuning of instruments. In a few moments the cameras would start to roll and the announcer's voice would herald the start of the broadcast. Backstage, pageant officials, contestants, the musical director, the choreographer, camera teams, lighting and audio engineers, set designers, and numerous other stage hands anxiously waited for the director's signal.

Francine, dressed in a beige pant suit and a blue silk blouse, stood in the wings, well away from the other backstage hostesses, who were responsible for maintaining order and ensuring that the contestants adhered to the rigid television schedule. Her heart was pounding with anticipation. And anxiety. That morning, Frank's photo had appeared in every newspaper and on every television station in the state. And although it was an old photo, taken at the hospital in New Orleans when Frank was a gaunt, gangly boy of 18, the resemblance was strong enough to pose a potential threat. She would have to be as inconspicuous as possible.

At two minutes to air, the dressing room doors flew open and the contestants, the reigning Miss Empire State, a professional dance ensemble hired for the final, and the host, singer/actor John Davidson, quickly took their places in the wings. Francine smiled encouragingly as she helped her young charges get into position. In a few hours one of them would not only win a crown, but would also earn the privilege of becoming her partner in the most daring and macabre *pas de deux* ever seen on live television.

The stage manager called for silence. The orchestra, elevated at the rear of the stage, launched into a fanfare. The director, whose console was located in the orchestra pit, cued the on-air announcer.

"Live, from the fabulous Radio City Music Hall in New York City...it's the 1997 Miss Empire State Pageant! Now, here's your host, John Davidson!"

*****

Robert Molinaro, who was seated with the other judges behind a black-velvet-covered table at the foot of the stage, to the right of the temporary runway that extended across the orchestra pit, watched the opening production number with all the interest of a longshoreman at an Elizabethan poetry recital. His thoughts were fixed on Frank Ryman, who was somewhere in the auditorium. Molinaro was certain of this because he'd finally figured out the riddle.

He'd stumbled onto the answer just before the start of Friday night's evening gown competition. He'd been idly staring at the inside cover of the pageant program, specifically at a photograph of the Radio City marquee. Eventually, his eyes focused on the word 'Radio.' Then, through some inexplicable trick of synaptic switching, he recalled the original name for radio was 'wireless.' This immediately summoned up Ryman's riddle: What is wireless, is located in a metropolis, and produces vibrations in an auditorium,

That's when it hit him. The damn thing wasn't a riddle at all, but a code. His original assumption that the answer had something to do with a musical instrument was largely correct, but he'd made the mistake of taking the clue too literally. Rather than the vibrations produced by a particular instrument, Ryman was alluding to music in general. From there, the rest of the solution quickly fell into place. 'Metropolis' was another word for city, while 'auditorium' was another word for hall. Radio. City. Music. Hall. Ryman was targeting the pageant.

This revelation triggered another brainstorm, a variation on his original plan. Instead of ruining Rachel's chances, he would do everything in his power to help her win. If she didn't, no big deal. He'd notify security about Ryman's presence and still get credit for his capture. But if Rachel *did* win, he'd race to her rescue himself; the stubborn little vixen would be in his debt for the rest of her life.

The odds were definitely stacked in her favor. She'd already won her group's talent competition — which represented the largest single block of points in the pageant — and, considering that he'd given her top marks across the board, had probably also scored well in the private interview, evening gown, and swimsuit segments. He was certain she had made it into the final. Unless she fell on her ass, her chances of winning the crown were excellent.

There was only one hitch. He would have to come up with some way of explaining how he knew about Ryman's presence. And why he didn't notify the police earlier. But that could wait.

Molinaro's attention was drawn back to the stage by a burst of applause signaling the end of the production number. After waiting for the dancers to leave, John Davidson walked to center stage and began to introduce the contestants. Once that was done, the reigning queen would take her final stroll down the runway, the judges would be introduced, and Davidson would open the envelope containing the names of the ten finalists.

When it came to Rachel's turn to be introduced, Molinaro fidgeted in his chair in an attempt to get her attention. But she wouldn't bite. How like her, he thought. Proud as a peacock right to the bitter end. Leaning back in his chair, he placed his right hand inside his jacket pocket and fondled the canister of mace he'd brought along for his possible confrontation with Ryman. How ironic. He no longer cared whether Rachel slept with him or not. All he wanted now was to make her choke on a fat slice of humble pie.

*****

Rachel Curran held her breath as she waited for John Davidson to announce the last finalist. For the hundredth time since the start of the competition, she found herself questioning her sanity. Only an idiot would expend so much time and effort just to stand under a bank of hot lights in front of millions of people, flash a vacuous smile, and politely applaud each time someone else's name was called, all for the privilege of taking part in yet another round of torment. At least the ordeal would be over soon.

Dispelling these negative thoughts, Rachel glanced toward the left side of the auditorium and scanned the section that was reserved for family members. Her mom and dad, as well as two of her brothers and their spouses — the oldest had stayed home to care for a sick child — were seated in the third row, gazing up at her with eager anticipation. Her dad caught her eye and gave her a discreet thumb's up. She allowed herself a brief smile and sought out Tom Brennan, but couldn't spot him.

Back on stage, John Davidson folded his hands in front of him and turned to gaze paternally at the assembled contestants. "And finally," he said, with a broad smile, "from Buffalo, bearing the banner of Miss Erie County...Rachel Curran!"

"Oh my God!" cried Rachel, covering her face with her hands. For one frightening moment, she couldn't move her legs. Her eyes darted from her feet to John Davidson's face, to the audience, then back to her feet. Thankfully,

Deborah Wong, who was standing behind her, leaned forward and gave her an encouraging hug. Rachel felt a pang as she read the disappointment on her friend's face. She kissed Deborah on the cheek and walked to the front of the stage to join the other finalists. Then, as the audience cheered and flash bulbs popped, the ten women clasped hands and basked in the glow of victory.

"Ladies and gentlemen," cried Davidson, accompanied by another fanfare, "here they are! Our ten lovely finalists!"

The cameras continued to roll for a moment, then cut to a commercial. The stage manager stepped out of the wings, thanked the losers, and cleared the stage for the next production number. The contestants, many in a state of shock, drifted back toward their dressing rooms. For Rachel and the other finalists, it was time to prepare for the first event of the evening: the swimsuit competition. For the losers, the dream was over. They'd be watching the rest of the pageant on a dressing room monitor.

*****

When Lionel Jackson showed his detective's badge to the young usher who greeted him in the Radio City foyer, he thought the kid was going to lay an egg. The staff had been told to be on the alert for trouble so it was not surprising to find them a bit skittish. After easing the boy's mind by explaining he was there on a personal matter, Jackson accepted a program, entered the auditorium, and took a position at the top of the last aisle on the right.

The house was packed. Up on the stage, which was framed by an arched, brightly lit proscenium designed to resemble a sunburst, the swimsuit competition was under way. From where he stood, some 160 feet away, Jackson had to squint to make out the face of the contestant, a leggy blonde in a yellow suit. She looked tiny and forlorn as she strolled across the vast stage to pose for the judges.

Jackson leaned against the wall and surveyed the sumptuous auditorium. He'd been inside Radio City only once, in 1993, to see the annual Christmas Spectacular with his wife and kids. For months afterwards, Cassie and Janet both swore they would become Rockettes some day, and spent numerous hours practicing their dance steps. He didn't have the heart to tell them there were no black Rockettes. The theater claimed it was a question of uniformity and esthetics, not race. But how do you explain that to a child?

He closed his eyes and ran a hand across his scalp. Thinking about his children always unleashed deep feelings of guilt. Maybe now that the Sardonicus investigation was winding down, Hawthorne would finally give him some time off to visit them in Chicago. It had been so long he was afraid they'd forgotten what he looked like.

As the next competitor walked onto the stage, Jackson wondered if Rachel had taken her turn yet. If not, he'd have to move closer for a better look. Although he knew that contestants wore one-piece suits, he tried to imagine what she looked like in a string bikini. It was a very pleasant picture.

He glanced at his watch. It was 7:25. He had a meeting with the FBI at 9:30, to discuss how to best utilize the new data supplied by the New Orleans Police Department. He should've remained at the station house, reviewing Ryman's file. Instead, thanks to a sweet young thing who was probably lonely and saw him as some kind of father figure, he was cooling his heels at a beauty pageant. What the hell was he thinking?

*****

Francine let out a long sigh as the swimsuit segment finally came to an end and the stage was cleared for yet another inane production number. It was taking forever, she thought, wiping her palms on the back of her slacks. And it was far from over. She still had the talent competition, *another* production number, and the evening gown competition to endure before the judges finally got around to naming the winner.

Her legs were tired and she wished she could sit down, but it was forbidden. Backstage hostesses had to remain standing at their posts for the entire two hours, to ensure that the contestants made their entrances on time and in the right order. They were also expected to help their young charges cope with the pressure.

Placing a hand over her mouth to mask a yawn, Francine leaned against a storage crate and reviewed her plan. She intended to strike the moment the winner's name was announced and the others flocked around her to offer their congratulations. It would take a few seconds for people to figure out what was going on, more than enough time for her to make her escape.

Like Southern patriot John Wilkes Booth's extermination of the villainous Abraham Lincoln, she would strike a blow for righteousness in a crowded theater then disappear during the ensuing confusion. Unfortunately, Radio City had no private boxes for her to leap up to, but it had something just as useful: a pair of choral staircases. Built along the base of both side walls in order to soften their curvature, the 'staircases' were actually a series of platforms that rose toward the back of the hall with the incline of the floor. Each platform had a draped entrance that allowed performers to reach them from backstage for special production numbers.

Once behind the nearest entrance, she would discard her jacket, false eyelashes, and wig — she had fashioned her real hair into a pageboy and had dyed it brown — race toward the nearest exit, and meld into the surging crowd. By the time the police got their act together, she'd be on her way to the airport, where a suitcase full of Frank's hard-earned money awaited.

*****

Lionel Jackson took advantage of a commercial break to search for an empty seat. He strolled down the aisle and was lucky enough to find one about 20 rows from the stage. Squeezing past half a dozen annoyed spectators, he sat down just as the first finalist appeared for the start of the talent competition.

Flipping open his program, he turned to Rachel's biography and discovered she would be performing on the piano. Chopin. Jackson frowned. Long hair music. The stuff was okay in small doses, but he wondered how the mostly white, middle-aged audience would react to a loud, rollicking blast of Fats Waller. Acting on a hunch, he quickly thumbed through the rest of the program. It was just as he'd suspected. There were only two black contestants, and neither had made the final.

He'd done some research and discovered that no black woman had won a state title until 1970. It took another 13 years for judges to select the first black Miss America, the magnificent Vanessa Williams, who was then forced to resign when *Penthouse* magazine published a batch of nude photos she'd modeled for a few years earlier. As it turned out, her successor, who'd finished as first runner-up that year, was also black, so she became the second Miss America of color. The next black winner didn't appear until 1990.

Jackson thought pageants were little more than a trivial pastime. But they did serve as a bellwether for some of the social changes that were taking place in the country. From that perspective, blacks were at least making progress.

*****

"And now," announced John Davidson, flashing a mouthful of dazzling white teeth, "the final contestant in the evening gown competition...Miss Rachel Curran!"

Robert Molinaro's eyes widened as Rachel strode — no, floated — onto the stage. True, the woman was as stubborn as George Steinbrenner, but there was no denying that she was drop-dead gorgeous. Hair. Makeup. Posture. Even the cut of her gown. It all came together to create a distinct, harmonious whole. A man had to be blind not to see she was the class of the field.

Smiling broadly, Rachel looked completely at ease as she took her place next to John Davidson.

"Hello, Rachel," said Davidson, opening the envelope that contained her platform question. "How are you holding up?"

"It's a little nerve-wracking, but I guess I'm okay."

"Well, you look like a very capable young woman. I'm sure you'll do just fine. All right, then. Are you ready?"

Rachel nodded.

Davidson pulled a white card out of the envelope. "You've identified naturopathy as your platform issue. What are the specific reasons you feel naturopathy is a viable alternative to conventional medicine?"

"First," said Rachel, inclining her head toward the microphone, "I'd like to point out that naturopathic medicine is not seen as an *alternative* to conventional medicine, but as a complement. Naturopathic doctors strive to aid the healing process by incorporating a variety of natural methods based on the patient's individual needs. These methods include acupuncture, hydrotherapy, herbal medicine, nutritional counseling and supplementation, massage, and lifestyle counseling, among others.

"Naturopathic medicine is geared toward treating the whole person, by stimulating the body's inherent ability to heal itself. Where conventional medicine treats the *effects* of an illness — with drugs and surgical techniques that often produce serious complications — naturopathic doctors treat the *cause*. Let me give you an example. If a person is suffering from asthma and—"

Molinaro shifted position and rubbed his aching neck. All this waiting was getting on his nerves. And allowing him too much time to think. Only now was he beginning to appreciate the full implications of what he was planning to do. It wasn't some macho game. He was about to confront a serial killer; a man consummately skilled in the taking of human life. There would be no room for mistakes.

Pursing his lips, he peered intently into the shadowy spaces at both sides of the stage and wondered where Ryman could be hiding. It had to be some place where he'd have quick and unobstructed access to his target. Maybe he intended to slide down on a rope. Or pop up out of a trap door in the floor. Hell, the son-of-a-bitch could even be masquerading as a member of the orchestra. No one ever paid attention to classical musicians unless they were soloists.

Then again, perhaps he wasn't in the theater at all. Given the strict security, both inside and outside the building, it was possible he had changed his mind. Molinaro took a deep breath. Who was he kidding? The Tivoli had been rigged with as much security as Fort Knox and Ryman *still* managed to get in. The guy obviously had the smarts, and the balls, to pull this thing off.

By now, Rachel had finished her speech and was standing near the apron, posing for the judges. Again she managed to avoid his gaze. Lifting the hem of her gown, she sauntered down the runway, turned, and walked off the stage. Molinaro picked up his pen and scribbled a '10' on his ballot. The spotlight shifted back to John Davidson.

"Ladies and gentlemen, we've come to the end of the competition. We're now minutes away from the moment we've all been waiting for. The judges have marked their ballots and they're now being collected so they can be given to the auditors for tabulation. We'll have the results for you right after these commercial messages."

Molinaro pushed his chair back and stood up. Placing his hand inside his jacket pocket, he gripped the canister of mace for assurance and slowly walked toward the nearest exit.

*****

Lionel Jackson cast a quizzical glance at the departing Molinaro then looked at his watch. It was 8:45. If he didn't leave soon he risked being late for his meeting. Then again, it would be a shame to miss the coronation. He decided on a compromise. He'd return to the top of the aisle and watch the finale from there.

That way, when the pageant ended, he wouldn't have to fight his way through the crowd.

As he stood up, he became aware of a minor disturbance at the left side of the auditorium. Molinaro, who was standing near the exit, was having a hushed but heated discussion with a pair of security guards. The man was obviously concerned about something, because his face was flushed and he kept pointing toward the stage. He tried to wedge himself between the two guards, but was gently repulsed. More gesticulating followed. Finally, they relented and allowed him to pass.

Jackson's brow furrowed. Pageant judges ordinarily stayed in their seats during the announcement of the winner's name. Something was up. Although logic suggested it was probably just some minor snafu, his gut told him otherwise. He decided to investigate.

*****

"Come on, girls," shouted Francine, ushering the finalists back onto the stage for the grand finale, "quickly now. You know your places. Don't forget to keep your head straight and your eyes pointed forward at all times. And let's see those smiles!"

The ten women strode gracefully to the center of the stage, formed a line, and clasped hands. Francine turned to one of the other hostesses and whispered, "My God, they're about to announce the fourth runner-up and I've got to pee!"

"Can't you hold it for a few minutes?"

"No!" she replied, backing away. She headed for the stairwell leading down to the washrooms but once she was sure she wasn't being watched, turned and hurried toward the opposite side of the backstage area. When she got there, she took a deep breath and approached the head of backstage security, a burly, middle-aged ex-cop named Phil. He and a number of other people were crowded together in the wings, eagerly waiting for John Davidson to open the envelope that contained the names of the winner and her court of honor.

Francine tapped Phil on the shoulder. "Excuse me," she whispered. "I don't want to sound like a worry wart, but as I was leaving the washroom just now I saw a man loitering near the door of the scenery dock. I didn't get a good look at his face, but I'm pretty sure it wasn't anyone I recognized."

"Did you notice if he was wearing an ID badge?"

"Not really. I just saw him in profile as I was walking past. I'm sure it's nothing, but I *was* told to report anything that seemed even a tiny bit suspicious."

"Okay," he said, obviously peeved by the possibility that he'd miss the coronation, "I'll check it out. But don't say anything to the others just yet. We don't want a goddamn panic."

He used his two-way radio to notify his team then quietly rounded up a few of his men and hurried toward the stairwell. The rest of the backstage security detail remained scattered along the perimeter. Francine was confident that once she made her move the resulting rush of people toward the wings would neutralize their ability to interfere with her plans.

Francine returned to her post, arriving just as John Davidson announced the name of the fourth runner-up. There were only four security guards now close enough to foil her plans; the ones standing near the two side exits on either side of the auditorium. But they would never risk a shot from that distance. In fact, by the time they realized that something was happening, she'd already be scaling the nearest choral staircase.

Francine slowly unbuttoned her jacket and caressed the outline of the straight razor nestled in the inside pocket.

*****

Robert Molinaro felt the bitter bile of disappointment rising in his throat as he stood alone backstage, oblivious to the cheering and clapping that greeted the announcement of the second runner-up. It appeared he wouldn't get to be a hero after all. A few minutes earlier, someone had spotted an intruder, prompting security to go to high alert.

To make matters worse, the ubiquitous Sergeant Jackson had shown up. The cop had seen him leave the judges' table and had followed him backstage to see what was up. When told about the intruder, he immediately joined the hunt. Regardless of the outcome, Jackson was bound to ask a lot of embarrassing questions when he got back.

"Shit!" hissed Molinaro, under his breath. His carefully wrought plan was crumbling around him like a sand castle at high tide. All he needed now was for Jackson to catch Ryman and for Rachel to win the crown. Wouldn't that be a kick in the teeth?

A hush settled over the auditorium as John Davidson prepared to announce the name of the first runner-up. Realizing he didn't have time to get back to his seat, Molinaro hurried to the right side of the stage so he could watch the end of the show from the wings.

"And now for the first runner-up," said Davidson, pausing a moment for effect. "From Albany...Miss Paula MacKenzie!"

Another burst of applause as an obviously disappointed brunette in a shimmering blue gown bravely accepted the congratulations of her fellow finalists. Fighting back tears, she walked to the side of the stage to join the other three women who would comprise the eventual winner's court of honor. The six remaining finalists, Rachel included, clasped hands again and waited to hear which one of them would be crowned *Miss Empire State* for 1997.

Stuck with a poor vantage point, Molinaro began to elbow his way through the knot of people crammed together in front of him, earning more than a few dirty looks, as well as an angry order to keep still from the stage manager. He persevered and eventually managed to find an unobstructed view. Then, like everyone else in the auditorium, he fixed his eyes on John Davidson. The seconds ticked by. Someone in the audience coughed, momentarily shattering the tense mood.

A movement a few yards to his left interrupted Molinaro's concentration. One of the backstage hostesses, a tall blonde he'd seen once or twice from a distance, was inching her way onto the stage. She had her right hand tucked inside her jacket. From where he stood, Molinaro could only see the side of her face. Even so, there was something familiar about her profile.

"And the winner is," said Davidson, pausing even longer than usual, "from Buffalo...Miss Rachel Curran!"

"Jesus Christ!" cried Molinaro, as the blood rushed from his face. He'd found Frank Ryman.

*****

A roar erupted in the auditorium as Lionel Jackson rushed up the stairs toward the stage. He'd given up the chase for the intruder in order to find the hostess who'd made the sighting. There were only three ways an unauthorized person could've gotten to the scenery dock and they were all heavily guarded. He also wanted to have a chat with Molinaro. Maybe it was a coincidence, but there was something fishy about his sudden rush backstage at the very moment the intruder had been spotted.

He had another reason for returning to the stage. The most important one of all. If Frank Ryman *was* in Radio City, that's where he'd be heading.

Just then, he was startled by a series of loud screams, not of joy but of fear. Jackson broke into a run. By the time he arrived backstage the area was in a state of pandemonium. Dozens of people, including a number of shrieking contestants, were running for the exits in a mad panic. He looked for Rachel, but couldn't find her.

Unholstering his revolver, he elbowed his way through the surging crowd and raced onto the stage. The first thing he noticed was the pungent, unmistakable odor of mace lingering in the air. What he saw next, at the far end of the stage, froze him in his tracks. Robert Molinaro was grappling with one of the hostesses! He then noticed something else. The woman was wearing a wig, which had begun to slide down the right side of her face, and she was wielding a straight razor! Jackson finally understood how Frank Ryman had gotten so close to some of his victims.

He planted his feet and took aim, but he was too far away and Molinaro kept getting into the line of fire. He lowered his gun and raced toward the combatants. Half way there, he saw Molinaro lose his footing and fall to his knees. The razor slashed through the air. Molinaro slumped to the floor, great gouts of blood gushing from his neck. More screams as people in the front rows surged into the aisles.

Where the hell was backstage security, wondered Jackson. Then he remembered. Most of them were still downstairs looking for the phantom intruder.

He stopped and took aim again, but someone got in his way. When he looked up, Ryman was gone. A moment later, he spotted him a few yards further downstage, moving with the stealth of a leopard stalking its prey. He was heading for one of the contestants, who had fallen near the edge of the orchestra pit. Her face was turned away. In his agitated state, Jackson initially failed to recognize the dress. But now there was no doubt about the woman's identity. It was Rachel!

Jackson cut to his right and raised his gun. This time, he had Ryman in his sights. But as he squeezed the trigger, a clarinetist, screaming and still clutching her instrument, crashed into his side, causing the bullet to slam harmlessly into the folds of the curtain and knocking the gun out of his hand. In the same instant, a million slivers of pain rammed into his spine. His knees buckled and he collapsed to the floor.

Clenching his teeth in agony, Jackson shook out the cobwebs and tried to locate Rachel. She was running toward him. Ryman was right behind her, the razor poised to strike. Gripped by a sense of *deja vu*, he watched helplessly as the killer grabbed her by the hair and flung her to the floor. It was the botched hostage incident all over again.

Jackson struggled to his feet and lunged at Ryman, but only managed to grab the hem of his jacket. He watched in horror as the killer opened a gash across Rachel's sternum then lifted his arm to strike again. Jackson punched him in the abdomen as hard as he could. It was like punching concrete.

Ryman made a noise like a wounded animal. Letting go of Rachel's hair, he spun around and twisted his mouth into an evil snarl.

Jackson grabbed Ryman's arm with one hand and his throat with the other. Their faces were less than an inch apart. Jackson looked into the killer's cold blue eyes and knew dread.

Roaring with rage, Ryman easily wrenched his arm free and slashed Jackson's shoulder. The detective stumbled and fell to the floor. Ryman jumped on top of him and pinned his arms with his knees. Grinning, he poised the razor directly above Jackson's throat.

Jackson closed his eyes and winced. He saw the faces of his children. As he took what he thought would be his last breath, a loud explosion reverberated through the auditorium. Jackson felt something wet land on his hands. He looked up. Ryman was staring straight ahead in wide-eyed surprise. A crimson circle appeared at the center of his forehead. It became larger, then quickly began to lose its shape. His knees wobbled and he slumped sideways onto the floor. The back of his head was missing. Jackson rolled away from the body and looked for the shooter.

He spotted Rachel standing two yards away, still frozen in the Weaver combat shooting stance, left foot slightly forward, both hands wrapped around the handle of his .38. Her face was a pale, grim mask. Blood was streaming from her wound. Dropping the gun, she looked at him and crumpled to the floor.

Jackson crawled to her side, lifted her head, and cradled it on his lap.

*****

When Rachel opened her eyes, it was like looking through a gauze filter. The house lights were on and a forest of legs surrounded her. She saw her mom and dad bending over her with pale, drawn faces. Except for a few stragglers near the exits — she thought of ants swarming into their holes — the auditorium was almost empty. A number of security guards were coming down the aisles in slow motion, guns raised in readiness.

She blinked and turned her head slightly. There was something shiny lying on the floor a few yards away. She squinted until the object came into focus. It was her crown. Rachel wondered why it was on the floor. A sudden, searing jolt of pain ripped through her, dispelling her momentary confusion. She stared at her blood-soaked gown then looked up at Lionel Jackson and squeezed his hand.

"Am I going to die?" she asked.

"Not on my watch, young lady," he replied as he pressed a towel someone had handed him against Rachel's wound. "Not on my watch."

Acknowledgements

This book was made possible by the generosity of the following individuals — including two who wish to remain anonymous — all of whom contributed to my crowdfunding campaign. In a very real sense, this is as much their book as it is mine.

Lena, Daniel & Lisa Bruno

David Carey

Judi Chambers

Gary Cox

Ellen Gardner

Ron Glen

George Hale

Steve Lloyd

Susan Maclean

Mario Miceli

Gary Rier

Gary Tannyan

Frank, Monica & Matthew Volpentesta

Jim & Lauretta Wood

www.ingramcontent.com/pod-product-compliance
Lightning Source LLC
Chambersburg PA
CBHW021122190726
48288CB00008B/2458